The Journey to Vapor Island

By Robert Stark

Special Thanks to:

Francis Nally, Mark Velard, Alex Goldstein,

Ashley Messinger, and Brandon Adamson

The Journey to Vapor Island

By Robert Stark

Disclaimer: This is a work of fiction. Names, characters, businesses, places, events and incidents are either the products of the author's imagination or used in a fictitious manner. Any resemblance to actual persons, living or dead, or actual events is purely coincidental.

Printed in the United States of America

First Printing, 2017

ISBN 978-0-692-98008-8

“My name is Noam Metzenbaum. I am 15 years old and live in New York City with my mother in this tiny apartment. I know I am destined for great things and will one day escape these confines. You see, my father was a great aristocrat and I shall someday carry on his legacy, but for now I am in hibernation awaiting my ascension, my moment to rise up to my rightful place in this world. I am the emperor of mankind, dammit! I will save mankind from its hedonistic desires, crush false social orders, and annihilate all that is ugly in this world. I shall establish a new order that will bring justice to this broken world where the vile and wicked rule and the noble and greatest minds are crushed and made to suffer in silence. I am the only one standing in the way of utter nihilistic violence. This world was never meant for me! You see, God has put me on this earth for one thing only, and that is to save mankind from their sins and to find my one true love.”

Noam’s mom interrupts his writing, “Noam, hurry up! You're late for school.”

“I don’t want to go!” Noam replies.

Noam puts down his journal and looks out the window of their one-bedroom apartment from the 23rd floor, which overlooks the Lower East Side, the East River, and the skyline of Midtown in the distance.

He thinks, “I feel so magnificent up here in my tower, observing the useless plebs down below like insects. Someday this will all be mine, but today I would rather stay home and write in my journal.”

"Noam! Get ready, don't you want to make something of your life?" shouts his mom.

Noam replies, "I am being held back in this penitentiary of plebeians."

"Aren't you being a bit overdramatic?" replies Noam's mom. "Now get ready, you don't want to be late again."

Noam reluctantly gets ready for school.

Barely making it in time, he hops on a city bus which is full of homeless people, ghetto blacks and Puerto Ricans and elderly Chinese immigrants. "I don't belong here," Noam quietly mutters to himself.

Noam prefers walking to the slow and crowded bus. He doesn't mind the subway, but there isn't a stop close enough to his home. His mom told him that he if he has another tardy she will cut off his allowance.

Noam arrives at school. He looks around anxiously, knowing he is out of place. He thinks, "I feel so meek and small around these wild beasts, yet they are so far beneath me. One day I will grow strong and crush them like ants. They have no value to this world. They are a waste of space!"

Noam walks to class trying not to make eye contact with the thugs in the halls.

He hears taunting, "Yo white bitch, come give me some sugar!"

Noam gets to his history class, which is his favorite subject. The teacher, Ms. Latisha, is a sassy overweight black woman. Noam has utter contempt for her lowly intellect and crude demeanor.

He looks at the other students in disgust.

Noam thinks, "I'm not a racist. If they could only see my visions they will follow me to greatness. Wishful thinking, perhaps? Maybe I should stop listening to my mom and her silly friends."

There is a group of black kids making noise in the back of the class. Noam always sits at the front to avoid them, since the front rows are always empty.

Ms. Latisha proclaims, "Today's history lesson is the legacy of slavery and its effects on inequality in modern-day American society."

One of the black boys shouts out "Down wit da white man!"

Ms. Latisha says half-jokingly, "Calm down Jerome, we'll get to that shortly."

She starts her lesson talking about the housing projects across the street, which are mostly filled with underprivileged blacks and immigrants.

Jerome interrupts, "And them rich white Jews be chilling in their penthouses uptown."

Ms. Latisha doesn't know how to respond.

Then she replies reluctantly, "Well yes, Jews are white and can be privileged, but they have also suffered great discrimination like African Americans and Latinos have."

The black kids in the back start booing her.

Noam finds the situation amusing. Even though he is Jewish, he was never really accepted by the rich Jewish kids growing up. He thinks, "They are nothing but petite bourgeois little brats, not true aristocrats like me."

Ms. Latisha continues, "Well class. There's a lot of inequality in America today. We are still recovering from the legacy of Slavery and Jim Crow. We need to address white privilege and end all inequality by removing the White Patriarchy from power."

Noam gets up and proclaims "White Patriarchy? This city is owned by rich bankers. Bankers can be Jewish, Chinese, and Indian. This city is ruled by the false-money elites and those who produce cultural filth and manipulate the lowly masses of slaves to do their bidding. The genuine elites are being suppressed and …"

A black girl cuts him off. "Check yo privileged white ass!"

"Look at that preppy ass cracker in his Ralph Lauren Polo!" another black boy chimes in.

Noam gets up and shouts "I live in a studio apartment with a broken heater in the middle of winter and no air conditioning in summer. I have no friends. My mom can barely pay the bills. I'm not accepted by those rich fuckers … fake elites! And you are all nothing but their pawns. Some of you may be lucky enough to get affirmative action and a cushy government office job, but most of you will end up unemployed or incarcerated, all disposable slaves!"

Noam is about to cry but manages to hold it in.

The class ridicules him, "Fuckin' cracker ass bitch" "Stupid white boy" "fuck off Jew."

There is an awkward silence. Ms. Latisha is giving Noam a nasty look but doesn't know how to handle the situation.

A shy black girl who sits by herself in the row behind Noam gets up to speak. She explains "Maybe he does have a point. My uncle who lives in Georgia is African American and he owns his own business and a big house in the suburbs. He worked hard his entire life to get where he is. White people did a lot to help him succeed in life, but he pulled himself up from poverty through hard work. He is my personal hero. He has told me that in his town, on the outskirts, there are many whites living in trailer parks, addicted to meth. All their jobs have been sent to China, and if they are lucky they can get a job at Walmart, but most are on welfare, drinking themselves to death."

Jerome is having none of it. "Lazy ass white crackers!" he hoots. "We was slaves. We paid our dues. Those whites are too damn lazy!"

Ms. Latisha still doesn't know how to respond, but luckily for her the bell rings, and class is over.

After class, the shy black girl approaches Noam in the hallway.

She says, "Interesting class, huh?"

Noam replies awkwardly, "Yes … I think so."

She giggles, "My name is Vanessa. Want to catch a bite of pizza after class?"
"Sure, why not," Noam says.

Noam notices the black boys from the back of the class staring at them in shock and jealous rage, the nerdy white boy talking to the cutest black girl in class. Noam gives them a smug grin. He sets up a time to meet with Vanessa after class.

After class, Noam is out on the school yard for lunch break. He is reading a book by himself while eating a bagel with cream cheese. He is approached by the black and Hispanic boys from history class. Jerome approaches Noam and says, "What yo doing with Nessa?"

Noam replies "I don't know."

They start laughing. Jerome says, "What yo mean you don't know fool? I saw you with my home girl Nessa. She ain't into no white boys."

Noam replies "She's a nice girl. We are just friends."

Jerome says, "Yo trying to stick yo tiny little white dick into Nessa? Dat ain't right."

"Leave me alone," Noam responds.

Jerome pushes him, "Fuck off white bitch!" One of Jerome's friends grabs his backpack and says, "What you got in there white boy?" They empty out his backpack, which is filled with books. They pull out his favorite book, which is a collectible of old photographs of New York City that his grandfather Saul gave to him.

Jerome proceeds to rip the book up in into pieces. Noam begins to cry. That was his favorite book, which reminded him of his late grandfather and gave him great aesthetic inspiration. Noam thinks, "They have no appreciation for civilization or beauty."

Noam yells at them in tears, “You are all descended from slaves, while my father is a great aristocrat!”

One of the boys, who is a Dominican named Angel and a baseball star, taunts the black boy “Whacha gonna do bout dis white boy, Holmes?”

Jerome replies “He’s dead nigga!” and then punches Noam in the stomach. Noam cries as they continue to taunt him.

“Die, niggers! Die!” Noam cries out.

“Dat’s a hate crime. We gonna sue you ass white boy!” the Dominican replies. The blacks are about to continue punching him but an administrator catches them and breaks up the fight. Noam leaves abruptly in tears.

As Noam is walking home from school he sees Angel making out with the only pretty blonde white girl in the school. His greasy brown skin, kinky hair, and ugly face desecrating the perfect blonde beauty. Noam thinks, “I’ll chop off his balls and murder the beast with my bare hands if I ever find out they consummated the vile act!”

After a bit of snooping, Noam found out that she is Italian American by her last name, but she has the look of the blonde Jewish girls Noam has always lusted after, the ones who go to the private schools uptown.

Noam was never in class with her but would stare at her from a distance in the yard. She never even acknowledged his existence. He saw her socializing with a group of Dominican guys, one of whom threatened to beat him up if he didn’t stop staring at her, but he never imagined she would ever actually stoop to dating beasts like them.

"A beautiful rose floating alone in a sea of raw sewage, now sullied and disintegrating into the waste," Noam thinks.

Noam stares at them in rage and wonders "Why would a girl like that date such an ugly subhuman beast and not a true aristocrat like me? The fairer sex apparently has no sense of justice. I will sort things out once I get into power!" Still in tears, Noam chuckles. It begins to rain.

Noam walks past the Pizza joint and sees Vanessa with her head down in tears after being stood up. He feels bad, but is in such rage. He thinks to himself, "I don't need those niggers and spics. They are a useless race of slaves."

Noam starts writing down notes in his journal, "A true elite would not have to rely upon such filth. A society not ruled by profit and sexual brutes but true justice, true order, true aristocratic radicalism! I will achieve great things, realize grand aesthetic visions of the past and the future. Let society decay. Burn it all down! 99% of humanity has lost its usefulness! A great cleansing of the filth!"

As Noam writes in rage, he accidentally bumps into an elderly Chinese woman carrying a bucket of stinky fish, which splatters onto Noam's shirt. She starts shouting gobbledygook at him in Cantonese.

Noam continues to walk through the pouring rain, still aching from the beatings, and stinking of fish. He stumbles across a Japanese bookstore, and steps inside to get out of the rain. He is enamored and overwhelmed by all the aesthetic imagery. He has a hundred dollar bill which his mom had given him for his birthday. He buys a copy of Yukio Mishima's "Confessions of a Mask," some teen hentai, which some call lolicon, a book of futuristic photographs, illustrations from Japan in the 1980s by Roger Blackstone (who is running for president), the manga "The Poem of the Wind and the Trees," and an illustrated Japanese text book based on the story of Anne Frank which he knows will piss off his mom.

Noam had always seen himself as a European aristocrat, but there was something about the Japanese aesthetic that intrigued him; the bright neon colors, the perfect harmony, grand visions for the future, yet respect for ancient traditions.

Filled with sadness and rage, Noam walks home alone in the rain, passing by the concrete public housing blocks of the Lower East Side, back to his mom's small apartment. He imagines the grim concrete towers covered in bright neon like the images of Tokyo from the 80s.

Noam arrives home, soaking wet and covered in bruises, crying. Concerned, his mother asks him, "What's wrong?" Noam complains about the niggers and spics that beat him up. She is upset that he got beaten up but is more horrified by his racism and reminds him that his grandfather Saul fled the Nazis from Austria as a little boy.

She says, "He came to America to escape bigotry and we must be kind and tolerant to all people and understand that not everyone has the same opportunities we do."

"Saul was a great man," Noam retorts. "He contributed a lot to civilization. These beasts are worthless scum. They have no value to society."

Somewhat taken aback, Noam's mom emptily replies, "What have you done to help society? Why not be nicer to the other kids and they will give you a chance."

Noam laughs sarcastically. "They are low-IQ thugs who only respond to strength, power, and violence."

Noam's mom is disturbed by his comment and sits in awkward silence thinking of something to say. "They are nice kids. They just didn't have the same opportunities you did," is all that she can manage to come up with.

"What opportunities?" Noam says. "They are filth but have strength in numbers. I am left to rot alone in filth, not a single friend in this world, even though I am the best student in my school. Straights A's but nothing to show for it except being a kissless virgin with bruises on my face. Look at me in this tiny little apartment. Goes to a school in the ghetto, getting beaten up and humiliated, and I have it good?"

"You have a lot of potential, Noam. You just need to put yourself out there," she lectures.

"Not when I am surrounded by savages with the collective intellect of a cockroach," he fires back.

Clearly offended, his mom scowls disapprovingly and says, "Where did you learn that rhetoric?"

"It's just basic common sense," he replies. "Something you and your colleagues from 2nd rate liberal arts universities who make 30 thousand a year, yet think they are the intellectual elite, don't comprehend." Noam runs into his room and slams his door.

Once in his room, Noam takes out the VHS tape of the poem of "The Poem of the Wind and the Trees." Noam is lucky to still have an old Sanyo VCR, which his mom had from before he was born.

Noam just bought the videotape randomly on a binge, but discovers it is a beautiful love story between two boys around his age at a boarding school in 19th century France, which has a very aristocratic aesthetic, the kind of world Noam dreams of living in.

Noam wishes he could have a friend like Gilbert to share his deepest secrets, to hold and caress on dark and lonely nights. There are graphic illustrations of naked anime boys, Japanese visions of the Aryan physique.

Noam so wants to swim naked with these boys and share the strongest male bonding, but sadly he never has had the chance to experience those pleasures in reality. He was repulsed by all the beastly ghetto boys at his school. Just seeing them in the locker room was rape to his pupils. Bad enough there were very few pretty girls, and the few that there were, were already taken by ugly beasts and mutants. Worst of all he was never even allowed to view the male form in its pure beauty. What a crime against nature!

Noam takes out the Anne Frank book and opens to a section where there is an anime illustration of young Jewish girls in the showers. Noam originally bought the book for shock value but is turned on by the graphic illustrations of the cute young girls; Cute young Jewish girls but with the faces of anime characters.

Noam starts masturbating to the images. He imagines himself in the gas chamber, rescuing the girls from their fate, kissing them

Just as Noam is about to cum, his mom walks in on him masturbating. She finds the book and is horrified. She confiscates it and gives him the silent treatment for the remainder of the evening.

He cannot sleep and lies in his bed all night staring at the broken ceiling fan, the sound of flies, the stench of sweat, and his own dried semen which had built up on his sheets over countless lonely nights.

Noam looks out the window and fantasizes of his dream world. The Japanese futuristic city from the Blackstone book fused with the Art Deco film noir aesthetic of old New York from the book his grandfather Saul gave him.

Noam imagines he is with a beautiful anime blonde Jewish girl dressed in a colorful silk kimono, sharing the magical experience looking out over the lights of the city, holding hands, savoring each other's bodies, licking every inch of her sweet smooth skin, and going down on her for all of eternity. Noam falls asleep fantasizing about his dream girl.

As Noam's mom wakes him up, he is still making the tongue gesture from while he was dreaming about giving his fantasy girl pleasure for all of eternity.

Noam's mom laughs, "Got a fly in your mouth again? This place is infested, but our disgusting slumlord won't even call the exterminator." Noam blushes awkwardly but realizes his mom does not understand what just happened.

Noam wonders if the girl from his dream is out there somewhere, and if she is, he has to go out to find her. He knows he isn't going to as long as he's stuck at the school he is at now.

At breakfast Noam tells his mom that he decided to quit school, which upsets her, but she has come to accept that Noam can't go to a school where he is constantly tormented.

After Noam's mom leaves for work, he prances around the kitchen in his bathrobe, holding up a cup of tea and pretending to be an aristocrat while eating stale croissants.

After breakfast Noam turns on the TV. It is the film Clueless. He thinks, "Stupid 90s chick flick about spoiled rich brats." Then he sees the girl in the film, Cher Horowitz. Everything about her is perfect. He has never seen a creature so beautiful and wonders, "Is this the girl I saw in my dreams?"

"If only she could civilize those stupid brats with her beauty," he says to himself, but then Elton comes along. He sees Elton put his arm around Cher. Noam is terrified that Cher is going to end up with Elton, whom Noam sees as the typical obnoxious popular guy. But no, she has the dignity and honor to reject his deviant request. Noam is relieved by her apparent purity.

After she leaves the party, the neon clown looks down on Cher with menace. She is all alone just like him, no longer the rich popular girl, just a beautiful lost soul looking to be saved.

Then Cher mentions she is still a virgin, waiting for the right guy, the perfect gentleman who dresses well and isn't a crude, obnoxious oaf. Noam thinks, "Is she saving her virginity for me, still frozen in her prime teen years, saving her purity, waiting for the perfect gentleman? Yes, she is that girl from my dream. If only I can save up enough money to travel to Beverly Hills I can be with her."

The film is interrupted by a public emergency announcement about a terrorist threat in the city. Noam wonders how the film will end. He knows she is out there somewhere waiting for him. Still 16, still a virgin, in her mansion all alone by herself waiting for Noam to save her, and ride off in a golden chariot to his father's palace like Cinderella.

Noam spends the rest of the day home, alone in his room while his mom is at work. Noam can't stop thinking about Cher. But then he comes to the realization that Cher is signaling to him to find his one true love, the girl of his dreams, the blonde Jewish girl whose eyes he once glanced into one fateful night.

"I'm not even worthy to say her name," Noam tells himself. "I must first prove to her that I am a great aristocrat like my father. Then we shall marry."

Noam continues writing in his journal and reading philosophy, including Nietzsche, Jünger, and Schopenhauer. He takes out the manifesto of Alistair Blackstone, which was given to him by his grandfather Saul who knew the Blackstones. Saul told Noam to keep the book a secret and not tell a soul, especially his mother.

Alistair was a controversial British aristocrat and father of the presidential candidate Roger Blackstone. He wrote a secret manifesto titled "Why the True Aristocrat Must Rule," which had given Noam the will to power to rise up from being just a meek pathetic loser. The book spoke to him on the deepest level, and he knows that he is the true aristocrat the book is referring to. Every passage he reads makes him feel more powerful and special knowing that he is one of the few living mortals to possess a copy.

The manifesto states *"There are three kinds of men in this world, those who were born to serve, natural born slaves. They have no free will, blindly follow orders, blindly consume, and conform to the values of a decaying civilization.*

They are not merely the proletariat rather they make up much of the Petite Bourgeoisie; those who have just enough material comfort that they are enslaved to the elites, either out of coercion or conformity, foolishly convinced that they will one day be part of the elite.

Then there are the exploiters, the parasites; those who control and manipulate the conformist masses." Noam thinks about the bankers who rig the economy yet contribute nothing to civilization, the politicians who convince stupid people to vote for them, the trashy pop icons who make millions off of stupid plebs, and all the stupid popular kids who are handed everything on a silver platter just for existing, yet add nothing of value to society."

It goes on to say that *"They have the skills to manipulate the masses but lack the intellect, character, creativity, and grand aesthetic visions to rule. They must be exterminated by the true Aristocrats.*

You see the true aristocrat is suppressed, forced to rot in silence. We must rise up and annihilate the false elite, and establish true order, true justice, true Aristocratic Radicalism. We shall build a new imperium that will replace this decaying society, and remove the worst parasitic elements from the human race.

This new elite will breed with the best women, taking the daughters of the enemy while they are still young so we can reprogram them to serve the new master race.

Young nymphets will swim nude in a garden paradise, while great artists and philosophers will observe them, paint them, and draw inspiration from their beauty of true romantic ideals that drive man to reach the pinnacles of greatness.

The Question here is how do we get to this utopia? Do not fear violence; ruthless actions are necessary when going forth in bringing about a new order based on justice and true aristocratic ideals.

The slaves must also be stripped of their rights and sterilized because they serve the parasitic elites.

Right as we speak, the treasonous elites of our nation, the liberal capitalist class along with their accomplices in the supposed aristocracy are in the early stages of importing a new slave class from the Commonwealth nations on top of our domestic slave class. We must prevent this at all costs.

And in the future, technological advancements will allow for machines to carry out most basic human tasks. Therefore most of humanity will no longer be of use. But we must not let the capitalist class take hold of these mechanisms before the revolution. Therefore we have a limited time frame to carry out our objectives.

All modern falsehoods must be dismantled; democracy, capitalism, and egalitarianism. A new priest class descended from a lost ancient civilization shall decide who is fit to rule. All wealth and capital of the parasitic class will be confiscated and given out to those who are worthy, and they shall be given the finest young fecund females to breed with."

This was music to Noam's ears. His entire life he had been tormented and belittled by both the false elites and thuggish slave class. He knows deep in his heart that he is the "True Aristocrat" the manifesto is referring to, and he has been chosen by a higher power to receive this great manifesto and implement its grand visions for a utopian society.

Noam looks at the manifesto; there is an illustration of a girl who resembles a princess from some lost Middle Eastern civilization. But she has blonde hair, a pointy nose, and the same features as his crush. Perhaps it is a sign that she is out there waiting for him to restore this ancient order.

Noam had read a lot of political and philosophical writings, from Ayn Rand to Karl Marx, but nothing ever spoke to him on such a deep level. He thinks, "These faux elitist scum only have their power because they convince stupid ugly people to buy their junk, who then have more stupid ugly kids to buy even more junk, and then they rig the financial markets so no one else has a chance to thrive. I am the one destined to carry out these grand visions once I become emperor of mankind! I just need to find my aristocratic father and my one true love, the blonde Jewish girl from my visions."

Noam daydreams about his father, a European aristocrat who impregnated his mom at a cocktail party, whom he had never met and knows little about other than overhearing his grandmother shouting at his mom for getting impregnating by that "fascist s.o.b." when she should have married a nice Jewish doctor and moved to Long Island and had three kids.

Noam thinks of the life he could have lived if his father had married his mother. He blames his mother for not being good enough to keep his father. He envisions his father with his new family at their chateau in France, eating caviar and sipping champagne, while reading the best literature and looking at their collection of the finest art. He wonders if they even know of his existence. Is he nothing but a speck of dust floating in the wind?

Noam's mom feels bad about leaving her son home alone all day by himself and decides to let him go with her to a cocktail party for her work, even though Noam has made scenes in the past in front of her friends and colleagues.

Noam is at the cocktail party with his mom, hosted by her boss, publisher Mr. Bloom at his penthouse on the Upper East Side overlooking central park. He is an arrogant, balding middle-aged man who acts like he knows everything, just like the parasites Noam was reading about in the manifesto.

Mr. Bloom shows everyone a picture of his daughter Natalie, who has dark golden blonde hair, almond shaped hazel eyes, a pointy nose, and a dimple smile. The minute Noam sees her picture his heart sinks and he has butterflies in his stomach. She is the blonde Jewish girl from his dreams.

Noam recognizes her from her Bat Mitzvah at the Russian Tea Room from about a year ago which was Noam's favorite place where his grandfather Saul used to take him for his birthdays as a kid. Whenever he ate there with Saul, he was the young prince eating caviar, while Saul would comment on the Art Deco and Czarist Russian aesthetics, but that night changed everything, and he vowed he would never return until his wedding to Natalie.

When Noam first saw Natalie that night at her Bat Mitzvah, he was immediately mesmerized. He had a crush on her ever since the moment he laid eyes on her, but Mr. Bloom put him at the table with all the nerds. Noam despised Mr. Bloom, but had a feeling in his gut that he was not her real father, that she was also descended from great aristocratic stock like him. She had mixed Jewish Aryan features and didn't resemble her vile father the least bit.

Noam remembers staring at her while she sat with her rich popular friends, and he was stuck with the ugly nerds. He lucked out by getting to hold hands with her while they danced the horah, but she was grabbed off by one of the popular boys whom Noam found repulsive. He thought, "He was loud and obnoxious, had a massive Jewfro, hooked nose, and swarthy complexion; the first to be sent to the gas chambers. Not a true aristocrat like me."

After all the hip hop and twerking which Noam found repulsive and a desecration against the great aristocratic setting, the DJ announced "Here is a slow dance, a golden oldie." It was the song "I Want to Know What Love Is" by Foreigner. Noam looked over at his crush at the other table with the popular kids. He didn't have the courage to ask her to ask to dance, and the dance was stolen by that disgusting pig. But Noam knew it was his destiny to be with her, and he would do everything in his power to make her love him.

Noam ran off to the bathroom stall to cry, still able to hear the song in the background while he was sobbing. After the song was over, he could hear a teen couple fucking in the stall next to him. He could recognize by the moaning that it was one of his crush's close friends who was also a hot blonde Jewish girl. Noam thought, "Only 13 and already sexually active while I will rot in celibate hell for all eternity!" He couldn't stand the thought of such a beautiful girl being violated and feared for the fate of his crush.

Noam left to look for his crush, but she had left with all the popular kids for the after party. He greatly feared that his crush would be defiled by the pig she was dancing with. He spent the next week alone in his room sobbing listening to Foreigner.

After that night, Noam refused his grandfather Saul's birthday invitation, and Saul died of a heart attack the night after his birthday. Noam never got over the guilt. He was the only relative Noam felt any special connection to.

Noam's grandfather Saul Metzenbaum from Austria was an architect who designed many of the skyscrapers that glittered on the New York skyline; magnificent buildings that were tainted by the corrupt elites they housed. Noam thought he was a man who actually built great things. Noam would visit him in the winters in Palm Springs at his house that he designed. He also designed the casino for Roger Blackstone in Las Vegas which Noam's mom was horrified to admit to her friends.

Saul had great knowledge of European art, history, classical music, philosophy, and he could speak German, French, and Russian. He taught Noam everything he knew about being culturally sophisticated, unlike his grandmother who knew nothing of great culture and sophistication and only cared about money.

While Mr. Bloom brags about how great his daughter's school Chadsworth Academy in Greenwich, Connecticut is, one of his colleagues teases him, "Why do you send your daughter to such a goyish school when there are plenty of good Jewish ones in the area?"

Mr. Bloom replies "I was going to, but my daughter is going through a rebellious stage, and wants to be a shiksa. She's taking horseback-riding lessons and talking about all the cute blond boys, oy vey!"

Mr. Bloom expresses concern that his daughter is under too much pressure to fit in with the popular crowd, and all the horny Chads. An older man asks "What's a Chad?"

"It's Chadsworth slang for all the popular, attractive blond jocks that get all the girls," Mr. Bloom explains.

"She's a strong independent young woman and can handle herself," Noam's mom interjects.

Mr. Bloom gets slightly offended and dismisses the comment, "You don't understand boys."

"My son's a sweet young man. He would never act crude around a girl," Noam's mom chortles.

Mr. Bloom laughs arrogantly and replies, "Girls that age go for the jocks and popular boys, not geeks like your son who have probably never even kissed a girl." Noam's mom is upset but holds it in.

Noam decides that he is going to prove that asshole wrong and find a way to meet the girl of his dreams.

He can't stop thinking about Natalie. Just by the picture, something magically transforms him. He knows it is his destiny to be with her. He must find a way to get into Chadsworth Academy, even if he has to move to Greenwich and become a butler after school, or just guilt trip his mom until she gives in.

Noam sits alone on the couch reading his Blackstone book of Japanese futurist illustrations from the 80s. His mom sees the book and says, "Blackstone's a fascist pig! Put that book back in your backpack!"

Before Noam leaves the party he steals a photo of his crush that was taken at her Bat Mitzvah and hides it in his backpack. He will cherish that photo until the day he reunites with her.

When Noam and his mom get home from Mr. Bloom's party, they sit on the couch eating popcorn, watching TV together. He tries persuading her to talk her boss into pulling some strings to get him into Chadsworth. She just can't afford it and tells him insincerely she will "consider it."

As Noam and his mom are watching TV together, a commercial for Roger Blackstone comes on. He is an eccentric billionaire whom Noam has been enamored by ever since reading his father Alistair's manifesto and looking at his book of futuristic cities from the 1980s.

Blackstone is a tall slender man with wavy blond hair, round glasses, and a pointy nose; very aristocratic in a futuristic sense. He is dressed in a black shirt and an 80s-style gray blazer, vest, and slacks. He looks as if he just stepped off a space ship from a more advanced and civilized planet; an alien here to bring civilization to the lowly human race.

The intro music comes on, and it's 80s synthwave. In the background, there are images of futuristic cities. They are much more clean and sterile than that of the noir aesthetics from his book from the 80s, but Noam understands that Blackstone has to present a more palatable message to the masses.

Blackstone speaks as if he were a god, "I'm Roger Blackstone. I have dedicated my life to advancing civilization and furthering human progress, from finding cures to deadly illnesses, to radical life extension, to building utopian cities. Imagine a world where you can get on a fast train in Miami and be in New York City in 30 minutes. Imagine an end to aging and illness. I have the power to rewrite the human genome and end all human suffering. Imagine an end to all ecological degradation, preventing utter ecological catastrophe. I have the solutions to end our petroleum based economy, implementing high speed railway and monorail networks; vertical farms and renewable energy from unknown energy sources. I will help rebuild our suburban wastelands into magnificent walkable communities, accessible to mass transit and parklands; but most importantly true freedom. The freedom to live in the utopia you desire, whether it is a vertical garden-city, a neon-lit retro wonderland, or a European-style village. I've actually built these things and understand that true freedom will only occur when people can live in their very own utopia."

Noam's mom scoffs, "Sounds like just another one of his commercials for his real estate developments, rather than an appeal from a public statesman. He wants to turn all of America into one giant theme park. He doesn't give a rat's ass about ecology."

Blackstone continues, "Imagine no work! Robots will do all the work, and there will be a guaranteed basic income. People will no longer be slaves to dead-end jobs and will be free to pursue their dreams and reach their full potential. Imagine no ugliness! I will offer economic incentives for the most attractive women to have multiple offspring and implement an immigration policy limited to only the most attractive women; the best looking European models and economic incentives for all young blonde Israeli women to immigrate to avoid military conscription. I will further human enlightenment with the legalization of LSD and DMT. I will fix our broken economy with a repudiation of all debt, home mortgages, and student loans, and an end to all interest with nationalization of the banks. Vote for me. I will make your dreams come true!"

Noam's mom interrupts, "Faux populist fascist pig! His gaudy casinos prey on the working class, his tastes are stuck in the 80s, he objectifies women, and he has done nothing to empower women and minorities! His father Alistair wrote this bizarre creepy fascist manifesto advocating for the aristocracy to enslave the proletariat, and I know Roger is influenced by that fascist shit."

"He sounds interesting," Noam replies.

"You're too young to understand," she responds dismissively.

"What do you mean?" he asks.

Noam's mom's tone becomes unhinged, "He's a fucking child molester. He screws little girls and leaves them broken!"

She breaks down in tears. Noam is confused. He leaves his mom to cry and goes to bed. He feels a bit guilty that she has to sleep on the filthy old couch while he gets the one bedroom. He thinks, "Even though my mom is not on the same intellectual level as I, I know she cares about me and will help me find my one true love."

Noam lies in bed fantasizing about Blackstone, and how he will restore civilization once elected. Noam imagines living in a futuristic city, where artists, writers, and true aristocrats have a basic income, blonde Israeli girlfriends, and blonde teens swim naked in the lakes. There will no longer be any use for the parasitic elites and thugs, a true aristocratic utopia.

The next day Noam and his mom are at breakfast. "Look, Noam, you can't just stay home all day," she says. "I'm going to talk to Mr. Bloom and see if he can help get you into Chadsworth, but you are going to have to stop acting so immature. I'm willing to make a big sacrifice, but you have to meet me half way."

Noam, (now sporting a big grin) says, "Sure, I can't wait. I will do all my chores and study all day."

"That's what I want to hear," she says. "I heard they have a creative writing scholarship. Maybe you should submit one of your journal entries?"

Noam agrees and decides he will submit a creative writing entry. He is confused what to write about and was thinking about writing a fictional story about an aristocrat who graduates from Chadsworth and goes on to create great poetry, art, and literature, but then he thinks, "That's a little passé."

His mom tells him to, "Write from his heart."

Noam decides to pour his guts out. He writes about his years of loneliness, how he was not accepted by the rich kids uptown and was bullied by the ghetto thugs at his high school. How he will prove to the world how great he is, that he has the best taste in culture, highest philosophical ideals, and grandest aesthetic visions, and how he will remake the world into a utopia for true aristocrats.

Noam spends the next week in his room waiting in anticipation. He is so nervous, he can't eat or sleep.

Finally Noam's mom brings him the mail. She says, "You got a letter from Chadsworth. Open it up."

Noam looks at the wax seal on the letter for Chadsworth Academy. Noam thinks, "How very aristocratic." Noam's hands are sweating and shaking nervously.

He is about to open it, but his mom hands him his grandfather's antique letter-opener jokingly saying, "For a true aristocrat."

Noam opens the letter with a sense of importance. He pulls out the letter, his hands still sweating. He puts it down. He turns to his mom: "I can't open it!"

"Relax," she says. Then she takes out the letter and turns to Noam with tears in her eyes. There is an awkward silence. Then she smiles and says, "Noam, you got in!" and gives him a big hug.

In the note, Principal Greenstein from Chadsworth writes, *"Ms. Metzenbaum, this is one of the most brilliant critiques of white male privilege and toxic masculinity I have ever read. We can't wait to have your son here at Chadsworth. It is an inclusive and nurturing environment for students from all diverse backgrounds."*

Noam is delighted but finds it odd that the school thinks his journal entries are a parody. He thinks, "Stupid rich dilettantes, but hey, at least I get to be with my one true love."

Noam and his mom pack for the move to Greenwich. She asks Noam to sort his stuff into one pile to take and one pile to give away to charity. Noam is distracted, lying on his bed daydreaming about reuniting with his dream girl at Chadsworth.

Noam's mom hires some Dominicans to help move. Four men show up who can hardly speak English. One of them asks in broken English, "What you wanna us move?"

"Noam is your stuff together?" she screams.

Noam replies "Just a minute."

He finds an old box in his mom's throwaway pile. She looks at it and says, "Noam, that's junk. Go sort out your stuff. Please!"

Noam takes one of the boxes into his room and opens it. It is a pile of an old video game series called "Leisure Suit Larry." Noam is fascinated by the aesthetics of the covers. It's a cool dude who looks like an adult version of himself surrounded by hot chicks in an 80s retro tropical paradise.

He still hears his mom in the background screaming, "Noam, get over here!"

"Just a moment," he replies.

Just as he is about to turn on his computer to play the game, his mom barges in to his room and sees his mess. "We have to be out of here by tomorrow!" she says.

Noam puts the game back in the box and hides it under his bed.

One of the Dominicans breaks Noam's mom's antique lamp. She breaks down in tears. "That was my mother's! It's priceless." She then pays them and says, "Thank you! Just go." Noam helps his mom clean up and puts his pile in order.

"You don't need those dirty spics," he assures her. "I'm the man around here."

"Whatever. Now go get some rest. Tomorrow is a big day. I made a lot of sacrifices to get you into Chadsworth," she says, exhausted.

Noam goes to his room and opens up the box he kept under his bed. He stays up all night playing "Leisure Suit Larry." As he continues to play every single game in the set, he falls asleep, becoming one with the game in his dream. He is Larry. Larry is a man of action. Noam finds himself in a tropical paradise; girls lounging in bikinis, girls topless, but why won't they talk to him? After all, he is Larry, the master of his own universe. He explores the island's many resorts, rainforests, and beaches; a magical world of exploration where everything is pink, purple, and turquoise neon colors. Maybe his crush is out there waiting for him. Then he sees her, but no it's not his crush; it's Alicia Silverstone from Clueless, but she is no longer a teen, rather a grown woman with a well-developed body sitting on a pink surface, topless, wearing see-through pants and displaying a smug upside-down smile. Perhaps she's already lost her virginity, cheating on him for countless years.

Then he asks her if she wants to make love to him. She explains that she has been too busy in her studies to worry about men and has little sexual experience. Noam is relieved that she is still a virgin. He says he wants them to be together.

“Yes I would like that,” she replies.

Just as he is about to kiss her, she disappears and he finds himself inside a sleazy casino. He looks around. Everyone starts laughing at him. Some old dirty drunk says, “Larry you’re almost 40 and still a virgin?” He rushes out to escape but realizes he is out of money for cab fare. He runs back into the casino and over to the slot machines hoping to make a fortune. All at once the word “virgin” appears on the slot machines and casino marquee. The sleazy overweight man turns to him and says, “There is only one way to end this madness,” and hands him a gun. He takes the gun and shoots himself in the head, drowning in his own blood.

Noam wakes up and thinks, “I’m not Larry, I’m not going to be some 30-something virgin. I’m going to hunt down my one true love. We shall lose our virginity together on a romantic warm summer night to the sounds of crickets and the waterfall of the country club serenading our love. Just like in the movies Dammit! I will find her and propose the very moment I lay eyes on her!”

The next day Noam and his mom drive up to Greenwich from New York City in her ‘88 Beamer. While driving, they fight over music. Noam wants to listen to the 80s station, while his mom wants to listen to NPR. As they drive up the East River Expressway, the song “What’s On Your Mind (Pure Energy)” by Information Society comes on. Noam looks back and admires the New York Skyline. He can remember the name of every Skyscraper in Manhattan from his grandfather Saul; the Empire State Building, the Chrysler Building, Rockefeller Plaza, the Seagram Building, the Pan Am Tower, the UN Building, and Trump Tower. Noam dreams of becoming an architect and beautifying every city in America. He thinks, "Real power is in creation, and those who build great things are the masters of civilization; gods among men."

As they drive by the Upper East Side, Noam admires all the luxury high rises and fantasizes about all the blonde Jewesses who live up in the towers, but he cannot make out the tower where his crush and Mr. Bloom live. Noam remembers Mr. Bloom talking about how his daughter would spend most of her time with Mr. Bloom's ex-wife in Greenwich but would spend holidays with him at his Upper East Side penthouse. Whenever there was a school break, Noam would beg his mom to take him to Mr. Bloom's place, but she had no idea his true intentions and didn't feel comfortable randomly inviting Noam over.

As they drive past the housing blocks of East Harlem, the song "I Want to Know What Love Is" comes on, which brings him back to that night, the night when his crush was stolen from him.

Noam's mom interrupts the song and turns the station back to NPR where some ethnic fusion music plays.

Noam turns around and takes one last look at the Manhattan skyline. Part of him misses the city. Despite all the obnoxious proles and trashy fake elites, this was his home; a place of exploration, the center of the universe, but he was on a mission to find his crush and establish a new aristocratic order.

As they leave the city, a radio segment on Roger Blackstone comes on. The radio host is interviewing a spokesman from the Republican Party. The radio host says, "This man, this lunatic is going to ruin this country with all his empty promises. Unfortunately, a lot of progressives are buying into it. They want a basic income, free healthcare, legalized drugs, and alternative energy, but at what cost? They are willing to overlook Blackstone's psychosis, fascist background, and lewd behavior towards teens. Plus he's letting his sexual perversions influence his immigration policies, which are flat out racist and misogynistic. This is how tyrants get elected, with grandiose visions and empty promises."

The Republican replies, "Blackstone's a progressive, a liberal fascist. He is one of your guys. The fascists were progressives, utopians, eugenicists, but the Republican Party is the party of true freedom. Blackstone does not believe in the free market. He wants to shut down private banks, give free handouts without a plan to pay for them. He will just give everyone LSD so they are too tripped out to realize their country has been taken over by a madman. He's the psychedelic Hitler! Not to mention most of his supporters are unemployed, racist, pedophile virgins who jerk off to Nazi Lolicon."

Noam starts laughing, thinking, "Psychedelic Hitler. Love it!"

As they approach Greenwich, the song "Invisible Touch" by Phil Collins comes on the 80s station. Noam feels like a true aristocrat, just like Phil Collins in his British manor. Noam starts humming "She seems to have an invisible touch yeah. She seems to have ..."

Suddenly a Mercedes SUV cuts them off. Noam's mom flips them off, shouting, "Fuckin' asshole."

"No way for a true aristocrat to behave," Noam says. "I shall have the filthy cunt beheaded."

Noam's mom turns to him, "Don't be silly, Noam. We are far from the aristocracy. Aristocrats have always been assholes. Nothing new here."

"My father was a great aristocrat," Noam says. "Tell me about the night you met."

"I don't want to talk about your father," she blurts out. "He was a prick, just a sperm donor. You have your whole life ahead of you."

As they pull off the freeway, Noam is appalled by all the boring suburban office parks run by hedge fund companies. "Where are the palaces?" Noam wonders to himself.

In front of them is an antique Rolls Royce driven by an older man with a white beard and Blackstone bumper sticker, which is black with gold lettering. "Finally, a true aristocrat," Noam thinks.

They park their car in downtown Greenwich. Finally, they've arrived somewhere Noam finds aesthetically intriguing. He is enamored by the magnificent setting of the town and all the attractive blonde girls. It is Indian summer, and the weather is warm and balmy. All the teen girls are wearing short skirts, revealing their long smooth legs. He feels as if he has been transported to a fairy-tale setting, somewhere in England perhaps, where he has faint memories of visiting as a small child; the English colonial architecture, the old Victorian clocks and lamp posts, the immaculate landscaping, the magical forest-like setting, and the warm moist scent of marigolds; the scent of what young blonde pussy must smell like.

Noam is wearing a buttoned dress shirt, which his grandmother gave him for his birthday, but when he sees the opulent clothing of the townspeople, he feels out of place. He begs his mom to give him money to shop for clothing but she says, “You’re fine. You’re a handsome boy. You don’t need all that designer stuff.”

Noam eventually convinces her to take him to the department store, which dates back to the Gilded Age. Noam admires all the marble columns, gilding, the giant old clock, and crystal chandeliers. It is packed with rich teen girls, his concubines. He felt like this was his palace and everything was his for the taking.

Noam asks his mom to buy him Armani sun glasses which she refuses to get, but he convinces her to buy him a pink Lacoste polo shirt and a yellow Alfani sweater, which he ties around his neck which makes him feel like a million bucks.

Noam tells his mom that he is going off to explore the town. He walks around town showing off his new clothes. He feels very aristocratic, but is self-conscious that no one is paying attention to him. He thinks, “I have finally arrived. This is my place to shine and rise to the top!”

He accidentally bumps into a platinum blonde, forty-something rich woman with fake tits and a face that's morphed by excessive plastic surgery. She gives him a bitch face.

“Whore!” Noam shouts

She walks away sniggering.

Noam thinks, "She's nothing but a cheap gold digger from Jersey who's sucking off some 90-year-old banker."

He walks into an ice cream shop. In front of him in line are a group of blond teen couples around his age. The boys are dressed in preppy style clothing and the girls in short skirts.

Noam wishes he could be their friends and share erotic experiences with them. He knows he has finally found a group that will appreciate his magnificence.

He is enamored by the good looks of the young teens: perfect smooth skin, golden blond hair, and no cares in the world. Noam orders a mango sorbet waffle cone but is very self-conscious with the group of teens behind him.

Noam leaves the ice cream shop and sees a group of boys around 14 and 15 hanging out in front of the ice cream shop to meet their girlfriends who were buying ice cream. They are all blond, athletic, and wearing tank tops after working out. They are still sweating. Noam over hears one of the girls say, "Oh my God … it's the Chads!"

The Chads start to flirt with the girls. Noam feels a bit of jealousy but assures himself he will be accepted by them once he is in school. Noam can't get over how good-looking the boys are.

Noam is confident in his heterosexual credentials, but one night his mom took him to a cocktail party hosted by an avant garde gay photographer in Chelsea. He was very controversial but became friends with his mom after she was the only journalist to give him a fair interview.

At the party when all the adults were drunk, Noam decided to snoop around because he wanted to steal something controversial. Noam gulped down a glass of Merlot and worked up the courage to sneak into the photographer's study.

Noam found his private collection of art photographs of naked blond teen boys in saunas, skinny dipping in forest lakes, taking showers, and changing in locker rooms; mostly taken in Germany and Scandinavia. Noam masturbated to the photos but the old gay man walked in on him and told him to get lost. He stole one of the photos as a souvenir and something to jerk off to.

Noam was never attracted to the ugly beasts at his old school, but these boys remind him of the boys in the photos. He dreams of pleasing both the boys and the girls, having a ménage à trois as they call it in the movies. He has to convince himself: "I'm not a faggot! I just appreciate aesthetic perfection in the male form, just as great artists like Michelangelo did."

Noam's mango sorbet waffle cone starts to melt in the sticky warm evening air. It is the sensation of erotic juices. He licks his fingers, fantasizing he had just fingered and jerked off the young couples.

Noam notices a group of young teen girls who are around his age, probably high school freshman like him sipping smoothies next to a fountain. Noam always found fountains to be the most romantic setting, with the sound of the water on a warm summer night. He imagines himself sitting with the girl of his dreams sharing the waffle cone as the spigots of the fountain squirt the erotic juices of his lover.

Noam tries to work up the courage to approach one the young blonde girls. She has the same blonde Jewish look that always appealed to him; something about the golden blonde hair, almond eyes, dimple smile, and cute pointy little nose. Just like his crush.

He remembers hanging around his cousins in Long Island. His mom's sister had married a wealthy Middle Eastern car dealership owner. Noam despised the man. He was always rude to Noam, wore a gold chain and had bad body odor.

Noam couldn't understand how such an obnoxious, low class man could be so wealthy. They are all trashy wannabe guidos, not true aristocrats like him and his father. He had two male cousins around his age whom he also despised.

One of his cousins, who bullied Noam when he was younger, had a cute blonde Jewish girl friend. He loathed his cousin for being able to attract such a girl.

"Why did he get such as cute blonde Jewess and not me? I am the son of a great aristocrat!" Noam thought. Still, Noam never had the guts to talk to his cousin's girlfriend and had to watch them make out whenever he visited them in the summers, but one time when she was spending the night, he sneaked into her room, and got a hold of her lacy panties, soaked in her aroma. He sniffed and licked her scent, which transported him to another world where anything was possible; the sweetness of a blonde girl, but with an exotic spice to it. Noam thought one day "I will get a girl like that and I can drink her sweet nectar all night."

Noam stands in front of the girls awkwardly in silence. He smiles.

“What do you want?” one of the girls says.

“Hi, my name is Noam. I just moved here,” he replies.

“Ok, that’s nice,” she responds dismissively and resumes chatting with her friends.

Noam has a feeling that these girls must know his crush.

He interrupts them, “Do you know Natalie Bloom?”

They laugh. One mocks him, “Do you know Natalie Bloom?” in a nasally voice.

“Well I thought you might know her. Do you go to school around here?”

The girls just ignore him and continue chatting.

Noam drops his waffle cone and walks away humiliated.

Dejectedly, he walks back to meet up with his mom and on the way overhears an old rich couple on the street talking about the election.

“I can’t believe the American people would fall for such a con artist,” the woman groans. “I have lost all respect for the people in this country, the people in flyover country. They just aren’t well, uh, informed.”

“I just care about the industry. Blackstone is going to shut down the entire banking industry,” the man replies.

“I know all about that fascist prick,” the woman goes on.

The gentleman interrupts, “Listen Babs, he’s going to destroy us, but not just us, this town, the entire American way of life.

He's talking about nationalizing the entire banking system. I'm thinking about putting all our assets into the Cayman's account. The man's a lunatic."

"I know dear, but we have the means to survive. Aren't you concerned about the most vulnerable in society? I mean the Blackstone's father was an outright Fascist, and he's a racist, misogynistic pervert! What about the immigrants and the vulnerable teenage girls, I'm very worried Irving!"

"Immigrants? I don't think Blackstone's really serious about that," the man replies. "He just wants to keep the good-looking ones, and I can always get a robot to replace Maria. And the teen girls will be just fine. I mean Blackstone's a choir boy compared to all these horndogs running around from Chadsworth. I just think his financial proposals are flat out fascistic, not to mention communist. It's the 30s all over again."

"Well I just think his tastes are horrendous," she says. "I mean French Rococo meets 1980s Casino Chic? Come on! With all that money, can't you at least hire a decent interior decorator or architect like Daniel Liebeskind to design your buildings? The very fact that Saul Metzenbaum designed all his early work makes me ashamed to be a Jew! Worst architect of the 20th century by far!"

"I kind of like the Blackstone style," the man says with a smirk.

She responds, "I can't even look at you right now Irving!"

Noam laughs to himself, "These stupid old rich people think they are the aristocracy. Ha! They need to drop dead and let the real aristocrats take over. Blackstone is onto something!"

Noam meets up with his mom by her car. He gets hungry and asks her to take him to The Brasserie for dinner. "I want champagne and escargot, Dammit!" he demands.

"Noam come on, be sensible! We are on a tight budget, and besides you're way too young to drink, and escargot isn't Kosher. I have a TV dinner I can heat up at home."

"Kosher?" Noam replies. "First of all, I'm not a Jew, and second of all, I saw you eating week-old frozen pork chops the other night. You are just too cheap. We need to prove that we are worthy if we want to be respected in this town."

"I thought you didn't care about impressing nouveau riche petite bourgeoisie filth," his mom replies mockingly.

Noam runs off to take a peek into The Brasserie. It's a Friday night, date night, and the place is packed with groups of rich blonde teen girls on dates with their boyfriends. "If only my mom would let me eat there," he thinks. "I could have a girlfriend like that. All that great food wasted on those stupid spoiled little brats!"

Noam's mom has to get an extra job as a personal assistant for a wealthy old British woman who lets them stay in the tiny guest house behind her mansion (which is in the style of a Georgian manor).

Noam befriends the woman, and she invites him over for Lady Grey tea and crumpets. Noam says in his fake British accent, "Oh yes, Lady Grey, Sasha Grey, Lady Sasha Grey! Not quite a lady but a …"

The woman interrupts him "Who on God's green earth is Sasha Grey?"

"She's, uh, a famous artist!" Noam replies.

"Oh she sounds lovely, I'd love to see her work. Is she on the internet? I'll have to give her a look later." The old woman gets up to get the fresh crumpets out of the oven.

Noam laughs, spitting out his tea on to the table and quickly cleans it up with a cloth napkin. He doesn't want to make a bad impression. Noam had never had someone so important show interest in him. He assumed she was going to be another typical old rich woman like many of his mom's friends.

They discuss philosophy, and Noam tells her that he is reading Alistair Blackstone's biography. She confides in Noam that her late husband was a controversial British politician and personal friend of Alistair Blackstone.

She refuses to reveal his name but says he was accused of Nazi collaboration. "I have a lot of respect for the Jewish people," she says apologetically. "And I don't condone his actions, but people have to understand that was a different era. He was a good man and loving husband and that's all that really matters in life, not status nor politics. I have preferred to keep a low profile in this town. This town is run by dirty money, but we shall not discuss politics. Noam, feel free to explore my library. I see something special in you. You remind me of a young man I once knew, who went on to do great things."

Noam is honored. He finds a copy of Alistair's manifesto in her library, the same one his grandfather gave him. Then he finds his grandfather's photo book of old New York that was destroyed. The woman turns to Noam, "That is a superb photo series. It is yours."

Noam thanks the woman. It even has his grandfather's signature. "Watch your back at Chadsworth," she says. "My eldest son went there. It was founded as an all-boys school in the late 19th century and wasn't integrated until the 1960s. My son told me they have still kept the old British boarding school customs. But I shouldn't worry you, you will have a splendid time. You're a bright young man, Noam. Now go, get plenty of rest. The future offers boundless possibilities for you."

Noam is bewildered, and thinks, "Old British boarding school customs? A world where they respect and honor the true aristocrat? Sounds like my place to shine."

Noam goes back to the guest house, which has one bedroom and a living room. The night before school, Noam's mom kisses him goodnight. He is embarrassed that she still treats him like a little boy.

Noam falls asleep and dreams of Chadsworth. He is dressed in his fancy school uniform. He walks through the countryside and opens up a gate and walks into a magical garden filled with Roman statues until he finally reaches Chadsworth Academy, which resembles Oxford. All the students in their blue blazers rush up to greet Noam.

"Noam welcome to Chadsworth!" "You are the greatest intellectual!" "We are just mere mortals in your presence." Then he hears the most beautiful harpsichord music playing in the background. He searches the premises to see where the angelic symphony is coming from.

The rooms start twisting around, getting wider, and turning upside down like an M.C. Escher maze. Then he finally reaches the location of the sounds, it is a large baroque concert hall, and up on the stage is a beautiful blonde girl in a puffy dress playing the harpsichord. Then she turns her head and notices him. It is her, his crush, his one true love, playing just for him, his inauguration to Chadsworth! The angelic sounds are interrupted by his alarm. He bangs his alarm clock, “Dammit! Not again.”

After breakfast, Noam starts writing in his journal, “Today is the beginning of a new start on the journey of life. Youth, all of them have over a million paths from which to choose from in this forest of bountiful opportunities. The path awaits you. This is it, your time to triumph.”

"Noam, the bus is here! Go now!" His mom commands him to get out of the house and stop writing in his journal.

Noam steps onto the bus as if he were a prince entering his chariot. He notices the cute blonde Jewish girl from the fountain. He stands there awkwardly, about to ask her if he can sit down.

The bus driver, who is an older black man, says, “Hurry up kid, we need to get going.” The boys in the back laugh.

“May I …” Noam asks the girl awkwardly.

“Huh?” she replies.

“Sit down here?” he continues.

“Sorry, seat taken,” she replies and puts her purse down on the seat.

Noam is humiliated, but he tries not to let this one incident ruin his pride.

He walks past a group of handsome blond boys smirking at him. There is one available seat left at the back of the bus.

Looking out the window, he sees his mother drive off in her car. Noam doesn't want to draw attention to himself. It is just him now, all alone on the beginning of a new journey.

Noam takes out his journal and continues writing where he left off. Noam was not sure if he should write in it again. He begins to feel nauseous from the motion of the bus, the constant stops, and being surrounded by the other students. "Are they talking about me behind my back?" he wonders.

Noam looks out the window, trying not to make eye contact with the boys in front of him who are moving around in their seats. He watches all the mundane people in the neighborhood, feeling lonely and longing to find his one true love.

He takes out his journal and starts to write, "I am on my path to greatness and to love that one person in life, the Jewish girl with the blonde hair. We have a special connection that no other living being can comprehend. I love her. I love everything about her, her hair, her smile, her eyes, her heart, her soul. She is mine! She doesn't think I'm a dweeb, I swear, I will find her wherever she may be. I will hunt her down, she shall fall in love me, and I will propose to her when the end of the earth happens, even if my final days on this earth are coming. I will propose to her. 'Marry me,' and she will say 'Yes!' I will win her heart!"

Just as Noam is about to write a new sentence he is interrupted by a cruel voice, "What are you writing, dweeb?"

Noam looks up and sees a handsome blond jock type, the same type whom he saw all the pretty blondes swooning over earlier.

Noam's first day on the yellow bus and his plans for popularity, world domination, and plans to woo over his crush have reached a road block. This was indeed a crucial moment to prove his worthiness.

Noam closes his journal and holds it close against his heart.

In front of him is a mop of golden blond hair covered by a backwards white baseball cap like the rest of the boys wore with the Chadsworth logo on it. Noam thinks, "Really? Backwards baseball caps are for niggers."

The boy gets up and turns around to see who is sitting behind him. He takes off his white cap revealing his mane of golden hair. He is one of the most handsome boys Noam has ever seen; cute face and the smooth skin of a girl, but with the athletic, masculine power that commands attention.

"Hey kid, what's your name?" the boy says.

This was Noam's time to shine.

"My Name is Noam," he replies. "… Noam Metzenbaum! I am the greatest person who has ever lived!"

The boys all start laughing.

"Oh wow. You sound like a cool dude." the boy replies sarcastically. "Yo! Hey Chad! Come over here and see this new kid!"

Noam feels as if he were trying to gain some respect from a newly found African tribe, "The Chad."

The other boy turns to the boy talking to him and says, "Yo Nick, this kid's name is … uhh?"

"Noam!" Noam finishes for him.

“Yeah whatever, dude,” he scoffs. He leans over to Noam and grabs his polo shirt, “What’s your favorite color? Do you like pink?”

Noam doesn’t respond and smiles awkwardly.

“Pink? Are you serious? Isn’t that a girls’ color?” Nick asks.

“No, of course not,” Noam says defensively.

“What are you, a fag?” Nick says, his face beginning to appear more menacing.

More blond-haired boys turn around laughing at him.

“Pink is the color of vagina! Do you like Pussy?” Nick says.

“What? That’s vulgar,” Noam responds.

“Hahaha! What the hell is wrong with you? Don’t you like pussy? Oh wait, are you gay bro?”
Nick continues, “Carlos is gay, but he’s cool. This kid’s just a little virgin dweeb. But I have nothing against gays.”

Noam doesn’t know how to respond. He is on a quest to lose his virginity with his crush and she is out there waiting for him, saving her chastity for a special gentleman, not some lewd obnoxious brat like these boys.

Noam tightly holds his journal.

“What’s that, your diary?” Nick asks.

The other boy says, “Guys are not supposed to have diaries.”

“No! It’s a journal! A *men’s* journal,” Noam insists.

"Who the fuck cares?" Nick says. "You probably write emo stories in that book and plot to shoot up the school!" All the boys are laughing.

Another boy in front of him turns to Noam. This boy has to be the youngest looking of them all and is constantly munching on candy. He looks down at Noam. This Chad seriously has anime-like eyes that catch Noam's attention. Noam thinks, "Surely this kid understands I am being bullied by these idiots!"

The boy mumbles with his mouth full of candy, "Hey, are you gay? I heard you like sucking dick?"

"Why the hell do you think I am gay? I already have a crush!" Noam gets up and shouts.
The bus stops abruptly to pick up more students.

"So who's your crush?" Nick asks.

"None of your damn business!" Noam responds combatively.

"Tell us! Or are you too gay?" one of the other boys says.

"Is your crush a guy?" Nick asks. "That's cool, bro. We get it. Just don't check us out in the shower."

They all burst out laughing.

Noam realizes that he has to prepare for taking a shower after gym class because he never had the opportunity in his entire life to be around such good-looking guys naked. He thinks, "What if I accidentally get an erection? Don't stare at their dicks."

The other boy responds to Nick, "Shit! Like totally bro!"

"No! I don't like guys," Noam says. "So stop asking if I like guys or not!"

Nick puts his hands on Noam's shoulder and says sarcastically, "Maybe this kid hasn't even gotten his first erection yet. It's going to come this semester. Watch out, this kid is probably going to become a monster around school. His potential is rising. He just doesn't know it yet."

The bus stops at school. He has arrived at his final destination. He is on a mission, and he isn't going to let these morons stand in his way.

The boys continue laughing and block his entry.

"Get the fuck out of my way!" Noam shouts.

Nick starts doing a humping motion towards Noam, grabbing his dick, "Yeah bitch. You like what you see? Wanna suck it?"

The other boy says, "If you don't reply, that means yes."

"Then I guess that means yes," Nick says. "No worries. I got my dick sucked by Stacy last night with her retainer on. I doubt he can give worse head than that."

Noam gets up and trips on the candy, landing right on Nick's lap, with his dick brushing against his face.

Noam rises again, hunching over trying to hide his erection.

"What's wrong with your back? Stand up straight," Nick says.

Noam gets up, and they all notice his erection.

One of the boys says, "Looks like the new kid likes dick!"

They all chuckle.

"I don't blame him." Nick responds. "All the bitches want a taste of my golden seed."

The bus driver shouts, "Knock it off kids! Now get off my bus!"

The boys walk off the bus. The bus driver says, "See ya later punks!"

Noam is one of the last in line to walk off. One of the Chads pushes him, causing him to trip on the curb while the bus driver watches, ambivalent to Noam's torment. The driver closes the door shut and drives off.

Noam has finally arrived at his destination, his place of conquest. This is a whole new experience for him.

The school resembles an exclusive British boarding school with the aesthetic of old brick colonial style architecture. The sign on the front read "Chadsworth Academy, Established 1897."

Noam enters the school. He is all alone. He thinks, "Who needs others who will only stand in my way. I am a great aristocrat, a Roman emperor alone in this world that was created for me to conquer."

The green lockers stand side by side, left and right. The hallway went on so far that Noam cannot see the end. If he was to make it to the very end, a new endless hallway would appear soon after. "When I finally reach the end? When will I …" he wonders.

Noam bumps into a student. His journal falls to the floor, along with his pen.

"Yo ese! Amigo Amigo, where the hell ya think you're going?"

Noam looks at him. He is a chubby Puerto Rican boy with a stylish haircut, pink sunglasses, a pink tee shirt, and turquoise nylon pants (as if he weren't already flamboyant enough).

Noam says, "I'm sorry. I have to get to class."

The boy says with a big smile, "Chill out, Holmes. You need someone who can watch your back around here."

"I don't need anyone. I am on a one-man mission to find my crush," Noam thinks.

Noam hurries to get his books and put his pen back into the exact spine of his journal. He hurries off to class.

The Puerto Rican boy blows him a kiss in the air and says, "See ya later hot stuff. My name's Carlos by the way. Carlos de la Boca."

Noam runs to his first class. He is already late.

He bumps into a group of senior Chads.

One of them says, "Yo! Watch where you're going, punk! What are you, a freshman?"

Noam saw this coming. If he were to tell the truth, he knows the Chads will ridicule him. He is stronger than that. He is going to trick them. Give them a taste of their own medicine.

The Senior Chads stand there waiting for an answer. Unlike the Freshman Chads on the bus, these are big men with big muscles who could crush him with one touch, but he still won't let these monsters stand in the way of his quest to save his princess.

"Umm, no! I am a senior!" Noam says. I am an honor student of Roman History! What makes you plebeians thinks I am not?"

Carlos comes by to check out the situation. Noam is shocked that he is accepted by them. He doesn't fit the mold of a Chad as a chubby, gay Puerto Rican. He thinks, "How did he earn the respect of these racist homophobic beasts?"

The Chads looks at Noam's buttoned up color and geeky polo.

One Chad says, "I bet this kid's a virgin!"

Carlos puts an arm around Noam's shoulder and says, "No way! My homie here gets fine ass tail. I mean he has to fight the bitches off."

The Senior Chads are bewildered. One of them remarks, "I haven't seen this punk around here."

Another says, "Really? Who's your girlfriend? I know every chick in this school. So I can tell if you're lying."

Noam says, "I don't need a girlfriend! I have real work to do."

“What buddy? Yo lyin’!” the boy says. “You are so a freshman. Tell me, you had sex before?”

Noam says, “Get out of my way. I need to get to class.”

The Chad says, “Look if you don’t have a girlfriend you’re either a virgin or gay. And I got nothing against gays. It would be a hate crime if I did, but we don’t tolerate virgins around here.”

Noam didn’t want to hear that. He holds his notebook to his chest and puts his nose up in the air and walks off to class.

The Chads start laughing at him and shouting, “Virgin! “Never even kissed a girl!”

Carlos chases him and says, “Yo! Where you going?”

This kid really wants Noam’s attention. As Noam goes off in the distance, Carlos shouts, “If you ever need a buddy, I’m here for ya, Holmes.”

Carlos looks down and thinks, “That boy ain’t right.”

Noam finds his history class at Room 143. He looks at his watch. He is 26 minutes late. Noam stands in front of the door in a nervous sweat. His hands are shaking. This is it!

He peeks into the room. Everyone is sitting down waiting in boredom for the class to start. Noam looks away and takes in a deep breath. This was too much to bear.

Then he looks in again. There they were, the “Chads,” the popular arrogant blond freshman boys who had tormented him earlier that morning on the bus ride, all sitting together on the left side of the class facing the windows. Noam thinks, “Pull yourself together. This is my domain, my place to shine. Academia is no place for loud, obnoxious meat heads."

Noam takes in another deep breath and looks in again. He sees a group of pretty blonde girls sitting in the middle of the class, including the girls he recognizes from the fountain earlier.

But then Noam notices someone else. Up in front in the second row, in front of the other girls sits: his crush, his maiden, the girl with the mixed Nordic and Jewish features. The girl he had been searching for and dreaming about every breathing moment since he laid eyes on her that magic fateful night. There she was! Noam feels butterflies in his stomach, shortness of breath, and his entire body is shaking in a cold sweat. He thinks, "Noam, you're a warrior king, a great philosopher, and a perfect gentleman just like Plato and Socrates! She was put on this very planet just for you. She is yours for the taking."

Noam takes in another deep breath and slowly opens the door, not to bring attention to himself. He tries not to make eye contact with her and sits down in the front row a few seats to her right.

Noam just sits there, staring at the clock waiting for the teacher to arrive. His crush is only several feet away. He is breathing in the very same oxygen, her DNA particles entering his lungs with every deep breath, yet he does not want to blow things and stare at her.

He thinks, "Just one look." He takes in another deep breath and quickly glimpses at her. Every dream he has ever had, every romantic fantasy replayed at this moment. The vivid visions of her saved in the back of his mind, like discovering a lost treasured lolicon image of a blonde Jewish anime girl on the hard drive of your computer.

Noam settles in at his desk, takes out his note pad and starts organizing for class. He thinks, "If I am going to get this girl, I have to prove myself honorable in school! I must get an A+ in this class!

Noam could hear the arrogant blond Chads in the background talking. One of them says, "Yo, who's the new girl?" "The other says, "Oh that's Natalie Bloom. She's fine. I heard she's still a virgin."

"Fresh meat!" another responds.

Noam is terrified and relieved at the same time. He knows in his heart that she is pure, waiting for him, but now the Chads have their sights on her. He is now engaged in a battle, a knight prepared to use lethal force to defend the honor of his maiden.

Soon the fat history teacher walks into the room. Some of the Chads laugh. Class was to begin. The fat teacher is half-deaf and cannot hear anything around him.

"Look at this fat fuck," one of the Chads sniggers.

"Yeah I know, when's the last time he's seen his dick?"

"Never. This guy's probably a virgin, like that kid over there!"

That Chad was pointing to Noam of course. Noam thinks, "Is this my future? A middle-aged virgin, teaching a bunch of rich, hedonistic brats? No! Noam, stop thinking negative thoughts. You are great. You are fabulous, a true aristocrat!"

"Oh my God, dude!" the Chad says. "He's gonna be like the fucking teacher's pet! Just watch, dude!"

The fat teacher starts roll call.

“Molly Katzenberg.”

“Here.”

“Lisa Goldberg.”

“Here.”

“Audrey Johnson.”

“Here.”

“Wendy Silverstein.”

“Here.”

Noam looks over and recognizes Wendy as the blonde girl he had the encounter with at the fountain.
“Nicholas Anderson.”

“Yo, bro.”

The Chads laugh.

The fat teacher says, “Calm down. Let’s get off to a good start.”

“Chad M.”

“Here boss!”

“Got it,” as the teacher marks off his name.

“Chad S.”

“That’s me bro!”

"Yep, got that."

"Let's hear again, Chad S.?"

"Yo!"

"Ok. Now let me hear … Chad B."

No answer.

One of the other Chads says, "Chad B is getting done with lacrosse practice. He will like, be coming in a few minutes."

"Got it." The teacher marks him "present" even though he is not.

Noam is nervously preparing for the teacher to call his name. Thoughts stream into his head, "Don't screw this up Noam! Get ready to pronounce your name like a true aristocrat that is prepared for battle."

The teacher continues roll call.

"Natalie Bloom"

"Here."

Noam flinches. He thinks, "Did she notice?"

His entire world sank. It was as if time froze and one second became an eternity. Every heartbeat he could hear like the slow ticking of the clock.

His significant other is in the very same room as him, just a few feet away, as if their hearts beat together as one.

Noam looks over his shoulder briefly. Then quickly looks back at the fat teacher. He can hear the Chads laughing in the background, "Oooooo, someone's got a stalker crush."

Then he hears the popular blond girls giggle. "What a weirdo," one of them remarks.

He looks over at his crush again. She looks uncomfortable. "Did I screw things up?" Noam thinks. "No, she is disgusted by those subhuman Chads. Stop thinking negative thoughts. Noam you are fabulous and she will be impressed by you great knowledge of history."

The awkward situation is interrupted as the teacher continues taking roll.

"Kei Inoue?"

"She waves her arm. "You can call me Katie."

"Got it."

Noam looks over again. Katie is sitting right next to his crush. "Perhaps they are close friends?" he theorizes. "Perhaps that's one way of getting to her heart; know her, then know my crush. Brilliant thinking, Noam."

Because Noam is getting excited over the thought of his crush and her best friend, that cheesy song by the Spice Girls comes chiming in, "If you want to be my lover, you gotta get with my friends."

"Dammit! Don't think about lame pop songs! You're better than that Noam! You're a great aristocrat! Dream of Bach, Mozart, Phil Collins! Not that crap! What if I accidentally hum that lame song out loud and the Chads find out. They will kill me because

I've lost my honor to defeat them! Just shut up Noam and pay attention to class! This is it!"

"Noam Metzenbaum"

Noam stops breathing. He feels like he is going to die. He thinks, "This is your moment Noam. You need to get your act together."

The teacher calls out, "Noam Metzenbaum. Do we have a Noam Metzenbaum present?"

Noam proclaims, "Here I am! I am so glad to be here!" As he stands there erect like a Japanese soldier ready to die as a kamikaze pilot.

The teacher says, "Did your mom name you after Noam Chomsky? Smart lady."

"Ah, I don't know," Noam stutters.

"Ok, got it," the teacher says.

Noam looks back. Everyone is laughing at him. Even his crush, who is putting her hands over her mouth trying to hold in her giggles.

"Did I fuck up my one chance?" he wonders. "Fail at my mission? Dammit Noam. I'm going to make her love me, even if I have to drag her out of her room and take her on to my space ship to our own special planet that was created just for us to populate."

The teacher stops taking roll and goes over to the computer to set up a power point presentation. It is these moments of awkward inaction that make Noam the most vulnerable, like a soldier without a general.

Nick whispers to the other Chads, "Dude, that kid is totally going to shoot up the school! I called it earlier. I will bet you a thousand bucks he shoots up the school by Friday."

Chad S. says, "Yeah I know dude, watch, it will totally happen bro. They should do a test to see if you're a virgin. Cause like if they expelled all virgins we wouldn't have any school shootings."

Nick says, "Dude. That's genius, bro. We should tell the principal that kid's going to shoot up the school."

"Yeah bro, I don't wanna get shot up. I want to live, dude, so I can get laid every night," replies Chad S.

Noam is enraged. He assumed that everyone would be a virgin at such an exclusive institution. Not like his old school, where thugs were constantly getting hood rats pregnant, and they even had an STD clinic on campus.

Noam despised his old school but took great pride in knowing that he was superior; that he came from a prestigious pedigree; being the son of a great aristocrat and carrying on that legacy through his philosophical contemplations.

Noam thinks, "But now at this utmost elite institution, where the movers and shakers of American society send their offspring, not only do they lack the true aristocratic credentials to rule; to add insult to injury, they do not even afford me the most basic decencies. And on top of it all, all these hot rich blonde popular girls, perhaps the daughters of billionaires, throw themselves at these vile disgusting creatures, the Chads."

Noam looks back at them; their golden blond hair, perfect bodies, and cocky arrogant smiles as they joke about which girl they are going to deflower next.

He fantasizes, "If I can't win them over with my intellect, charm, and charisma, I have to kill them first! No one is better than me!"

The teacher turns on the power point presentation. The class calms down. The social chitter chatter is over. "This is the time for the real academic to shine," thinks Noam.

He regains his pride and is ready to demonstrate his knowledge of history. He knows everything about the subject, and knows that all great historic events in history were leading up to his very own rise to power. He thinks, "All this great philosophy was created so I could study it and rule over the lowly masses. And I shall take these historic events and rewrite history in my image. My princess is right here waiting for her prince to kill his rivals and declare himself emperor! This is it dammit!"

Unfortunately, the teacher announces that today's class is about the school's rules and decorum. Noam thinks, "Rules are for plebs; Aristocrats make the rules! Oh so boring. I can write a better code of decorum in one second!"

After a long boring discussion of the school's rules, which Noam daydreams through, not paying any attention to them in the slightest, the bell rings and the class is over.

Noam sits in his chair watching the other students leave, waiting for his crush. First the Chads and their perfect athletically toned bodies, then he sees his crush walking from behind; her golden blonde hair, her yellow sweater which shows off her figure, and her pink skirt which shows off her shapely buttocks. Noam stays in his chair fantasizing about burying his face into her bare buttocks.

Now Noam is getting an erection, which handicaps his ability to get up but the teacher is motioning for the kids to leave. After most of the class has left, the fat teacher says, “Okay Noam, time to get on with your day.”

Noam gets up, hunching over to hide his erection, but luckily for him the entire class is gone. He doesn’t want to run into the Chads again. Just get the rest of the day over with and go home to write in his journal.

Noam gets up and waits outside the room. He looks around, “No Chads. The coast is clear.”

He walks down the hallway to drop his books off in his locker. Just as he thinks no one is standing in his way, he sees the freshman Chads hanging out around his locker. He thinks, “That is my locker! How dare they stand in such close proximity?”

Noam thinks about just holding on to the books but they are too heavy and are causing his back to ache. He decides to go right to his locker, quickly deposit his books, and not make eye contact with the Chads.

As Noam is walking to his looker, with his nose up in the air and eyes staring at his destination point, he bumps into the Chads; his books falling all over the floor.
Nick says, “Watch where you're going, virgin!”

Noam looks up at Nick. He hates himself at this moment, but he can’t get over how good-looking Nick is. He thinks, “At my other school all the bullies were ugly beasts, but how can such a handsome boy be so cruel?”

Noam just stands there admiring Nick's mane of golden-blond hair, smooth skin, and Adonis chest; just a freshman like him but with such prowess.

Chad S. says, "What you reading?"

"Just my philosophy books," Noam replies.

Nick says, "Ah yes, the Virgin Philosopher!"

They all laugh at his cheesy joke.

"I am a great aristocrat and you are nothing but slaves," Noam declares.

Chad S. replies, unimpressed, "Whatever, dude. My dad is loaded. He's a hedge fund manager. What about you?"

"My dad's an aristocrat, in fact descended from the British monarchy," Noam replies.

Nicks says, "What's his name?"

Noam pauses. He had never met his dad, and his mom refuses to talk about him.

"Ah. Sir. Uh … Nigel Metzenbury IV."

The all start laughing.

Nick says, "This kid is the biggest loser I've ever seen. My fat middle-aged Mexican maid Juanita is way cooler then this dude. I mean she's even given me coke in exchange for not reporting her to ICE."

They all laugh again in sync.

Nick says, "Let's see what virgin boy here is hiding in his big pile."

Noam reaches down to pick up his stuff. One of the Chads pushes Noam aside causing him to stumble on his shoe laces.

Nick pulls out a picture. It is the picture of his crush that Noam had stolen from Mr. Bloom. Noam expects them to mock him but they all stare at him in an awkward silence. They whisper among themselves about how to handle the situation. Noam is mortified.
He thinks, "Will they tell the entire school? What shall my crush think of me? No, I'm not a stalker dammit! That was an act of pure love of a perfect gentleman who can appreciate pure beauty. She will understand. No, not only will she understand, she will fall in love with me, knowing that I had given my heart to her on a platter. Yes Noam, things are going to work out just fine!"

After about five minutes of deliberation, Nick slowly comes up to Noam with the look that he wants to kill him and talks right in his face, "What are you doing with that picture of Natalie Bloom? Are you some kind of Psycho Stalker? Are you going to rape her, virgin?"

"No!" replies Noam.

One of the other Chads says, "Yeah, let's not let that happen. If he rapes her he will technically lose his virginity. I want this loser to die a virgin."

"I'd like that too," Nick says. "But we have to be mature about this. I don't want virgin boy to go on a shooting spree."

The other Chad replies, “Let’s tell the girls about this creep who’s after Natalie.”

“No, I can handle it,” says Nick.

Noam says, “Wow let me get my stuff. I have another class to go to.”

Nick turns to Noam, “It’s not that simple. We don’t respond to that kind of sick shit here at Chadsworth. Didn’t you listen to the rules in class today? We could get you expelled for this. Just one call to Principal Greenstein and you’re finished.”

Noam pleads, “Please don’t. I didn’t mean any harm.”

Nick says, “Look kid, I kind of feel sorry for you. I mean you're in high school now and still a virgin. I’ve been getting my dick sucked since sixth grade. There’s nothing more pathetic than being virgin. So I won’t tell Principal Greenstein on you, but here’s the deal. From now on you are our bitch. You have to do whatever we say.”

Noam says, “Ok! Just give me my pictures back.”

Nick laughs and tears up the picture.

Noam had stared at that picture every night. It was the one physical souvenir he had to connect to his true love. He felt like his heart was just torn in half.

“You got that, bitch?” Nick asks.

Noam reluctantly agrees, “Ok.”

Noam goes off to math class, luckily for him there are no Chads in the class, but he can't find his crush either. He wonders, "Is she avoiding me?"

While most kids find math boring, Noam was able to use his mathematical skills to dream of new killing machines; machines that could wipe out two thirds of humanity. But he never had access to the funding to build such mechanisms, and this causes him to despise the Chads even more, for spending their vast fortunes on hedonistic pleasures.

While he is daydreaming about using geometry to create the ultimate Chad-killing machine, a nerdy Indian boy, Sanjay, gets up to announce the tryouts for the Mathletes. Noam thinks, "What a waste of time. I have better uses for my math skills."

Noam leaves class to go to lunch. He doesn't have much of an appetite. He is in battle mode and he shall not eat until he accomplishes his mission. His mom has packed him a bagel and cream cheese, a Perrier, and a black-and-white cookie. Then his stomach starts to growl and he thinks, "Perhaps one bite won't hurt."

Noam enters the lunchroom, looking around like a mouse watching out for owls. He sees all the social cliques. The blond Chads, the blonde cheerleaders, the token black jock who hangs out with the Chads and cheerleaders, the popular Jewish kids, the nerdy Jewish kids, the Asian nerds, the wannabe cool Asians who try to hang out with the popular Jewish kids, and then he sees her, his c r u s h.

She is sitting with the popular Jewish kids, right next to Wendy Silverstein, the blonde girl he recognizes from the fountain, the other blonde girl Lisa Goldberg, and their friend Molly Katzenberg, who has reddish brown hair, blue eyes, and a curvy figure.

There she is, his crush, sitting with them. But she is not talking, just listening to their chitter chatter. Noam thinks, "Is she alone just like me? I knew we were destined to be together; two lone individuals, Übermensch who the common homo sapiens cannot relate to?" Noam thinks about approaching his crush, but this isn't the right time.

Noam looks around for a place to sit. He thinks about sitting down next to the nerds but just listening to their nasally, whiny voices makes him want to vomit. He thinks, "What? No table for true aristocrats?"

Noam decides to sit alone. He assures himself, "I am above all this clique bullshit."

Noam finds one empty table left. He sits down. The table is messy with gum underneath the table, everything is sticky.

Noam takes out his bag lunch. He closes his eyes and imagines he is alone in a serene location, up on top of a mountain, a world where the human race had been annihilated and it was just him and the mountain top looking down on the depopulated landmass. Noam takes in a deep breath and is about to take a bite out of his bagel, but then someone puts their arm around him.

"Was up amigo?"

Noam looks up. It is Carlos de la Boca, the chubby, flamboyant Puerto Rican homosexual whom he had run into earlier.

Noam replies, "Not much."

Carlos says, "You don't look all right, Holmes. Why you sitting all alone?"

"None of your business," replies Noam.

"You look like you could use a friend right now," says Carlos.

Noam disagrees, "Look! I'm sorry, but I am not into guys. I am not … I am not a faggot!"

"Whoa! That's homophobic, Holmes," Carlos responds.

"I just want to eat my lunch in peace," says Noam.

"Look, I know what you're going through," Carlos says. "You're insecure, totally confused, Holmes. You haven't had sex yet so you don't know if you like dudes or chicks."

"Look, I am not gay," Noam insists. So please just leave me alone."

"Ok. I get it, you straight," Carlos says. "You just need some confidence."

Noam says, "What do you mean? I turn my nose up to these useless plebs, but I can't stand being around these beasts … these Chads!"

Carlos bursts out laughing, spitting his cream soda all over the place.

"You think this is funny!" says Noam.

Carlos continues laughing, "Yes I do. You see, I got Chad Thundercock wrapped around my finger, eating out of my hand. So don't let them intimidate you, you got to stand up for yourself, Holmes, if you want respect. Where you from?"

“Uh. New York City, the Lower East, but my father was a great …”

Carlos interrupts, “Lower East Side? That’s gangsta man. You’re a real New Yorker for shits! So don’t let these pansy ass small town white boys push you around. You gangsta, Holmes!”

Noam says, “So how do you deal with the Chads? What’s your secret?”

Carlos stands still for a minute looking all gangster and chilled out and then says, “Look, I’m a senior, and if some new fresh meat comes in, well first of all, if he’s a newcomer right? I want him to suck my ass with jelly, which we call toss the salad, it means sucking my ass, with jelly. Some people use syrup, but I prefer jelly!”

Noam is repulsed and horrified. He is about to lose his lunch. Then Carlos takes out an old packet of grape jelly someone had left over from breakfast and says once again, “I prefer jelly.”

“Look, I ah don’t want to … anything to do with this,” Noam replies.

Carlos burst out laughing, spitting soda all over Noam’s pink polo shirt. “I’m just fucking with you, Holmes. It’s from Chris Rock. You know Chris Rock?”

Noam replies, “Yes of course. He’s that funny black man on TV. He’s always like 'You got black people, and then you got niggers.' That sort of thing.”

Suddenly, the black jock overhears Noam. “What did you just call me?”

“None of your damn business,” Noam says. “I was talking to my friend Carlos.”

Carlos says, “So this dude wants nothing to do with me, and now he wants me to cover his ass?”

Then Carlos puts his arm around Noam and says, “He’s my bitch. Now fuck off, or I am going to call Grande Master Chad D to chop off your big black balls.”

The black boy says submissively to Carlos, “Yes, sir.”

Then Carlos pats the black jock on his frizzy hair as if he were a little dog.

Noam starts giggling, “Wow! That was fuckin' awesome! How did you do that?”

Carlos says, “I told you, I run things around here.”

Carlos starts running his thick greasy fingers through Noam’s hair. Noam is uncomfortable but doesn’t know how to respond. He realizes that Carlos is useful in dealing with the Chads. He gently pushes Carlos’s hand away.

Carlos asks, “You know Nick, right?”

“Yes, of course,” Noam replies. “He’s the biggest asshole, but he’s so …”

Carlos interrupts him “Hot! Damn straight, Holmes. Let me let you in on a little secret. Well Nick likes getting his dick sucked, but none of these little white freshmen bitches know how to get the job done. So I give him the sugar, and I control him. All the other Chads do whatever he says, so I’m gonna do my new friend a favor and tell the Chads to lay off you. You got it,

Holmes, that New York 'tude. You gonna be all right. Do you like anime?"

Noam replies, "Love it. Have you seen "The Poem of the Wind and The Trees?" It's about two boys who fall in love at a French boarding school in late 19th century France. The aesthetics are superb."

Carlos says, "You sure you ain't gay, Holmes? I'm more into Patalliro. Gangsta as fuck! You got this little boy king, telling everyone what to do, making them his bitch. That's how I roll, homie!"

"That sounds cool," replies Noam.

Carlos says, "I want to give my new friend something special." He hands Noam a rare collectible copy of Patalliro.

Noam takes it out and admires the colorful queer aesthetic. Like with "The Poem of the Wind and The Trees" he can tell there is an aristocratic, art nouveau influence, and ever since reading Blackstone's photography book he is fascinated with everything Japanese.

He turns to Carlos. "Thanks a lot. You're a true friend."

Carlos replies "You don't need to thank me. That's what friends are for. Whenever you need a favor don't hesitate to ask, and by favor I mean anything if you catch my drift." Carlos starts licking the inside of Noam's ear but Noam is worried the Chads or the popular girls will notice. He thinks, "I don't want my crush to think I'm a faggot!"

Noam interrupts the situation and asks Carlos, "Do you like Roger Blackstone?"

Carlos replies "Hell no! That man's racist, Holmes! He just likes blondes, especially blonde Jewish chicks. He said he wants to deport all the chicks he ain't into. And I don't think he's into Ricans. He don't appreciate the booty. He just wants these blonde Jewish chicks like those bitches over there," pointing to Wendy Silverstein, Lisa Goldberg, and Noam's crush Natalie Bloom.

Noam is offended. He says, "Well, I like blonde Jewish girls!"

Carlos says, "You need to get over those stuck up rich bitches. You need a nice chica. I can hook you up."

Noam refuses, "No thanks. I have a crush!"

"Who's your crush?" Carlos asks.

"Never mind!" replies Noam.

Carlos says, "I know who you like; you crushin' over that blonde Jewish chick, Natalie Bloom."

"Shush!" says Noam.
Carlos says, "Relax, chicks like a dude who's chill. If you really like Natalie I can help you win her over. You just need to listen to every word I say, and I mean everything." Carlos gives Noam a big hug, his sticky hands leaving grease marks all over Noam's new polo shirt.

While Noam and Carlos are talking, the Chads look over at them joking around together. Nick can tell his sweet deal is under threat. He turns to the other Chads, "We got to take care of the virgin once and for all, and I know how to destroy him."

"How's that?" replies another Chad.

Nick says, “We need to fuck that new girl. Natalie Bloom.”

Chad S. responds, “That’s not a bad idea. Every year we get new crop of freshmen virgin pussy. Deflower her, and destroy that creep.”

”I love you guys.” Nick confides. “You're like brothers to me, and I won’t let anyone stand in the way of our brotherhood, especially some loser virgin wannabe school shooter.”

After lunch Noam goes to English class. There she is; his crush again in the class. He looks at her, admiring her perfect beauty. She catches him staring, looking uncomfortable. Noam sits down quickly, thinking, “Oh fuck. Not again!”

The teacher, Mrs. Smith introduces the class. “This semester we will be focusing on philosophy.” Noam is excited because they are reading Schopenhauer, and that is his area of expertise. Noam is exhausted from the long day, but this is his chance to prove himself once and for all.

Mrs. Smith calls roll. After going through names, she says, “Natalie Bloom.” Natalie replies “Here” in her cute voice. Noam can’t get over that sweet angelic voice. Noam looks over. He can’t help himself. He has to look at this beautiful creature that he has been dreaming about every night since the moment he laid eyes on her.

She looks very uncomfortable. Then Noam shouts out “Dammit, Noam,” and slams his face down on his desk.

The Chads start laughing, “Oooo, psycho stalker here has a thing for Natalie Bloom. Is he going to rape her, kidnap her, and take her down to his secret dungeon?”

Mrs. Smith goes over to Natalie and asks her if everything is ok. Natalie leaves the classroom with Mrs. Smith to speak to her in private.

The Chads start laughing, “You blew it loser virgin, now everyone knows you’re a creep!”

Noam looks back at the Chads. He says, “You shall pay for your crimes!”

Nick replies, “Oh I’m so scared. Virgin gonna shoot up the school? Or just go home and cry and write in his diary about what a loser he is, and how no girl is ever going to love him.” The bell rings. The day is over. Noam decides not to take the bus and walks home instead. He sees the Chads getting on the bus; he takes out his finger and pretends it is a pistol, shooting every single one of them.

He thinks, “Perhaps they are right. Maybe I will shoot up this school full of worthless rich brats! If only I can make her love me, then maybe, just maybe there can be peace in this cruel world.”

Noam walks home from school, trying to hold in his tears. He walks down a residential street lined with McMansions, noticing teens from his school pulling into their driveways in their expensive cars. He sees popular blond boys skateboarding in the street, and teen couples holding hands. He can’t take it anymore and is about to explode in tears.

He sees a trailhead and decides to take a detour through the woods. Once he is in the woods he takes in a deep breath of relief. He walks through the woods listening to the sound of the birds chirp, and the rustling of the trees. It is early autumn and the trees are beginning to change color.

Noam hadn't been out in nature since visiting his grandfather Saul at his cabin in the Catskills right before he died, but he felt at peace; no humans to interrupt his train of thought.

Noam's moment of serenity is disturbed. While walking through the woods he sees group of blond, popular boys hanging out. He doesn't recognize them. Perhaps they are freshman from another school or eighth graders from the middle school who had developed early.

He overhears one of them mentioning that he is still in eighth grade and can't wait to tap some high school ass next year.

Noam stares at them for a few minutes in rage. He notices one of them already has a girlfriend.
"My future adversaries," he thinks. "Future Chads! I should just kill them right now before they can surpass me!"

They catch him looking at them, and he decides it's best to avoid them. He thinks, "I'll deal with those little brats latter!"

He continues walking through the woods until he hears the sound of water rustling. He sits down by the creek and tries to meditate listening to the sounds of the frogs and the bubbling creek.

After some time, he gets up and continues walking home. Noam reaches a clearing in the woods. He notices the trees are being destroyed and sees the wood frames of some new McMansions going up.

One of the Mexican construction workers in his tractor shouts at him to get out of the way. Noam thinks, "Stupid rich assholes and their slaves have no respect for this planet. I can't wait to burn this town to the ground!" Noam flips out at the construction workers and blocks their tractor and yells, "Stop it! What do you think you're doing?" One of them curses at Noam in Spanish and throws an empty Corona bottle at him.

The contractor, a fat middle-aged Italian American man comes over to check out the situation. He comes over to Noam and says, "Look kid, we got work to do. We don't want any trouble. Now scram!" Noam flips him off and continues running. He hears the contractor yelling at him, "Who the fuck do you think you are?"

Noam finds himself back in a residential neighborhood. He is lost at first but then recognizes one of the street names. He continues down it and finally finds his way back home.

Once he gets home, his mom's says, "Noam, you're home late. How was your day?"

"Fine," Noam says in a deadpan voice.

"Great, did you study after school?"

"Yes," Noam replies.

She says, "Good for you. I knew it was worth sending you to Chadsworth."

Noam slams the door to his room and cries on his pillow.

He starts writing in his journal:

"My first day at Chadsworth Academy in Greenwich has been an utter catastrophe. My first chance of re-uniting with my one true love has been sabotaged by subhuman barbarians. It is time to get into battle mode Noam! You are a great warrior! No! A great aristocrat! A great warrior aristocrat! These rich brats at Chadsworth are way beneath you. They are subhuman scum!

The entire human race is scum! Noam, you are not a lowly homo sapiens but a human alien hybrid. That's right! That is why the lowly human race does not understand your greatness. Your father came down from outer space, choosing one human female to impregnate. Noam you are of a great master race. You have the power to enslave the lowly humans. You just have to outsmart them with your wit. Perhaps there are others out there just like you? Just not at Chadsworth. Therefore, I Noam Metzenbaum, offer a declaration of war against the institute of Chadsworth Academy and swear on the lives of the entire human race that I will be with her. My crush! Natalie Bloom! I wrote it dammit! I'm good enough for her. I can say her name! Yes! Natalie Bloom! Natalie Bloom! Natalie Bloom! She is mine, and I know she loves me. And if our love cannot be, then the entire human race shall parish in a sea of blood!"

Noam wakes up, "No time to write in my journal. Today is war!" Noam gets on the bus; he looks straight ahead trying not to make eye contact with the Chads, his sworn enemies.

The old black bus driver says, "Hurry up kid, we don't have all day!" The Chads laugh.

Noam ends up sitting next to an overweight, nerdy kid. The kid has a runny nose and is constantly blowing his nose, with snot going everywhere.

"Why don't you watch where you blow, you fat fuck!" Noam yells.

"I'm sorry," the boy says.

"Well you better be," replies Noam.

Nick gets up and turns to the fat kid, "Yo Elliot! Is this new kid bothering you?"

"No, but thanks for the concern," Elliot responds.

Nick looks toward Noam. "You see, Noam, even Elliot here has lost his virginity; in fact to a cute Asian girl from the Mathletes. So before you start shit, you need to tell everyone what a pathetic loser you are."

Everyone in the bus starts chanting, "Virgin! Virgin! Virgin! Virgin!"

Noam's first class is history, his best subject. This is his chance to prove himself, "The Chads know nothing about history! I shall prove my greatness, my knowledge, and annihilate their empty skulls. Yes, behead them with my knowledge!"

The teacher walks in. He is a tall skinny older British man with a dry wit. He takes roll. Noam knows that he can't screw this up again.

The teacher calls Noam Metzenbaum.

"Here sir," replies Noam.

Well then "Natalie Bloom."

Noam does not look at her, just stares straight at the white board, but he hears the Chads mocking him. "Oooo Natalie Bloom! Virgin's got a crush on you. Watch out for psycho virgin killer boy!"

The teacher turns to the Chads and says, "Knock it off, lads."

After taking roll, the teacher introduces himself. He says, "I'm Mr. Cockfoster." The class bursts out in laughter. Mr. Cockfoster says, "You can laugh all you want but I graduated from Oxford University and went to the top boarding school in the UK, so I know quite a lot about discipline."

Chad S. says, "Oh I'm really scared."

Mr. Cockfoster turns to Chad S., looks him right in the eye and says, "Do you know what they did to lads that stepped out of line at my old boarding school?"

He stands there in silence. Mr. Cockfoster continues, "Well if a pupil were to disrespect any staff member, the headmaster would take him into the broom closet and sodomize him with a broken broomstick!"

The entire class was in horror, even the strongest Chads were trembling in fear. Noam finds the situation quite amusing.

Mr. Cockfoster goes on, "Silly boys. Do you really buy that? Well then. That just proves how stupid you are. Now time to learn about history!"

Nick gets up and says, "Yo, I don't care who the fuck you are, but that's sexual harassment. I'm going to tell on Principal Greenstein. My dad's a prosecutor and he can throw your old ass in jail."

Mr. Cockfoster responds, "I don't care if your father is the Queen of England. Now sit down! We have work to do!"

The class settles down and Mr. Cockfoster starts his lesson and proclaims "In honor of Sexual Education Awareness Week the lesson for today is the history of fellatio." The class giggles. Mr. Cockfoster bangs his stick on his desk and continues "First of all what is the most important thing to know about fellatio?"

Wendy Silverstein gets up and says, “That you should always make the boy wear a condom when giving a blowjob?”

“No!” replies Mr. Cockfoster. “The most important thing about fellatio is pronunciation, and I warn you there will be severe punishment for any student who shall mispronounce the term. As you will learn, there is great history behind the practice of fellatio so it is crucial that you do not mispronounce the term! For starters, the A in fellatio is pronounced ‘Ah’ as in awful not ‘Ai’ as in ‘atheist.’ Now let’s here everyone repeat after me. A, atheist, ate, aim, anus.”

As the class repeats the words they all giggle after anus. Mr. Cockfoster says, “There is nothing funny about the human anus. For starters it is a crucial part of the human digestive track and I doubt you would find it funny if someone were to shove a stick up your anus. So get the pronunciation right, or pay the price!”

The class is silent.

Mr. Cockfoster continues, “The next step to pronouncing fellatio is getting down the ‘tio.’ Now we are talking about Latin; the language of love, law, and the foundation of Western Civilization, but also severe punishment. The Romans didn’t take kindly to anyone who would dare disrespect their language. So to get the pronunciation of ‘tio’ you have to use the sharp T, not the ‘sh’ sound which I hear often and just makes me ill; it is fellatio not fellatio for heaven's sake!”

After the class spends the next ten minutes practicing the proper pronunciation of fellatio, Mr. Cockfoster says, “Now that you have mastered the pronunciation, the proper lingo, you have proven yourselves worthy of learning about the great history behind the act of fellatio.”

Nick gets up, bows and says, "We are ready, sensei, to learn of the great ancient art of fellatio."

"I don't think they practiced fellatio in ancient Japan," Mr Cockfoster says, "but as for the practice of the ancient art of bukkake, that was especially reserved for young lads like you who stepped out of line, but we shall save that for another lesson!"

Mr. Cockfoster continues his lesson, "The act of fellatio in ancient Rome, was not just an erotic act between two individuals, it was an act of power, an act of pure domination of one participant over the other. For the receiver of fellatio, the individual had to be of high social standing, but for the fellator it was a disgraceful act, an act of shame, an act of submission!"

The Chads laugh. Chad S. says, "Yo, I go this bitch to fellate me last night, she even swallowed."

Mr. Cockfoster resumes, "It was also quite common for a man to receive fellatio from a male servant."

The same Chad interrupts again, "Yo, that's gay, dude."

"Only for one fellator," the teacher replies. "It was not considered homosexual for a man to receive fellatio from a man of lesser standing. The mouth was considered to be of great importance; it is what you speak with. So once your mouth is sullied with the DNA of another more potent man you are no longer a man, you are nothing but a sissy. But there was nothing homosexual about receiving fellatio from a man, when that man was nothing but a sex toy, a sperm receptacle there to drink the semen and urine of a superior male."

Unmoved, Chad S. insists, "Yo, I still think that's gay bro. Why let a dude suck my dick when I've got bitches lined up begging to suck me every Friday night."

Wendy Silverstein rolls her eyes in disgust and raises her hand.

"Yes Wendy," replies Mr. Cockfoster.

She asks "In ancient Rome was there any pleasure for women? You know when a guy goes down on you? What do you call that?"

All the girls giggle.

Mr. Cockfoster responds, "Oh you mean cunnilingus! Oh no. It was considered quite a disgraceful act. A man who performed cunnilingus was considered less than a man, no better than a fellator. However, archaeologists have found murals in Pompeii of women receiving cunnilingus from their male servants, but again those were not real men, just human dildos. He was forever subject to humiliation and mockery. A real man who was respected in Patrician Roman society would never even dream of the dreaded act of cunnilingus!"

Wendy sighs in disappointment.

Mr. Cockfoster reassures her, "Well Wendy, you don't live in ancient Rome. You are a bright young woman, a future leader!"

Wendy blushes. All the other girls giggled, "You go girl!"

Chad S. interjects once more, "Ew gross. Why would a dude want to put his mouth where piss and blood come out of?"

Wendy says, "Shut up!"

“That’s ok.” Mr. Cockfoster says. “This is a learning experience. I take great pride in educating naive young minds about pleasure and punishment! The other act in ancient Rome besides fellatio was irrumatio. Irrumatio was the act of fellatio but by force; the act of thrusting one man’s genitalia into another man’s mouth. It was an act used both to prove one’s virility and as an act of punishment! For instance, if a young apprentice wanted to avoid falling victim to irrumatio he must obey his professor under all circumstances!”

“Yo, irrumatio!” Nick blurts out. “That sounds gangster, bro!”

“What are you gay, bro?” Chad S. interjects.

“Hell no! As the professor said, it’s all about domination!” Nick replies.

Mr. Cockfoster continues, “While the ancient Romans perfected the art of Irrumatio, the primitive Etoro tribe of Papua New Guinea had their own take on the practice. Keep in mind that this tribe is still in existence and has resisted the inroads of modern civilization; therefore the practice is rumored to still be in place. However few brave souls dare venture into the foreboding jungle territory of the Etoro. In the Etoro tribe a young warrior must fellate an older more experienced warrior, taking in his seed; a right of initiation to be a stronger warrior. You see the Etoro believe that the warrior spirit is passed down through the semen of each generation of warriors to another. However unlike the Romans, where the act of fellatio was considered to be quite disgraceful, for the Etoro tribe it is considered to be the greatest honor to orally receive the sperm of a great warrior!”

“Yo! I’m the greatest warrior here,” Nick boasts. “My seed is gold!”

Mr. Cockfoster says, "That's enough for today's lesson. I'm sure you would fare well against the brave Etoro warriors, but anyhow go on and enjoy your day and soak in the knowledge."

Chad S. laughs and says, "Yeah! Soak in my cum, bitches!"

"That's enough! Class is dismissed!" Mr. Cockfoster commands.

Noam looks at his class schedule. His next class is swimming. He is terrified about being alone in the locker room with the Chads and decides to ditch. He doesn't know where to go. He even thinks about escaping into the air vents but decides that is not a good idea owing to his intense claustrophobia. He continues to pace aimlessly down the hallways, back and forth, staring at his own reflection in the shiny floors.

Then suddenly he is reprimanded, "Where do you think you're going?" Noam looks up; it's the fat nerd Elliot whom he got into it with on the bus earlier.
"Well, well, well, look who we have here," Elliot says. "Noam Virgin Metzenbaum skipping class."

"Leave me alone you fat ugly kike!" Noam replies.

Elliot says in his nasal voice, "Ha! You just committed a hate crime! That's grounds for expulsion!"

"Look, I'm Jewish too," Noam replies. "I mean Metzenbaum, come on. It's just like how black people get to call each other nigga! So we cool?"

"Well I could get you expelled but since I'm in a good mood after my Asian girlfriend gave me a blowjob last night, I'm going to go easy on you. It's your lucky day, Noam. Now let me see your class schedule!"

Noam reluctantly takes out his class schedule and hands it to Elliot. Elliot looks it over, "Let's see. Swimming! That's in our new state-of-the-art swimming complex. Right down the hall and take a left turn, then walk down the stars which lead to the changing room." He then he blows his nose into the schedule.

Noam thinks, "Changing room? Just me and a bunch of naked Chads? What if they beat me up? Or try to rape me? Or what if I accidentally stare at their dicks and get a boner? No! Noam, you're at war now. You need to think like a warrior. A great a warrior would not be afraid of a silly changing room."

"Enjoy the rest of your day, asshole!" Elliot says, handing back the snot-covered schedule.

Noam walks down the long hallway past all the identical green lockers. Then he turns left at the end of the hallway. He slowly walks down the stairwell down into the boy's locker room. He takes a deep breath and enters. It smells like a cross between chlorine and Chad sweat. Noam looks around anxiously but no one else is there. He takes in a big breath of relief but the smell of the locker room makes him nervous again.

Noam finds his locker and changes into his swim trunks. He leaves on his underwear underneath in case someone walks in on him changing. He slowly walks down on a march of death to the swimming pool. Noam can hardly swim, just barely doggie paddle. He thinks, "Everyone will be there, the Chads, the girls, and possibly my crush!"

Noam enters the pool. He looks in and sees the Chads in their speedos showing off their bulges and perfectly toned bodies, all the hot popular girls in their one-piece swimsuits that reveal their buttocks and bikini lines, and then there she is, his crush, swimming perfectly like a dolphin, her perfect buttocks popping up out of the water.

Noam is terrified of getting an erection but anxiety can be a strong boner-killer.

The swim instructor, who is a middle-aged flat-chested lesbian with short gray hair, blows her whistle, "You're late for class! What's your name young man?"

"Ah, it's uh. Noam Metzenbaum," Noam stutters.

He hears laughing in the background, and all the Chads come over to mock him, "Looks like virgin boy is afraid of the water."

"Natalie is going to find out he can't swim."

"I bet he has a small penis."

The instructor blows her whistle again, "Boys, knock it off! Noam, get in the pool!"

Noam was terrified of swimming ever since one his cousins nearly drowned him in their pool on Long Island, while he was visiting over summer vacation. Noam thinks, "My asshole cousin tried to kill me, and he gets a hot blonde Jewish girlfriend while I'm a virgin who can't swim. How am I supposed to impress my crush?"

Noam slowly walks on the slippery surface in his flip flops, his towel covering him. He puts his towel and flip flops on an empty bench, away from the bench where the rest of the class put their stuff. Noam slowly walks towards the shallow ends. The Chads continue to mock him, "Just jump in loser!"

Noam puts his feet in the pool, one foot at a time. Luckily for him the pool is heated at a comfortable lukewarm temperature.

Noam just stands there in the shallow end and watches the rest of the class swim in the deep end.

The instructor blows her whistle and points to Noam, "Stop messing around and come over here to the deep end."

The Chads continue mocking him "Virgin scared of a little water?"

Noam thinks, "Do you really want your crush to see you like this; a pathetic virgin who can't swim? Come on Noam, this is a maritime battle not play time!"

Noam rushes over to the deep end. The water is now up to his neck. He gets pushed by the currents further out until he can't touch the ground with his feet.

One of the Chads says, "Do you need water wings, virgin?"

Noam sees his crush swimming like an angelic mermaid. He must prove he is a great swimmer. He starts dog paddling, but isn't able to keep up with the currents. He looks over to the side and realizes he is in 6 feet of water. He starts panicking; water rushes into his mouth down into his lungs. He tries to gasp for air and screams "Help!" as the Chads continue laughing and splashing water towards him.

The water currents overwhelm him and push him further out into the deep end. He frantically paddles and gasps for air to save his life but it is no use and he goes under.

He finds himself floating on a calm ocean by a tropical beach at sunset. No Chads, just him on the water; all his stress, worries, and physical discomforts gone. He wonders if he has died and gone to heaven.

Then he sees her, his crush, a mermaid with a giant seashell behind her. She says motioning with her hands, “Noam, come to me, my love.”

Then she reaches out to give Noam a kiss on the lips.

Suddenly Noam wakes up to the old lesbian swim coach giving him mouth to mouth. The Chads are laughing hysterically; Wendy, Lisa, and Molly are giggling, and even his crush is trying hard to keep a straight face.

The instructor lectures Noam loudly in front of the class, “You should have had your mom write the school a letter saying that you can’t swim.” Everyone explodes in laughter, even his crush.

Noam has never been so humiliated. He thinks, “Now the love of my life thinks I’m the biggest dweeb. It is over. I lost the battle, now is time for a kamikaze mission.”

The instructor blows her whistle. “Go to the lockers,” she says.

Noam is terrified. He thinks, “What if the Chads find out I have a small dick and tell my crush? What if I accidentally see one of their dicks and get an erection? Ah, their perfectly chiseled bodies. Stop it, Noam! Stop thinking gay thoughts!”

Noam decides to wait to enter until all the Chads are gone. The teacher yells at Noam to go get changed. Carlos comes over to Noam and asks “You all right, Holmes?”

“Yes, Carlos. Just fantastic!” replies Noam.

Noam enters the locker room; it is packed with Chads in their speedos, and the next class of sophomore Chads are coming in to change. “Don’t stare Noam!”

Noam looks over briefly, like looking at the sun without burning one's eyes. He sees one of the Chad's dicks. Noam starts to get hard. "You disgust me, Noam! You're not a faggot!" he reassures himself.

At Noam's old school he was always terrified of the locker room and avoided it at all costs. Being the only white kid with rough black and brown kids was a terrifying experience. It reminded him of watching cheesy late-night prison dramas where the scrawny white guy ends up in the shower, surrounded by savages waiting to pummel his ass.

Noam had only showered once at his old school, and the sight of those disgusting naked beasts just made him sick to his stomach, their dicks like giant turds.

As much as Noam despises the Chads, this was his first exposure to the male figure in an aesthetically pleasing form. "You're not a homo, Noam. It's the feminine qualities that are bringing you to arousal. The blonde hair, smooth skin, cute faces. Yes, like girls. Exactly! Oh but the toned muscles and big dicks. Stop it, Noam! Stop thinking homoerotic thoughts! You disgust me!"

Noam rushes over to his locker and changes quickly with his towel around him to hide his small dick. Luckily for him he doesn't see any freshman Chads, but a group of good-looking sophomore Chads are changing out of their school clothes into their speedos. Noam accidentally looks at one of their massive cocks. The Chad doesn't say anything but gives Noam a dirty look.

Noam is about to leave but hears Carlos giggling and joking around with the Chads. He looks over at the shower. He can't believe his eyes. There is Carlos surrounded by a group of naked Chads, joking around together. Noam tries really hard not to look at their dicks. Then suddenly one of the Chads smacks Carlos on the ass as if he was homosexual, too.

Noam thinks, "Perhaps the Chads are homosexuals, and they are just bullying me because they have a crush on me. I'm way better looking than that fat ass, Carlos."

Then Noam accidentally gets a glimpse of Nick's dick. It is one of the most beautiful things he has ever seen; cute and smooth, yet powerful and masculine; a pale tan line from his speedo and a nice dark bush that makes it pop out, and it was uncircumcised too. Noam gets a massive erection and is about to cum his pants. He thinks, "Stop it, Noam! You should be thinking about chopping the monster off, not fantasizing about fellating it!"

Noam quickly leaves because he does not want to risk bringing attention to himself. It is lunch time and his mom had packed him a dry croissant, an orange, and a ginger ale.

Noam looks over at the lunch room. It is the same as the day before with all the social cliques occupying their territory. There are the Chads, all arrogant and cocky with their blonde cheerleader girlfriends, and then he sees the one black jock making out with a blonde cheerleader. Noam thinks, "Stupid nigger! He's descended from slaves yet he gets to hang out with the Chads and make out with a blonde cheerleader while I, a great aristocrat, am forced to suffer alone. They see me as a threat! I know it. They want a house nigger they can control, not someone who will challenge their power. I doubt she's even touched his nigger cock; she's just with him for show, to prove the she's not racist, and all cool with the latest MTV fads."

Then Noam sees the nerds and that fat Elliot with his Chinese girlfriend. Noam thinks, "Even he gets a cute Asian girlfriend. Maybe I should just join the Mathletes and date a cute Chinese girl. I heard they appreciate a guy who gets straight A's. No,

Noam! Don't go down that path. You deserve a nice blonde, but not just any blonde."

Then Noam looks over at Wendy and Molly's table and notices something new, "Shit, Noam, there's a threat in town," he says to himself. Noam sees a popular boy just sitting there bloviating, with Wendy on one side, and Molly on the other, staring into his eyes, and rubbing his shoulders.

Then he sees his crush on the side. Shy and quiet, but staring at the new boy like she's curious to find out why her friends think he's so cool. "I have a new threat to eliminate," Noam quietly realizes.

Carlos sees Noam standing by himself and says, "Yo amigo, come sit down!"

Noam sits down with Carlos, who asks, "You all right, Holmes?"

Noam replies, "Who is the new boy over at the table with Wendy and Molly?"

"Oh that's Zack Rosenblatt. He's a junior. His dad's a billionaire banker, dude. The richest kid in the entire school; even richer then Chad S."

Noam looks over to the table and sees Zack flirting with Natalie. Natalie is too shy to talk to him, but she is smiling, signaling that she likes him.

Noam says to Carlos, "That's enough, I'm going to go give that fucker a piece of my mind."

“I would watch it if I were you,” Carlos replies. “Zack has major clout around here. I wouldn’t fuck with him, Holmes, but I will let you in on a secret.”

“What’s that?” says Noam.

Carlos continues, “Zack is the sworn enemy of Nick Anderson. I know because Nick tells me everything after he blows his load in my mouth and breaks down in tears and cries about his ex, while his sperm swims around in my mouth. Zack and his friends defiled Nick’s girlfriend at their party at Zack’s dad’s mansion, and ever since then Nick has been plotting revenge against Zack. Nick used to be a sensitive boy with a nice girlfriend, but that incident turned him into the monster that he is. So look Noam I can help you with the Chads but Zack is like a Chad on a whole other level. The apex of Chads. Sorry, Holmes. I can’t help you on this one.”

“I've got an idea,” Noam says.

“Que?”

“I’m going to start a race war!”

“Whoa! Chill out, Holmes. You're starting to scare me,” Carlos replies.

Noam thinks, “I’m like Charles Manson, I'm going to get the goyim to go kill the kikes, and the kikes to kill the goyim! Wipe them all out, so it’s just me and my crush alone without the filth of humanity standing in our way!”

Noam continues to stare at Zack, seething in rage. Then he sees him playing with his crush’s golden hair, talking to her as if he’s asking her out on a date.

Noam got up from the table. "Where ya going, Holmes?" Carlos asks. Noam ignores him.

Noam stands there hiding behind a column waiting for lunch to be over, spying on Zack and his crush. Then he sees Zack reach in for a kiss. His crush avoids the kiss but giggles and blushes innocently, like a perfect angel who has yet to be defiled.

After the lunch bell rings, Noam follows Zack down the hallway. When he gets to him alone, he approaches him from behind and says, "Hello Zack."

"Yo. What's up?" Zack answers, then turns around looks at Noam and says, "Do I know you?"

"Hello, my name is Noam Metzenbaum. I am new here. I just moved here from the Upper East Side. My dad is in hedge funds."

"Yo, cool bro. Who's your dad? I know everyone in the industry."

"Uh … Moshe Shekel Metzenbaum?" Noam replies.

"Never heard of him, bro. I got to get to class," Zack says.

As Noam continues following him, Zack begins to get annoyed, "Yo bro. What's your problem?"

Noam replies "It's the gentiles?"

"Huh?" replies Zack.

Noam says, "The gentiles! We Jews have to stick together. We can't trust them especially blondes, Chads, and blonde Jewish girls too. They are basically shiksas!"

“What have you been smoking?” Zack says. “I have a date set up with a hot blonde Jewish chick. Now if you will, I have to get to class.”

Noam is about to ask about his crush, but he doesn’t want to let Zack know he has a crush on Natalie.

Noam says, “Well I just hate them! They have been persecuting us for centuries. It’s time to strike back, deal with those Chads! They only let them into this school because they are good at sports; lacrosse and Water Polo. They are no better than niggers!”
“That’s racist, bro,” Zack says. “Besides, my mom’s a gentile and so are a lot of my friends. I got it made. My dad’s worth billions, I get to bang all the hottest blondes so I got nothing to complain about, now if you will I got a date with a fine blonde Jewish girl after school.”

As Zack walks away after Noam’s failed attempt at starting a campus race war, Noam says under his lips, “You’re dead, Zack.” Zack doesn’t hear him and continues on to class.

Noam thinks, “Is tonight the night; the night that my crush, my one true love shall be defiled? No! I won’t let that happen. Forget the Chads; number one target is Zack Rosenblatt.”

Noam goes to his math class, a subject which he is usually good at, but he is too distressed to concentrate. The teacher asks Noam if he is feeling all right.

“I think I’m coming down with bad stomach flu,” Noam says.

“Ok, go to the nurse’s office,” the teacher replies and hands him a slip.

The nurse checks his temperature which is normal but can tell he is distressed.

She asks him if everything is fine.

“Yes, everything is fine,” replies Noam.

The nurse tells Noam that she is going to call his mom to pick him up. Noam doesn’t want his mom to come because that would derail his plan to track down Zack and stop him from defiling his crush.

The nurse sends Noam to lie down in a bed in a private room which resembles a small bedroom.

Noam thinks about ways of escaping, but it is no use. The nurse is right in front of the door, and his mom would be there within the hour.

Noam is so anguished and sickened by the thought of his crush being defiled that he starts to feel like he is going to throw up, but he doesn’t. He just lies there in distress until his mom arrives to pick him up.

As he walks out with his mom, he looks around. All the students are still inside their classes.

“Noam, are you ok?” his mom asks.

“I’m all right, just an upset stomach,” Noam replies.

She says, “Come home and get some rest. I think it was a mistake to send you to Chadsworth. All the schoolwork and pressure to fit in is putting too much strain on your health. I don’t know what to do, Noam. I can’t really afford to send you here, and it’s putting a lot of strain on both of us.”

"Look mom, I'm fine!" says Noam.

"I'll let you rest, but I'm seriously considering moving back to the city," she insists. "Mr. Bloom told me he wants me back in New York, and he's complaining about this creep stalking his daughter."

Noam thinks, "Is she talking about me? Dammit! If I can't win her over, I have to capture her and take her off to a private Island."

Noam looks out the car window. There is Zack in his Porsche with his crush next to him listening to load rap music, *"If you want it bitch, come suck on the nigga! If you want it bitch, come suck on the nigga!"* Noam puts down his head so they don't see him.

His mom screams, "Noam! Are you going to vomit? Do it out the window! Not in my car!"

The windows are down and Zack turns down the rap music, overhearing Noam's mom. Noam can hear Zack chuckling and ridiculing Noam in front of Natalie. He thinks, "This is it, the night my life is over. I shall never love again."

Noam gets home. His mom offers him some Pepto Bismol and sends him to bed.

Noam starts writing in his journal:

"Dear Journal, this may be my very last entry. You have been a good friend, perhaps my only friend. The only one who has listened to every word I said and truly understands me. You see, I went to Chadsworth on a mission, and that mission was to find my one true love. After years of torment; a lonely childhood followed by an adolescence filled with torment at the hands of

subhuman beast, my life changed when I saw her. The moment I laid eyes on her I knew we were destined to be together, that she was my soul mate. I did everything in my power to reunite with her but I have failed at my mission and am not worthy. Tomorrow will be the last day on this planet because this world was not made for me. I know I am a superior being, not of the human race. I thought I had a chance at defeating the Chads and came close. Then that dirty rat comes along and desecrates my one true love. I shall say goodbye to this planet, jump off the roof of Chadsworth and return to my home planet. So long humanity; you had your chance to prove your worth, but you are a cruel, cold, ignorant race."

Noam turns on his computer. While watching tribute videos to famous school shooters he stumbles across a bizarre music video. It is titled "Aryan Imperium: Gas the Kikes." Noam thinks, "Perhaps a little dark humor is in order before my departure."

Noam expects the usual skinhead music with some white trash meth addict screaming about Jews, but instead it is cool images of futuristic cities, neon swastikas, with 80s-style synthwave playing in the background. Then an image of Blackstone appears. Noam thinks, "That's a bit odd. Isn't Blackstone half Jewish like me? Why do these Nazi freaks like him so much?"

Noam scrolls down the seemingly incoherent comment section, "Hail Blackstone, gas the Jew bankers," "Shut up! Blackstone's a New World Order Occultist Jew shill!", "Yeah, he's controlled opposition." "Import Blonde Israeli Aryan Woman! Deport ugly shitskins!" "Israeli Aryan Imperium!" "

Noam thinks, "Israeli Aryan! Like me? And my one true love? I shall defend my maiden from that creep! How dare he defile pure Israeli Aryan beauty!"

Noam falls asleep and finds himself in a city. He looks around. It resembles New York but in the future or some alternate universe. All the skyscrapers are covered in giant neon swastikas, while stormtroopers march to synthwave. Then he sees Blackstone as a hologram on an electronic billboard in a military uniform giving the Nazi salute.

Then all the soldiers approach Noam. He thinks, "Are they after me for being a Jew?" Then he sees them dragging Zack's naked bloodied body in the streets. They face him and salute "Heil Herr Metzenbaum! Heil our Fuhrer! Israeli Aryan Imperium!" Then Noam's sees Jewish bankers being executed by the soldiers, while their pregnant blonde teen daughters are being taken as wives by the soldiers. Noam follows them and watches Zack being dragged naked screaming "Noam, save me!"

He follows them to what looks like Grand Central Station. There is a giant neon swastika above the clock. He follows them inside to the main concourse, which he had visited many times as a kid. Inside is a great palatial setting. There is Roger Blackstone on his throne. The soldiers all line up and place Zack's bloody naked body in front of Blackstone.

Blackstone turns to Noam, "Are you the great Noam Metzenbaum?"

"Yes," Noam replies humbly.

Blackstone says, "Did this boy here try to defile your maiden?"

"Yes, Fuhrer!" Noam replies.

Blackstone says, "Then I shall grant you the honor of taking care of this piece of garbage."

Noam follows the soldiers down to the lower train concourse. The soldier, who had a thick German accent, turns to Noam, "Dis train goez straight zu Neue Treblinka!"

The soldier hands Noam Zack's body, which Noam is about to place on the train. Suddenly the door closes and Noam is trapped inside the train, while Zack is still on the ground. He hears the train start. He sees other Jews on the train, including his family, his mother, and late grandfather Saul. Noam turns to them and screams, "Help!"

"You did this to yourself, Noam," Saul says. "You betrayed your ancestors who died so you could live. You are a worthless disgrace."

"You are no longer my son," Noam's mom says.

Noam starts to cry as the train speeds faster and faster. Then he looks out the window and sees his crush in the other train. "Natalie! Natalie! Wait, I'll save you!" he screams, but it is too late. Her train goes off into the dark. Mr. Bloom turns to Noam, "You killed my daughter, you son of a bitch!"

The train goes through a tunnel. A red neon sign reads "Wilkommen zu Neue Treblinka." Then the train fills up with toxic gas.

Noam wakes up in a cold sweat, suffocating, and feeling sick to his stomach. He looks at the clock. It is 4:30 AM. He tries to go back to sleep but can't.

He thinks horrible thoughts about what could be happening to his crush at this very moment. He has graphic visual images in his mind of Zack fucking his crush and cumming all over her face.

Noam's mom comes in to check on him at 7am and says, "Noam, you look ill. Your face is green. You should stay home today."

Noam begs his mom to take him to school so he can carry out his final mission but she refuses, considering his state.

While his mom is talking to the older woman from whom they are renting, Noam sneaks out and decides to take the city bus. He looks at the bus schedule, but the next bus doesn't arrive for another 20 minutes.

He thinks, "For a town with such immense wealth and prosperity, they can't even invest in decent transit. No high speed rail, monorails, or even a basic subway system. No! Stupid slow city buses for the plebs, while the fat cats live in their McMansions driving their gas guzzlers, with no concern for civilization!"

He starts running down the street but runs out of breath. He feels like passing out, but pushes himself to carry out his final mission; suicide of his mortal carcass, while his soul is sent into outer space back to his home planet.

Noam thinks, "I shall miss my mother for all that she has done for me to try to re-unite with my crush, but she is a mere homo-sapiens, who my father happened to miscegenate with. I am of a higher being that no mortal shall ever understand, not even my very own mother."

As Noam runs, accelerating, he feels the strain on his lungs. He thinks, "Perhaps my half mortal body won't survive the fall, and my species will reject me for not being a pure blood; accepted by neither species, just a lone atomized particle floating in space in eternal sorrow."

Noam sees a bus and sprints to the next bus stop to catch it. He enters, panting, out of breath and puts in a few quarters. The bus driver turns to him. "Hey kid, aren't you supposed to be in school?"
Noam ignores the bus driver and sits down. The bus is mostly empty except for a few Mexican maids. He realizes the bus doesn't go to Chadsworth, so he gets off and takes the route through the woods.

He goes by the creek and stops to check on the frogs but doesn't see a single frog or even a tadpole. He thinks, "The water must be polluted from the construction. The Frog God shall come down and exterminate the vile human race for their crimes against nature!"

He continues running through the woods. He looks at his watch. He has already missed his first class, but if he gets there fast enough he might make 2nd period.

Noam finally arrives at Chadsworth. He notices Zack's Porsche is parked in the student parking lot. He takes out his Swiss Army Knife, pierces the tires, and carves a swastika on the side with the words, "Chads rule, Jews Drool!"

He then sneaks into the school through the back entrance, thus avoiding security. He walks down the empty hallway past the green lockers thinking, "This is it Noam, your last day on earth!"

Noam makes it on time to his 2nd period class. He enters the door to the class, "Oh great! It's the Chads, Wendy, and my, my crush! This may be my last chance to see her. I shall bid her farewell, wish her a good life, to marry a nice churchgoing virgin before the Chads get to her first.

"Oh well. Perhaps I shall find a female of my own species when I return to my home planet?" Noam thinks. "Some day we shall conquer planet earth and enslave the lowly humans for their crimes and show them no mercy."

Noam sits down. He hears the Chads mocking him in the background but is able to zone them out. They don't matter anymore since he is leaving this planet to go to a more advanced civilization where virtue and wisdom are respected and fornication and obnoxious behavior is not tolerated.

The teacher, who's an overweight lesbian with the feminist symbol on her sweatshirt, introduces herself, "Hello my name is Miss. Vulvis." The class giggles.

She continues, "I will be teaching your Sex Ed course this week. Mr. Cockfoster was dismissed from teaching Sex Ed for making crude misogynistic and homophobic remarks in front of young impressionable minds. I am here to enlighten you and most importantly teach you about the joys of safe sex."

Chad S. says, "Yo. She's never taken dick. What does this rug muncher know about fucking? She's knows about as much as virgin boy here," pointing to Noam.

Wendy chimes in, "No girl would ever let that creep's mouth anywhere near her sacred lady parts."

Chad S. replies, "Only losers with small dicks go down on chicks. Bitches want a nice big cock!"

Noam thinks, "Are they are implying that I'm even lower than a loser, not even registering as human, not even worthy to be a sex toy to some hot popular girl?"

Ms. Vulvis explains, "That is the exactly the kind of unenlightened thinking I want to get out of you boys. I'm here to re-program you. For starters, there are many ways to express one's sexuality. Penises are not even necessary. If anything, they are dangerous and can lead to unwanted pregnancies and STDs. I will teach you about alternatives to the obsolete male member."

"Thank you!" says Wendy Silverstein.

One of the Chads turns to Wendy and says, "That's not what you said after I came on your tits last night."

"Enough!" Ms. Vulvis says. "Let's talk about cunnilingus! Cunnilingus is the oral stimulation of the female genitalia. It is a safe alternative to intercourse. There is no risk of pregnancy and only a small risk for STDs, and most importantly it feels fantastic! Sexual intercourse is ineffective because most of the nerve endings are on the clitoris, and unless you are planning on having kids someday, I would recommend avoiding it completely!"

The Chad B. starts making a crude tongue gesture.

"Chad B, go to Principal Greenstein's office!" Ms. Vulvis orders.

Chad B. gets up while wiggling his tongue in front of all the girls in the class.

"I think he may have learned something today," Molly says sarcastically.

Ms. Vulvis continues, "Now that we got those distractions out of the way, we can continue our lesson. Before one goes for the final act, let's start with some foreplay."

One of the boys asks, "Isn't cunnilingus foreplay?"

“No!” replies Ms. Vulvis. “Cunnilingus is the be all and end all. There shall be no intercourse!”

Wendy and Molly start cheering.

“Yo. This bitch is trying to convert all the girls into dikes!” Chad S. says.

“Chad S, go to Principal Greenstein’s office!” Ms. Vulvis points to the classroom door.

Noam was repulsed by Ms. Vulvis at first, but he admires her ruthlessness in dealing with the Chads.
He thinks, “Maybe she is onto something. With the Chads and their filthy penetrative sex out of the way, I should propose to Ms. Vulvis that we start a cunnilingus club on campus. It will be just me pleasuring all the hot popular girls.”

Noam raises his hand.

“Yes, Noam,” replies Ms. Vulvis.

“I support what you're doing,” Noam says. “You are right. Yeah, who needs intercourse? Cunnilingus is the only acceptable sex act!”

Wendy looks at Noam with disgust while her friend Molly giggles.

One of the other Chads says, “Don’t be such a suck-up Noam. Get it, suck up?”

“Principles Greenstein’s office!” Ms. Vulvis dismisses yet another Chad from class.

Ms. Vulvis continues, "With foreplay, the best way to start off is to rub your girlfriend's feet, then slowly kiss her inner thighs, then bury your face in your girlfriends pubic hair, savoring her feminine scents."

Another Chad says, "Eww, gross. Should she at least wash and shave?"

Ms. Vulvis responds, "No! It's misogynistic to expect a girl to shave. It's important to respect and worship the female anatomy in its natural state."

The students notice a gray pubic hair stuck in Ms. Vulvis's teeth and start giggling hysterically.

Noam thinks, "Cunnilingus should only be reserved for the female elite. I feel bad for Ms. Vulvis munching down on that disgusting gray bush. Blackstone is right to ban uglies; he should extend that policy to cunnilingus! And appoint every hot teen girl a personal tongue slave!"

Ms. Vulvis is confused but continues her lesson with the gray hair still wiggling in her teeth, "Now after savoring the scents, lightly tickle the urethra with the tip of your tongue. If a little bit of urine comes out, that's ok."

"Barf, I'm out of here!" another Chad interrupts.

Noam is pleased that Ms. Vulvis is getting rid of all the Chads. He didn't care much for feminists but thinks, "Maybe I should become a male feminist, castrate all the misogynist douchebags and Chads and be a tongue slave to all the popular girls. Who needs patriarchy? Having to play competitive sports, hold a 9 to 5 job, and compete with other males for girls and status. I just want to eat out hot girls all day. They can have their high-paying careers, while I just sit under their desk eating their pussies and asses all day long. That's how it should be!"

Ms. Vulvis continues, "After tickling the urethra, move on to the clitoris. The clitoris is very sensitive and has multiple times as many nerve endings as the entire worthless penis in a tiny little region, so it's important to be gentle. First lightly flick the clitoris with your tongue, and then gradually make circular motions around the clitoris. Then once the clitoris is fully engorged you can suck on it like a blowjob, while continuing to flick it with your tongue. Then stick your finger inside the vagina to stimulate the G-spot. This will cause the most intense orgasm imaginable!"

Wendy asks excitedly, "What about positions?"

Ms. Vulvis explains, "The best position for cunnilingus is face sitting. The woman has absolute control and does not have to look at the pathetic face of the man beneath her. It is awkward for many women to have to look at their partner eat them from below. You should not have to feel self-conscious about your body. He is only there to give you pleasure. His comfort is of little importance. Now enjoy yourself ladies and remember: safe sex and say no to the penis!"

Noam looks over at his crush and notices she is getting aroused by all the talk of cunnilingus, face sitting, and orgasms. He then looks down to her skirt and long legs, fantasizing about burying his face between them, savoring her nectar.

He thinks, "Those Chads will never go down on her. This is my chance! I will invite her over for cunnilingus after class."

After class, Noam overhears Wendy and her popular friends chatting in the hall. He sees his crush sitting on the sidelines, not quite in their inner circle yet.

Lisa Goldberg says, "Wow that was a really informative class."

Molly replies, "Yeah. My useless boyfriend won't even go down on me."

"You know at the party one unlucky girl is going to have to blow all the Chads," Lisa responds.

"Eeeww gross," says Molly.

Noam's crush looks nervous, but Noam doesn't understand.

Wendy suggests "Why don't we turn the tables on them?"

"What do you mean?" Molly replies.

"Every year one unlucky freshman must service all the Chads at the first party of the year," Wendy says. "Why don't we set up a cunnilingus party?"

"How do we go about setting up this party?" Molly replies.

"We will find a boy, not a Chad, but not total dweeb either," Wendy says. "Just an average guy who is desperate to fit in with the popular clique and good with his tongue. We will trick him into thinking he's getting an orgy; in a sense he will get an orgy just not what he expected." The other girls giggle.

Wendy continues, "At the party we will tie him to the sofa and force him to service all of us."

"We shouldn't even wash or shave," Molly suggests, excitedly.

The other girls gasp. This was a new idea to them.

Molly continues, "I want to make sure the bitch suffers. Last year some freshman girl had to have her stomach pumped from all the Chad cum. She quit school, never to be heard from again. I want him to know he is here just for our pleasure. His mouth and tongue only exist to give us orgasms. His discomforts are of little importance."

There is an awkward pause but afterwards they are in consensus.

Noam fantasizes about being the boy, but thinks he won't have a chance. His crush has a look of arousal but hasn't said a word.

Lisa points out, "Guys are pigs. They will let any girl, even the fattest most grotesque creature slobber their cock, but we are not like that. We save cunnilingus for a special guy."

"Screw all that! I'm for real gender equality," Wendy exclaims. "Those whores go for the opportunity to drink the cum of all the popular boys, and incubate one ultimate Chad in their belly. Why not give the same opportunity to some loser dweeb who hasn't even seen a vagina. Give him the honor of giving us pleasure and tasting our most intimate areas." They all giggle.

Then they notice Noam eavesdropping.

"Ha!" Wendy says. "He actually thinks we'd grant him that honor. I don't want his filthy mouth anywhere near my beautiful cunt."

So much for Noam's ultimate cunnilingus fantasy.

Noam heads off to lunch. All the talk of cunnilingus made him forget about his mission. He looks around and sees Wendy over at the nerd table talking to a boy.

Noam thinks, "What is a snob like Wendy doing talking to a bunch of dweebs?"

After Wendy leaves, Noam goes over to the nerd table. Fat Elliot says, "Look who we have here! The great aristocrat who thinks he's above it all but now realizes what a loser he is and comes to us begging for mercy. I shall grant him mercy if he kisses my onion ring."

"Fuck off!" replies Noam.

The other nerds are annoyed with Elliot. One of them says, "He can sit here if he wants. It's a free country."

Another nerd says, "Free country my ass. This is Chad-occupied territory. CHOG; Chad occupational government, and we are the resistance. Welcome, fellow dweeb."

Noam scoffs, "Me? Dweeb? Ha! Dweeb Nationalists who are looking for a leader, a true aristocrat to lead their measly little corner of the lunch room."

"Relax, we are just really into anime and World of Warcraft," the nerd replies.

Noam looks over at the boy Wendy was talking to. He isn't a total nerd; in fact he's not even bad looking, just a bit shy and not able to fit in with the other social cliques.

Noam introduces himself, "Noam Metzenbaum, a pleasure to meet you."

"Hi, I'm Justin," replies the boy.

Noam asks, "Why were you talking to Wendy Silverstein? You know, the popular hot blonde girl?"

"Wendy just invited me to her party with all her popular friends," he replies.

"Traitor! You were never one of us to begin with," one of the nerds says.

"They are just playing a prank on you; probably some kind of hazing ritual," another interjects.

"No! It's an orgy! I get to fuck all the popular girls. Get my dick sucked. Experience what it's like to be a Chad!" Justin says.

"Keep dreaming, sugar tits," Elliot says. "More likely, they will make you dress up like a clown. Then when the Chads are all wasted, they will take turns cumming on your face; watching a concoction of clown makeup, tears, and cum droop down your face in humiliation. I've been watching a lot of clown bukkake lately; clown chicks getting facials."

The rest of the nerds are shocked. A nervous Justin says, "That's just a rumor."

Elliot continues, "Think what you want, but you're in for a world of hurt. Every year the Chads pick one unlucky freshman to humiliate. Last year they invited the nerdiest freshman to their party, then when he was passed out they filmed him while they took turns tea bagging him and then pissed on his face. He ended up committing suicide. Don't fall for their tricks."

"He's right, Justin," the other nerd replies. "That's why Elliot is such a prick, because the Chads killed his best friend. He used to be really cool and not all passive aggressive and whatnot."

"No way!" Justin replies. "Wendy's a sweet girl; she would never do such a thing. She even told me she has some special game planned, and because of my smaller stature I can fit into her secret sex chamber!"

They all laugh while chocolate milk squirts all over the place out of their noses.

"Good luck," Elliot says. "It was nice knowing you, friend. I'd love to attend your funeral, but I have a World of Warcraft convention that day."

"The only video game I play is Leisure Suit Larry," Noam says. No response as the nerds continue rambling.

Justin turns to Noam, "Do you think Wendy loves me?"

"No!" Noam responds. "She's just a cruel whore trying to take advantage of an inexperienced loser. No offense."

"I've touched a girl's vagina in eighth grade," Justin boasts. "Have you even kissed a girl, Noam? Wendy wants to know if I'm good with my tongue. Ah. Making out by the poolside on a romantic full moon lit night."

"The only full moon you will be seeing is the Chads asses on your face!" Elliot says.

Noam realizes that this boy is the designated pussy licker. He feels a great deal envy at the boy for being granted the honor of orally pleasuring all the popular girls, even if it means his tongue will be so sore that he won't be able to talk for a week. Noam thinks, "I'm much better looking than him and a true aristocrat. How dare he have more romantic experience than me! What makes him so special?"

The Chads walk by and see brown milk stains on everyone's shirts, including Noam's. One of the Chads remarks, "Did you guys shit yourselves, virgins?"

“I’m going to deal with them!” Noam says.

“Oh no. Don’t tell me you're gonna shoot up the school,” Elliot says.

“Of course not,” Noam replies. “I have more creative ways to deal with these fuckers. Give them a taste of their own medicine.”

But in reality, Noam doesn’t have a concrete plan for dealing with the Chads or reuniting with his crush, and he is getting distracted with all this talk of cunnilingus.

He thinks, “Pull yourself together, Noam. Stupid Chads trying to ruin everything, poisoning my reputation with my crush and her hot blonde friends. As much as I despise Wendy, all I wanted was to eat her pussy and ass since the moment I met her at the fountain. No, Dammit! Stop thinking dirty thoughts Noam! You shall preserve your honor and purity for your crush. Then you shall lap at her golden labia for all eternity! Forget that filthy whore Wendy. She’s probably blown over a hundred Chads!”

Noam looks over at the popular table but doesn’t see his crush, just Wendy, Molly, and Zack. Zack looks angry and upset while Wendy and Molly are trying to comfort him. Noam can’t hear them because of the nerds rambling about World of Warcraft.

Noam walks over to the popular table and hides behind the column.

Noam overhears Zack saying, “Those fuckers! Nick and his bros trashed my car! He carved a fucking swastika into my brand new Porsche. I mean my grandmother was in the Holocaust, and Nick was extremely disrespectful when she spoke to the school.”

Wendy says, “Yeah I know Nick can be insensitive, but I don’t think it was him. I think it was that virgin creep. What’s his name?”

“Noam?” says Molly

Zack says, “That kid's a creep but he has no motive. Besides, he’s Jewish. Nick has had it in for me since I dated his ex after they broke up. He’s been spreading false rumors that I date raped her. I mean, come on, I can have any girl in this school. I'm not some loser virgin creep like what’s his name.”

“Noam,” says Molly.

They all laugh.

Lisa asks, “What happened on your date with Natalie?”

“I don’t know. She’s kind of shy,” Zack sighs. “She came over to my place, but she seemed uncomfortable.”

“Did you make a move?” asks Wendy?

“I was a perfect gentleman,” Zack says. “We watched TV, I made her popcorn, brought her the finest Champagne, rubbed her back, then I just unzipped my pants and asked her for a blowjob, but she refused, and asked to be dropped off at home. Is that too much to ask for?”

Wendy laughs, “What a prude. I thought she was cool. Maybe you should go down on her first, get her in the mood. I could tell that she likes getting eaten out by her reaction in class today.”

Zack says, “I’ll see how things go. I asked her to come hang out at the boathouse this weekend, but she said her father’s visiting from New York. She’s cute, but I mean she’s just not into it.

You know, sex. She wouldn't even let me give her a goodnight kiss!"

Wendy puts her arm around Zack, "Forget about her. You can do better."

Noam is relieved. All his worst fears have been dispelled, but he still had to finish off Zack and then deal with the Chads.

After everyone leaves the lunch room, Zack and Wendy start making out. Noam takes out his camera phone to film it as evidence, but while filming Noam sneezes, thereby bringing attention to himself.

"What's that?" says Zack.

"Nothing," Wendy says. "You're good with your tongue. Now get back to work!"

Zack gets up and catches Noam with his camera phone and says, "Well, Well, Well. Look who we have here. I guess Wendy was right. It was you, virgin creep. Look, kid. There's a surveillance camera in the parking lot. I'm going to have you expelled and tried for a hate crime." Zack then takes out Noam's camera phone and smashes it on the floor.

Nick and the Chads show up. Zack turns to Nick, "Look bro. I'm sorry about accusing you of screwing up my car. It was this virgin creep here."

"Yeah, Noam!" says Molly.

"Yeah Noam's been a blemish on this school since the day he set foot on campus this week," Nick replies. "Don't worry Zack; I'll take care of the virgin once and for all."

“Thanks, but I have enough evidence to put him away,” Zack says.

“That’s letting him off easy,” Nick says. “He will just go on to stalk and rape more chicks. We need to destroy him so bad, that he will lose any ounce of confidence he has, and most importantly remain a virgin forever. I have a plan.”

“Ok bro,” says Zack. “You take care of that creep.”

“I've got it all taken care of,” Nick assures.

They give each other a bro hug.

“Ah sweet,” Wendy says.

Noam leaves in tears. His plan to destroy Zack and Nick by turning them against each other has failed miserably and has only brought them closer, and now they are both united to destroy him. His only solace is that his crush has yet to be defiled. Now he knows he has to perfect his cunnilingus skills to win her over. “But how?” he wonders. “Practice on an ugly fat girl? Eww gross. Never! Or I could practice on one of the Asian girls from the Mathletes, but I heard they have fishy fire vaginas. I don’t need practice. Nothing pleases a lady better than an eager unsullied tongue.”

Noam has to take the bus home. The only remaining seat is next to fat Elliot. Elliot turns to Noam and says sarcastically, “Well hello there, princess!”

“Shut up Elliot!” replies Noam.

As the bus starts moving Noam can feel the vibration under his seat. Something about the stimulation makes him fantasize about what it is like for a girl to receive cunnilingus. Noam starts daydreaming about giving cunnilingus to his crush, while simultaneously feeling the orgasmic pleasures himself as the seat vibrates.

Just as Noam obliviously starts making tongue gestures, Nick gets up and grabs him by his polo collar.

"Looks like virgin boy is doing his homework from class today," Nick says. "But there's no need to practice since no girl would ever let that filthy tongue anywhere near their pussies, so you might as well start practicing for eating fat Elliot's asshole."

Elliot turns to Noam, "You know, Noam. I broke up with my Asian girlfriend because she refused to eat my ass. I can't say I'd turn down a nice rim job after a long day. Nothing sexual, it's about good hygiene, wouldn't want to sit around all day with a filthy ass."

Noam looks at Elliot in disgust, "You are one of the vilest creatures I've ever met!"

"Well thank you princess. Oh sorry I mean aristocrat!" Elliot replies.

The Chads all laugh. Nick turns to Noam. "I'm not finished with you bitch! We are going to take care of you once and for all. It's for the public good. Destroy a virgin, prevent another school shooting."

Noam just ignores Nick. He has no idea what plan he is talking about but has to focus on the final mission of winning over his crush.

Noam gets home, briefly finishes his homework. He thinks, "Busywork for future office drones! Quickly get it out of the way. Get an easy A+ and then get to the real work!"

Noam's mom gives him a big smile. "I'm so proud of you, Noam! All the hard work. I'm sorry I even doubted you. Chadsworth is the perfect place for you. Next stop Yale!" He smiles back and goes to his room.

He takes out an art book about the 18th century French artist Achille Devéria. There is an illustration of an aristocratic lady pulling up her petticoats exposing her hairy bush standing, while a man on his knees pleasures her orally. Noam starts masturbating to the image. He thinks, "Cunnilingus, the act of true aristocrats! Fellatio is for stupid bros and Chads!" Noam masturbates to the image imagining the aristocratic woman is his crush, and that the man on his knees is him.

All this pleasure gives Noam inspiration to write in his journal. He quickly takes out his journal. While he continues to masturbate he starts writing:

"There shall be a new order. That is the order of the true cunnilingus aristocracy! But no, this is not some libertine sexual free for all. There shall be rules to enforce this new order. For starters, all those disgusting Chads, those filthy misogynists who are always getting their dicks sucked shall be castrated. What is the point of fellatio if it only benefits the most crude and vile of the male species? There shall be a new aristocracy of men, men of high caliber who are chaste and refuse such vile acts of fornication and debauchery. There shall also be a new female elite of only the most beautiful women. No uglies or sluts! And most importantly all women who sleep with Chads shall be

executed! All reproduction shall be done through artificial insemination. No penile penetration! Cunnilingus shall be the only acceptable act for pleasure! Cunnilingus is about true aristocratic power, complete control of the female orgasm! Fellatio is the real submissive act. Letting some whore slobber your knob? Granting her filthy mouth, which has sucked off thousands of Chads complete control of your manhood? No! It's all about cunnilingus!"

Noam lies in his bed and fantasizes about his crush sitting on his face while he eats her pussy and buttocks. He can vividly imagine how every particle of her anatomy smells and tastes, even though he has never seen human female genitalia up close.

Noam falls asleep fantasizing about pleasuring his crush.

He finds himself walking on a bridge through the sky. The sky is pink with a perfumy smell of sex. The perfume scent becomes more intense; filling his nostrils, and fogging up the sky. Finally the fog clears and the bridge leads to a Roman palace in the sky. There she is, his crush, a Roman empress sitting on her throne with her legs open.

"Kneel before me, Sir Noam," she orders.

Noam remembers what Mr. Cockfoster had said about ancient Roman sexual etiquette, but now he has the power to rewrite history.

Noam gets down on his knees beneath his crush; he can smell the intense perfume coming from between her legs.

"Eat me, Noam! I know you've been dreaming about it ever since we first met eyes."

She opens up her legs and Noam starts kissing her inner thighs. "Further in. Eat me, Noam!" she encourages him.

Just as Noam is about to bury his face in her bush he starts falling down a deep dark hole until he finds himself trapped in a small dark concrete chamber that he can barely move in.

It is pitch black, but up above he can hear Wendy and her friends chatter; their voices muffled. Trapped in the dark, it is as if Noam had been buried alive in a coffin.

Suddenly a light pours in through an opening. Noam looks up and can see into the girl's dressing room. He had always fantasized about what it would be like to sneak in; all the hot popular girls changing out of their panties after gym class. Perhaps they have a personal butler to clean them up and spray them with perfume so they always smell like roses.

Noam looks up and is blown away by how luxurious it is. Even though he can only see up through a hole he can see the fancy pink wallpaper.

He can hear the girls talking in the background but still cannot make out what they are saying. He thinks, "Is it their usual gossip, or are they planning something sinister?"

Suddenly a nice plump pair of buttocks sits down covering the hole. It is now pitch dark again, but he catches a glimmer. They are the most perfectly shaped, smooth buttocks. Then he feels himself gradually move upwards, his face smothered in the girl's buttocks and hairy pussy.

He feels compelled to start licking, even though he has no idea who the mystery girl is.

The girl then cums and pisses right on his face. She gets up as if she were simply using the toilet. It is Wendy Silverstein. Then another girl sits down; her buttocks and pussy are even more beautiful. He licks out the girl's pussy and buttocks. After every lick the girl starts humping his face, rubbing her hairy cunt on his mouth, while his nose is stuck up her perfect buttocks. Following the routine, the girl cums, then pisses on his face. She gets up. It is Lisa Goldberg.

Then another girl sits down. She has a nice plump pair of buttocks and a thick reddish-brown bush. His face is now fully suffocated in her buttocks, and he can hardly breathe. He starts lapping at her ass while his entire face is submerged, still struggling to breathe. He can feel the floor moving upwards pressing his face further into the girl's buttocks. Like the others, the girl relieves herself in his mouth, causing him to gag.

She gets up, and it is Molly Katzenberg, who gives him a look of disgust and then spits on his face. He is now several inches deep in urine.

Noam realizes there is a long line of girls waiting to use him; all the hot blonde cheerleaders wanting their sweaty buttocks licked cleaned after cheer practice, the nerdy girls with their hairy unwashed bushes, and the Asian girls with their fishy-smelling pussies.

After all the girls have orgasmed and relieved themselves on Noam's face, he is now submerged in urine all the way up to his face. Anymore girl piss and he would drown. He thinks, "If I start drinking it all, I might survive."

Then he hears another long line. He overhears Wendy talking to a group of the town's rich housewives, who are paying her big bucks just to use him. He thinks, "Is this the end?"

One of the women sits down. His face is now completely submerged to the point where the only way to survive is to breathe the stale air out of the woman's cunt.

After she orgasms and relieves herself, Noam is completely submerged. Piss starts pouring down his throat. He can see nothing but an endless sea of yellow.

Noam wakes up in his bed struggling to breathe. Everything is soaking wet, and he feels stickiness in his pajama pants. He thinks, "A wet dream so wet you drown to death."

He opens his eyes and realizes there has been a fire, setting off the water sprinklers, which were spraying water right into Noam's mouth. Noam coughs up the water from his lungs. He can hear fire sirens outside. He quickly puts his pants on over his pajamas.

The firemen burst in to check out the situation. Noam's mom just awoke from her sleep, "What's going on?"

The fireman says, "A fire alarm went off in your guest house; we have to do an inspection to see if this old place is up to date."

A fire inspector shows up and inspects the guest house. The older British woman comes out screaming, "What's going on here?"

The fire inspector says, "Your guest house is not up to date to the new standards. I'm sorry, but I will have to fine you $4000 for fire code violations."

The old British woman approaches Noam, and his mom and says, "I'm sorry but I'm afraid I'm going to have to ask you to leave for a while, while I get this place up to code. I don't want to be held liable. You have one day to pack your belongings."

Noam and his mom have to spend the weekend at a hotel. Fortunately, they have a gift certificate for the Blackstone Plaza Hotel in Greenwich that Noam's mom won at her workplace's holiday party. It was given as a joke by the office prankster, and she was embarrassed to use it, but at this point it was a relief to have a free week at a five-star hotel and spa.

Noam and his mom drive off to the Blackstone Plaza Hotel. They drive under a grand gilded gate through a wooded area called the "Blackstone Preserve," up to the hilltop hotel which resembles a French chateau, featuring a giant gold-neon roof sign reading "Blackstone Plaza" and purple neon along the edges. In front of the hotel is a giant fountain by the loading zone where hotel patrons are getting out of their chauffeured limos and luxury automobiles.

Noam notices a bunch of teenagers getting off a luxurious black bus which has the gold Blackstone logo, perhaps rich kids taking a school field trip to the spa.

Noam gets out and admires the Blackstone. He has a strange feeling that he belongs here. He looks over at the teenagers. One of the girls smiles. Noam wonders, "Is she smiling at me?"

They enter the grand lobby, which has marble floors, a giant gold clock, crystal chandeliers, and all kinds of European antiquities; what you would expect at the finest hotels in London or Paris.

Noam's mom remarks, "Tasteful for Blackstone's standards. I heard he bought the forest around the hotel as a wilderness preserve, saving it from a planned subdivision. Probably the only decent thing he's ever done in his life, even if it's for selfish reasons."

They check in at the concierge desk and are handed their room keys while the bellhop takes their luggage up to their room.

Past the lobby, they walk through the shopping arcade, which resembles something you might expect to see in Paris. Then into the massive atrium, which has a glass ceiling and 12 levels. They get on the glass tube elevator which has a gilded art nouveau style gate and an old style elevator indicator.

As they go up the elevator, Noam can see down into the pool and spa area which is packed with teens.

Noam's mom comments, "That creep Blackstone created this place just so he can gawk at the teens. What a perv! He's probably up there in his private observation deck as we speak."

Noam looks down and notices some of the teen girls are topless, like some kind of fantasy resort you read about in France, but this is in his very own backyard.

The elevator door opens at the 4th floor and a group of blonde Israeli high school girls get on. Noam feels awkward being surrounded by such beautiful girls while his mom is there because she would often embarrass him.

They get off at the next stop, the 7th floor. Noam looks out over the balcony down into the pool area. Noam's mom yells, "Noam, get over here! You'll have plenty of time to check out the pool. I need your help." Another group of teen girls giggles at him as they walk by.

Noam walks over to their room and the bellhop hands them their stuff. They enter the room, which is spacious and filled with European antiquities.

Noam notices something odd. There is an old portrait of a boy from the 18th century that resembles him. He thinks, "Perhaps I am descended from a great aristocratic bloodline after all? I knew it!"

"Noam! Sort your stuff out!" his mom yells. Noam takes out his suitcases and quickly organizes them. It is time to head down to the pool. But then Noam realizes something; he didn't pack any swimwear. He searches his luggage frantically and shouts, "Mom, I need a swimsuit!"

His mom says, "The swimwear at the hotel boutique is too expensive. I'm afraid we're all going to have to make some sacrifices. Why don't you skip the pool and catch up on your homework."

Noam is furious. There is an entire pleasure spa down there waiting for him, and he is going to use it one way or another.

He gets on the elevator but it won't go down. He then pushes the down button frantically but the elevator goes up instead. An attractive rich woman who is about 30 gets on at the 11th floor. She appears to be either a high-powered businesswoman or a trophy wife, wearing a power suit and a short skirt revealing her legs. Noam thinks, "Perhaps Wendy Silverstein in a decade or so."

Noam smiles at her awkwardly, admiring her plump buttocks and smooth legs. She ignores him. Then she takes a phone call, "Yes, Patricia! I'll be at the spa all afternoon, so don't disturb me. What? That's none of your business! What? Don't tell anyone I was at the spa or I'll have your head on a platter!"

She has a look like she is up to something sinister. Noam asks, "What's at the spa?" She gives him a look to fuck off.

Noam gets off on the ground floor and walks towards the pool and spa area past the lush tropical vegetation. He can hear the sound of the teens playing in a distance. He thinks, "Most resorts I've visited were full of disgusting fat old people or annoying little brats. A resort for hot teens? Maybe Blackstone is onto something here."

Noam arrives at the gate to the pool, puts in his room chip to open the gate. A pool attendant comes by and says, "Excuse me sir, but you must be in swim attire to enter the pool area."

Noam is honored that someone would refer to him as "sir." He thinks, "They know who I am! A great aristocrat, Sir Noam Metzenbaum!" Noam stands there in silence basking in his sense of aristocracy.

The man says, "Excuse me, sir, do you have swim attire? If you don't, we have a swimwear boutique right down the hall and to the left."

Noam replies, "My swimwear is with my mom in her bag."

He thinks, "Big mistake. Now he knows I'm a loser virgin who vacations with his mom."

"Ok", the man replies, "there is a changing room down below."

Noam puts up his nose like he imagines an aristocrat would and walks around the pool area which is packed with rich teens, even better looking than the ones at Chadsworth. "Well except for my crush, of course," Noam thinks.

After all the torment Noam experienced at Chadsworth and at his previous school, he finally has a break. He can simply just enjoy himself and relax. No Chads or high school clique bullshit to stand in his way. This is his place.

Walking around the pool area, Noam sees the group of topless French teen girls, a group of teens from Germany, and then the blonde Israeli girls he saw earlier in the elevator.

He is overwhelmed with lust. He thinks, "Should I go after the European teens like a true aristocrat, or the blonde Jewesses whom I have always craved? Why not both? The world is my oyster."

Noam quickly rushes to the changing room so he can find a swimsuit and get in the pool and start hitting on girls.

He walks down the stairs into the changing room. He steps inside to look around. He can hear a group of boys joking around in German. He walks over and sees a group of blond teen boys changing out of their day clothes into their speedos. While admiring their perfect bodies he sneaks over and steals one of their speedos which have been left on the bench.

They are too busy joking around and taking their time, basking in the nude, to notice him.

Noam has never worn a speedo in his entire life and feels great shame about his tiny penis but he is eager to get to the spa.

He goes into a stall, quickly changes, leaving his clothes inside, then walks out in his new speedo. He looks at himself in the mirror. He is self-conscious about his scrawny arms and tiny penis but thinks of the painting of the aristocrat, "This place is mine dammit! You are fabulous, Noam. *Sir Noam* that is!"

Noam walks out back to the pool area past the group of topless French teen girls. He decides to follow them over to the hot tub, which is already filled with a group of German teen girls. He watches the French girls get in. One of them says something in French. They all laugh and then take their bikini bottoms off and put them to the side.

Noam wants to find a way to see their naked pussies and buttocks but feels awkward getting in the spa with them.

He hides in the bushes then grabs their bikini bottoms, sniffs and licks the insides and then throws them into the bushes where they can't find them.

He waits about five minutes, then gets in. The hot tub is crowded but he manages to slip in. The girls don't pay any attention to him but continue to brush up against him as they mess around in the hot tub.

He continues to sit there and watch them play, staring at their tits, but they are oblivious to him. One of them says something in French again. They look around for their bikini bottoms but can't find them.

Eventually they get out naked, exposing their plump naked buttocks and thick bushes. They walk around the spa area fully nude as if it's no big deal. Noam is in awe and has never seen anything like this in his life.

Noam is now alone with the German girls. They giggle and talk in German. Noam doesn't know if they are making fun of him or laughing about the naked French girls walking around the pool area looking for their bottoms.

The girls still don't pay any attention to him and continue to talk among themselves. Then their boyfriends come over. Noam recognizes them from the changing room all in their speedos. They are carrying beers with them. They all get in the hot tub and hand the girls beers.

Then one boy comes over naked holding a towel over his dick. He takes off his towel and puts it on the side bench and gets in; his dick right in Noam's face as he jumps in, completely oblivious to any sense of personal space, but Noam can't help but stare at his large penis and Adonis chest.

Noam is terrified the boy is going to notice that Noam has his speedo and tries to cover it with his hands but the boys just drink beer, joking around with the girls not paying any attention to him.

Noam is concerned that none of the girls are paying any attention to him, but thinks, "Perhaps it's just the language barrier."

Noam remembers his mom warning him not to trust Germans and that most of them are still Nazis. He thinks, "If they find out some Jew boy stole their speedo they'll kill me!"

Then the naked boy looks down at Noam and starts laughing. Noam is in fear for his life.

The boy says in perfect English, "You have my speedo. Yes?"

Noam doesn't respond.

The boy says, "All is good. We are socialists. What's mine is yours, what's yours is mine. We share?"

Noam thinks, "I like the part about him sharing but as much as I dislike Jews, I still am one, and we just don't share."

Noam smiles and says, "Hello my name is Noam Metzenbau … ah Metzenbauer." "Still too Jewy?" He thinks.

The boy hands him a beer, "Hello new friend. My name is Jürgen."

All the German girls giggle and say "Hello Noam."

Noam is surprised at how nice the teens are. He thinks, "They are rich, popular, good-looking, and hanging out with me? Accepting me as one of their tribe? I don't need these stupid Americans. I'm a true European aristocrat and have found a slice of heaven in this dreadful place they call a country."

Jürgen says, "Noam, the girls are heading to the spa, why don't you join me and the guys in the sauna?" Jürgen says, "Auf Wiedersehen ladies," and they head off to the sauna.

Noam has never been in a sauna but remembers one of his mom's friends' joke that that's where old homosexual men hang out to have sex. "Or was that a steam room?" wonders Noam.

Then he remembers that old gay photographer whose study he sneaked into, taking art photos of naked young teens in saunas. Noam is a little nervous, but this is his chance to experience some real male bonding that he missed out on at school.

When they arrive at the sauna, a staff member hands them all fresh towels. Noam puts the towel around his wet speedo. The boys laugh. Jürgen turns to him, pointing at the speedo, "You need to take those off first."

They all take off their towels and place them down on the Sauna to sit down. Noam looks at them, admiring their naked bodies but doesn't know what to do.

Then Noam sees the smoke rise in the sauna and remembers his grandmother talk about how Jews were tricked into the ovens at Auschwitz. He thinks, "Are they trying to trick the silly Jew boy into the oven? No way are these guys so nice to me for no reason."

Jürgen hands Noam another beer. He takes a sip, still in his speedo. The boys are laughing at him but not in a cruel way like the Chads but like close bros.

Noam finally drinks enough to get the courage to take off his speedos. "Do they think my dick is small," he thinks and then looks at their giant uncircumcised dicks.

Noam continues standing there naked in front of them, not sure whether to sit down or not. Then Jürgen points to an empty space right in the middle, sandwiched between them.

Noam sits down, his skin rubbing up against their muscular sweaty bodies and his legs close up against theirs. He starts to get an erection and takes his towel to cover up his dick.

Jürgen says with his legs open wide and dick hanging out, "Chill bro," then puts his arm around Noam, and hands him another beer. They all drink beer with their arms around each other like they've been best friends forever. For the first time in Noam's entire life he feels accepted, like he is part of a tribe.

While they gulp down beer a drunken Jürgen gets up and stands on the sauna's bench. He starts walking around naked in front of the other guys, who are leaning back to avoid getting his dick in their faces.

Jürgen then leans in towards the wall, his naked hip brushing against Noam's face but just barely sparing him his dick as he starts humping the wall.

Then he turns around again and stands up in front of Noam, his dick less than an inch away from Noam's face.

Noam is confused. He thinks, "Is Jürgen gay and wants me to suck his dick, or is he just taunting me like the Chads. No! It's just natural male bonding!"

Noam is about to lean in to kiss Jürgen's dick, but he jumps down and starts laughing. All the boys laugh and start talking in German.

They all notice Noam's massive erection. He is terrified that they are going to ridicule him or worse.

Jürgen notices Noam is upset and turns to him, "It's ok if you're gay, but we're just playing around, bro. I'm not gay. I have a girlfriend." The boys all laugh. The other one say says something in German.

Jürgen sits down next to Noam again and remarks, "Its ok bro, we joke around like American Chads."

The other guy says, "Yo! I am an American Chad. Get laid, bro!

Noam is disgusted. He thinks, "Are the Chads infecting the entire world with their crude uncivilized ways?"

Then the boys' girlfriends enter the Sauna. Noam is mesmerized by their beauty, their golden blonde hair and perfect bodies.

They have an expression on their faces like they have just orgasmed. Then the girls take off their towels, exposing their perfect tits and golden bushes. Noam fantasizes about the blonde Jewish girls and their golden bushes, but these were real European girls, girls in touch with their aristocratic femininity. Noam stands there in awe.

The girls giggle and say something in German and the boys laugh.

Noam thinks, "Are they talking about me?"

Then the girls sit down next to their boyfriends, with Noam sitting on the side feeling completely sidelined.

Noam so wanted to sit next to the naked girls but they are sitting so that Noam is still sandwiched between two guys.

Noam turns to one of the girls and asks her how the spa was, curious about what he had heard from the woman on the elevator.

There is an awkward pause, and then all the girls giggle.

One of the boys puts his hand on his girlfriend's crotch, but she pushes it away as if she was already satisfied from her experience at the spa. One of the other girls gives him a handjob to make him feel better.

Then Jürgen's girlfriend gets down on her knees and starts giving him a blowjob, her perfect tits and buttocks bouncing up and down as she sucks him off.

They continue to joke around, playing with each other's perfect bodies, completely ignoring Noam.

Then Noam asks if he can join in. Jürgen replies, "Sorry, new friend, go find your own girlfriend."

Noam leaves the sauna in tears. He thinks, "So much for socialism. Sharing the wealth? My mom was right about trusting those krauts. I'm going to look for the blonde Israeli girls. I have to be with my own kind."

He gets lost walking around the sauna complex, ending up at a door with a sign saying "Women's Day Spa." He assumes that men are not allowed but sneaks in anyway. He thinks, "Perhaps I will find the blonde Israeli girls there."

He walks down a long hallway. There is something very secretive and discreet about the place.

As he walks down the corridor he cannot see anyone but can hear what sounds like the faint sound of an orgasm. "Is this some kind of secret sex club?" he wonders.

There are curtains on the side of the walls, which he can hear strange noises from inside. He walks up closer to see if he can peek in.

Suddenly the attractive businesswoman from the elevator steps out wearing a bathrobe, almost bumping into him. She looks at him with the utmost disgust.

Noam is terrified she recognizes him from the elevator, but she just throws her sweaty towel at him as if he were a bin for disposing used towels.

Noam is insulted. He thinks, "I'm a great aristocrat, not the help. There must be some confusion!" He notices the towel has a yellowish stain and dark curly pubic hairs on it. He tries to uphold his dignity but just can't help himself. He buries his face in the towel, breathing in the women's scent, noticing it has a weird fishy smell mixed with stale urine. He feels disgusted and humiliated for sinking so low.

He then hears someone walking down the hall. He hides in an empty stall behind the curtain. Once he gets inside, he finds it is a small space with a cushy bench, a clean towel, and stirrups at the bottom like you would find at a gynecologist office.

He wonders if the woman's towel smelt so rank because she was seeing a doctor for an infection and was ashamed to tell her assistant. He feels nauseous thinking about how he just licked an infected medical towel.

While he hides out inside he hears a strange sound coming from the stall next door. There is a wall separating the side like a bathroom stall with a small area to peek through.

He is terrified of peeking through but puts his ear to the side of the stall. He can hear a woman talking on the other side.

He has to find out what is going on and peeks through the narrow space into the other stall. He sees a beautiful young woman, about 20, who resembles Sarah Michelle Gellar from Cruel Intentions and is wearing a bathrobe. She is on her phone, yelling at her boyfriend about what a loser he is, but he can tell by her facial expression that she is in great pleasure while she bosses her boyfriend around.

Then she quickly hangs up the phone and has the most intense orgasm. Noam looks down and sees a small young Latino man on his knees, with his face buried between her legs, acting as though he was her personal vibrator.

After she has orgasmed, the man leaves. Noam watches her change into a clean robe, admiring her naked body and hairy pussy.

He thinks about sneaking into her stall to steal her used towel but decides it is too risky. He leaves and continues wandering down the corridor leading to another room where there is a young blonde woman lying down naked on a massage table waiting for her masseuse.

Noam notices her face is buried in the table and she cannot see him. Noam thinks about pretending to be the masseuse but is terrified of touching the naked woman. He continues to stand over, her staring at her plump buttocks, which are pale from her tan line.

He then gets down on his knees to get a closer look, staring straight at her buttocks. He examines her perfect buttocks, then inspects closer and underneath he can see her labia and pubic hair. He is tempted to lick it but is terrified to do so, even though he suspects that might be what she wants, having seen what he has just witnessed in the stall.

He starts hyperventilating in arousal and gets close enough that she can feel his warm breath on her labia.

"Lick it!" she commands. Not caring who it is, just demanding pleasure. This is his chance.

Noam contemplates going for it, but just as he slowly moves his face closer to her ass, a small South East Asian man catches Noam and starts shouting at him in some jungle Asian dialect. The woman catches Noam and screams, "Get that pervert out of here. I want full service at no cost! Or else I'll sue this resort for sexual harassment!"

The man gets down on his knees and starts eating the woman's ass. Another staff member comes over, putting a curtain around her, and sees Noam checking out the situation. He orders him to leave.

Noam is surprised a place like this exists. He had no idea that attractive, high-status women had these desires and acted on them, but he also realizes that he is still viewed as a loser by high society and has no place.

He thinks, "Blackstone's just another fat cat capitalist who profits from the most debauched elites! He's just another phony like the rest of them."

Noam goes back to the pool area to look for the blonde Israeli teen girls, but his mom catches him. She says, "Noam, I've been worried sick about you. You've been gone all day without even telling me. Go to the room, I got Chinese takeout!"

A group of teen girls in the pool sees Noam and his mom and laugh at him, "What a loser, and probably still a virgin."

"Yeah, like totally."

Noam goes up to their hotel room with his mom for dinner. Noam's mom can smell the beer on him and says, "Have you been drinking beer? That's it you're grounded for a week. No leaving this room unless it's with me, and especially no going to the pool!"

Noam has hot and sour soup, chow mein, and ginger ale. His mom says, "Just a minute. I have call, and if I catch you sneaking out you're dead meat!"

She goes into the other room to talk. This is his chance to sneak out to look for the blonde Israeli girls.

Still drunk, Noam wanders down the hallway to the elevator. He goes back down to the pool to look for them, but they are nowhere to be found. After searching for about 30 minutes, he gives up on the pool area.

He goes over to the spa again thinking they might be there. He sees a group of attractive women, perhaps models, going in. He thinks, "No uglies. I would think some desperate women would want to use these services, but they are unworthy. That is smart thinking on Blackstone's part."

The security guard recognizes him from sneaking into the spa and warns him, "If I catch you snooping around here again, you are banished from the hotel!" Noam walks away and thinks, "This is my place. I shall do as I please."

He remembers his mom joking about Blackstone having a secret room to observe all the girls. He thinks, "Perhaps if I get into the surveillance room I will be able to find the location of the blonde Israeli girls."

He gets on the elevator and takes it to the 12th floor. He sees a sign saying "Observation Deck" with an arrow pointing in the direction. He takes one last look down at the pool. From this vantage point, the swimmers just look like blobs of beige. He then follows the sign down a hallway, which leads to a spiral staircase.

He walks up the stairs to the clock tower observation deck. He looks out and admires the view of the town and the sun setting over the sea. He can even make out Chadsworth in the distance, still haunting him in his place of refuge.

He fantasizes about being in his palace's fortress, shooting cannon balls down onto Chadsworth but thinks, "What is there to protect when I am all alone in such a romantic spot? I should be here in my royal tower with my maiden."

As he watches the sunset, he can see the lights of the town and the glow of light from the hotel's neon sign.

He hears steps going up the stairwell. He turns around and sees one of the blonde Israeli girls. He is speechless. "Did she come up here just for me?" he wonders.

They awkwardly make eye contact with each other. Noam doesn't know what to say. She then walks away to look out at the view.

Trying to quickly make a move he says, "Nice view?" The girls smiles awkwardly.

He says, "My name is Noam, *Noam Metzenbaum*. This is quite an exquisite locale?"

"Yes," the girl replies. Noam thinks maybe she can't speak good English.

"What's your name?" he inquires.

"Shir," she responds.

"Nice to meet you, Shir," he smiles.

She smiles back at him awkwardly.

They both look out at the sunset.

"Very romantic," Noam says.

The girl looks uncomfortable, "Oh, I know. I'm meeting my boyfriend."

Noam looks away in despair, trying to hold in his tears. He tries not to make eye contact with her.

He hears steps coming up the stairs. Her boyfriend appears, and he is a swarthy Middle Eastern looking guy.

He ignores Noam and says something to his girlfriend in Hebrew. Then they start making out. Noam rushes back down the stairs in tears, thinking, "How does such a disgusting pig like that get such as beautiful blonde!"

He heads back to the hotel room and his mother is furious.

"Noam! I told you that you were grounded," she says. "You deliberately disobeyed me! I had no idea where you were. There are all kind of creeps lurking around this hotel, and you put yourself in danger when you wander around aimlessly on your own. Not to mention, you're drunk! You're a handful, Noam. You know that? And it's not easy raising you alone! Your

Grandma Rosa is visiting from Long Island tomorrow, so you'd better be on your best behavior. Now go to sleep!"

Noam starts to cry. He says, "I don't want to see her!"

Noam's mom shouts "How dare you! Your grandma loves you very much and has done a lot for us. You'd better show her the utmost respect tomorrow!"

Noam ignores his mom, quickly changes into his pajamas, and goes to bed.

His mom yells, "Don't ignore me, Noam! What were you up to today? Were you doing drugs?"

"No, mom," replies Noam.

"Goodnight, Noam! Your grandma is coming first thing in the morning!"

Noam has trouble sleeping. He thinks about his missed opportunities and disappointments at the resort; a place that was supposed to be a refuge from the torments of Chadsworth, and how he has to go back to school on Monday to face the Chads. He wonders what his crush thinks of him, if she even knows he exists.

Noam's mom wakes him up at 6am, "Noam, get up! Your grandma called. She's driving up from Long Island, and she will be here in an hour. Now get ready!"

Noam is tired from being up all night and falls back to sleep. His mom continues to yell, "Noam, get up! I want to make a good impression. We are meeting downstairs for breakfast at the cafe."

Noam reluctantly gets out of bed. He asks, "Can't I just sleep in? You can meet her for breakfast and I'll be ready by lunch time."

"Are you fucking kidding me?" his mom replies. "Look Noam, I know this is all one big joke to you, but my mother has always looked down on me since I was a girl. My sister was always the favorite growing up. In college I got into drugs, and dated bad boys, while my sister always dated the guys in pre-med. The final straw was when I got pregnant! Ever since then she's always favored my sister, fawned over her kids, and her husband is always scheming over the inheritance. This is an opportunity to make a good impression, and as much as I love you, you don't always make the best impression."

"I don't want to see her!" Noam is defiant. "I want to go to the pool! This is my last day to do something nice. Your sister's a psycho bitch, and I hate her bratty kids and her filthy sand nigger, oops I'm sorry sand kike husband!"

Noam's mom, for the first time since he was a little boy, spanks him on the ass. She screams, "How dare you disrespect your family like that. Your grandmother, aunt, cousins, and yes even your uncle all love you and care a lot about you! And I shall have zero tolerance for your racist crap. Where are you learning that? The internet! No more internet, unless it's homework related! I've seen which sites you visit, and I'm not pleased!"

Noam is humiliated to be shown that much disrespect and have his privacy violated. Noam starts to cry.

"Stop sulking," his mom scolds. "Let's head downstairs to meet your grandmother in the lobby. She will be here any minute."

As they head down to the lobby, Noam looks down through the glass elevator down into the pool admiring the fresh crop of teens.

His mom says to herself, “What’s with this place and teen girls? I bet that creep Blackstone is using it for some kind of elite sex trafficking ring. I should talk to Mr. Bloom about doing an exposé.”

She turns to Noam. “Speaking of Mr. Bloom, how’s his daughter Natalie doing?”

“Ah, I don’t know. She’s fine, I guess,” Noam replies.

“That’s good to hear,” she replies. “Mr. Bloom is concerned about her getting into the wrong crowd and thinking of transferring her to an all-girls school. I mean, Mr. Bloom, the publisher of the top progressive online publication and the biggest womanizer I know doesn’t want his own daughter to experience her own womanhood. What a misogynistic hypocrite!”

Just thinking about her causes Noam’s heart to sink; butterflies in his stomach. He has to come up with a plan fast, but his grandmother’s visit has derailed his day, and he has to face his fate tomorrow totally unprepared.

They head over to the café, which has a Parisian theme. Noam asks his mom to buy him an apricot tart, but she says, “No, we are waiting for your grandma, and we will eat together.”

She gets a ring on her cell phone, “Hi mom. You're in traffic? Ok see you then.”

She turns to Noam, "Your grandma is still in traffic. I guess all of New York City is heading up here for the weekend. I suggest you catch up on your homework."

Noam is too upset to work on any school work. His only homework is his mission to conceive of a plot to win over his crush.

The group of French girls he recognizes from the hot tub walk into the café. There are about 30 of them; must be on a school trip.

Noam is embarrassed to be seen with his mom and can't stop staring at the girls in their designer fashion and miniskirts; the images of the bare asses and bush still stick in his mind from the day before.

Then Noam's grandmother shows up. She comes over to him, "Noam! Give you bubby a kiss! You've grown a foot since the last time I saw you."

Noam feels insulted because he is short for his age. The last time he saw her was at his grandfather's funeral, and she blamed Noam for his death while his aunt's family schmoozed with her hoping to get a chunk of the inheritance.

Noam's mom says, "Great that we are all here together. Now let's get something to eat. How about Quiche Lorraine and fresh squeezed orange juice for brunch?"

Noam's grandmother looks at her watch. "Brunch? Its 12:30, and besides, this place isn't even kosher! Let's go into town! I'm not paying a penny to that Nazi, what's his name?"

"Roger Blackstone?" Noam says with a smirk.

His grandmother looks upset and his mom gives him a dirty look.

Then a group of German tourists come in and walk up to the counter to order pastries. His grandmother gets uncomfortable.

She says, "Are they talking about …?"

"No, of course not," replies Noam's mom.

Noam's grandmother says, "We need to leave now! Your generation doesn't get it. Your naiveté is appalling, and you're raising your son with no connection to his heritage!"

"Relax mom," Noam's mother says. "We will find you a nice kosher deli. There are plenty downtown. This town has changed a lot."

"I'm glad to hear that," she replies. "I haven't been here in ages. This town used to be quite WASPy."

They walk outside. Noam's mom offers to drive her Beamer but Noam's grandmother refuses, "I won't drive in that death trap from the Reagan Era. And besides, I won't ride in a German car."

A group of German tourists walk by and say something in German. Noam's grandmother screams, "Valet, get me my Lexus!"

They bring over her Lexus. Noam's mom drives while his grandmother sits in the front passenger seat, and he has to sit in the back, which he hates because he gets carsick.

While they drive through the woods, Noam's grandmother remarks, "Look at all this empty space. I mean they could make a fortune in real estate, but it is just sitting there full of trees!"

"It's called conservation," replies Noam's mom.

"Oh you and your silly hippie stuff," Noam's grandmother says. "You never got over your pot-smoking college days, running off to join Green Peace because you fell for that dirty hippie while your sister was dating a nice dentist. No wonder your life is such a mess. You're past 40, a single mom, and your chances at marrying a doctor and buying a nice house are diminishing."

Noam's mom doesn't respond, but her mother's rants cause her to drive chaotically.

They drive into town to find a place for lunch. As they drive around town, Noam starts to get carsick and feels like he's going to vomit.

Noam screams, "Pull over. I'm going to puke!"

"Watch your language young man. Now let's find a good kosher place," his grandmother says.

They have lunch at a kosher deli. Noam's grandmother proclaims, "We have to try the white fish on rye!"

Noam looks over and sees Zack on a date with Wendy, but they pretend not to notice him. Then as his mom and grandmother start yelling and his grandmother rubs Noam on the head, they can't help themselves and start laughing at Noam.

Noam whispers to himself, "You're dead, Zack, and I'm going to tongue rape your girlfriend!"

They sit down at the table. Noam still feels sick to his stomach from the car ride and running into Zack and Wendy. The waiter comes by and asks them what they want.

He turns to Noam's grandmother, and she orders a white fish sandwich on rye, a side of potato salad, and matzah ball soup, while his mom orders a bagel with cream cheese and lox.

The waiter turns to Noam, "I'll just have saltines and ginger ale."

His grandmother looks at Noam, "You have to have something to eat. You're on the Auschwitz diet. Look at you. No girl is going to want to date such a weakling."

Noam is disgusted to hear his own grandmother talk about his desirability to the opposite sex. He remembers the time when they all stayed at his aunt's house in Long Island and she would gloat about how handsome and muscular his cousins were and how lucky they were to have girlfriends, "Not just any girlfriends, but blonde fucking Jewish girlfriends dammit!" Noam thinks bitterly.

He is going to vomit; he rushes off to find a bathroom. He finds the men's room and rushes over to the stalls. He looks in and most of the available ones are small and stink. He finds the handicapped stall which is spacious enough. He doesn't want to get near the toilet thinking about all the disgusting handicapped people who have used it.

He goes over to the corner and is about to hurl but nothing comes up, just a dry heave. Then he hears something in the stall next to him. It's Wendy having an orgasm.

He thinks, "She must be with that asshole, Zack!" As much as Noam despises Wendy he fantasized about her sitting on his face while he ate her out ever since meeting her at the fountain on his first day in Greenwich.

Noam can't help himself and starts masturbating. His feeling of nausea is overcome with an intense feeling of eroticized rage, wanting to rape Wendy with his tongue or have her fuck his face, while Zack lies there on the side castrated and bleeding to death.

After masturbating to the sound of Wendy's orgasms, Noam cums all over the toilet seat.

He gets out of the stall and sees a morbidly obese man in a wheel chair and a colostomy bag waiting to use the handicap stall.

The man scowls at Noam, "You fuckin little prick! If I ever get out of this chair, I'm going to make you regret the day you were born!"

As Noam washes his hands he hears the man screaming in the stall.

He thinks, "Eeew gross. Now my aristocratic seed on the seat is contaminated by that fat old man's shit!"

As he is about to dry off his hands, he sees Zack and Wendy leave the stall. Wendy rushes out of the men's room giggling with an orgasmic expression on her face.

Zack comes over to wash his hands next to Noam. Noam can smell pussy on him. They both stare into the mirror trying to avoid making eye contact with each other.

Then just as Noam leaves, Zack says in a calm but threatening voice, “I know it was you, virgin. You're going to pay one way or another. Oh and by the way I just got laid. Something you’ll never get to experience.”

Noam leaves the bathroom to go back to the table. His grandmother screams, “Noam where have you been? Did you have diarrhea?”

Noam can hear Wendy giggling in the background.

His grandmother looks at him disapprovingly, “No wonder you're so ill. You don’t eat. I got you everything on the menu.”

Noam looks at all the food in front of him. He feels ill. He slowly sips on his matzah ball soup and nibbles on his bagel.

His grandmother says, “Noam dear. I got you something.”

She takes out a box with a card on it.

Noam opens the card. There is a ten dollar bill in it.

Noam stares at it.

“What do you say, Noam?” his mom says.

“Thank you,” Noam replies with a fake smile.

Noam feels insulted. He knows she had inherited $4 million when her husband died. She was somewhat nice to Noam as a kid but ever since her husband’s death, she had always behaved passive aggressively towards him.

Then she hands him the box which doesn’t even have wrapping paper on it. “Open your present, Noam.”

Noam opens it. It's a tacky sweater.

He looks at his grandmother. "Thanks."

"Try it on," she says.

Noam smiles awkwardly. "I'll – I'll try it on when I get home."

"I want to see you with it on right now! I saw it at a flea market and knew the moment I saw it that it would suit you perfectly."

Noam thinks, "She bought the sweater just to humiliate me, knowing that I am pressured to fit in with the rich kids at Chadsworth. She's been around superficial rich people her entire life!"

Noam puts on the sweater. It is oversized and stretches out like some fat guy wore it.

He can still hear Zack and Wendy laughing at him, their laughter getting louder and louder as if they are sitting right behind him.

There is an awkward silence at the table. He can tell his mom and grandmother are upset with him.

Noam breaks the silence, turning to his grandmother, "So I know Grandpa Saul was close friends with the Blackstones."

His mom whispers in his ear, "Zip it, Noam."

His grandmother responds, "Well, I don't want to think about that horrible man right now, but since the day has already been ruined I don't think we can make it any worse, so here goes."

Noam is waiting in anticipation while his mom is rolling her eyes.

His grandmother continues, "So Noam. Roger was a close associate of your grandfather. As you may know he designed Blackstone's casinos in Las Vegas and his new hotel in San Francisco. He even designed one for New York, but the project went bankrupt. I never felt comfortable with that man around the house, with his Nazi connections and all, but Saul was my husband, and they were good friends, so I had to honor my husband and just stay out of the way."

His mom interrupts, "Not to mention his lewd behavior around young girls!"

Noam's grandmother goes on, "Well, I always suspected he was a homosexual, but Saul told me he was actually quite conservative, insisting on only marrying a virgin. That's why he liked them young, but he stayed single and rumor has it he was a virgin well into middle age. But let's not talk about that evil man. I could sell that information to the tabloids for millions but I have to honor my late husband's wishes."

Noam's mom puts her hand down: "He's a fascist prick, and anything it takes to bring that creep down, so be it! And of course Saul was oblivious. He didn't always have the best judgment about whom he would have around his family. It was always all about his career and schmoozing with his prestigious colleagues."

Noam's grandmother shouts, "How dare you talk about your father that way! He loved you so much you would never understand; so enough with this nonsense. Let's head down to the sea. I can use the fresh air. This place is stuffy.

As they leave, Noam takes one last glance at Zack and Wendy as they are sharing a strawberry milkshake.

They get into his grandmother's Lexus. She says, "Now let's go check out the sea."

Noam's mom suggests there's a nice spot near the light house. Noam has not been there yet but has heard that the light house is notorious for the Chads taking girls up to de-virginize after a night of drinking and partying on the beach.

As they are driving to the beach his grandmother starts ranting again to Noam's mom, "Look at yourself. Is this how you want to live? Raising your son in an unstable living situation. Your sister just remodeled her house in Long Island."

Noam's mom whispers under her lips, "With money you gave her."

Noam's grandmother continues ranting, "Moving back and forth, from that tiny little apartment in the city, to renting some shack in someone's backyard, to staying in hotels. You just can't live like nomads. Like animals!

Noam's mom is upset, but she is used to her mom. She says, "There's the beach down there. Let's get some fucking fresh air!"

Noam's grandmother says, "What kind of a role model are you for your son? No wonder he's such a loser."

Noam's mom replies, "Look you can talk smack about me all day, but leave my son out of this! Now there's the fuckin' ocean!"

"I can't believe you," Noam's grandmother snips. "Your sister has never talked to me that way, and how are we going to find a place to park? The entire city is here for the weekend."

Noam looks out at the water; it is packed. As they are looking for parking he sees a group of teen girls in skimpy bikinis, which reminds him he really wants to get back to the Blackstone and hang out at the pool.

His grandmother points to them and says, “And their fathers let them dress that way? These days, girls grow up without fathers around, and their stupid hippie mothers let them do whatever they want. You have girls losing their virginity at 12 these days!”

“You don’t know what you're talking about,” Noam's mom says. “It’s all about guys putting pressure on girls to put out, and then the marketing companies exploiting girls from a young age. I fight for women’s rights at my magazine, and I raised my son to be the perfect gentleman!”

“No you raised your son to be a spoiled brat; a wimp who will never make a suitable husband!” the grandmother replies.

“Let’s head back to the hotel. It’s getting late,” Noam's mom suggests.

They all get into the car. There is an awkward silence.

As they drive by the light house, Noam sees Nick and the Chads with a group of cute blonde freshman girls. He wants to die.

When they get back to the Hotel after a long awkward silent drive, Noam’s mom asks, “Mom, do you plan on spending the night, or are you headed back to Long Island?”

“Well it’s too late to head back to Long Island,” the grandmother replies. “And I don’t like to drive in the dark, and I’m not staying at the Blackstone. I had enough of that man as it is. How about this? I have a friend who owns an apartment complex. I'll give him a call and see if he has any available rooms. My treat!"

"That's a good idea," Noam's mom says. "Noam's been getting into too much trouble there."

Noam sighs in disappointment. His hotel adventure has come to an end and he is totally unprepared for his return to Chadsworth.

The grandmother calls her friend. He has an extra apartment available which he can rent out for a month.

The grandmother says, "I'll cover the cost, but you don't need to thank me!"

They arrive at the apartment, which is a brand new four-story brick building just outside downtown.

The man briefly introduces himself to Noam and his mom. He mentions that he is a real estate developer and has worked with Saul in the past.

While the grandmother schmoozes with him, he says, "Nice to see you again" to Noam's mom. He briefly shakes Noam's hand and heads off.

They enter the two-bedroom apartment. Noam rushes to the bedroom to get some alone time. Just as he starts masturbating, his grandmother bangs on the door.

Noam finishes up. "Let me in, Noam!" she yells. "I need to get to sleep so I can be fresh for the drive tomorrow!"

Noam opens the doors for her. Noam's mom comes to check on them. His mom turns to him and says, "Sorry Noam, but you're sleeping on the sofa for tonight."

Noam is not able to sleep; the uncomfortable sofa, the thoughts of failure at the resort, and having to face his adversaries at Chadsworth tomorrow keep him up all night. He can hear his grandmother snore in the bedroom.

The next morning they have coffee and stale bagels for breakfast. His grandmother complains to his mom, "I get you this nice apartment, and you don't even bother to get any food? I can't drive on an empty stomach."

"I'll drive Noam to school, and when I get back I'll take you out for brunch," Noam's mom says.

Just as Noam is about to leave out the door his grandmother asks, "Aren't you going to give me a hug goodbye?"

Turning to Noam's mom she says, "Is this how you raised your son to be the perfect gentleman?"

Noam walks over to his grandmother. She kisses him on his cheek, leaving a lipstick mark. She jokes, "Maybe the other kids will think a girl kissed you. Ha! I highly doubt it."

Noam rushes out. "And he didn't even say goodbye. How rude!" his grandmother's voice trails off.

Noam takes a tissue and wipes off the lipstick. His mom turns to him and says, "I know your grandmother can be difficult, but you don't need to make things worse for me."

Noam asks his mom to drop him off two blocks away so he isn't seen.

"All right Noam, but you better hurry so you're not late."

Noam gets out of the car and walks down the street to Chadsworth. As he is walking, he takes out his journal and starts writing:

"This is my 2nd week at Chadsworth Academy. My first week has been an utter failure: complete humiliation, failure to establish my social standing, and inability to initiate any meaningful contact with my crush. Over the weekend I have missed out on social activities and am not up to date on the latest matters dealing with my crush. Off to battle again."

Noam reaches the entrance to Chadsworth, puts his journal away in his backpack and walks in as a soldier prepared for battle. He goes to his first-period class, which is history.

He enters the class and sees Principal Greenstein. He thinks, "Am I in trouble for something? Did Zack snitch on me about his car?"

He takes a deep breath, contemplates hiding out or skipping school, but decides there is no coward's way out. He thinks, "Noam, you must face your adversaries! A true aristocrat would not cower in fear!"

Noam steps in. Principal Greenstein, a slightly overweight middle-aged woman, smiles and says, "Welcome, Noam!"

Noam is relieved that he isn't in trouble.

Then he looks out at the class and sees the Chads laughing at him. Wendy, Lisa, and Molly are sneering, with Zack looking at him like he's going to destroy him. Then he hears the door open, and he turns around. It's her, his crush.

His heart sinks. Everyone in the class is looking at him, knowing about his feelings for Natalie. She walks right past him, completely oblivious to his existence, then sits down next to Wendy and Lisa. Wendy whispers something in her ears. His crush starts giggling. Noam is devastated.

Mrs. Greenstein says, "Please sit down, Noam." The entire class starts laughing.

Mrs. Greenstein explains, "Unfortunately your history teacher Mr. Cockfoster has been dismissed, and we have yet to find a replacement. Today we have Sanjay Patel on behalf of the debate team here to run a special mock debate for history class."

Sanjay gets up in front of the class. One of the Chads yells, "Yo, Sanjay! Where's my slurpee!"

Mrs. Greenstein says, "There shall be zero tolerance for racism and bigotry at Chadsworth. We are a welcoming and inclusive environment for students of all backgrounds."

Noam thinks, "What a load of bullshit."

Sanjay gets up and speaks: "Greetings to all, on behalf of the Chadsworth debate team. We are hosting a mock debate. This is how it will work. I will assign a presidential candidate, give each of you a paper on the candidate's platform, and then put you into groups. One student will represent the candidate from each group. I shall declare the winner, and they will earn extracurricular credits for their great verbal and persuasive abilities!"

Noam smirks, thinking, "Politics as usual; stupid foreigners deciding our elections."

Sanjay proclaims, "The first group is for Democratic candidate Senator Dave Cohen-Rodriguez from the state of California." Zack, Wendy, Lisa, Molly, and Fat Elliot join the group.

Then Carlos joins in. He turns to Noam, "Sorry Noam, but I got to support my candidate. Still love you, Holmes." He blows a kiss at Noam. The Chads laugh.

Sanjay says, "The next group is for Republican candidate Governor Wilbur Rex Jackson III from the state of Oklahoma." Nick, the rest of the Chads, and a nerdy rich kid with a bow tie join the group.

Then Sanjay announces, "Next we have entrepreneur Roger Blackstone from the state of Nevada."

There is an awkward silence.

Zack says, "Who's going to step up to represent this fascist? I'll kick his ass!"

"Yeah what a commie bro," Nick replies.

Noam gets up. He is the only one to represent Blackstone.

The class laughs at Noam. Carlos gets up and says, "Even though I hate Blackstone I admire Noam's courage; standing up for what you believe in instead of going with the herd."

Then one of the nerds joins the Blackstone group.

Suddenly Noam's crush gets up. She is about to walk over to the Blackstone group, but then Wendy says, "Over here," and she joins them at the Cohen-Rodriguez group.

Noam is devastated. His first chance to talk to his crush one-on-one, sabotaged by peer pressure and the herd mentality.

"I think we are through here," Sanjay says. "But does anyone want to represent Libertarian Adam Brown, state senator from the state of New Hampshire?"

Justin Green, the boy whom Wendy invited to the party, volunteers.

"I will give you all 30 minutes to deliberate," Sanjay announces. "Study the platforms, and then vote on a leader to represent your group."

Zack is selected to represent the Democratic candidate Dave Cohen-Rodriguez. Wendy, Lisa, and Molly gush over him.

"You're our hero, Zack!" Wendy fawns.

"Yeah like future president of the United States," Molly replies.

Noam can tell by his crush's facial expressions that she doesn't like Zack anymore but is in the group thanks to the social pressure.

Nick is selected to represent Republican candidate Wilbur Rex Jackson III. Nick steps up with his cocky grin.

Chad S. shouts, "Chads in da White House!"

Then Noam is selected to represent his idol, Roger Blackstone.

The class ridicules him.

Noam steps up, thinking, "I am jaguar stepping up to devour those stupid donkeys and elephants."

Then Justin gets up to represent the Libertarian, but no one really cares.

Sanjay announces the candidates one more time and explains the format, "You will each start with an opening statement. After that, you will be given a question; each response will be granted one rebuttal. First up is Dave Cohen-Rodriguez."

Zack states, "I am Dave Rodriguez Cohen. I am committed to upholding the values of diversity, equality, and social justice that have made this country great but are now under threat from forces of fear, bigotry, and intolerance. I honor both my Jewish and Chicano heritage and cherish diversity with my commitment to the Jewish people by protecting the state of Israel from enemies both foreign and domestic and providing a safe and tolerant environment for marginalized minorities, including women, the LGBT community, and undocumented immigrants."

Wendy, Lisa, and Molly cheer.

"Thank you Zack," says Sanjay with a big smile.

Zack turns to Sanjay, "And I will make sure that South Asian American contributions to the tech industry are fully respected and supported through comprehensive legislation."

Sanjay says, "Next is Wilbur Rex Jackson III."

Nick puts on a fake southern accent, imitating Francis Underwood from House of Cards, "I'm Wilbur Rex Jackson the III. Our very American way of life is under attack. The Democrats want to raise your taxes, make you poor, and give your hard-earned dollars to lazy slackers. I come from a business background and understand the need to cut regulations on corporations and put Americans back to work. I will re-establish law and order, throw the scum off our streets and put them behind bars, strengthen our national defense, and protect our allies in the Middle East. And most importantly, I will protect our Judeo-Christian values, which are under siege from the towelhead bastards and the commie left, and I'll bomb the shit out of any nation who threatens those values!"

The Chads chant, "USA! USA! USA!"

Justin interrupts him, "If by Judeo-Christian values you mean deflowering a new freshmen girl every night, then yeah I suppose."

Sanjay says, "Enough, you will have your turn."

Nick turns to Justin in his regular voice, "Look, I'm not some autistic libertarian. I've had real-world experience. Yeah I like to get laid! Those are red-blooded American values that this nation was founded on. Washington, Jefferson, Lincoln, and MLK; those dudes liked pussy. They were probably getting their dicks sucked while writing the Constitution."

Justin says, "You know nothing about the constitution. You're a retard. MLK had nothing to do with the Constitution. Name just one amendment!"

Nick says, "Yo dude, that's racist bro. Black people built this country!"

"Let's move on," says Sanjay. "Next is Roger Blackstone."

Both Nick and Zack look at Noam like they are going to destroy him.

Noam stands up straight, "Roger Blackstone here. I am here to bring the American people the great civilization that has been denied to them by corrupt parasitic elites. I will implement grand aesthetics visions, technological innovation, and further the advancement of human enlightenment. I have done great things, and will bring great …"

The Chads start mocking him, "Who would ever elect a virgin!"

"How can you win a war if you can't even get laid bro?"

Sanjay dismisses Noam and says, "Adam Brown?"

Justin steps up. "Hi there, I'm Adam Brown. Our Constitutional liberties are under threat. I will shrink our massive bureaucracy, reduce the size of government, and let the American people be free to live their own lives as they choose; not politicians or social engineers. All three of my opponents here are statists who have no regard for the principles of individual liberty and small government."

Sanjay says, "Our first issue is economics. How will you fix our nation's economic crisis and address income inequality?"

Zack says, "For starters we need to get more women into the workforce and end the gender pay gap."

"Aawww, you go Zack!" Wendy smiles.

Zack continues, "And end racial inequality by enforcing quotas to mandate that employers hire women and minorities, and full amnesty for all undocumented immigrants."

He gets a massive round of applause from the class.

Noam responds, “Look at this. The son of a billionaire parasite talking about income inequality. He’s a lazy spoiled brat who knows nothing about how the economy works. He hasn’t addressed how he will create jobs, how he will reform the financial system. Oh I forgot, your dad’s a fuckin hedge fund manager! We need to break up the banks, give their unearned wealth to the real innovators and intellectuals! Implement smart socialism! Aristocratic socialism!”

Fat Elliot says, “Yeah, national socialism you Nazi fuckwit!”

Sanjay says to Noam, “No personal insults! Zack, you get a rebuttal.”

“Thank you Sanjay, I can handle the creep myself,” Zack boasts. “To quote the great stateswoman Hillary Rodham Clinton: ‘If we broke up the big banks tomorrow, would that end racism? Would that end sexism?’ Of course not. Yes, my dad’s a hedge fund manager, and I am proud of him, and for what he’s done for our community. He has donated millions to his charities, The Coalition for a Diverse Connecticut, the Greenwich Social Justice Alliance, and the New England Open Society. The solution isn’t to shut down the banks or corporations but to ensure that they serve the diverse and open society we are building for the 21st century.”

Noam responds, “Bullshit! Those are all ...”

Sanjay interrupts, “Enough, Noam. Nick, do you have a response?”

Nick responds in his southern accent, “Yessir. I will cut all taxes to a flat tax of 2%, end all welfare for the lazy poor, end all regulations on corporations and banks, sell off the national parks, and open them up to mining, logging, and domestic drilling. Get our economy working again!"

Noam says, "Yeah, destroy the environment, and make the 1% richer at the expense of advancing civilization, the 99% and all that stuff."

Nick says, "You damn right, virgin. I'm part of the Chad 1% and we're getting 99% of the pussy at this school. If you got a problem with that, then you're a damn commie!"

Justin says, "May I speak for a second. We need to end crony capitalism, subsidies to corporate special interests. Both Blackstone and Jackson are proposing false promises that will lead us to authoritarianism. Yes, even fascism!"

Sanjay says, "Our next question is how would you handle the war on drugs?"

Noam says, "We need to implement the mass scale usage of LSD and DMT, transcendental experiences that will further human enlightenment and unleash creative potential."

Nick butts in, "What do you know about LSD, virgin? You've never even been to a party. But let's get serious here. We need to get tough on crime! Clean up our streets, send all those drug addicts to prison. Life sentences for drug dealers, and we can save a bundle with private prisons."

Justin interjects, "Yeah, let's start with your drug dealer," Carlos smirks shamelessly, pointing to himself.

Justin continues, "I'd love to see a major drug bust at one of your parties, Nick. Your dad's a corrupt prosecutor, and besides, how are you going to pay for all this? Look, the war on drugs isn't even working. It's a colossal waste of resources and tax revenue. You Republicans talk about small government, but the war on drugs is one of the worst abuses of state power."

Nick says, "I'll beat the shit out of you and have you arrested if you speak about my dad like that again! You're just jealous you never get invited to our parties."

Wendy smirks and whispers in Lisa's ear, "Oh he's invited all right."

Lisa gives out a sinister little laugh, "Yeah we'll put him to good use."

"Enough," Sanjay commands. "What say you, Zack?"

Zack clears his throat, "The key issue is not whether drugs are legal or not but the racial disparities in sentencing. I will mandate that any white person caught with drugs shall be prosecuted to the same standards as a person of color."

Sanjay says, "Ok, next topic: immigration. What will you do about the status of undocumented immigrants, and how will you fix our broken legal immigration system?"

"We need full amnesty for all undocumented immigrants," Zack states confidently, then turns to Sanjay, "Increase the skilled labor for the tech industry from India."

Sanjay starts to get annoyed by his pandering.

Zack continues "And dramatically increase legal immigration, streamline the process, and end racist discriminatory laws that keep out people of color."

Noam replies, “Massive immigration has had a devastating effect on the environment. It has dramatically lowered wages for the middle class, making the corporate fat cats and parasites like your father richer. We need to expel illegal immigrants and reduce the high levels of legal immigration.”

Nick scoffs, “Who cares about the stupid environment. We need the cheap labor to keep business going. I mean we need those damn Mexicans to do those dirty jobs. Like cleaning the shit out of our toilets!”

Zack replies, “Well that’s extremely racist. But on the other hand we do need cheap labor to keep our economy going and to ensure a more diverse America. I just want to point out that Roger Blackstone is a massive hypocrite and fraud. On one hand he says he is against immigration but what Noam here fails to point out is Blackstone’s extremely misogynistic immigration proposal favoring women based on their looks, and Blackstone seems to favor blonde women. So yeah that’s racist too. Basically a whites-only immigration policy. Plus, he doesn’t seem to care much about overpopulation when he wants to turn quaint suburbia into a sea of skyscrapers. He’s just a racist and misogynist. That’s all there is to say.”

Justin butts in, “That’s all part of UN Agenda 21. Blackstone’s not a real populist as he claims, but just another New World Order shill. His dad was an occultist who hung out with Crowley.”

Noam responds, “Nonsense. For starters, rebuilding suburbia is a way to save on energy, ending our dependence on automobiles, and Blackstone is not a white supremacist. I mean he likes blonde Israeli models. So what? I mean you are all about Israel, Zack."

There is an awkward silence. All three of the blonde Jewish girls Wendy Silverstein, Lisa Goldberg, and Noam's crush Natalie are looking at him awkwardly.

Zack says, "Yeah Noam. We all know about your creepy stalker fetish, and it's not cool. You're just objectifying women like your idol who's going down big time."

Nick pulls out a piece of Noam's manifesto that he stole when he wasn't looking. He turns to Zack, "I got it from here."

Two false rivals destroying the real threat to the established order.

Nick starts reading imitating Noam's voice, pretending to cry, "I dream about that blonde Jewish girl every single night. Her golden blonde hair, almond shaped eyes, and pointy little nose. I want to lap at her golden labia and kiss her buttocks. I love her, my crush, and I know she loves me, too. The moment I laid eyes on her I knew she was mine! It is destiny pure and simple truth."

All the girls start laughing. Noam's crush looks mortified.

Noam screams, "I love you, Natalie Bloom!"

Natalie runs out of the class utterly humiliated.

The entire class laughs at Noam. Noam runs over, grabs his manifesto and leaves the room.

This is the final straw. Noam thinks, "Now that my crush hates me, I have no reason to live."

He heads off to the bathroom in tears.

He sees Carlos in there taking a piss. Carlos hears Noam crying and turns around, “You all right, Holmes?”

Noam wipes his tears with a paper towel. “Yes. I’m just fuckin' fine.”

“You don’t look all right, Holmes. Wanna talk about it?” says Carlos.

Noam sulks, “I think this may be my last day on earth.”

Carlos replies, “Wow, chill out, Holmes. You talking about killing yourself over Natalie, Right?”

Noam breaks down sobbing.

“It’s not worth taking your life over some dumb hoe,” Carlos says.

Noam continues bawling.

Carlos puts his arms around Noam, “I’ll look out for you, Holmes. I got something that will make you feel better.” He hands him a pill.

Noam takes the pill. He starts to feel dizzy and light headed. Then he sees the walls of the bathroom vibrate, moving in and out. His vision blurs and he starts seeing strange colors.

Then he feels a powerful force of energy inside him; starting at his heart and then moving down to his crotch. It is as if he has some kind of magical sexual powers that cause the entire world to turn magical colors.

Then the warm feeling in his crotch get more intense; like an explosion of energy and bright colors emanating from his crotch.

He sees himself break up into atoms. It is as if he is no longer Noam Metzenbaum, and that there are no longer any Chads, or girls, or even his crush. Just the universe as a multiplicity of atoms uniting in one powerful erotic force.

Then the lights dim down and he feels the walls coming inwards; a strange claustrophobic feeling. Everything is dark, and he is all alone again.

Noam wakes up and finds himself passed out on the bathroom floor in the large handicapped stall. He feels something moist on his dick and notices his fly is unzipped.

Noam stays in the stall with a feeling of intense anxiety and confusion. He hears talking in the background. He slowly starts to come back to his senses.

He overhears Chad S. talking to Nick, "Yo Nick, that Natalie chick is fine."

Nick replies, "Now is our chance bro."

"Yo, my party Friday Night," Chad S. says intently.

Nick laughs, "Last day a virgin."

All the Chads laugh.

Noam realizes that he has missed several classes but at this point he doesn't care. He had humiliated himself in front of his one true love, who is now in mortal danger for her purity. He thinks, "If I can't have her, no one shall, especially those vile Chads. Chadsworth shall see a massive bloodbath before I let anyone desecrate her!" Noam breaks down in tears again, but the Chads have left and he is all alone again.

Noam stays in the stall to recover. About an hour later he heads back out into the hall. He sees the Chads pretending to comfort his crush, who is distraught from the incident earlier. Nick sees Noam spying on him and walks up to him and says, "If you ever fuck with Natalie again, I'll fuckin' kill you."

Noam feels the instinct to fight, or at least hide behind a nearby column.

Chad S. says, "Yo Natalie. I'm throwing a big party at my mansion Friday night. You should totally come."

"I don't know," Natalie says.

One of the cheerleaders says, "You know Wendy isn't really your friend. She's just using you to get to Zack. She's been spreading rumors that you're still a virgin or a massive slut. Forget which one. But you need to think about your reputation. Like, seriously."

Chad S asks, "So are you in?"

"Sure, I'd love to go," Natalie replies.

The Chads all high-five each other. Natalie still looks uncomfortable.

Noam realizes that his mission is to find out the location of the party, save his crush, and exterminate all Chads once and for all. Save future generations of freshman girls from being defiled and win over his one true love by proving his courage.

Noam goes home. He doesn't even bother with homework since he has more important things to do. He starts writing in his manifesto but feels the side effects of the pill Carlos gave him and falls asleep while writing.

Noam is standing there on the battlefield. He is a Roman emperor who has just defeated the barbarian Chad hordes. The sky is dark from the smoke rising from the corpses of dead Chads on fire, the heads of Chads on spikes, and Roman soldiers walking groups of naked Chads on chains like dogs.

In the distance he hears a cry, "Help me, Noam!"

He looks out into the sea of fire and smoke and can see his crush through the carnage. She is standing on top of a Roman column with a golden flower around her for protection. There is a group of naked Chads tied up in chains climbing up to grab at her.

Her voice gets louder and more desperate, "Save me, Noam!"

Noam runs toward her, but she keeps moving further away into the distance. He continues forward, beheading the Chads who are in his way, but there are way too many. He trips over the head of a decapitated Chad and looks up. It is too late. One of the naked Chads grabs her and takes her off into the fire.

Noam wakes up from his dream. He looks at his clock. He has overslept and missed his first class. He looks around the apartment. His mom is gone, but he finds the keys to her car. He doesn't know how to drive, but his uncle let him drive one of his used cars that he ended up crashing into a tree. Later that night, Noam was humiliated in front of his cousins by his uncle, who pointed out that "He even drives like a virgin."

He finds some coffee his mom made and puts it in his thermos. He needs energy for battle.

He takes the keys and gets into his mom's '88 Beamer, which is parked in front of the apartment complex. Noam feels like a millionaire driving around Greenwich in his Beamer. He takes out his Coffee and turns on the radio. It's the 80s song, "Heaven is a Place on Earth" by Belinda Carlisle.

Noam is moved by the music, which reminds him of his crush and starts singing to the lyrics:

"When I feel alone, I reach for you
and you bring me home
when I'm lost at sea I hear your voice
and it carries me."

He closes his eyes and imagines he is driving through the clouds with his crush next to him and starts swerving.

Noam hears a police siren behind him and the cop on his speaker says, "Pull over to the side of the road!"

Noam slams on the brakes and turns off the radio, while nervously shaking, causing him to spill his coffee all over his crotch.

The cop walks out of his car and asks for his license and registration.

"I'm just headed off to school," Noam says.

"Aren't you a bit late?" the cop replies. "Now, I still need to see you license and registration."

The cop is distracted by a call. To his relief, the cop is called to an emergency situation, and the cops says, “Go to school kid, but If I catch you driving around here again, you're in deep shit.”

Then the cop sees the brown stain on Noam’s crotch and starts laughing, “Oh shit. What a loser,” and gets back in his car puts on his siren and drives off.

Noam shows up to school with a massive brown coffee stain on his light khaki pants. Just as he rushes off to his next class he sees her, his crush, and quickly covers his crotch with his text book.

She looks at him uncomfortably.

“Hello Natalie,” Noam says.

She doesn’t respond and smiles awkwardly.

Then Nick and the Chads come by.

“I fuckin' told you to stay away from Natalie,” Nick blurts out.

Chad S says, “Virgin boy. What’s with the book? Are you hiding a boner?”

“Why don’t you take the book away to show Natalie what you got there,” Nick says.

His crush starts giggling, then sees the brown stain and looks disgusted.

“Looks like virgin boy shit himself,” Nick says.

Noam starts to cry. His crush looks at him like he’s the biggest loser.

“Ooow virgin boy gonna shoot up the school?” Chad S. laughs.

They all laugh, while his crush tries to hold in her laughter but can’t help herself and starts giggling hysterically.

Fat Elliot, the hall attendant comes by and turns to Noam “Noam Principal Greenstein wants to see you in her office.”

The Chads all laugh, “Oooow you're in trouble virgin boy.”

Chad S. puts him arm around Natalie and says, “Don’t worry, Natalie; you’ll never have to deal with that creep again.”

Noam suspects Natalie is under their spell.

“I got class,” says Natalie, and she walks off.

“See you at the party, Natalie,” Chad S. yells as she's walking away.

When she’s not looking, they all grab their crotches and do humping gestures, then look to Noam as if to say, “Yeah, we got her, bitch!”

Fat Elliot grows impatient, “Noam! Principal’s office!”

Noam walks down the hallway to Principal Greenstein’s office. He slowly marches down past the green lockers, thinking about all the scenarios; “Is this about Zack’s car? No way, that was settled. This is about me and my crush, my manifesto? It’s all over for me.”

Noam thinks about sneaking out, but the Vice principal sees him “Hello there Noam, Principal Greenstein wants to see you in her office.” He escorts Noam to the office.

Noam arrives in the office waiting room. Principal Greenstein is with another student. After waiting for about 20 minutes which feels like an eternity, one of the Chads comes out. He looks to Noam and whispers, "You're dead, bitch!"

Principal Greenstein says, "Noam, you can come in now."

Noam walks in to the office and sits down. He is expecting the worst.

Principal Greenstein says, "Noam, I'm concerned about you. You have had multiple tardies and absences. When you first arrived here, I saw great potential in you, but if you continue skipping class I'm afraid I'm going to have to strip you of your scholarship. I also got a call from your mother, and she's very upset that you took her car, driving without a license. She's heading over here right now. This is your final warning. If you have any personal problems, feel free to speak to the counselor, but I expect better from you. Now go to the waiting room, and your mom will pick you up there. Do you understand Noam?"

Noam nods his head and leaves the office. He waits in the waiting room for his mom to pick him up.

She finally gets there in about an hour. She screams, "Noam, you have no idea how disappointed I am with you. You took my car and could have gotten yourself killed. You are on thin ice here. You could lose your scholarship, which means back to public school, and if that's the case no more complaining. You've done this all to yourself, so no more playing the victim! I had to take a taxi over. Do you have my keys?"

Noam doesn't respond, but hands her the keys from his backpack.

They head over to the parking lot and get in the car. Noam looks over and sees Natalie talking to the Chads in front of Nick's brand new Beamer. He doesn't feel special anymore in the passenger seat of his mom's old Beamer. He thinks, "I'm an aristocrat. I don't need bourgeois materialism! I shall prove my status through violence, not driving some flashy automobile."

If things couldn't have gotten any worse Noam's mom says, "Oh there's Mr. Bloom's daughter Natalie." She rolls down the window and yells "Hi, Natalie Bloom!"

Noam gets down low to avoid being seen, but the Chads see him and laugh.

Noam turns around and sees Chad S. rubbing his fingers through Natalie's golden hair to taunt him, while Nick and the other Chads grab their crotches.

Noam's mom gives him the silent treatment for the rest of the day.

Noam goes to his room thinking, "I have reached a dead end. There in only one solution now."

He starts researching revenge and famous serial killers and mass shooters online, from Dahmer, to Ian Brady, to the Columbine killers.

He writes in his manifesto: *"Ah yes, Columbine; two young men on a battle against the wicked jocks and sluts, preparing to cleanse the world of all filth, but that stupid redneck Harris had to screw up their master plan. Klebold was the real mastermind; an Aryan Jew just like me, But guns are so 20th century. I need to think of more creative ways to annihilate my enemies. Carve out their eyeballs and fuck their eye sockets. Perhaps a bit archaic? Take a laser beam from outer space and burn right through their hearts ... Ah! Dammit! They have no heart, nor soul! Pure evil! I will hunt them down, every last one of those rich spoiled brats! Rape and torture their slutty blonde girlfriends too! Exterminate them all like rats! They have lived lives of pure hedonistic pleasures; all of which have been denied to me, but I am superior to them, which I shall prove. I am the only one here with the power to take life, and prove its worthlessness. I will not let them desecrate her, my crush, my one true love. From the moment I laid eyes on her, I knew she was mine. We were destined to be together, to dance in the stars and make love for all eternity, and anyone who stands in the way of our love shall know the wrath of Noam Metzenbaum!"*

Out of nowhere a strange computer virus causes an angry cartoon frog to pop up on his computer screen, screaming "Reeeeeeeeeeeeeeeeee!"

Noam thinks, "Did I just summon the Frog God to bring wrath upon the human race?"

That night Noam continues to dream of vengeance, war and apocalypse; piles of dead bodies, buildings in flames, and the heads of Chads on spikes. The one true leader, the destiny of mankind in his hands, and then he looks up, up to the heavens, the clouds, angels playing harps, and there she is waiting for him, her savior from the wickedness of mankind; the last two survivors of the apocalypse living out their eternal youth in the Garden of Eden.

Noam wakes up from his dream, his anxiety put to the side, just a cold-blooded killer on a mission.

He writes in his journal: *"Today is the day that will determine the destiny of mankind. The day when the gods rain justice over the sins of mankind; the day when the wicked shall pay for their crimes, and I Noam Metzenbaum am the chosen one selected to purify the earth of its filth."*

Noam goes to math class. The teacher says in a dry tone, "Nice having you back, Noam." The class giggles. Then he listens to the lecture on calculus while daydreaming about the number of dead Chads piled up after the apocalypse he will usher in.

After math class, he runs into the Chads again. They don't even bother tormenting him. They just look at him like he has already been defeated. He thinks, "But they know not of the plans I have in store for them. They don't know the true meaning of pain and suffering, but I will make them suffer. Oh yes I will!"

Noam heads off to lunch. He sees Natalie at the table with the Chads and cheerleaders instead of with Wendy, Lisa, Molly, and Zack.

After Zack leaves to go to the bathroom Noam overhears Wendy say "I'm so sick of Zack. Just because his dad's a billionaire he thinks he's so cool. But he's he such a whiny pathetic little bitch, and he hasn't even gone down on me yet!"

Lisa turns to her and jokes, "Yeah that really sucks, oops, I mean *he* doesn't suck." They all laugh.

Molly says, "We're going to have a lot of fun Friday night. I haven't shaved or washed down there this week. Do you think Justin knows?"

"I doubt it," Wendy says. "That dweeb is totally oblivious."

"I think Justin's kind of cute," Molly says. "Not in a hunky way. He's like a cute little fluffy pink vibrator. Like he's there for us to use when we need him but doesn't expect anything in return."

"Yeah, like totally," Lisa says. "We shouldn't have to put up with shit from guys. They are here to serve us!" Pointing to her genitals, while grinding her crotch and spreading her legs.

One of the nerdy girls comes over, "Wow! I couldn't help overhearing your conversation. I'm starting a feminist club and I've just got to say …"

Lisa interrupts, "Who the hell are you? We didn't give you permission to talk to us!"

"Yeah get lost lezzo," Molly says, making a face at the girl.

Wendy continues on, "Anyways, we're really on to something here. We are rewriting the entire gender script. If this works out, I'm starting a new secret club."

"You should charge clients. Like a pimp," Lisa suggests.

They all laugh.

Zack comes back from the bathroom. The girls talk to him like they usually do, pretending their little chat hadn't happened.

Noam suspects that Zack is still interested in Natalie. He thinks, "Should I try to sabotage him again by getting him to fight the Chads? No! I'll just kill them all!"

Carlos sees Noam standing there all by himself. He says, "Yo amigo, over here." Noam sits down with Carlos, who can tell something is wrong with him.

“You all right, Holmes?”

Noam replies with a cold blank stare, “Yes everything is fine.”

“You don’t look fine,” Carlos says. “You still crushin' over that blonde Jewish chick?”

Noam nods.

“Look, since I’m your bestie,” Carlos says, “I’m gonna do you a big favor. I know about Chad S.’s big party. Look, I can get you in but you got to be discreet, Holmes, and do whatever I say.”

Noam’s eyes light up, “Wow Carlos! Thank you so much. So what’s the catch?”

“So here’s the deal, Holmes. After Nick is done fucking all the new freshman bitches, I suck his dick clean. I know. Disgusting, right? Getting pussy juice in my mouth, but it’s the price I pay to be in with the in-crowd. So Friday night’s party at Chad S.’s house is gonna be a themed masked ball. But they don’t just let in any strange homies, but I can get you in as my bitch.”

Noam is offended, “What? I told you I’m not a homo!”

Carlos says, “You're just gonna have to roll with it, Holmes, if you want to save your girl. The only catch is you dress up like a girl and I’ll slip you in the door.”

Nick and the Chads see Carlos and suspect something is up. Nick comes over and asks “Yo, wassup?”

Carlos replies, “Yeah, I was just telling this virgin here that he has no chance with Natalie, and that he should just kill himself.”

Nick laughs, "Good, he's better off dead. We can celebrate the virgin suicide at Friday night's party after we de-virginize the new girl." The rest of the Chads laugh. Then Carlos takes his milk and pours it over Noam's face.

Chad S. says, "Looks like Noam likes cum on his face after all. Unfortunately for him that's his crush's fate; his is worse."

The Chads leave. Noam looks at Carlos in anger.

"I told you, Holmes. You got to roll with it."

Just as Noam leaves the lunchroom, he sees Wendy, Lisa, and Molly talking to Justin again. Zack comes over and screams at Wendy, "Why are you talking to this fucking dweeb?"

"None of your business Zack!" Wendy says.

Noam heads off to gym class, which is his least favorite class because it is the domain of the Chads. He thinks, "What have sports done to advance civilization? They reward the most bestial of the male species the sexual status that should be awarded to those who create civilization. When I'm emperor, the only sport allowed will be hunting Chads for sport."

Noam walks outside to the track field. He signed up to be on the track team after he quit swimming. Most of the Chads are on the lacrosse team and he has to watch them work out while he runs. He is a mediocre runner, but it is the only sport he can do.

He looks out and sees the cheerleaders talking to his crush. He sneaks under the bleachers to spy on them.

He hears the head cheerleader, Stacy, mention to his crush, "Natalie, if you'd like to try out for cheer squad, you have to go through the initiation Friday Night."

"What's that?" Natalie asks.

The other cheerleader says, "Oh it's something. Just a silly drinking game."

"I don't really drink," Natalie responds.

The cheerleaders all laugh at her. She smiles awkwardly, trying to fit in.

Then the Chads come over in their lacrosse uniforms and start flirting with the cheerleaders. Chad S. notices Natalie and puts his arm around her, but she is very uncomfortable.

Stacy says to the Chads, "We have to go to cheer practice, see you at the party."

The cheerleaders leave and Natalie goes off with them to avoid being alone with Chad. S.

Noam, still hiding under the bleachers, hears the Chads joking around by themselves, unaware that he is in onto their plans.

Chad S. proclaims, "After Friday's party, she will no longer be a sweet innocent girl."

They all laugh.

"I got first dibs on her," Chad S. says.

"No, we have to bet on her," Nick insists. "Whoever wins at a game of poker at the party gets first dibs."

They all laugh wickedly.

Then the coach blows his whistle to call the Chads over to lacrosse practice.

Noam's track coach catches him under the bleachers and shouts, "Noam! We already warmed up. Get on the track!"

Noam starts running. For some reason all the rage gives him the power to run like a maniac. The coach is impressed and smiles, "Noam, I never knew you had it in you."

For some reason the sense of power causes him to do something crazy. He runs right through the field through the lacrosse practice. Some of the Chads laugh at him, while others are pissed off "Move dweeb," "Get the fuck out my way virgin!"

The fat lacrosse coach comes over to Noam and shouts "Hey kid, what the fuck to do you think you're doing? We got practice here. Now go run off like a girl!"

Noam feels so weak and fragile, totally humiliated. The fat coach says, "Yo kid! I'm not going to warn you again!"

Noam walks off the field thinking, "That fat coach; perhaps he was once a Chad? His bulging belly sticking out like every other middle-aged gym coach. Gross! A crime against humanity. Reliving his youth watching these strapping young lads play silly games. They get to fuck prime pussy while he goes home to eat Cheetos and drink bud light, and fuck his fat disgusting middle-aged wife. Definitely not a role model for anyone!"

Noam walks around the track. He feels like he doesn't exist. He thinks, "Is this supposed to be the life of the average high school student?"

The track coach blows his whistle. “It’s time to go,” he says.

Noam tries to get his attention, while the coach is checking out the hot cheerleaders.

“Coach! Coach! Coach!” Noam yells.

Pissed off that Noam is distracting his view, he replies rudely “What?”

“I need to … go right now. I have to meet with, um, a …” Noam stutters.

“Take a shower before you leave! Got it?” the coach orders. He points to the door to the locker room like he doesn’t even care. He is too busy checking out the cheerleaders.

Noam sees the lacrosse team finishing up. He thinks, “Perhaps I can finish up really quick, get ready before the Chads come in, but then there are also the Chads from basketball, and maybe some have water polo practice?”

Noam rushes over to the locker room. Anxious, he rips through his locker, taking off the stupid uniform he is forced to wear. A shower. That should help. He feels like bursting into tears right now.

He looks around the shower, “Hopefully no one is in here.”

He steps in the shower wearing nothing but his underwear. He can hear the Chads rattling their lockers, and joking around with each other. He has to finish up before they find him alone and vulnerable in his soaking wet tighty whities.

A group of Chads enter the shower naked. He doesn't recognize them. "Perhaps they are upperclassmen from the basketball team," he guesses.

He tries not to make eye contact with them or their junk.

Then he hears Nick and his friends from the lacrosse team.

He is about to leave but another large group of Chads enters the shower, blocking the exit as if they are part of some grand scheme to entrap him in the shower.

Noam freezes in fear. He knows he has to leave but is blocked by the large group of upperclassmen Chads, all naked. Their big muscles and giant cocks standing in his way.

He closes his eyes and just stands there trying to enjoy the warm water, imagining he is alone under a tropical waterfall. "Perhaps solitude isn't so bad after all," he thinks to himself.

He opens his eyes, realizing he is surrounded. He only has on his underwear, but they are all naked!

Naked, dancing around and enjoying it. Completely self-confident in their bodies. He thinks, "Hot girls see them naked all the time, so what's the big deal if another dude sees their dicks."

One Chad soaping up the other Chad's butt! "What's going on?" he wonders, "They are even more beautiful in the shower then when they are playing games."

Noam stays in the shower's corner, his eyes focused on a small crack in the wall tiles. He thinks about just waiting until they leave, but realizes it is inevitable he will have to face them.

He thinks, "Noam! Don't look at them! Too tantalizing."

One Chad is abusing the soap dispenser, pushing it again and again. Some blond-haired Chad comes over and pushes Noam out of the way.

None of them looks interested in taking private showers. This is another bonding time for the Chads. "So graceful," Noam thinks.

"Those butts; so round, a crack right down the middle. Not hairy or anything. Almost like a girl's butt. Sexy and … big and muscle like. Do these guys shave at such a young age?"

And then their tan lines; the pale skin around their crotch area and buttocks in contrast with their slightly tanned muscles.

Noam thinks, "Must be from their speedos from water polo practice, spending the summers in their luxurious swimming pools, or just hanging around shirtless."

Noam can't take it any longer, but then the Chads from the freshman lacrosse team enter the shower. Noam tries to avoid them, but they were too busy frolicking in their perfect bodies to notice him. Playing ball, but without a ball, and their hanging balls.

Noam has to eavesdrop on their fun. He thinks, "Am I a Chad, too? Maybe it would be fun to be one. Get invited to Friday night's party and enjoy some male bonding in the hot tub. Then my crush and I will lose our virginity together! Wishful thinking perhaps?"

Noam soaks his face in cold water to set his mind and senses straight. He thinks, "None of this is happening at the moment. Just another dream? Wake up Noam!"

Noam's underwear is getting soaked. You can see his small penis right through it. One of the Chads notices.

"Ha Ha! What the hell are you doing here?"

It was Nick, his arch nemesis standing there in all his glory, towering over him, Noam still trying to avoid making eye contact.

Noam really doesn't want to answer, but he says, "Nothing."

"Really?" Nick replies. "What the hell, dude? Your cock is showing out of your pants!"
Noam's cock is evident. Everyone is naked except him. Way to ruin the party.

"Take it off, dude!" Nick says. "What are you, gay?"

"No!" Noam says like he is ashamed.

Nick says, "You don't do anything right! Too scared? What's like, your problem bro?"

Noam looks down on himself. Then he looks at the Chad's cocks and back at his.

"My penis is too small," he says to himself with a whisper.

Three other Chads look in his direction. Something is about to go down.

One of the Chads yells out, "Small dick? Who you callin' small dick?"

The entire group of Chads (with more in the background) are all hovering over little Noam.

“Does this little kid even have a dick like ours?” Chad S. says.

“I don’t know, but you can see it right through his underwear!” Nick points to it.

All of them are laughing.

Noam’s state of consciousness drastically changes, now looking down on the floor with his arms crossed against his nipples as if he were a girl.

Chad S. pushes into him.

Noam slips and falls onto the hard wet floor, hurting his knees. He is unable to get back up.

Chad S. commands, “Take off that underwear of yours and let me see it! Prove you're a man!”

Did Noam do something unethical against the tribe? He was bird-watching a few minutes ago, now a captive political prisoner, reduced to a thing they can manipulate. Noam can’t run away! This time, it is confrontation!

So swiftly, one Chad grabs him, while the other Chad forces his underwear down.

It sticks out; his tiny circumcised prick, bonging little thing, wet in the shower. The Chads frown on such a thing.

“Haha! Small dick! Small dick!”

The noises are all directed at Noam.

“It is circumcised, not small!” Noam insists.

One Chad comments, “I’m circumcised anyway, but you don’t even have a dick. Pathetic, bro.”

Ashamed, Noam gets angry. His girly consciousness switches on. Still covering his nipples, shouting like a little Japanese girl at them all, “Stop it! All of you! I’m not like you! I can still be myself.”

Noam is about to cry.

Another Chad pushes Noam. “Fuck off, loser!”

Tension is growing.

A war among the penises is about to break out.

Noam feels even more belittled. He is on the ground. All of them are hovering over him while more Chads from the sophomore, junior, and senior classes walk in.

There are now well over 100 of them, all crammed into the shower naked to watch, like the crowd at a Roman coliseum rushing up to watch a man being fed to a pack of lions

An older Chad says, “What’s going on, dude?”

“This little bitch thinks uncircumcised dicks are gay!” Nick says

“Well, I got a bigger dick than his! Watch this!” the older Chad replies.

The older Chad throws off his towel and starts wiggling his staff like the cock of a grown man.

Nick comes up to Noam, whipping out his own dick, feeling the need to prove himself in front of the senior Chad.

Noam has never seen a dick like it in his entire life. It is massive like a man's, but cute like a boy's.

Even the senior Chad is jealous.

Nick taunts, "Hey! Hey! Do you like my big cock! Do you like it?""

Noam can't look at such a thing.

"Look at this dick! You like that? Dude, what about this part?"

Noam looks down and sees white, dead skin from his dick; smegma.
Nick continues to taunt, "Want to lick this? Want to lick this awful shit? Yeah, I know you would weirdo!"

Nick starts touching himself, pretending he has something in his fingers, shoving it right it in front of Noam's face.

"Smell it! Smell it!"

Noam twitches. Disgusting; unreal, like a scene from *Ren & Stimpy*, being humiliated, like Sasha Gray but gay. He has had enough of this.

Noam gets back up and shouts, about to cry, "You! All of you!"

The Chads looking at him, Silent.

Noam proclaims, "You will all get your punishment! All of you! You motherfuckers! Don't you know who I am?"

A tear falls from Noam's eye, sprinkles of water upon him.

Chad S. says, "I know who you are, you're pathetic, bro. But if you want to be like us, we're getting our dicks sucked at the party. You got a dick, I got one too. But if you're a virgin, you can't be like us."

He was serious as he said it.

Noam starts to cry.

Nick says sarcastically, "His dick is not that bad. I've seen worse. It's actually a little cute. He just needs experience."

Angry, teeth clenched, Noam lunges out against Nick.

Nick loses his patience for Noam. He lashes out and pushes him on to the floor, Noam falling on his back.

There is an awkward silence as Noam lies there on the hard, cold, wet floor of the shower, his back in pain. He looks up at Nick, admiring his tall stature, Adonis chest, golden-blond hair, and cute but cruel face.

Nick looks down at Noam as if he were a piece of garbage. Noam feels completely powerless.

Then Noam makes eye contact with Nick's dick, which is now about a foot away from his face. A nice long uncircumcised dick, dark pubes with golden highlights, and a pale tan line above his dick making it pop out right in Noam's face.

Nick looks down to Noam in an angry but calm voice, "There is only one way you can join us."

Noam replies, crying, barely able to speak "What is that?"

“You want to be a man right?” Nick asks.

”Yes,” Noam replies.

“You remember history class dweeb?” Nick asks. “When a wimp wants to become a great warrior, he needs to take the seed of a superior warrior.”

Noam is confused and asks, “What the hell are you talking about?”

Nick orders Noam, “Get on your knees!”

Noam still confused, asks, “Why?”

“Get on your knees little, bitch!” Nick shouts.

Noam gets on his knees which are still hurting from his fall, his eyes now directly in contact with all the Chads' giant dicks; right in his face like a firing squad.

Nick orders, “Now suck it bitch!”

Noam starts to cry.

The Chads start chanting, “Suck it bitch! Suck it bitch!”

Nick grabs Noam by his hair and says, “Don’t make this more difficult than it has to be.”

Noam is on his knees sobbing, “No! Please! No!”

Nick orders, “Lick it! The balls first.”

Noam is hesitant but realizes he has no choice. He knows now is not yet the right time to fight or resist. He must take one for the team now, so that he will have a chance to battle the Chads on his own terms later when they least expect it – at the party.

Noam gives in, and does his best to mentally block out the many unspeakable acts that occur in the shower with the Chads that afternoon.

An eternity seems to go by.

After Noam is done servicing and showering, Nick approaches Noam, "Hope you enjoyed your shower. If you tell anyone, you're dead, bro! And don't worry, we'll take good care of Natalie tomorrow night."

The Chads laugh at Noam one more time. Then they get changed and leave.

Noam is too traumatized to leave and just stands there alone in the shower. The Chads are gone, and Noam is alone again, too humiliated to even care about anything, not great aristocratic power or even his crush. He just feels like a piece of garbage with no will left to fight.

Realizing that he left his clothes on a bench, he looks for them. They are now missing. He can't ask for help and has no way off getting out without people seeing him naked.

Noam freaks out and runs down the hall naked in tears. Wendy, Lisa, and Molly see him and look at him with complete and utter shock and disgust.

Noam tries to escape Chadsworth and heads out into the woods but is apprehended by the campus security. Another staff member comes over and gives him a towel to cover himself up.

All the Chads and popular girls are there laughing at him.

The security escorts him to the counselor.

Noam sits in front of the counselor, who happens to be an attractive blonde woman in her mid-twenties. He is completely humiliated.

She asks him, "What happened?"

Noam is frozen and unable to speak.

She says, "Look Noam, I can't help you unless you tell me what happened. Were you bullied?"

Noam doesn't respond.

"I will have your mom pick you up, but if you don't tell me what happened I'm afraid I will have to tell Principal Greenstein and recommend suspension until we sort things out."

She escorts Noam to the nurse's office. The nurse examines him and can smell the piss on him.

The nurse says, "Look Noam, something like this happened here at Chadsworth several years ago, but I'm afraid there's nothing I can do about it."

She gives him a towel and lets him rest in a private room until his mom picks him up.

Noam's mom comes to pick him up and brings some clothes for him to change into. Noam walks with his mom to the car. The

Chads see him but he is too traumatized to even notice. He feels like he is already dead.

While driving in the car, Noam's mom says, "Noam! What's wrong? Are you being bullied? This is very disturbing."

Noam just sits there in silence.

Noam's mom says, "I can't help you if you don't talk. I'm taking you straight to the hospital!"

Then Noam remembers his mission. If he is hospitalized he won't be able to stop the party and save his crush. "Nooooooo!" he screams.

Noam's mom takes him to the emergency room. Noam tries to run away, but his mom calls the hospital security, and they restrain him.

After waiting in a straitjacket for several hours, the security escorts him to see the psychiatrist. Noam refuses to speak and is shaking in fear.

The psychiatrist comes over to Noam's mom: "Does your son have any history of mental illness?"

She replies, "Well, not really, but he has struggled to fit in with other kids. He's always been a bit, well odd."

The psychiatrist says, "I've examined him extensively and it looks like he suffering from post-traumatic stress disorder. Has he had any history of sexual abuse?"

She replies, "No! At least not that I'm aware of, but he has experienced severe bullying."

Noam's mom breaks down in tears.

The psychiatrist says, "Your insurance doesn't cover hospitalization for mental health, and I can't commit him unless he has threatened to hurt himself or others. I can prescribe some anti-psychotics, but I recommend you keep a close eye on him."

His mom yells, "What the fuck is wrong with this country? No basic health coverage for mental health! No wonder we have so many crazies shooting up schools! Because of the greedy insurance companies!"

The doctor tells Noam's mom to calm down and gives Noam a pill which makes him feel woozy and fall asleep.

Noam wakes up back in his own bed. His mom comes over to comfort him, "Noam, I really need to know what happened to you yesterday. I'm not angry, just very concerned. If you were bullied, you have to let me know."

Noam still feels woozy from the drugs, says, "I'm fine," and falls back to sleep.

Noam dreams that he is already dead and looking down upon the universe. He is just a lost soul in limbo awaiting judgment. He contemplates the meaning of his life, "Am I worthy to move on to the next stage of existence? What have I accomplished in this life other than writing my ideas in my journal? Ideas that I have failed to implement. Am I just like every other being who just consumes resources and does nothing to further enlightenment? Am I truly worthy to be selected to judge mankind?"

He feels a sense of rejection for failing to live up to his ideals and then starts drifting back towards planet earth, zooming in like a satellite until he can see the house of the party.

He gets closer to the house and can hear the party going on. He sees a bedroom and can hear his crush crying in pain. Then darkness falls over him, and he is stuck in a void with no way out.

Noam wakes up and his mom comes over to check up on him. She says, "Noam! I'm taking a week off from work to take care of you. I decided to permanently remove you from Chadsworth. I talked to Mr. Bloom, he's ok with me taking time off, and he's also concerned about his daughter getting in with a bad crowd. Chadsworth is a toxic environment."

Noam realizes that he is stuck at home. And on this day, Friday, the day of the big party, stuck at home with him mom, unable to escape or even find the location of the party.

Noam goes over to check his computer but realizes his mom has confiscated it. His only option now is to get in touch with Carlos.

He looks for his cellphone, but his mom has also confiscated it.

He remembers that Carlos had written his number on a crumpled up piece of paper. His only option is to find the number and call Carlos on a landline if his mom leaves the house.

Noam starts looking through his messy backpack.

He hears his mom open the door. He is terrified she will take his backpack, but she just says, "Noam I'm headed off to the grocery store. Is there anything you want?"

"I'm fine, maybe just a mango smoothie," Noam says.

"Ok, Noam," she replies.

Now is his chance. He finally finds the paper but it has been smudged. He goes over to the landline and tries calling different numbers but keeps getting the wrong number.

He eventually gets Carlos's number, but he doesn't pick up.

Noam realizes his only chance now is to sneak out. He remembers that Carlos said it would be a masked costume ball, and he had to go as a girl to get in.

He steals one of his mom's old dresses and finds a Venetian mask that his grandfather Saul had given to him as a birthday gift from his trip to Italy.

Noam quickly puts on the dress and mask and rushes out before his mom gets home.

He then goes behind the apartment complex into the alley way and puts the dress and mask in his backpack but sees his mom's car pull in. He hides behind a dumpster.

He hears his mom get inside the apartment and screams, "Noam!"

Noam runs down the alley way. At this point he has no plan. It's still around noon, and he has no way of getting in touch with Carlos or finding the house.

He continues to walk around aimlessly but trying to avoid cops who are looking for truants or in case his mom reports him missing.

He runs out of breath and leans on a brick wall. A snooty woman turns to him, "What do you think you're doing here?"

He recognizes the woman as the businesswoman from the spa. She is apparently the town's top real estate agent.

He gets a massive erection knowing her dirty secret. Noam says, "I know your secret!"

"Get lost or I'm calling the cops!" she replies.

Then Noam notices something. It is an article posted on the wall of the real estate office. It is the house he had recognized from a photo while snooping on one of the popular girls' phones of the party location. It is Chad S.'s dad's house, who is a wealthy hedge fund manager.

The woman says, "I'm not going to give you another warning. I have clients!"

Noam leaves, thinking, "Yeah, clients? Some servant who eats your cunt."

Noam runs off, but he now has an address. He has an idea of where the house is located from his explorations of the town but realizes it is located in an exclusive community with tight security.

He decides it is best to hang out in the woods until the party. He thinks about getting lunch but is too nervous to eat.

He heads down to the creek to contemplate. He looks down and finds a used condom thinking "Gross!" But the students are still in school, and he has the place to himself.

Noam takes out his journal and writes his final entry: *"This is it, the moment I have been preparing for. For years I've had to endure torment and humiliation from those who envied and feared my great intellect. Then one day I met my maiden and she changed my life forever. We met eyes, and we had a special connection. I changed the course of history just so I could be with her. Suffered the worst atrocities imaginable, just so I could stay at Chadsworth. Then the Chads stepped in the way and threatened our love. Tonight shall be the apocalypse, the night the hellfire rains down on the wicked, and I am the one living mortal that shall survive the apocalypse and rescue my one true love, and we shall fly off into paradise away from the evils of this world."*

After hanging out in the woods, Noam starts to get hungry and finds an old Tiger's Milk bar in his backpack.

He decides to head over to the house. He has a vague idea how to get there but has a long way to go.

He finally gets to the area which is off an inlet surrounded by golf courses and mega mansions. He watches the sunset over the inlet. Soon it will be time to attack.

But he also realizes that the mansion is in a gated compound and the only way to get in would be to find Carlos, but Carlos will be in disguise. Noam starts panicking.

He overhears something. He hears the Chads in the distance. He hides in the bushes so they don't see him.

He looks out and sees Carlos handing the Chads large quantities of narcotics right out in the open; bags of cocaine, pills, and weed.

The Chads leave and head off to the party.

Once they are gone, Noam jumps out from behind and says, "Hello, Carlos."

Carlos says, "Wow! You scared me, Holmes. I heard you offed yourself, but I'm happy you're still alive."

"What do you mean, Carlos?" Noam asks.

Carlos says, "Well, the Chads told me that you killed yourself after Natalie rejected you, but I get it, they want you out of the way. The party's starting in an hour, but you've got to chill, Holmes. Be sly like a cobra."

Noam puts his dress and mask on.

Carlos laughs, "You look fine, bitch!" And smacks Noam on the buttocks.

Noam hides his backpack behind a bush. He thinks, "Whether I come out of this alive or not, once the world reads my manifesto things will never be the same."

They finally arrive at the location of the party, a magical location, a palatial estate in a Greco-Roman style that is out of place besides all the old colonial and English Tudor-style mansions. It is located right on the water, with a forest on one side and a golf course on the other.

There is a security checkpoint. Carlos chats with the security guard. Apparently, he is Carlos's older cousin and he gives them the go-ahead.

They approach the front of the mansion, which has pink neon around the Roman archway, which leads to a fountain that spurts out fluorescent-light-colored water.

Carlos says, "Yo this this like Scarface, Holmes! We're livin' it up Miami style!" Carlos puts his arms around Noam. "Someday this will all be ours!"

"I know, I have a plan," Noam replies.

A group of hot cheerleaders walks by. Carlos tells Noam to step to the side and chats with them. One of them says in a snooty voice, "Eeew who's that?"

Carlos says, "I'm just supplying some freshman ho for the Chads."

The cheerleader laughs, "You the pimp, Carlos!"

Then Wendy, Lisa, and Molly walk in as if they are princesses in their cocktail dresses, not even noticing him.

Even though they have masks on, he still recognizes them. This is a sign of hope that he can recognize his crush, and he wonders where she is.

Then a large groups of girls rush in wearing costumes. Carlos whispers in Noam's ear, "Now's your chance. Go!"

They rush into the party. Noam says in a nasally voice, "Wow! This is spectacular!"

Carlos smacks him and says, "Shut the fuck up! I said be discreet, Holmes!"

Carlos says, "I got to go hang out with the Chads. Enjoy yourself. I hope you find your girl. Just don't go psycho, Holmes."

Noam doesn't say anything and just blows Carlos a kiss.

He is now alone, surrounded by his adversaries on a mission to find his one true love, and defend her honor with lethal force if necessary.

Then Noam thinks about how he has no game plan to fight the Chads but is too overwhelmed by the whole experience.

He looks around, realizing he is out of place. He is wearing his mom's dress while the girls are all wearing thongs and are topless, while the Chads are wearing skimpy underwear. A few are even wearing nothing but a sock-like codpiece over their dicks.

Noam can hardly see and keeps bumping into people. He bumps into a girl feeling her tits and causing her to spill her drink. She shouts, "Watch where you're going bitch."

Then he bumps into a Chad who grabs his chest laughing, "Yo this bitch is like totally flat, bro! Like a tiny dude!" His friend says, "I would still like totally fuck her, bro!"

The Chad attempts to grab Noam's crotch, but Noam manages to avoid being caught.

He walks around the room looking for his crush in the crowd of masked girls.

Then he heads out to the pool area where the main party is happening. The DJ is a famous rapper whom he recognizes from TV.

The music is loudly blaring, "Yo nigga! Yo nigga! You got to get down on the floor! Twerkin' that ass, knows where it's at. That's how you get with the nigga! You gotta suck it bitch,

Noam wants to spy on them to find out if they know anything about his crush.

To get over his anxiety he guzzles down a bottle of vodka, which someone had left on the ground half drank.

Noam walks over to the cheerleaders. The lead cheerleader looks at Noam and says, "Look at this clueless freshman bitch dressed like she's attending to a funeral."

Her friend says, "Like whatever. She's probably one of the nerds the Chads bring in to humiliate for the first party of the year."

Noam says under his breath, "Perhaps they will soon be attending a funeral. Better get started shopping for nice funeral gowns bitches!"

Noam looks around. There she is, his crush dressed in a long expensive silk gown, a tiara which he recognized her wearing at her Bat Mitzvah, and like the cheerleaders, a mask covering her eyes.

One of the cheerleaders sniggers, "Playing princess? Grow up! You're not a little girl anymore!"

Noam's heart sinks. She is the girl that he would do anything for. He thinks, "There is no more time for distractions. It is time for action!"

The cheerleader turns to her, "Natalie, loosen up. Have a drink," handing her a shot of vodka.

Noam can tell she's nervous.

The other cheerleader tells her to take off the silk gown.

Natalie refuses, “Oh no! My dad bought it for me. It cost him like several thousand.”

“Like whatever, your dad’s loaded, he can by few a million more,” the cheerleader responds.

Her friend chimes in, “Don’t be such a prude. Take it off and show us what you got!”

Natalie opens up her silk gown revealing her skimpy lingerie.

Noam is aroused to see her smooth bare skin exposed for the first time but upset and humiliated that the sweet virginal girl he had fallen in love with had allowed herself to be debased.

The cheerleader turns to her, “You know Natalie, Chad S. is waiting for you upstairs.”

“I don’t know,” Natalie replies. “I kind of like him, but I've heard the stories.”

The cheerleader replies, “Don’t be so lame. Chad S. is like the most popular boy in our year, and if you're like seen with him that will totally boost your reputation.”

Natalie says, “I don’t know. I think he wants to have sex and I’m still …”

The cheerleader laughs, “A virgin?”

“I’ll just go up to see how he’s doing,” Natalie says. “Nothing like that.”

After Natalie leaves, the cheerleaders laugh, “She like totally has no idea what she’s in for.” They put their shot glasses together for a victory cheer.

Noam knows this is the moment he has been preparing for.

When they are not looking he steals a cocktail from one of the cheerleaders. He needs some more liquid courage for his final battle.

The cheerleader catches him, “What the fuck, bitch!”

Noam sees his crush walk towards the house. Now is the time to move.

Noam follows her into the house but the first level is packed; he mustn’t lose sight of her.

He sees her walk upstairs but is blocked by a large group of kids.

He gets to the bottom of the stairs but has lost his crush. He thinks, “She could be anywhere in this massive house. She could be defiled right this very moment! No! She’s still a virgin. You have to act fast, Noam! Time is of the essence!”

Noam walks up the stairs, feeling tipsy from the liquor.

The stairwell is packed with a large line of boys blocking his way; some are in nothing but their underwear, while others are completely nude. Some must be from other schools he doesn’t recognize. “Must be every hot popular blond boy from within a hundred-mile radius,” he thinks.

He finally gets to the 2nd floor and sees the line continue further down the hallway. They are all grabbing their crotches with one hand, while holding plastic cups of beer with the other.

Noam assumes there’s a long line to the bathroom. He sees a boy on the side pissing right on the wall. Then he sees a drunken girl on the side puking. The boys all laugh at her. One guy steps aside and pisses right on her face, and his friends join in. She is too wasted to even protest.

He continues trying to get through the packed hallway. Not an orderly line, just aggressive boys eagerly trying push their way through.

A group of guys walks down the stairwell with a look of celebration. One of them pushes Noam to the side into a group of horny Chads who start rubbing their dicks against him from behind.

Noam overhears one of the Chads, whom he remembers for making him gargle his piss, brag about the best blowjob he's ever gotten. Even the cute freshman who sprayed his name on him is there talking about getting his first blowjob, as if he is a little boy waiting in excitement about sitting on Santa's lap.

Noam gets to the end of the line and realizes there is a girl there giving blowjobs to all the boys lined up. Some trying to fuck her face while other just cum right into her mouth.

He observes that the Chads get off more from the act of watching her in this debased state than the sexual act itself.

He recognizes her from his freshman English class as the shy cute nerdy girl, except her face is drenched in cum and her mouth is overflowing like a Roman fountain.

She doesn't look too happy but knows she has to do her duty. Noam hopes this isn't his crush's fate.

Noam rushes past them to find his crush. The hallway is empty, but he can hear a strange noise. He wonders if his crush is nearby. He rushes down the hall, then turns left down another hallway.

He hears the noises coming from a room, noises of pure ecstasy and torment. But it is not his crush. He hears familiar sounds of a boy being tormented and girls giggling.

He thinks about opening the door but is hesitant. Then suddenly one of the popular girls comes out. She looks at him assuming he's one the nerdy girls, "We're having a private party. Stay out. You're not invited."

One of her friends walking over to the secret party notices Noam and says, "Eeew she must be one of the bukkake girls the Chads ordered. Wouldn't want to be her!"

Her friend, leaving, says, "Don't you feel at least a bit guilty for having all the fun, while the lesser girls get tormented?"

The girl says, grabbing her crotch, "Fuck them! That's the price they pay. Now if you may, I need service!"

Then she drunkenly, by accident, opens the door allowing for Noam to peek into the secret party.

Noam looks in and sees the same scenario in reverse. All the popular girls, the most beautiful young creatures lined up to sit on a chair.

Then Noam sees Wendy sitting on the chair with her skirt up like she using the toilet.

He looks underneath and sees Justin tied up to a board underneath with chains and his face tied to a hole carved out of the chair. Justin's body is covered up by a big blanket, so the girls don't have to look at him.

Lisa shouts, "I want another turn," and puts her ass over the hole. Wendy and Lisa are sharing the little pleasure hole, bouncing back and forth giggling.

Then they start to fight. Lisa shouts, "I want my ass eaten!" Wendy says, "You just had 15 minutes, don't be a selfish cunt!"

Lisa lightens up again, "Wow, we should really open up a spa. We could make a fortune. Think about all the horny rich ladies in this town."

They continue to giggle, bouncing up and down, Noam getting little glimpses of their hairy pussies and buttocks as their skirts fly up and down.

Noam imagines Justin there lying on his back in pain, his head trapped into the tight hole, razor sharp pussy hair cutting across his face, his tongue in agony being used as a sex toy by drunken horny popular girls.

Noam thinks, "What if the girls didn't even bother to wash their cunts. Perhaps some girl on her period is sticking her bloody tampon right in his mouth, while another girl cleans his face with her piss. Some girls just wanting their asses licked clean after a long day of sitting in their sweaty panties."

He thinks about how all the pussies of the popular girls taste. "Maybe they have sweet virginal pussies, or unwashed pussies stinking of stale urine, or maybe they have yeast infections."

Just as Wendy starts to orgasm Noam gets so excited he tries to bend over to hide his massive erection, accidentally bumping into the door making a large bang.

There is an awkward silence to all the noises of pleasure and pain.

Justin hears the noise and manages to break his head out of the seat. Wendy gets up revealing to Noam her perfectly plump pale buttocks and thick dark bush that he had wanted to eat out since the moment he saw her at the fountain.

Justin turns his head to the side bleeding from his neck and sees Noam, "Help! Noam, get me the fuck out of here! These bitches are psycho!"

One of the girls restrains Justin and Lisa tries to sit down in ecstasy from her multiple orgasms, ambivalent about Noam, but Justin's head gets stuck and she crushes his neck shouting, "Eat me bitch! Eat my ass!"

Justin screams in pain as his neck is crushed making a cracking sound.

Then Molly, who is next in line and eager to use Justin, notices Noam and runs over to the door. She is drunk from sipping on cocktails while waiting in the long line with her cocktail dress rolled up revealing her plump buttocks and thick hairy reddish brown bush. Noam can smell her odor and remembers her bragging about not washing her cunt for a week.

Noam is so turned on that he takes off his mask and walks right into the room hoping that some drunken horny girls will pin him down to the floor and take turns fucking his face.

The girls look at him in shock. One girl says, "What the fuck is this creep doing here?" Another says, "Who the fuck let him in? Isn't he like the wannabe serial killer?"

Molly slams the door on Noam, "Get lost pervert!"

Noam thinks, "Ah, perhaps one day?"

Noam hears Wendy scream, "He's broken! We need to find a replacement!" She starts to cry like a little girl.

Lisa says, "How about Noam? I don't care how much of a creep he is. At this point I just want a nice tongue in me!"

Noam had never been so tempted in his entire life. He thinks about Lisa's plump buttocks and hairy snatch smothering his face in her juices, but he has to rise above it. He is on a mission to save his one true love.

He looks at his watch and realizes that he has wasted about 20 minutes watching the spectacle and thinks, "I shall curse myself for betraying my crush, putting her sanctity in peril by being led astray by my own debauchery!"

He continues to run around the massive hallways looking for her, but they seem to go on forever. He is lost in the massive house which reminds him of a palace he once visited as a child on a trip to France.

He finds another stairwell and walks up to the third floor of the house, which is mostly empty. It is dark but with a dimmed eerie red light. There are all kinds of antiques, from Roman statues to Japanese samurai swords. Noam grabs a sword in case he needs it. He had a toy samurai sword that he practiced using watching Japanese samurai films.

He realizes that he has left his mask behind but he is prepared to face his adversaries. He thinks, “I want those scumbags to know the face of the great aristocrat who will end their wretched debauched lives! Noam fuckin' Metzenbaum, the great aristocrat!”

He stumbles upon the master suite. He hears a faint sound of crying. He thinks, “This is it!”

He tries to open the door, but it is locked.

He impersonated one of the cheerleaders’ voices, “Yo Chad S, I wanna lick you like a lollipop!”

One of the Chads opens the door to check what’s going on. Noam takes out the samurai sword, stabs him in the neck, pushes him aside, and barges in.

The master suite resembles a Roman palace with a giant hot tub and authentic Roman statues. Noam quickly hides behind the red curtain.

Noam looks out. There she is, his crush lying on the floor naked sobbing on her side. Noam notices she has a lush dark golden bush.

There are about a dozen Chads in Roman togas standing over her laughing with their dicks out jerking off. Noam can smell the stench of cum.

He has betrayed his true love. His worst nightmare has come true. At this point his only option is total annihilation. He doesn’t care about the consequences because all that is pure in the world had been sullied.

Chad S. declares, "Now you are a woman," while the rest laugh sadistically stroking their massive cocks, too ecstatic from their conquest to even notice Noam.

Noam, still hiding behind the curtain bumps into a head down below. It's Carlos down on his knees, rimming Nick's asshole while jerking him off.

Nick turns around to see who it is. Then Carlos down on his knees quickly finishes him off with a blowjob.

Noam grabs on to the red drapes but falls, ripping the drapes and landing on Nick and Carlos.

Just the moment Noam's lands on them Nick cums staining his blue dress with cum. Noam says, "Damn, I should have gone with the white one."

The Chads catch him. One says, "Get lost virgin! Who invited you?"

Noam takes the sword and beheads several Chads in one circular swoop except for Nick, who gets away.

Chad S. steps to the side looking for something to use as a weapon but Noam sneaks up from behind him and beheads him also.

Noam carries Chad S.'s head with him as a trophy. He notices there is an antique vase that is filled with cum. He wonders what kind of horrific rituals it was used for.

Noam takes the vase of cum and pours it into skull socket as if he's performing a Japanese tea ceremony.

Noam proclaims, "Chad S. you have lived a life of pure debauchery and defiled countless young maidens. May your eternity in Hell be spent being skull-raped by demons!"

Noam proudly holds the decapitated head as a trophy as a mixture of cum and blood oozes down onto the floor like ketchup and mayonnaise dripping out of a messy hamburger.

Noam looks out over his decapitated enemies. He says, "Vengeance is sweet, but it shall never reclaim the innocence and purity of my one true love!"

Carlos comes out from hiding and sees the dead Chads and Noam standing there covered in blood holding his trophy.

Carlos looks at Noam shaking his head in disappointment "Yo, I told you not to go psycho on me, Holmes!" Carlos leaves sobbing, "Don't tell anyone I know you. You're dead to me!"

Noam thinks about Carlos, "Was he ever my one friend at this horrid place or were we just using each other for our own personal goals?"

Noam is now there alone with his crush. Pure beauty defiled. He is speechless. His crush continues to sob.

Then Noam makes eye contact with her. She gives him a look expressing "Thank you for saving me." Noam feels a special connection to her for just that one second, even if they had never spoken.

He thinks, "She does love me! I knew it!"

Noam thinks about kissing her but cowers in fear. He is at the point where we had accomplished his main objective which was annihilating his adversaries but does not have a backup plan.

He thinks, “Where shall I go from here? Some day we shall be together, our purities restored, but I need to get the hell out of here!”

He looks at her one last time, but she continues to cry without noticing him.

Noam leaves the master suite and runs down the hallway, looking for an escape.

He hears, “Natalie! I love you! I’m sorry!” echo down the hallway. It is Zack.

Zack sees Noam with a sword covered in blood and screams, “Noam? What the fuck!”

Noam takes his sword and tries to do a fancy twirl like in the movies but drops it.

Zack runs away from Noam screaming, “Noam! Don’t do it bro!”

Noam takes his sword and slices it into Zack’s neck and says, “It was nice knowing you, Zack. Sorry it had to end this way.”

Noam realizes he has to find another disguise. He goes into a bathroom and finds another girl’s mask and a cum- and piss-drenched dress left on the floor.

Noam takes off his mom's dress and puts on the other dress, feeling all the Chad cum and piss oozing onto his bare skin. He feels more like a cheap whore than a great warrior, but at this point he just has to get out.

He continues running down the hallway and trips over a naked couple fucking right on the floor. He gets up and takes the sword, chopping of the guy's dick. The girl screams in terror as blood gushes out of his dick socket.

Then Noam slides down the stairwell, beheading all the Chads on the staircase lining up to get blowjobs. He looks up briefly and notices the girl is totally drenched in goo like a human snowman, totally unrecognizable.

He can hear people screaming and running away, police sirens in the distance. He hides the sword underneath his dress.

He gets to the main floor and sees people running outside to escape the mayhem, but they don't recognize him.

He runs down another hallway which leads to a stairwell that goes down to the basement. His childhood spent studying his grandfather's architectural blueprints has come in handy. He realized large houses were built like puzzles; there was always a pattern, which a great mind could find a way to figure out.

At the bottom of the stairwell, he finds a door and manages to escape and run down into the cellar and turns on the light.

He looks around and sees nothing but mysterious crates and vaults covered in sheets. He lifts up a sheet and finds the body of a little girl embalmed, with a bizarre occultist symbol carved into her chest.

He thinks, "What a sicko! Human sacrifices to the occult? Or just a wacko with unlimited spending money to buy shit online."

He thinks, "What is the purpose of our capitalist system if the excess profits are used to buy such useless debauchery? Why not end human suffering? Or use the revenue to build great civilizations to serve the true aristocrats!"

He thinks, "Noam, stop thinking about silly philosophical ponderings. You need to get the fuck out of here!"

He finds matches and gasoline in the cupboard.

He remembers hearing rumors about Chad S.'s father constructing a secret tunnel because he was paranoid about the Feds investigating him for insider trading, and now (as Noam has come to discover) a lot of other stuff, too.

He finds the tunnel behind a latch that is disguised as a furnace.

He thinks, "Now that his son is dead and house burnt down he can finally put it to good use."

He opens up the latch to the tunnel, but can see nothing but darkness. He had always been afraid of the dark since he was kid, fearful of what creature lurked in his closet at night, but he has worse things after him now.

He stares out into the abyss and slowly enters the dark tunnel. The door slams behind him. He checks it. He is now locked in, trapped in the darkness.

He walks down the long dark tunnel. He can hear someone in the distance banging on the door; "Perhaps the cops?"

He starts running as fast as he can to get away.

He finally gets to the end, where there is a ladder which leads up.

Noam climbs up the ladder and finds himself on the other side of the water inlet. He watches the house ablaze and gives out a chuckle, “Yes! I did it! I actually did it!”

He hears fire and police sirens and runs into the woods to escape. He continues running through the dark woods, but police helicopters start hovering over him and shine a search light down onto him.

He realizes at this point there is no escape, but he feels the urge to run for his life. He thinks, “Perhaps I will find a portal to another dimension, a world where everything is based on my visions and my crush still pure and innocent?”

He continues running as fast as he can, but his shoelace gets trapped in a branch, and he can’t get out. He’s stuck and hears the search dogs coming for him.

The helicopter search light shines right onto him and the cops capture and arrest him.

While in handcuffs, shaking in fear, and hung over from the vodka, Noam thinks, “I am now in captivity. I have accomplished what I have set out to do, which was to annihilate those who would dare desecrate pure beauty. I shall defeat this unjust system, the masses shall know the truth, and I shall be freed, lead the uprising, cleanse the world of all evil, and reunite with my one true love!”

A mean black cop sees Noam in the dress and laughs, “You gonna have a lot of fun in prison.”

Noam says, “Fuck off you dumb nigger.”

The black cop replies, "You gonna get fucked by a bunch of niggers where you're going boy."

Noam is terrified, but he knows that the cops are just useful idiots for the system, tools at the disposal of the elites, and once he is in power he would deal with them accordingly.

The next morning, Noam's mom turns on the news. The news anchor reports, "Last night a mentally disturbed freshman, Noam Metzenbaum, committed mass homicide and arson at a party at the home of a prominent hedge fund manager in Greenwich. There were 42 casualties, and many more with serious burns and life-threatening injuries. One boy died of a mysterious neck injury, but the cause is still unknown."

The co-anchor says with a big cheesy smile, "This is a historical event of pure evil, a cowardly act of terrorism that will forever scare this quaint New England community and send shockwaves throughout our nation's heartland!"

Noam's mom turns off the TV and throws the remote at the TV, cracking the screen. She breaks down in tears and thinks, "Noam was such a nice boy, how could this have happened? I gave him all my love and support. Where did I go wrong?"

Later that day Noam's mom watches a cheesy afternoon talk show. There is a discussion panel about the aftermath of the massacre. There is a conservative and a liberal pundit debating the causes of the massacre.

The liberal, who happens to be one of Noam's mom's colleagues from her online publication, says: "This is an act of white male privilege. This young man thought just because he was a white male from a wealthy upbringing he was entitled to girls, money, and power, but he never had to learn the values of equality. He lashed out at those who were weaker than him, primarily young women and people of color."

The conservative responds, "This is about class warfare and an assault on American values. This little brat was lacking in masculine virtues. He was a whiny, spoiled, entitled little piece of shit who couldn't stand the fact that some people through hard work, good social skills, and basic human decency had earned more than he did, so he lashed out like a commie and took their precious young lives."

The conservative breaks down in tears, while the liberal sits there with her smug grin.

Meanwhile an obese neo-Nazi shouts out in the audience, "This is no White Aryan! This fucking little kike killed these strapping young Aryan Chads. Spilled Aryan blood for his cannibalistic rituals! This is war! Chad Nationalism now!"

The obese Nazi starts gulping down a bottle of white goo which spills over his neckbeard shouting "I honor thy Chad brethren by drinking their Aryan seed."

Then a group of shirtless skinheads barge in covered in tattoos and backward baseball hats, throw down their beer from their red plastic cups and start chanting, "Chad Power! Chad Power!"

After the skinheads are removed by security, a psychologist comes on the show and says, "We really need to look into the deeper issues here of mental health. Did he have close friends; people looking out for him? Did he have adequate access to mental health and a strong support network?"

The talks show host interrupts the psychologist and says laughing, "I blame Roger Blackstone."

Both the liberal and conservative laugh and say, "I concur."

The funeral for the victims of the massacre is held at the local cemetery which is located next to the woods.

Presidential candidate Senator Dave Cohen-Rodriguez is the featured speaker, to whom Zack's father has donated millions.

There is a picture of Zack with the senator placed on his grave with flowers.

The Senator gets up to the podium to speak.

"This is a sad day, not just for the town of Greenwich but for all of America, and all of humanity. First of all I want to express my condolences to all the families here who have lost a loved one. I knew Zack and his father. Zack was the kindest young man you could ever meet. His young life ended in this cruel heartless act. But if we want to honor Zack's legacy, and the legacy of all these bring young lives that were lost that tragic night, we need to take action. We need to fight for justice. You see, my fellow Americans, this was not just a random act of violence, it was a bigoted attack against these sacred values we hold dear as Americans; values of justice, fairness, and equality."

Justin's mom gets up and interrupts the speech in tears, "What about my son? Where's the investigation? I don't know who did it but his neck was crushed! I don't think it was Noam."

The crowd gasps in horror as they hear Noam's name.

She continues, "The autopsy showed that he died of a neck injury. He wasn't killed by sword or in the fire like the other victims. I want answers!"

The police remove her from the funeral. She screams, "I blame all you superficial fuckers for this! You killed my son!"

The senator continues his speech, "Well, my condolences for your loss, but as I said this is not just about this tragedy but about the black cloud of bigotry engulfing our nation. You see the deranged young man …"

Justin's mom screams, "Noam!" as she is being put into the police car.

The senator continues, "This depraved individual didn't just learn to hate on his own. He had all the same opportunities as these bright young people, growing up in a peaceful compassionate community that values diversity. No, he was influenced by growing forces of hatred, forces that do not just exist in dark corners of the internet, but that are now put front and center in our presidential election, that threaten our basic values of democracy and equality. We need to honor the victims and survivors of this tragedy by fighting and squashing bigotry and make sure that acts like this never happen again. Thank you all and my deepest condolences."

There is a massive applause, but a few clap tepidly with a look of offense by the speech.

Nick's dad, Bill Anderson the district attorney, gets up to speak. He is tall, about 6'4", with dyed blond hair and a fake orange tan. He says, "First of all, I want to express my condolences to the victims and express how much I am moved by the senator's speech, but let's not kid ourselves here. It's nice to talk about justice, fairness, and equality, but our nation is at war. We have traitors living amongst us. We need to identify these domestic terrorists before they strike out, look for the early signs, and lock them up. Who am I talking about? I'm taking about loners, virgins, anyone with bizarre political theories. We need to put them away, classify them as mentally ill if needed before another tragedy like this happens. And I just want to say that I will do everything in my power to make sure that this little creep, this loser never sees the light of day again and never knows the love of a woman!"

The crowd applauds, his son Nick gets up and hugs his dad, both in tears. Nick turns around, showing his face, half-scarred from the fire. All the girls line up to hug him. Nick sees Natalie in the crowd and yells, "Yo Natalie!"

Natalie gets up.

"Get over here girl," Nick says.

The lead cheerleader says, "Like, what are you waiting for?"

Natalie gets up and walks over to Chad S.'s grave. She looks at his tombstone with a wicked grin then she runs off into the woods.

She sits down by the creek and cries, still hearing the funeral in the background. She finds an antique pocket watch lying by the creek.

She opens it and there is a photo of her. She puts it in her purse as a souvenir.

She listens to the running water and creaking of the woods and begins to cry.

Noam is taken to the courthouse to stand trial. While the bailiffs are taking him in, he sees a car parked. It is the vintage Rolls Royce with the "Blackstone for President" bumper sticker on it that he saw when he first moved into town.

He wonders if it is the judge.

Noam gets to the courtroom. His public defender sits next to him. Noam wonders where his mom is. His public defender informs him that his mom has been hospitalized after a mental breakdown. He gives Noam a look as to say, "You did this to your mom."

He is a short, scrawny, balding middle-aged man with glasses and a cheap suit.

Noam thinks "Perhaps this would have been me in the future if I chose the straight and narrow path and didn't fight back against the system. Put up with the torments throughout high school, no dates, no parties, just kept my head down and get straight A's. Get into a good College, still a virgin, no parties, and no hot blonde girlfriends. Maybe go on one date with a nerdy Asian girl who gives me an awkward hand job. Continue getting good grades and get into law school. After graduating, still a virgin, maybe get a job as a paralegal and work my way up. Once I start making decent money I get married at 35 to an aging slut who's fucked and blown hundreds of Chads. No, Noam! That's no way to live! You're a revolutionary. You can do better! You will survive all this and come out stronger and establish a new order!"

Noam sits in anticipation for the trial to start. He tries to avoid making eye contact with the other people in the courtroom; the journalist, the families of the people he massacred, the witnesses, and Nick's father, Bill Anderson, the prosecutor who is staring at Noam like he's going to kill him.

Finally the judge gets up to the bench. He is an old man with a white beard and glasses whom Noam recognizes as the man he saw earlier with the Blackstone bumper sticker. He looks over some papers then briefly makes eye contact with Noam. He gives him a stern look, not hostile, but not friendly either just saying, "This is an important day for you, young man."

The judge starts by letting Noam know the severity of the situation. Noam remains silent as his lawyer advises him. He just nods to let the judge know he understands.

The judge proceeds to list all the charges put forth by the prosecution: murder, arson, trespassing, stalking, hate crimes, terrorism, theft, and rape.

The judge calls up to the witness stand, Wendy Silverstein.

Wendy gets up in tears. She is dressed like a little girl in a doll dress with pigtails and glasses. She starts, "Noam was so mean to us. Every day he would sexually harass me and my friends. Then he sneaked into our party without being invited, and cornered me and my friends in a room. He saw us talking to Justin and got angry. He killed Justin and raped me!"

The judge replies, "How did Justin die?"

Wendy says, "Uh, well Noam tried to rape me and … uh, Justin tried to rescue me. Noam went over to Justin and like uh?"

“Yes” says the judge.

Wendy put on her best acting voice, “Well, Noam drugged me before he raped me but I saw Noam strangling him.”

She breaks down again in fake tears. “He raped me!”

The judge replies, “How exactly did the defendant rape you? Was there any penile penetration? I saw your medical tests, and I didn’t see any evidence of vaginal penetration.”

Wendy says in tears, “No, he didn’t use his dick!”

The judge probes further, “Well then, how did he rape you?”

She screams, “He used his tongue!”

The courtroom gasps.

“Explain exactly what happened.” the judge replies.

Wendy explains, “Well I was lying on the sofa, and he just pinned me down, lifted up my skirt, pulled down my panties, and started tongue-raping me for hours.”

The judge looks at her like he had never heard anything like that in his entire life.

Noam gets a massive erection and is actually quite pleased that Wendy is spreading rumors about the potency of his tongue, despite the fact that they are false and could potentially land him in prison for decades.

The judge says, trying not to laugh, “Tongue rape? Never heard of such a thing in my entire career.”

“Next to take the stand is Nick Anderson.”

Nick says, “That little fucker!”

“Excuse your language, young man,” says the judge.

Nick’s father, the prosecutor, gives the judge a nasty look.

Nick continues, “Yo! First of all he tried to sexually harass me in the shower, bro! I was taking a shower minding my own business and that little creep comes over and gets down on his knees and starts staring at my dick, and then he asked if he can suck it!”

The judge says, “Well, did you let the defendant perform oral sex on you?”

Nick, pretending to cry, says, “Hell no! I’m not a fucking faggot!”

The judge says, “That’s enough.”

Nick continues, “Wait! I have to tell you about the party.”

The judge says, “Go ahead.”

Nick goes on, “He broke into our party, bro! He was like totally uninvited. It was an act of sexual assault, bro, because he went into a place where there was like a ton of action; naked chicks everywhere. He didn’t get our consent. So yeah it was like rape, bro!”

The judge says, “That’s enough!”

The prosecutor demands, “Let him speak!”

The judge refuses, “Let’s move on to another witness. Sandra Green?”

Sandra, Justin's mom, gets up.

"Look, your honor, I can't speak for the other victims, but Noam didn't kill my son. My son was never part of the in-crowd."

Nick laughs, "That's an understatement."

She continues, starting to cry, "I overheard Justin talking to his friend on the phone. He was talking about being invited to some secret party by the popular girls."

She points to them, "Wendy Silverstein, Lisa Goldberg, and Molly Katzenberg. They were all in on it. They organized some bizarre hazing ritual that led to his death. The autopsy found that his neck was broken by …" She starts breaking down in tears, unable to speak.

A stranger in the background shouts, "Cunnilingus!"

The stranger is quickly taken away by the bailiffs.

Justin's mom continues sobbing, unable to speak.

The prosecutor says, "This woman here is clearly unfit to testify."

"I'll give Mrs. Green some time to calm down and have her back up to testify." The judge calls for a recess.

After a brief recess, the trial resumes. The prosecutor, Bill Anderson, gets up to make his case.

The prosecutor turns to Noam, "Look Noam, you mother fuckin' murdering piece of human excrement! You will never see the light of day again! You will get raped by your cell mate every single night! Then you will understand what it's like to truly suffer."

The judge reprimands him, "I won't tolerate this barbarism in my courtroom, and if I ever hear threats of rape or cruel and unusual punishment I will hold you personally in contempt of court. I have been a judge for over 40 years, and I have seen many important cases so I'm not going to take any threats from some amateur hot shot attorney."

The prosecutor sits down and apologizes reluctantly, steaming in anger.

Noam looks at him with a smug grin, then looks over at the parents of his victims mockingly.

The prosecutor is desperate. He takes out a piece of Noam's manifesto and looks at an elderly black woman in the jury in the eye and starts reading from it, "I hate niggers and Spics! They have tormented me every single day. They are a worthless race of slaves who have done nothing to advance civilization and are used to prop up the false elites!"

Noam's defense attorney interjects, "Well, I have another quote." He reads another piece from the manifesto, "I think Vanessa is a sweet girl. I once thought all blacks were cruel barbaric beasts, but she showed me kindness in this cruel inhospitable place. I shall enlighten her to my ways of seeing the world for what it is and she shall show her people my way and bring them to greatness. A new Afro-Futurist order where the colored race shall reach the pinnacle of civilization."

The prosecutor scoffs, "Yeah, I'm not racist because I have a token black friend. Yada Yada Yada."

Then the prosecutor goes over to an elderly Jewish juror who he notices has a tattoo on his arm from the Holocaust. He grabs his arm hard showing off his tattoo to the other jurors and reads from the manifesto, "I'm not a kike, I'm a real Aryan. You see those filthy rich Jews resent me because my father was a great European aristocrat. They are false elites who shall be annihilated and their unearned wealth confiscated. Hitler was right in a sense, but his only mistake was not impregnating the Jewesses and breeding a new blonde Nordic Jewish super race."

The man breaks down in tears, while the prosecutor looks at Noam to say, "I got you now!"

The defense attorney responds, "Look, Noam is Jewish himself, as am I. I don't take it personally, and my grandparents were survivors. The boy is clearly mentally ill, but he is not a racist or an evil human being. This is about mental illness not race or politics. He was briefly on anti-psychotic medication prior to the event."

Noam is furious that his defense attorney is marginalizing him by denying his status as a political revolutionary, but he knows this may be his only chance at freedom.

The judge asks the defense attorney to explain more about Noam's mental health history.

"Well, Noam was taken to the emergency room by his mother after a nervous breakdown but they refused to hospitalize him due to lack of insurance coverage. This is an indictment against our mental health care system. He was diagnosed with PTSD."

The judge asks, "Why was Noam taken to the emergency room? Why did he have a nervous breakdown?"

The defense attorney replies, "Well, Noam was experiencing some severe bullying. Every single day he was tormented by Nick and his friends. They tortured him in the shower before he had his breakdown."

The prosecutor shouts, "How dare you slander my son. I'll destroy you!"

The judge slams down his gavel, "I've had enough with you," then turns to the defense, "What exactly happened in that shower?"

Noam is terrified of his shower story getting out. He told his lawyer not to bring it up because it would discredit his honor as a great warrior, not some cheap piss whore, but his lawyer told him the humiliation he endured may be the only thing that could get him off.

The defense attorney desperately tells the story of Noam's experience in the shower, "Well, Noam was cornered in the shower by Nick and his friends. Nick's and his friend Chad S. –"

There is an awkward pause in in the court room. A man shouts, "How dare you speak ill of the victims, you scumbag lawyer piece of shit!"

The judge goes on, "Please continue."

The defense attorney says, "Well, Nick and his friends coordinated a hazing ritual where all the jocks at Chadsworth took turns urinating onto Noam, on his face, into his mouth, even making him gargle their urine."

Noam is relieved that his crush is not at the trial as a witness. He wants to reunite with his one true love under better circumstances.

The prosecutor interrupts, "Ah, a little piss play, that's nothing compared to what's going to happen to him in prison, the entire prison shower will be filled the blood from his rectum!"

The judge slams down his gavel, and for the first time raises his voice, "This is your final warning. I will not hear another word from you again!"

After listening to more witnesses regurgitating what Nick and Wendy said about Noam, the judge calls up the psychiatrist.

"Dr. Chang to the stand."

Dr. Chang, the psychiatrist who evaluated Noam speaks, "When Noam came to the emergency room that night, he looked very distraught. He tried to run away and security had to restrain him. He could barely speak and was shaking in terror. He showed signs of severe trauma. I finally got him to talk. He said there were monsters called Chads who were trying to rape a princess, whom he was going to propose to and take her off to his fantasy land. You see, this boy is clearly schizophrenic. He has delusions of grandeur, living in a fantasy world where he is a great knight on a journey to save his maiden from the Chad monsters. I prescribed him anti-psychotics, but he told me he had to kill the Chad monsters."

The prosecutor screams, "Chads? As in students from Chadsworth? He tried to kill my son, burnt off half his face! You knew and did nothing you chink bastard! I'll sue your ass and make sure you never practice in this town!"

The judge orders the bailiffs to remove the prosecutor for disrupting the trail.

He screams as he is being taken away, "You can't do this? This is unconstitutional!"

The judge smirks and says, "You're replaceable." Then turns to address Dr. Chang, "Dr. Chang, did the defendant have any mental health history prior to the incident?"

Dr. Chang replies, "Well, his mother told me that he was never officially diagnosed with mental illness but has struggled with severe depression, anxiety, and has suffered bullying since he was in middle school."

At some point between Dr. Chang's tedious medical testimony and the closing arguments for the defense and prosecution, Noam begins to get bored and slowly loses interest in his own trial. His attorney advises him not take the stand. Noam is annoyed that his lawyer doesn't recognize his masterful oratory skills and aristocratic eloquence enough to let him testify and give a passionate defense of his actions, but Noam is too beleaguered to protest. Detached from his own fate, he starts daydreaming and eventually nods off, as the trial ends and the jury deliberates:

At first, Noam is shaking in a cold sweat, but he blacks out and finds that the courtroom is vacated, and it is just him there alone in the dark. He finds himself at the judge's bench. He looks out over the court, but the floor is open and he can see down onto the town of Greenwich. He finds himself zooming in closer to Chadsworth. He can see the Chads practicing lacrosse on the field, the cheerleaders, and all the bullshit of high school politics. Then he can see the cafeteria, Wendy and her clique, the nerds, but then the school turns dark, and everyone freezes like statues.

A deep, powerful voice can be heard, "Noam Metzenbaum, the entire human race is on trial for its sins of debauchery, false social orders, and tormenting the one great mortal who showed them the way. You are the judge of the entire fate of humanity, what is your verdict?"

"Guilty!" Noam replies.

"Noam, wake up," his defense attorney alerts him that the jury is ready to read the verdict.

He feels as if a bolt of electricity hit him, awakening him to the fact that his entire fate is about to be determined by a bunch of senile old townspeople. Thoughts start racing through his head, "What if they do find me guilty," "What if I never get out of jail," "Will I survive prison?" "Will I ever see my crush again?"

The foreman for the jury gets up to read the final verdict. "I find the defendant Noam Metzenbaum guilty on counts of multiple homicides, assault, arson, and criminal trespassing, but unfortunately we cannot charge him for rape because our state's law does not recognize oral penetration of the vagina as rape."

Most of the courtroom gets up to applause and cheer. Wendy's mom scream's "What about my daughter? Where is the justice for her precious clitoris?"

The judge is bewildered. He says, "What is it with kids these days? In my day we used our dicks. No one would have dreamed of sticking their tongue down there."

The courtroom gasps. Wendy's mom screams, "You misogynistic fucker! Fuck you and this state's law. What is this, White Sharia?"

The judge laughs and gets up to leave, while Wendy's mom and her friends continue to scream.

The next day, Noam faces sentencing. The judge reads his sentence.

"Looking after this case, I have to take into account the severity of the crime. However …"

The courtroom hisses.

"However, on accounts of the severe bullying, the piss rape he endured, and his mental health history, I have taken all these events and factors into account."

The crowd continues to hiss.

The judge slams his gavel and continues with a smirk, "Look. I'd like to go easy on the kid for having to put up with the likes of you. Honestly, I don't blame the young man for his actions but unfortunately under mandatory minimum laws I have to sentence Noam Metzenbaum on behalf of the state of Connecticut to 16 years in the state psychiatric hospital. He never got the help he needed, and sadly our system is not in shape to provide it. He will probably come out even more deranged, but that is how our system works. Watch out in 16 years, but I'll be in my grave by then."

The crowd starts booing. "What the fuck!" "You're absolving this piece of shit of his guilt!" "Hang the bastard!" "Letting off a terrorist? You cunt!"

The judge smirks and addresses the crowd, “I’m ready to retire, so I can speak my mind. I grew up in this town, and you assholes ruined it. My family has been here since colonial times, old New England stock, and you trash come up from the city and ruin it with your mega mansions, replacing all the old stores with your chain brands, and you've turned the forest I grew up in into a golf course. You can all rot in hell as far as I’m concerned!”

The prosecutor, who is allowed back in for sentencing, shouts to Noam, “Don’t expect a walk in the park. You will face justice for your horrific crimes against our peaceful compassionate community.”

The judge rolls his eyes.

The prosecutor continues, “If you manage to survive prison, all the survivors of your cowardly act will hunt you down and make sure your entire life will be a living hell. Even if you manage to leave prison with your rectum intact you will remain a virgin for the rest of your life!”

The sting of the word virgin sinks into Noam’s mind.

The judge tells the prosecutor to “Calm down” and says, “Many mass murderers get plenty of female admirers from behind bars, and I’m quite sure our state allows conjugal visits.”

The prosecutor explodes in rage and tries to assault the judge, but the bailiffs restrain him. The judge says, “Feel free to join Noam in prison.”

Noam gives the survivors, journalists, and rich townspeople a smug grin before being taken into custody.

Noam wakes up in a strange small room feeling drugged, tired, scared, and confused. He doesn't remember anything since the trial. The room is small with linoleum floors and white walls with no doors or windows. There is a fluorescent light that permeates the room.

He is wearing a white hospital gown. His back and arms ache like someone has beaten him up but he doesn't recall anything.

He looks down and sees a small blue pill lying on a small table which is the only object in the room.

He feels as if he has been trapped in this tiny room without doors or windows for all eternity and everything that had happened to him was just a long dream.

Noam stares at the blue pill. He thinks, "Maybe if I take the pill I will know the truth, my true identity, and discover the world that exists outside this room."

He takes the pill.

Suddenly everything blurs and Noam feels woozy. He finds himself floating through the clouds. He thinks, "Am I dead and floating off to heaven, or has God played a cruel joke on me?"

The clouds subside and Noam finds himself in outer space. He looks down on the earth. He floats through the stars. He sees his crush on a magical star, floating towards him. He sees a tear in her eye. When he makes eye contact, she smiles, a smile of pure love and innocence.

Just as he starts to reach out to touch her hand, he finds himself falling. The intense feeling of dizziness overwhelms him, and he feels shots of pain through his muscles.

Noam wakes up in a cold sweat and hears sirens going off.

He is alone in his cell. His memory comes back to him after the drugs wear off. He thinks, “So this is prison?”

He looks at his small cell. There is nothing but a small foam mat on the floor to sleep on.

He hears banging on doors and yelling and screaming echoing down the cell corridor. He imagines all the criminals and psychos in the other cells. “Psychos who murdered and cannibalized their entire families, or perhaps they are eating themselves alive?”

Noam realizes he will be spending a long time here alone by himself.

He thinks, “My formative years, meant to learn great things, go on my first date, and the simple joys of breathing in the fresh air while taking a stroll in the woods. All gone. My youth stolen from me by a tyrannical system designed to crush great minds that challenge the existing order. I don’t belong here. I’m not a criminal. I fought for justice, true aristocratic radicalism!”

Over the next few days, time goes by in one big blur. Nothing really makes sense anymore. He keeps feeling drugged and then falls asleep and wakes up again, not even remembering taking the pills.

He thinks, “Is there something in the air ventilation? Mind control perhaps? I can’t think anymore. I am not a great intellectual. Just a drugged out zombie that society intended for me to be from the moment I was conceived.”

He spends hours staring at the ceiling, his mind empty of thoughts or emotions. Then he falls back asleep.

Noam wakes up and gets his first package. Inside he finds a journal his mom gave him. Inside there is a note.

It reads:

"Noam, I am sorry that I didn't see the early signs, but what you did was horrific. No matter how badly you were treated, there was no excuse for what you did. I feel a deep guilt for what happened, but it's too late now. I can't visit you and may not see you for a very long time but I want you to know that I do love you even if you don't understand. Some day we may meet again under better circumstances, but for now I want to get in touch with my spiritual side and away from all the bullshit of society. I'd advise you try to find your inner peace.

-Love Mom"

Noam breaks down in tears.

He tries to write in the journal but starts to feel drugged again. He now knows he has to avoid the pills at all cost.

Noam starts to fall asleep but forces himself to stay up a little longer so he can finish his train of thought.

Noam writes:

"It has been 7 days and 3 and a half hours since I have last made human contact. I am trapped in this tiny little box, but liberated from the ugliness that is the human race. My body is trapped but my mind is in ultimate control. The world is not

ready for me. One day I shall break free and restore order and justice to this sad pathetic place we call a society."

Noam finally falls asleep and starts dreaming. He is in a magical forest like a fairy tale. He hears birds singing, and sees giant flowers all around him that smell of the sweetest freshest young pussies.

He starts walking down through the woods, breathing in the fresh sweet air.

He hears a girl giggling. He looks behind and sees his crush, her golden blonde hair. She starts running away in the opposite direction.

He thinks, "Does she know it's me?"

He calls out, "Natalie!" She starts running away faster. He tries running as fast as he can but feels like there are weights stuck to his feet.

He can see her in the distance. He tries to chase after her but trips, falling down on the ground through the grass into a deep dark hole.

As he falls he looks around and sees penis-shaped mushrooms. He hears the voices of the Chads taunting him, "Virgin!" "Loser!" "No one will ever kiss you!" "Your crush gives great head!"

He looks at them closely and realizes they are not mushrooms, but the penises of the Chads which he can remember in graphic detail after having them shoved in his face at the showers at Chadsworth.

There are more penises, bigger ones surrounding him. They start spraying him with piss.

The spray pushes him further down like a waterfall; down to the bottom where he lands in a giant underground river of piss. He feels the warm piss in contrast to the cold air of the cavern which smells like a urinal that hasn't been cleaned in eons.

He can't swim so he starts to drown swallowing the piss. The currents push him further down the cavern; the currents getting stronger and faster.

He looks up struggling to stay afloat and sees her, his crush on a pedestal with light shining down onto her like an angel and her hand reaching out to rescue him.

Just as Noam is about to grab her hand, he wakes up and finds himself tied down to a medical table in what appears to be an operating room. He is in a restraint, some sort of suicide vest.

He looks at his arms, and there are deep cuts that are infected with blood and puss oozing out.

Noam looks around the room but can't see anyone. He is lying there in pain, no one there to help him.

An overweight black nurse comes in to give him a tranquilizer while he is kicking and screaming. Then she puts some disinfectant on his wounds, the sting causing him to scream out in pain. The tranquilizer comes in to effect but Noam doesn't dream. He just lies there alone in darkness.

When he wakes up, a psychiatrist, who is a nasty old man, speaks to him and tells him that he was caught trying to escape.

Noam asks, “Why was I injured?”

The psychiatrist says coldly, “You tried to off yourself multiple times before you tried to escape. We found you in a garbage dumpster. Ironic, isn’t it? You are garbage, properly disposing yourself as society should have a long time ago, but protocol is protocol.”

The guards come in and strap him to a gurney and put him in a giant elevator.

Noam asks, “Where are you taking me?”

They don’t reply.

When they get out of the elevator, they reach a long dimly lit corridor that resembles a dungeon. Noam realizes he must be deep underground.

He remembers hearing that the hospital was built over an old mental hospital from over a century ago and had heard a friend of his mom’s joking about the place being haunted. He realized he is in the remnants of the old hospital.

Noam can hear inmates talking to themselves about torturing their victims and others scream out in pain.

Noam is escorted to his cell, which is dark and barely the size of a closet. Unlike the other cell which had white walls and linoleum floors there is nothing but concrete.

A male nurse escorted by the guards forces him to take a black pill. Noam tries to resist but the nurse manages to force the pill down his throat.

He gags and can taste all the toxic chemicals from the pill.

The guards slam the cell door shut and it is now pitch black. Noam has arrived in hell.

He is now alone in his dark concrete cell with no bed, just a thin foam mat which reeks of dead flesh. He has no idea how long he will be down here.

He thinks, "Perhaps they will forget about me and leave me here to die. Wasn't that the plan all along?"

He sits down on the concrete floor. He gets up quickly, roaches everywhere. He tries stomping on them, but when he crushes them their guts quirt onto him.

He thinks, "Do they feed on human remains? How am I supposed to sleep? The roaches will devour me!"

Noam screams, "Help! Get me out of here!" No response.

After about five minutes of yelling, Noam feels the pills kicking in again.

Noam can here banging on the doors in the corridor.

He hears echoes of a crazy black inmate screaming. He starts to comprehend what the man is saying. He is bragging about raping, torturing, and decapitating a little girl.

Noam thinks, "How dare he! She didn't deserve to die that way. She was still innocent, not corrupted by the sins of lust, not a vile teen slut who blows Chads, one after the other. She had a chance at life, to be a good person, preserve her virginity for a great noble man like me, and this beast cuts her life short. And to think I have to share the same living quarters with the beast. Is this what society thinks of me? I decapitated for justice. I'm not some sick nigger molester who gets his jollies decapitating little girls. No! I am a political prisoner!"

Noam feels drugged and woozy from the pill, but this pill wasn't like the other pills he had taken. There is something about that black pill that brings upon feelings of death, as if he is crossing the void into hell.

He starts to feel sick, like his internal organs are rotting away. Starting with his gut, then his lungs, and then consuming his brain.

He gets down on the mat. Lies there, feeling the hard concrete against his back, staring into the abyss.

As he starts to drift off to sleep he can hear the beast rant in graphic detail about how he chopped off the body parts of the little girl and hid them away in glass jars.

Noam had always got off on violent fantasies of revenge, but they had a purpose. This was too much for him to listen to.

Noam drifts off from the drugs and reawakens, finding himself restrained in chains to the floor.

He thinks, "Did the beast break into my cell to decapitate me? I'm not a little girl. What does he want from me?"

Noam lies there in the dark, unable to move.

He notices his arms and legs are strapped to the floor. He feels hands grabbing at his legs. He looks down and sees naked creatures without faces or genitals with white skin and cuts and pins in their bodies which are illuminated in the dark.

He hears hissing, "Noam," getting louder, "Noam, Noam, we've come for you; come join us."

They start grabbing at him. He closes his eyes, trying not to look at them but feels their slimy fingers crawling around his body.

He thinks, "Are they trying to drag me off to hell or are they lost souls like me, never given a chance at life. Did they have the misfortune to stumble across a cruel puzzle box, trapped into a dark maze without an end, or are they just demons devouring my soul."

Noam opens his eyes and realizes that there are roaches crawling all over his legs.

He continues to scream in agony as he is strapped to his cells floor. As his eyesight adjusts to the darkness, he can see blood stains on the wall and the roaches crawling out of a crevice.

Noam manages to peek into the crevice and for a fraction of a second, he can see a giant cavern full of dead bodies.

He realizes that the stench of rotting flesh filling the cell is coming from the crevice and remembers hearing that the prison used to bury dead inmates in a makeshift cemetery.

He starts to hear the faint sound of voices screaming out in pain.

He thinks, "Are they the faceless genital-less creatures who attacked me?"

He cannot tell whether it is day or night since he is stuck in this dungeon, nothing but darkness, suffering, and misery.

Noam wants so much to speak to another human being. Even the asshole staff, but not even they would check on him. He feels like he is buried alive in a coffin.

For the first time in his life, he prays to God. He prays, for an end to the pain and suffering, he prays for salvation from the eternal darkness of hell, and he prays to be united with his crush.

Noam screams, "God! If you give me one more chance, I will be a good person! I will be kind, I shall feed the poor, comfort the weak!"

For a moment Noam is in peace; the faceless bruised creatures are gone. He is still alone in his dark cell, yet his mind is at ease.

Over the next few days Noam spends in his dark cell, he reflects on his life and why he was put on this earth? He thinks about how his mom must have felt being alone and having to live with her son being an infamous, incarcerated mass murderer. He even thinks about the families of the victims; compassion for their suffering? Noam thinks, "Is God bringing me to love thy enemy, have compassion for those I have wronged."

Then Noam pauses in contemplation. "No! They were evil debauched spoiled rich brats! They deserved everything they got. They deserve to suffer in hell for their sins, not me. I was put on this earth to cleanse it of its filth. I'm a good person. I tried to stop evil, even if it meant using lethal force. Is murder a sin when you are preventing greater evil? The most evil act is to defile pure innocence and beauty."

Noam feels his heart harden again, but he begins to grow stronger, tolerate the darkness, and loneliness of his underground lair.

He starts to befriend the roaches; holds discussions about philosophy, his dreams and ideals. They are, after all, a captive audience and make great listeners and would sometimes squeal in approval.

After several weeks in the dungeon, he is taken back to his original cell. He has become so accustomed to the dark that the fluorescent lights sting his eyes and he has to keep them closed for a while.

He finds a way to avoid taking the pills. He pretends to swallow them and then when the nurse is not looking he spits them in out into the toilet.

Once he is off of the medication the feeling of being drugged is replaced with terrible withdrawal symptoms of nausea, fatigue, and aching in his muscles.

But after about a week or so he begins to regain his consciousness.

He imagines what the world is like outside the prison walls and what the world will be like in the future when he gets out.

One day he notices a white pill instead of the usual black pills.

Out of curiosity he is tempted to take it but fears that it will control his mind, taking away his potential for contemplation.

He gives in to his temptations and takes the pill.

He feels calm at first, then he feels the sensation of floating.

He looks around and he is no longer in his cell but floating in air.

He looks down to see if he is still in prison but sees nothing but white clouds.

Out of nowhere, a frog goddess approaches him.

He feels a warm magical presence comforting him. He is no longer in agony. All his anxiety and fear are gone.

The frog goddess says, "I am Shadilay, I have come to teach you the gospel of KEK and show your species the way of your amphibian overlords." She takes out a harp and starts to sing. A group of young frogs sing in the background serenading Noam:

"Cosmic absolute, regular reality
Breath of an image/concept, syntony of civilizations
Confused descendants of rebel cells
I fly towards the universe, I'll pass through it
If you are a star, show yourself, I will stop
oooh oooh

Shadilay shadilay my freedom
Shadilay shadilay oh no
Shadilay shadilay oh dream or reality
Shadilay shadilay oh no
(You) fly into my life, no it's not finished
I will stop
Set my sails, in the sky or at the bottom of the sea
I WILL BELIEVE IN YOU

Metallic harmony, CONCRETE/REAL REALITY
Electronic video clip, praise of civilizations
Confused descendants of rebel cells
I fly towards the universe, I'll pass through it
If you are a star, show yourself, I will stop
oooh oooh

Shadilay shadilay my freedom
Shadilay shadilay oh no
Shadilay shadilay oh dream or reality
Shadilay shadilay oh no
(You) fly into my life, no it's not finished
I will stop
Set my sails, in the sky or at the bottom of the sea

I WILL BELIEVE IN YOU"

With the power of Shadilay, Noam flies through the stars, explores outer space, experiences other dimensions. Perfect visions for civilizations and ancient tribes lost in space looking for his guidance back to planet earth.

Once Noam returns to earth from his cosmic journey, the power of Shadilay gives him the mental strength to survive the rest of his sentence and new hope for the future.

He finally gets his journal back (which was confiscated) and begins writing. He has plans, fresh plans. He starts to write about his plans to rebuild society into something new, learning from his past mistakes.

Noam writes: *"As a young man I had fallen short. Yes, I Noam Metzenbaum, the great aristocrat, succumbed to my base instincts. If I did not partake in actions based on my crude sexual impulses I would have been better prepared. I failed my crush and got captured by the enemy but now is not the time to look back in despair over past shortcomings. Now is time to plan for the future! I will not be in this asylum forever. Listen up, mankind. Noam is coming back! All the sluts who rejected me will be old hags, and I will have a new crop of young nymphets to rebuild my utopia. I will teach them how to live, how to be the perfect maidens, to uphold civilization. I was once a kid but my experience in the darkest underbelly of society has given me a deeper insight into human nature and how the mechanisms are created to crush the human soul and psyche. I have learned from my enemies and will use those mechanisms to take power and enforce my will upon mankind."*

Noam spends the rest of his sixteen years of incarceration contemplating on life, writing in his manifesto, reading philosophical and political novels he orders from the prison library and dreaming about his crush.

The rest of his incarceration goes by fast in one big blur; a day becomes an hour, a week becomes a day, and a year becomes a week.

Noam's last day in prison he contemplates his prison experience. He imagined that he would have to fight for survival with the worst savages of society but after he got over the worst aspects; the drugging, the mean-spirited staff, and the boredom, it became an opportunity to sort things out in his mind. Now he anticipates a new world and whether his actions on that fateful night made an impact for better or worse. Regardless, Noam is ready to face the world as a new man.

Noam is released from prison. A white van picks him up to take him to New York City. Noam has nothing but his journal and money saved up from donations from his admirers that were put into a trust.

On the bus ride to the city Noam writes in his manifesto: *"I'm now free from confinement, back in the world that once threw me away. I fought back against injustice. They tried to annihilate me, but I have grown stronger and am prepared to wage battle against the world. Since my incarceration, many girls who were just born at the time of my great act of heroism have already been defiled, while I am 31 years old and have yet to even kiss a girl. But I am a stronger man now. My freedom from debauchery gave me the strength and purity to see the world for what it is and challenge its injustices. I know my crush is still out there waiting for me. I will hunt her down if I have to search every inch of the universe. I know that the Chads didn't deflower her because I exterminated them like rats before they even got a chance to lay a finger on her. She is still pure and innocent in her soul. Now is the time to wreak havoc on the wicked and establish a true aristocratic order!"*

Noam arrives in New York City. The bus drops him off at the bus terminal near Times Square. As a boy, he was always repulsed by all the cheesy commercialism, overweight tourists, and the sounds of obnoxious hip hop and twerking pop stars blaring from the electric screens, but his grandfather Saul used to show him pictures of Times Square from the 30s to the 60s and told him, "Noam, someday this place will be great again."

Noam looks up and sees a giant electronic screen. On top of it is the massive lettering "Vapor INC" in flashing neon like the signs in Blackstone's book from Japan in the 80s. A hologram appears out of the screen. It is a beautiful blonde Jewess in a kimono advertising Vapor Island, which Noam remembers Roger Blackstone working on as a kid when he was running for president.

The images of Vapor Island portray a tropical paradise with skyscrapers covered in pink, purple, and turquoise neon, ancient monuments, and magnificent palaces, while 80s synthwave with calypso steel drums plays in the background. It is that magical world where the past meets the future that Noam had always dreamed about. Then he sees a beach with holograms of beautiful teen girls in pink and turquoise 80s style bikinis that revealed their buttocks and bikini lines.

Then for a split second he realizes that one of the girls is his crush, the girl he had dedicated his life to finding is there lounging on the beach waiting for him. He has to find a way to journey to Vapor Island.

The commercial is interrupted by a large crowd of protesters. On one side he sees a group of middle-aged overweight women chanting, "We are human beings not robots," and "We have agency, we are not obsolete," holding up signs with images of sex robots crossed out.

On the other side he sees a group of men in frog masks. Many are overweight and wearing tee shirts with anime porn on them. They are chanting "Hail, Noam Metzenbaum!" "Death to the Chads," and "Beta Uprising now."

Noam thinks, "Are these my followers? I am no beta; I am the ultimate alpha, master of the universe. These creatures are not fit to be in my presence."

A group of large muscular, douchy men covered in tattoos, each with two blondes in their arms walk by and start mocking them, "Get a life, virgin," "Hit the gym," "Get laid, bro." Like older grotesque versions of the Chads who tormented him in high school.

Then the men in the frog masks start throwing junk food and soda cans at them.

Noam scoffs, "I would have them beheaded and use their skull as a toilet. Poseurs!"

A group of robot police round up the men in frog masks and throw them in a black police van. Noam overhears one them shout out, "Noam, go to the island!"

Noam thinks for a second maybe they are on to something.

Noam walks down 42nd street in Times Square. All the Broadway shows and tacky tourist shops are gone, replaced by adult entertainment, pornographic holograms, and the magic glow of neon illuminating the street.

Noam can tell that everything is designed by Blackstone's Vapor INC. He sees theaters with animated neon signage in Chinese and Japanese, advertisements for live hologram sex shows, even, "live hologram lolicon" shows, and glass pedestrian tubes outlined with neon connecting the buildings.

He looks up and sees a large tower that resembles a casino. It is a tall tower with dark glass and animated pink and purple neon grids, and an animated neon sign at top saying "Vapor Love Hotel." Noam notices packs of Chinese businessmen walking inside.

He walked inside underneath the neon marquee to find out what the place was all about. The interior of the lobby resembles an old New York Art Deco hotel with an Asian touch. The carpeting is crimson red and gold inspired by ancient Chinese patterns, and black marble walls with gilded Chinese patterns.

Noam remembers that Blackstone had collaborated with his grandfather Saul who was an architect. He gets a massive erection thinking about all the grand architectural visions that are being implemented.

Noam is so overwhelmed by the aesthetics that he decides to go to the bar for a drink. He orders a virgin martini. He has never had one before but had admired the elegance of the old New York socialites from his grandfather's photo albums sipping martinis and had always wanted to try one.

The bartender whom Noam recognizes as Scarlet Johansson (but has not aged a day) handed him his martini, "Virgin martini? Martini for a virgin? I can change that."

Noam is confused but soon realizes that she is a robot.

Noam thought Scarlet was hot growing up but had more of a thing for Alicia Silverstone. Watching her in Clueless and jerking off to her in The Crush as a boy reminded him that he had to find his own crush, and he also thought that Nick Eliot was the biggest imbecile for turning down Alicia Silverstone in The Crush. If only his crush would have been that forward towards him none of this chaos and carnage would have been necessary.

He is quite concerned that her image might be desecrated by being used as a sex robot for horny Chinese businessmen, but he isn't going to allow for that injustice.

Noam usually doesn't initiate conversations with strangers but he is curious about finding out more about the new civilization he has inherited.

He starts small talk with the Chinese businessman next to him, "Nice place."

The man replies, "Very nice. He he."

"Where are you from?" Noam asks.

"Shanghai," the man replies. "This here have best sexbots this side of Pacific."

"You're a rich man. Can't you find a mistress?" Noam asks.

The man looks insulted, "Fook you American white man. You had your chance, but you let Chad defile your women. You no find girlfriend. You no have waifu. You no fight Chad, but we in China had no choice. Government mandated one-child policy and female got aborted. We have no women, but you people disgust me!"

"Look, chink," Noam replies. "I fought back against the Chads, and they locked me away in the dungeon but now I'm back and this world is in for a rude awakening!"

The Chinese man realizes who Noam is and says, "I very sorry sir, please forgive me. I no idea who you are. Chinese men love Noam. We support you. You have admirers worldwide. Can I get selfie with Noam?"

Noam refuses the selfie but shakes the man's hand and says, "Thank you for the support," and walks away.

Noam has enough money saved up from the donations to buy a penthouse suite at the Vapor Love Hotel. He sits in his penthouse and admires the view.

He looks out the window and admires the skyline; like something out of his dream sequence, a futuristic film noir metropolis. All the tacky early 21st century buildings are gone.

The skyline is dotted with massive Neo Deco skyscrapers with golden spires, the animated signage gives a feeling of life to a once dead city, and the colorful glow of neon permeates the nightscape. It is that dream world he envisioned as a youth: Blackstone's images from the 80s combined with his grandfather Saul's book of old film-noir New York City.

He thinks, "These grand visions have been implemented. Architecture can be pleasing to the eye, however my utopia shall not be complete until I find my true love."

Noam falls asleep. For the first night since he was a young boy, he is able to have a good night sleep free from agony and torment. He dreams of the island, meeting Roger Blackstone, and finally reuniting with his crush in her prime teen years, pure innocence, still saving herself for him. Frozen in time like a butterfly in a glass jar waiting to be brought back to life by the magic touch of her one true love.

Noam wakes up feeling rejuvenated. A Eurasian sex robot with a French accent brings him fresh squeezed orange juice, coffee, and Belgian croissants. Noam puts on his silk robe, opens the curtains to let in the sunlight, and admires the skyline.

He can make out the Empire State Building, the Chrysler buildings, and Central Park. There are many skyscrapers of that style, connected by sky bridges and glass tubes for cars, trains, and pedestrians. A multi-layered metropolis that was built for him.

As he sips his coffee from the finest china, admiring the view, he opens up his massive pile of fan mail. They are mostly from countless sexually frustrated lonely men who admire him, as well as some female admirers who rant on about how the act of decapitation makes them wet.

Noam is impressed that he has so many admirers but is disgusted that most of these men are unattractive, overweight pigs who sit around all day eating junk food and jerking off to porn with no purpose in life, nor grand aesthetic visions other than massive bukkake orgies.

Noam thinks, "They are real losers. I am a great aristocrat deprived of my rightful place at the pinnacle of society."

Noam gets one letter with the official seal of Vapor Inc. on it. It simply reads "Come to Vapor Island. We have been waiting for you."

Noam decides that before he makes his pilgrimage to Vapor Island he has some business to take care of. He thinks, "While the city has reached its pinnacle of aesthetic perfection I must cleanse it of all its subhuman filth and debauchery."

Noam decides he needs a makeover if he wants people to take him seriously. He goes to all the top department stores and boutiques in the city.

He thinks, "If I truly am the one great aristocrat, I have to look the part."

He finds a tailor from Italy on the Upper East Side, who makes him a custom-made suit. Nearby he finds an antique store where he buys a Venetian mask, a burgundy silk cape, and a vintage Rolex watch from the 80s. He looks at himself in the golden mirror and proclaims, "I am the one true aristocrat!"

The store assistant sniggers at him. He takes out an old rapier sword and points it at her face and says, "Do you know who I am?"

She stands there humbled in silence.

Back in Times Square, Noam sees a giant hologram advertisement for Moosh. Moosh is an Israeli Dating Coach named Moshe Nazarian. He explains in his commercial "I am Moosh. Moosh can get you Koosh. Are you a fat, ugly perma virgin loser who jerks off to anime? Or just a nerdy businessman addicted to sex robots? For just $3000 American dollars I can take you to the most elite clubs in New York City and teach you the seduction skills necessary to get high quality Koosh."

Noam notices in the commercial that Moosh is surrounded by beautiful blonde Jewish girls while he is a slimy Middle Eastern man. Noam thinks, "He must pay for his crime of desecrating these blonde Aryan Jewesses. Not to mention preying on the most desperate of males, who unlike me do not have the fortune of not being slaves to their libido."

Noam signs up for Moosh's plan and shows up at the nightclub to meet Moosh. He has a swarthy complexion, shaven head, with a goatee, and thick Israeli accent. He is dressed in a white Armani suit, and has Armani sunglasses, the kind Noam always wanted as a boy but his mom couldn't afford to buy him.

Noam looks at all the pathetic men wasting their hard-earned money on the stupid seminar. Then he sees the models, all young blonde Israeli women.

Moosh explains, "When I was a boy in Israel, all the pretty blonde girls left for America on Blackstone visas. All our best women left for America, but I learned the skills from the best, the Krav Maga of pussy. I came to America and slept with them all. Not just blonde Israeli women but hot Asian girls, hot Latinas, and hot blonde shiksas. They all love my hairy chest and long schlong."

Noam is seething in rage but pretends to go along with the seminar. He thinks, "How dare he desecrate these Israeli-Aryan women? They belong to me dammit! I will show that sand creature!"

Moosh goes on with his first lecture, "The first thing about pussy is you have to put the pussy in the gutter. That's right. Think of pussy, not as something you desire but as droplets from a rainstorm passing down into the sewer, Cheap and plentiful! And never, I can't I can't overstate this, NEVER go down on a blonde Jewess!"

This fills Noam with rage. It was his life goal to go down on his crush, worship her entire body from her golden hair to her pussy, to lap at her golden labia and drink her magic juices.

Noam looks over at all the pathetic men awestruck at Moosh and thinks, "They have no clue of their enslavement."

Then the women come in; all blonde Israeli models, the kind of women that Noam lusted after since he was a boy.

While the men are listening to Moosh's lecturing, all the models notice Noam. They can tell by looking at him that he has the look of a murderer in his eyes. That's what gets them wet, not Moosh's cheesy talks.

Noam wants these blonde Israeli women but thinks, "They are all sluts, they've had their share of cock. They have been desecrated. I am on a mission and that mission is to find my crush who is still pure. I know it!"

After the seminar, Moosh comes over to Noam to tell him that he is impressed by how all the ladies were drawn to him and invites him back to his private bachelor pad to learn from Noam and his story.

After a few drinks, Moosh is distracted and Noam slips a roofie in his drink. Moosh wakes up tied to his bed naked with his testicles missing.

Noam proclaims, "The desecration of Israeli Aryan women will end!" He stabs Moosh in the chest with his dagger, missing his heart but causing a lot of blood to ooze out.

Moosh cries out in pain, "Why did you do this my dear friend? I saw something special in you. You have a gift; something that I have never witnessed in my entire life but you betrayed me for no good reason!"

Noam replies, "I am on a quest to annihilate all those who engage in acts of debauchery."

Moosh replies, "I was once a lost soul; a geek, a virgin. I envied those who got laid, but I learned game, and it changed my life. But you, you had all those blondes swooning over you and you still can't get over your adolescent rage from past rejections. You cannot reach the level of top notch game unless you let go of your past. Then you can fully comprehend game."

"I'm not about game!" Noam insists. "I'm about action! Establishing true aristocratic order!"

Moosh screams out, "It's all about game!"

Noam finds a small golden Egyptian frog statue on Moosh's desk. Moosh screams out, "You can kill me, but don't take that frog! It is cursed!"

Noam can sense it has some kind of special powers. He takes it and puts it in his pocket and leaves as Moosh bleeds to death in agony.

Noam puts on his disguise, his Venetian mask and burgundy cape and declares himself "the aristocrat!" He continues his campaign to cleanse the city of its filth and debauchery.

His frog statue gives him a special sense of power; all his anxieties and insecurities are gone. He feels like he can get any girl he wants, but his objective isn't to get laid but to use sex to woo his debauched adversaries and deal with them accordingly.

After all, there is only one girl for Noam and he knows that if he wastes his precious seed banging sluts he will no longer be worthy of her.

He starts off by going to seedy nightclubs in the back alleys of Times Square, where he beats up and drugs sexually promiscuous men and collects their testicles.

After he is done cleaning out the lower rungs of debauchery he decides it is time to cleanse the city's upper crust of its debauched elements.

Noam goes to an exclusive VIP club in SoHo, simply called "Naughties," that caters to Wall Street bros, trust fund kids, models, and other celebrities. The club has an early 21st century kitsch theme, which fills him with rage after witnessing all the grand new aesthetics in the city.

Now with the power of his frog statue he can seduce anyone in the club both male and female. He starts charming people with small talk. They buy into his persona that he's the prince of a fictional nation called "Kekistan."

He goes over to a table where there are a bunch of douchy trust fund bros with their model girlfriends. After they are all drunk and under his spell he slips them roofies and takes the men out to the back alley to castrate them and collect their testicles in a jar he keeps in his purse.

Later that night at the club he recognizes the Dominican guy who bullied him at his original high school, Angel. He is now a famous baseball player hitting on a blonde model.

Then another model comes over and Noam overhears Angel saying "Let's go over to my place for a threesome, bitches!"

Noam approaches them. The girls are enamored by his aristocratic persona, but Angel is annoyed that he is hitting on the models.

Angel declares, "Ladies, let's head over to my place. Now!"

The girls start giggling, "Ah, we want to play with the aristocrat."

"He's like some alien prince," the other girl says, smiling.

Her friend replies drunkenly, "I've never done it with an alien before. I heard they have big dicks. I could use a nice probing."

"Fuck that shit," Angel says. "I'm an alien, bitches. My parents brought me over on a raft from the Dominican Republic when I was a baby and my cock is ten times bigger than that tiny little prick!"

The girls start whining, "We want a real alien, not some dirty Mexican."

Angel is pissed but changes his strategy.

He turns to Noam, "Look dude, apparently the girls find you amusing. If you want to chill with us, we cool, but if you step out of line I'll kick your ass."

They all head over to the VIP lounge and get wasted on mojitos. Noam is able to impress Angel and convince him that his nation of Kekistan is opening its first professional baseball league and needs a celebrity front man. Angel is intrigued.

Then after he has Angel fully under his spell, he slips a roofie into his mojito.

He takes him to a restroom underneath the club, ties him up against the sink and takes off his clothes revealing his cock. He then proceeds to castrate him and chop off his dick (which is covered in genital warts).

He realizes that he can't hang out there all night. He bitch-slaps Angel in the face to wake him up. Then takes out Angel's cock and rubs it in his face.

"Remember me?" Noam says. But Angel doesn't recognize him.

Angel taunts him, "What you gonna do bitch!"

Noam replies, "Suck it! Put the whole thing down your throat."

"What the fuck, homie!" Angel reacts, confounded.

“If you want to live you have no other choice. Just think of all the poor girls who had to suck that disgusting thing!” Noam gives him an ultimatum.

Angel then recognizes Noam, “I remember you, bitch! You were that nerdy white boy who couldn’t get laid. I was banging every hot white chick in high school. Those blonde Jewish bitches gave the best head! I bet you graduated a virgin!”

Noam then puts a knife to his throat and forces him to suck his own chopped off dick, pushing it down his throat causing him to gag.

Afterwards, he sticks it in the toilet where someone took a massive dump and flushes it down, but it’s clogged and the toilet overflows.

Angel cries out pathetically, “My dick!”

Noam leaves him there to bleed to death, “Say hello to all the Chads in hell. Tell them Noam sent you!”

Noam continues to go to clubs in New York to pick up sluts, but instead of sleeping with them he ties them up and performs rituals on them using his frog statue.

The rituals are intended to deny them of all their sexual desires for Chads, all the sexual energy from the nerve endings from their clits consumed by the power of the great mysterious amphibian.

Noam doesn’t know anything about the history of the statue but it is able to understand and implement all his deepest and darkest desires.

He remembers Moosh saying it was cursed. He wonders if it is some kind of trick like in the movies where you sell your soul to the devil in exchange for powers without knowing.

He tells himself, “Don’t think about silly movie stuff. I have already been to the darkest corners of hell and back and survived the torments of demons. I am the one great mortal to escape and now I am on a journey to paradise to retrieve my one true love, and nothing shall stand in my way!”

While Noam is in his hotel room staring at his vast collection of testicles he gets a call from his old friend, Carlos de la Boca. Startled, he drops the jar of testicles, spilling them all over the floor and soiling his brand new Italian loafers.

Noam was able to steal the virility of the Chads through the act of castration and collecting their testicles but for a second now he feels vulnerable again, seeing all the testicles spilled out on the floor. However he takes great pride in knowing that he has got his revenge, turned his tormentors into eunuchs, and now it is time to set out on his quest to find his crush.

Noam takes the phone to talk to Carlos, who is now a major Hollywood producer. He explains to Noam that owing to the cult following of his manifesto, the director Ari Meschel wants to turn it into a high-budget production, all of which will be filmed on location at Blackstone’s Vapor Island.

Noam is skeptical at first because he views Hollywood as beneath him but sees it as an opportunity to implement his manifesto into reality and finally get the chance to go to Vapor Island to find his crush.

Carlos explains to Noam that Vapor Island is a very exclusive location, not accessible to the public like any other tourist destination. Therefore one must get special permission.

Noam knows the island was created for his greatness ever since he was a young boy and had visions of it in his dreams.

Later that day a limo picks up Noam in front of the Vapor Love Hotel in Times Square to take him off to the airport.

Carlos's British assistant, Harry, is in the limo to explain to him the situation. As they drive off, Harry (who is an eccentric tall skinny bald man with a flamboyant flair) talks about how much he admires Noam's work. As Harry continues to rant, Noam blanks out, daydreaming about holding hands with his crush on a tropical beach.

Noam and Harry get out of the limo and walk up onto the private jet with the Vapor Inc. logo. As they take off, Noam takes one last glance, admiring the New York skyline at sunset that his grandfather Saul helped Blackstone transform. He can't wait to see what Blackstone did with Vapor Island.

Noam looks down and notices that large chunks of Long Island have been submerged by rising sea levels. Harry jokes, "Maybe we should have listened to Al Gore."

The pilot replies, "He did have good taste in jets. I was his pilot."

A map on the airplane shows the island is located directly east of the Carolinas. "The Island is right outside the Bermuda triangle and enjoys a superb subtropical climate," the pilot remarks.

As they approach the Island, it appears to be a giant magical star floating in the night sky, made of elements of pink, purple, turquoise, and golden light. As they move in closer to the island they can make out it's a landform.

Noam looks out the window and admires the glistening, colorful skyline of the island. He has finally arrived in his electric paradise.

When they get off the plane, a DeLorean is there waiting to escort them to the tower to meet with Carlos.

Harry hears a ring on his giant cell phone. He picks up, "Hello there, Carlos. I am here with Noam. Yes. Ok Sir. I see. Yes? You are busy, sir? Very important business? Ha Ha. Noam is ready for you, sir. Ok. I see. Talk to you then."

Harry turns to Noam, "Well Carlos is busy. Probably up to his usual antics. We can give you a brief tour of the island if you desire."

"Yes, I would like that," Noam replies.

From the landing strip of the airport, Noam can see the skyline across the bay. He admires the uniform color pattern of the skyline: black glass with gold, turquoise, pink, and purple neon.

There is a giant black, gold, and pink, neon pyramid, and the tallest tower which resembles the shape of the empire state building.

Harry says, "Oh yes, that is simply known as the tower. That's where we are headed to meet with Carlos."

Noam takes in all the details of the aesthetics of the island; like rediscovering remnants from a dream.

Harry explains that "The Island has several main quarters. Outside the main city, there are private palaces, private beaches, and a tropical rain forest. Blackstone has preserved many species that are now extinct in their native habitats, and there is plentiful tight young untouched teen pussy. Anything in your wildest desires."

They drive across the bridge from the airport to the main island's waterfront, which is bustling with night life and lined with high rises and giant animated golden neon palm trees which shoot off beams of golden light like fireworks.

Noam was expecting the usual drunken loudmouths with their skanky girlfriends, but as the DeLorean slows down for the foot traffic he gets a glimpse of the people.

They aren't the trashy people whom Noam would see on his summer trips to Florida and the Jersey Shore. There are young, aristocratic-looking girls in luxurious gowns holding hands with true aristocrats like him, not disgusting filth.

Noam thinks, "The right fashion sense, the finest custom-made suits, perfect gentlemen who would never engage in acts of debauchery. I have arrived!"

Harry turns to Noam, "Ah, enjoying the eye candy. You are going to enjoy yourself here. You're a star! The ladies will love you!"

Noam looks to Harry and grins awkwardly. No one had ever said that to him in is his entire life. He was always told growing up to study hard, get good grades, be nice to people, treat everyone as an equal, and one day he would find a sweet girl who would appreciate him for the gentleman he is.

Then after years of rejection and abuse from the Chads, and later the prison staff, he finally realized that the world in which he lived in was just a mere illusion, and that there was a great utopia out there waiting for him to rule over.

They turn away from the waterfront up the main boulevard, which is lined with Parisian-style lamp posts, wide pedestrian walkways, palm trees, and a cityscape of black glass with animated gold, pink, and purple neon; the Blackstone color pallet.

They drive by the massive Blackstone Galleria which is all black glass, covered in the same neon color pallet, but as they drive closer, Noam notices a gilded glass atrium, golden statues and lamp posts.

Harry says, "Oh yes, the Galleria. It was inspired by the Galleria Vittorio Emanuele in Milan. Anything you can think of is there. Maybe if you're a naughty lad, Carlos will get you into the Erotic Emporium, but I shall warn you: It's not for the faint of heart."

Suddenly, a group of the most beautiful teenage girls walk up from the Galleria blocking the roadway, running over to the DeLorean. They start screeching "Noam!" Throwing their lacy panties at him shouting, "We love you, Noam!" as if he were an A list celebrity, the one true aristocrat.

They proceed to pull up their skirts, showing off their unshaven twats, screaming, "Eat our pussies, Noam! Let's have a cunnilingus party!"

Harry smirks, "Your manifesto has had quite an impact, Noam. Cunnilingus parties are now the it teen girl fad, and the bush is back in style, too. Feel a bit sorry for all the young lads with hair stuck in their teeth. My nephew is always complaining about his sore neck, his tongue so stiff he can barely even speak, but that's the price of fitting in with the popular girls. But for me I could never quite understand the appeal of the female anatomy."

The chauffeur jokes, "Yeah, he's into hot dogs, won't eat pizza if his life depended on it."

"Shut the fuck up or I shall have you banished form the Island!" Harry says.

Harry turns to Noam and explains, "The cars are all self-driving. A chauffeur is merely a status symbol, no real practical purpose. It's the same as people in your time riding horse-drawn carriages in Central Park."

They approach the tower, which is the tallest structure on the Island. It was modeled after the shape of the Empire State Building but with black glass, pink and purple neon, a golden crown spire, and a giant pink neon retro clock on the top. Much like many of the buildings Blackstone built in New York but on a much grander scale.

As they drive into the tower's roundabout, Harry proclaims, "The Blackstone aesthetic is quite intriguing. Aristocratic in the sense that it looks to the future yet pays homage to the past. Every great American city, starting in Las Vegas and from then on New York to San Francisco now has the Blackstone touch. Some say it's a tad gaudy, I say it's fab!"

Harry escorts Noam out of the DeLorean. The roundabout is lined with Roman columns with golden neon tulip crests on the top, and in the middle there is a giant fountain with a golden Neptune statue in front of a giant marble seashell, and seahorses squirting out water which turns different colors. Noam thinks, "Las Vegas, but for true aristocrats!"

Noam looks up from the base of the tower and admires its height and exquisite aesthetic. He notices there are golden motifs up and down the tower, and glass tube elevator shafts.

"An orgy of architectural genres," Noam thinks as he tries hard to hold in his erection. He has never seen something so magnificent in his entire life.

The entrance is all gold with details of ancient Egyptian icons and glass sliding doors. Up above a sign reads "Blackstone" in gold over the black glass, with two gold Art Deco Egyptian frog statues holding up a pink neon pyramid with a giant golden clock in the center.

Harry comments, "The clock was from an old department store in Paris. Blackstone bought a lot of the best antiquities from Europe, right before the great war."

They walk through the sliding doors into the massive atrium which has a glass dome with gilded beams, and geometric slabs of marble, waterfalls spouting out of golden statue heads into a giant lake surrounded by tropical gardens filled with pretty teens swimming naked.

Noam thinks that they don't look like the sluts he went to high school with, but rather like they had stepped out of an old master's painting.

Noam notices there is a glass tunnel that goes underneath the lake. He so wants to walk underneath it and admire the young teens swimming up above but Harry tells him that they will have plenty of time for that, and they have to meet with Carlos.

They step into one of the glass tube elevators, which have golden crowns with light bulbs and pink neon lights on the side. It has been reserved specially for him.

Once the elevator leaves the massive atrium, Noam admires the view of the lake, which reminds him of something out of a Hieronymus Bosch painting, with giant perfume bottle sculptures made from the finest crystal.

Then the elevator goes under a light colored waterfall and for a second Noam sees the image of his crush reflected in the water. The image that was frozen in his dreams is for this very second crystal clear right in front of him, like she is there with him sharing a special moment.

Harry looks at Noam, staring out with a look of longing. He explains, "The waters on the island reflect your deepest desires. Some have gone insane. Must be something about the electrical static patterns coming in from the Bermuda Triangle or perhaps it's just all the DMT Blackstone did."

Then they leave the atrium into a dark elevator shaft that leads to the outside view.

Noam admires the views across the city, where he can see the glistening colors of the skyline at night and the giant mysterious pyramid.

Once the elevator reaches the top, they enter the private penthouse lobby. It has gilded, vaulted ceilings with crystal chandeliers hanging from it, black marble floors and walls, Art Deco lamps, and gilded rococo mirrors.

There are giant portraits of Roger and Alistair Blackstone and their ancestors dating back to the 17th century. It is how Noam imagined the penthouse of his father's chateau in France but with a futuristic twist.

Noam looks out the window to admire the skyline. He remembers that dream he had as a boy where he looked out of his apartment window onto his utopian city, his crush by his side while he ruled over his fiefdom.

At the end of the hallway there is a giant gilded door with Egyptian iconography, a pink neon pyramid above it, and a golden clock in the middle, much like the entrance of the tower.

Harry opens the door, and they enter the rotunda which reminds Noam of many of the penthouse banquet halls of the old hotels his grandfather use to take him to in New York as a boy.

It has a fountain in the middle, a classical synthwave quartet, and there are many aristocrats sitting on the luxurious furnishings discussing art and philosophy. They all get up to pay homage to Noam.

From the rotunda they enter Carlos's office waiting room, which has glass brick and pink walls, a different aesthetic from the rest of the penthouse, much more Hollywood then aristocratic.

Noam looks around and sees pictures of Carlos posing with many famous actors, especially young male ones.

Carlos's assistant, who is a pretty young woman in a purple silk gown, tells them that Carlos will be with them shortly and offers them a drink.

Harry takes a gin and tonic and Noam demands a cup of Lady Grey tea in their finest china.

While sipping his tea Noam notices an old Art Deco Saturn lamp in the waiting room. He remembers his grandfather Saul having one in his study and was always fascinated with it as a boy. He asked his grandfather about the lamp and was told that it was a gift from a very important contact, but he would not disclose the name. He explained to Noam that one day Saturn and Jupiter would align, and it would change the entire course of history and Noam's life.

Noam always dismissed it as a silly story, but right before the massacre his grandfather came to him in a dream and warned him that he must wait for Saturn and Jupiter to align.

That night of the massacre Noam looked out into the night sky but did not notice Saturn or Jupiter, nor any great planets to usher in his great aristocratic reign, but he did what he had to do to save his crush and would often think he was being punished for not waiting for the sign.

Harry notices Noam staring at the lamp and tells him, "Get yourself together. Carlos is almost ready and you must be at your utmost preparation to make your case.'

Noam is annoyed that Harry is questioning his authority and restless after waiting for over an hour and barges into Carlos's office.

Instead of Carlos, there is a handsome young male actor, barely 18, sitting at the producer's chair naked with a weird expression on his face.

Carlos gets up from underneath the table with cum on his lips. Noam tries hard to keep a straight face. Carlos jokes, "These are the perks of the industry," and orders the young actor to leave.

Carlos is now overweight and balding, wearing a white suit, pink shirt, and a golden chain that is submerged in his hairy chest.

"Long time, old friend," Carlos says. He puts out his hand for Noam to shake, but Noam politely refuses.

"Let's cut to the chase, Carlos," Noam says.

"Relax," Carlos says. "You've had a long journey to Vapor Island. You should enjoy yourself." He offers Noam cocaine, but he refuses. Carlos is slightly offended.

Carlos explains again that the director Ari Meschel wants to make Noam's manifesto into a movie, owing to its cult following.

Harry jokes, "There is profit in despair. Sir Noam here has quite brilliantly managed to capitalize on the comic value of misery and death!"

Carlos tells him to shut up and get out.

Carlos explains that tomorrow they will meet with Meschel at his palace, and they will go over the details of the film. Carlos says that Meschel wants to reach a broader audience.

Noam responds, “What do you mean broader? Normies? Chads? Superficial little cunts? Consumption for the worthless masses?”

Carlos bursts out laughing, “Look Noam, you’re a genius, but you don’t get the industry. Meschel has great visions, and I’m sure you will be pleased by the results.”

Noam explains that he does not want anything in his manifesto changed. Carlos reassures him disingenuously.

After Noam is done with Carlos, Harry escorts him to his own private palatial suite in the tower, which is even grander than the one he stayed at in the Vapor Love Hotel.

The next day, Harry escorts Noam to meet with the director, Ari Meschel. Noam recognizes the name. When Noam was a kid, Meschel was known for making cheesy teen soap operas. The kind of stuff where the sweet innocent virginal teen girl would fall for the disgusting degenerate Chad, and she would accept him for his wicked ways thinking he had changed, that he wants romance and true love, while rejecting the nice quiet intellectual who was there waiting for her all along.

Noam thinks, “I doubt Meschel was ever a Chad. He was probably a fat dweeb growing up who was tormented by them. Is he just another sellout putting out rubbish for a quick profit, or is he using them to get back at the true aristocrats like me? Brainwashing vulnerable young girls into being concubines for the Chads. That is history’s greatest conundrum; economic profit vs. the sexual domination of the Chad? I shall be the first to break the cycle.”

Noam remembers that all the hot popular girls who rejected him in high school were fans of Meschel's work and Noam felt personally wronged by him. He doesn't trust Meschel one bit. No, he despises him, and is appalled that he is even allowed on an island built for true aristocrats, but he has no choice but to meet with him if he wants to get his manifesto implemented and re-unite with his crush.

The DeLorean picks up Noam and Harry in front of the Tower and takes them off to Meschel's Palace. As they drive along the palm lined coast, Noam can see the beaches are packed with young teens just like in the commercial where he saw his crush.

Noam thinks, "Is she out there somewhere playing in the waves or lying in the sun waiting for me?

They approach the massive pyramid through a glass tunnel filled with bright lights. Noam looks down and notices a giant gorge filled with tropical vegetation, the ground level flat as if a giant meteor hit it, filled with lakes, jungles, and ancient ruins.

He looks up and notices the sunlight coming in through the giant glass pyramid. There are glass spaceship-like structures perched up on the cliffs. Then the glass tube goes through a waterfall and into a lush tropical garden. There are grounds filled with flamingos and Roman statues.

They drive up to the front of the palace which has a Roman theme. Everything is marble with pink neon along the columns and ceilings. The marble floors are all white and pink checkerboard, and the vintage sound of Macintosh Plus echo in the halls.

Meschel's assistant greets them and says, "Meschel is busy at the moment, but you will all get a chance to meet him at the party tonight. Feel free to enjoy the palace for the day."

Noam walks around the palace admiring the ancient antiquities. He hears the faint sound of giggling, a sound so familiar yet distant after years of isolation and despair. He has to find out where it is coming from.

A butler approaches Noam and warns him, "I'd advise you to not go wandering off around these parts."

Noam ignores the man and wanders down a long spiral staircase. The man blurts out, "Do so at your own peril."

Noam again hears the sound of giggling echoing from down the stairwell. He continues to chase the noise down the stairs.

He looks up and cannot even see the top level. He thinks, "I know it! I can't leave unless I find her!"

Noam gets to the bottom of the stairwell and continues to explore the many corridors.

After a while, everything is dark and Noam can hardly see where he is going. Not knowing where to turn, he runs into a wall, turning on a switch which illuminates an animated neon grid pattern on the floors.

He just follows the motion of the animated neon grid, but then they reverse and lead him back where he was before.

Noam thinks it is all part of some live-action roleplaying game, but after several hours of exploring the many rooms and corridors, he finds himself lost in a massive labyrinth.

He eventually is unable to find his way back to the main part of the palace. He hasn't noticed a single person on his entire journey.

After a while, the animated neon grid starts stretching out further and further and he feels smaller and smaller. He tries to walk, but just feels like he is walking in place on a treadmill.

Instead of the giggling of his crush he can hear the sadistic laughter of the Chads echo in the distance, mocking him from beyond the grave.

Noam starts to freak out, “Is this really about my crush or is she just being used as a honey pot to lure me in, entrap me, and kill me before I can stage my revolution. Maybe she isn’t even out there after all, and this is the end?”

Then he feels a jolt of electricity and the floors stop stretching out. He walks through crimson velvet drapes which lead to a rotunda which has red and white checkered floors and is filled with bright light, a Roman bust, and a ceiling painted with a fresco of a sky at sunset.

It reminds him of the setting of his dream where his grandfather came to him right before the great massacre.

He looks up at the fresco and sees naked teenage girls floating in the clouds like angels. One of them is his crush. He isn’t quite sure if it’s a sign or all part of some elaborate scheme.

Suddenly the sky turns dark. Perhaps a power outage. But then he looks up and sees the stars. He sees the planets Saturn and Jupiter in the distance slowly moving towards each other.

Then the moon floats into the night sky lighting up the rotunda. Once Saturn and Jupiter align to their rightful place, everything blacks out.

He can a sense a strange vibe that brings back dark memories of the past, the musky scent of death, feelings of lost love, and separation from the entire human race.

Noam remembers his grandfather telling him stories that he read from an old occultist text that once the alignment occurs it will usher in either great lightness or darkness, depending on whether one is without fear.

Noam is on a journey to find his crush and establish true aristocratic order, but he is also scared and confused. He is trapped alone in the darkness thinking about whether he is spiritually prepared for the great alignment of the two great planets. He wonders if he will trap in the darkness for all eternity.

He tries hard to gather together enough strength. He thinks about all his victories, and times when he lacked fear and anxiety when dealing with his adversaries.

He remembers the frog statue that he took from Moosh, which gave him great power and that he had kept in his pocket but forgot about.

He takes out the statue and feels his strength return.

Then he feels the floor start to stretch downwards like an elevator.

When they stop stretching Noam reaches a long corridor lit with dim purple light. He walks down the strange corridor, which continues to become darker and narrower.

He continues walking down the long dark corridor and can see an eerie, dimmed blue fluorescent light in the distance.

At the very end of the corridor, he walks underneath an entrance covered by a pyramid leading to a bizarre shrine. There is an Egyptian frog god statue surrounded by statues of dead bodies, illuminated in the blue light like human sacrifices to a pagan god.

There is a pile of decapitated heads lying on the floor, a headless boy grabbing his genitals, and another headless boy receiving fellatio. Then he realizes all the statues are based on scenes from the night of the great massacre. He sees a statue of himself, victorious, holding up the head of the decapitated Chad as a trophy.

Then he sees the statue of his crush lying on the ground naked in tears, her facial expressions perfectly captured in time, an image frozen from that night. He had thought and dreamed about her every single night when he was alone in his dark cold prison cell.

He wonders if she was with him in his dreams, "Does time even exist in the dream world? My crush, still young, a virgin, yet I am a grown man who has grown stronger. Am I now worthy of her purity? Is time the adversary of true justice?"

Noam looks over the statues of the corpses of his decapitated enemies and himself as a great young warrior king and isn't quite sure what to make of this, "Are they worshiping me as a god or playing some cruel trick on me? Either way, I know that this alternative universe is dedicated to my existence, and I have to find out who the supreme being is who created all this just for me!"

Noam gets down on his knees to pay his respect to his crush and her chastity. He thinks about that fateful night that determined the fate of both him and his crush, as well as all of mankind. He sheds a tear; a tear of despair over being separated from his crush for years in hell, and a sweet tear of vengeance for those who sought to desecrate pure beauty and innocence.

He walks past the sculptures and notices a bright opening. Bright light pours into the dark labyrinth he was trapped in. As he walks out through the light, he can feel the aura of his crush.

He ends up outside by the sea at sunset. He looks out at the water imagining his crush is out there somewhere, floating on a seashell, playing a magical harp, singing songs of pure love, only for him.

He cannot tell whether he is indoors or outdoors by the sea. It is another world, the water still and eerie. There is bright turquoise light illuminating from underneath the water, like a giant indoor swimming pool.

He looks out and admires the giant moon, and can see the planet Saturn right next to it in the pink and orange sky. He wonders if the great alignment has already occurred and he has entered paradise.

He listens to the sound of the waves crashing against the shore and the seagulls and dolphins in the distance. The smell of the sweetest perfume in the air and the sound of classical synthwave music permeates the atmosphere. It is just like in that commercial for Vapor Island.

Then he notices a group of young blond teens swimming naked. He smiles at them and admires their perfect bodies.

As he is admiring the teens he sees a girl swimming with golden blond hair from behind. She turns around and there she is. After years of separation he sees her, his crush, his one true love, swimming naked, smiling, an innocent sweet smile of a virgin, not defiled by the Chads. Her perfect dimpled smile, golden-blonde hair, and perfect skin.

He is so in love with her and enjoying the moment that he doesn't even need to stare at her buttocks and bush. It is as if she were an angel, not a lowly human female.

He feels pure love, innocence, and beauty. Sharing a special moment in a magical setting that he had dreamed about for so long. There is no fornication, ugliness, nor debauchery. Just the two of them in paradise together forever.

She quickly glances towards Noam. Their eyes meet touching his soul after years of separation. She motions with her smile to come to her.

Just as Noam is about to jump in the water Carlos sneaks up from behind smacking him on the buttocks, ruining his magical experience and one chance to reunite with his crush.

Noam sighs, thinking, "Too good to be true. No, dammit! I will find her. I saw her out there and I will hunt her down! She belongs to me. She always has and always will!"

Carlos proclaims, "Noam, we have a big gala planned for you tonight. You're the belle of the ball."

Noam finds the otherworldly setting replaced by the poolside of the palace. The pool resembling a Roman bath surrounded by columns covered in pink neon and a giant marble sea shell with seahorse fountains on the side.

Naked people are packed in the pool like sardines, while on the side there is a massive orgy with people piled up upon one another in debauched acts.

Noam can't even make out what they are doing. Just a massive blob of human flesh, with cum and pussy juices oozing out of it.

Noam could appreciate the innocence of watching the teens swim naked, but this was too much. He thinks, "I the Messiah whom this new utopia was built for? Yet they know nothing of my work. No comprehension of the true meaning of my manifesto."

Carlos pulls Noam aside and says, "Let me introduce you to Meschel."

The director Ari Meschel is an overweight bald man dressed like a Roman emperor, sitting in his golden throne. There are two naked young women chained to his throne, fanning him with palms, while other naked women are on their knees hand-feeding him grapes.

Noam notices that the throne has the Blackstone family crest on it and is appalled that it is being defiled by such debauchery.

Noam thinks, "Even though I am not a Blackstone, Blackstone built this utopia making it possible for me to implement my visions. I have a duty to protect his honor."

Meschel gives Noam a big hug and proclaims, "Noam you are the star! We are going to make a movie together. Feel free to have your way with all the young ladies here. This is it! Your manifesto in action!"

Noam says sternly, "Have you even read my manifesto?"

“I’ve looked it over,” Meschel responds. “Lots of hot teen girl action. One massive orgy. I’ve recreated it all for you. Aren’t you pleased?”

Noam is disgusted. He thinks, “This fat pig doesn’t understand the true meaning of my manifesto, nor has he even bothered to read it.” He stands there giving Meschel a stern look.

Carlos interrupts the awkward situation and says, “Noam, tell Meschel about your shower experience.”

Noam replies awkwardly, “My shower experience?”

Meschel burst out laughing, “What? Was the boy ass raped in prison? No wonder he’s so stiff.”

Carlos responds, “Even better! When he was in high school all the cute blond popular boys gave him a golden shower. They even made him gargle their piss.”

“Love it!” Meschel responds. “This can appeal to the gay demographic. Lots of old fags want to see young twink pissing action.”

Carlos agrees, “I certainly would. I’ll take Noam to the Golden Spa tomorrow. Maybe that will help him re-ignite his creative potential.”

As Noam stands there in rage, Meschel says, “Lighten up, Noam. We’re all here to have a good time and pull in the dough. We’re going to break box office records!”

Noam replies sarcastically, “I look forward to working with you, Meschel,” then grabs Carlos’s margarita and gulps it all down at once.

Noam continues to walk around the palace tipsy and disoriented. Unlike his previous quest through the palace where he didn't see a single soul, the debauchery is on in full force. Noam walks around the long corridors stumbling over naked people fornicating.

He tries to find the corridor that led him to his crush but is stuck in a maze of pink walls and now with the full effects of the margarita he gulped down everything is a blur.

Like a puzzle box where there are many palaces within a palace, corridors are constantly in motion leading to new locales, making it impossible to trace one's steps.

Noam can hear his crush's faint voice in the distance, "Noam, save me."

He knows she is out there somewhere but everything is a blur of bright colors, and he cannot find his way around. Perhaps Carlos spiked the drink.

Noam trips and stumbles through the crimson velvet drapes into another room; a massive palatial suite. Everything is clear again, but he still feels a bit dizzy from the drink.

He looks up and sees a group of young handsome teenage blond guys dressed in togas lying around on luxurious sofas drinking beer from golden cups as if they were young kings. Just like the Chads he went to school with but better looking and more sinister.

Noam has a gut feeling to get the hell out, but he is intrigued.

He stands there in awe of their Adonis chests, golden-blond hair, and cute boyish looks, but they don't even bother to notice his presence.

Despite their appearance of young princes, their talk is identical to that of the Chads. They are talking about their lacrosse victory and how the entire freshman class gave them all head after the game.

One of them says, "I'm sick of all these teenage bitches. I want to fuck a real woman."

Noam is furious. He never had the experience of enjoying a sweet, young, fresh, innocent teen girl and these pricks are taking them for granted. He wants to kill them.

Noam almost explodes in a violent rage but knocks over a statue making a load bang on the marble floor.

The young men finally notice his presence. They look down at him as if he were a piece of dirt on the floor.

One of them asks, "Who the hell are you, creep?"

Noam looks up and sees their Adonis chests hovering over him and their cruel faces staring down. Their togas, which barely cover up their pricks offer a glimpse of their pubes below their perfectly toned stomachs. This is high school all over again.

The young man asks again, "Who the hell are you, and what are you doing in our palace?"

"Your palace? Ha! I am a great aristocrat, the emperor of this palace. Now if you may, I have to get on with my imperial duties. Ruling over an empire isn't easy work, but what do you brats know about aristocracy?"

Just as Noam is about to get up to leave, Harry walks in. He is surprised to see Noam but pretends not to notice him.

Harry says, "Well lads, what will it be this time?"

One of the young men shouts at Harry, "You're late, bitch."

Harry replies, "Please accept my sincerest apologies. I am here at your service, lads."

One of them orders Harry to get down on his knees and then bitch slaps him.

Another young man starts doing a humping motion towards Harry's face. Then his toga falls apart and his dick is exposed right in his face.

He shouts out, "Faggot tried to stare at my dick. Sick freak!"

"I'm so sorry, my deepest apologies," Harry grovels.

"If he likes it so much why doesn't he give it a little kiss?" the other young man replies.

Harry nervously replies, "Well I don't think that is quite appropriate behavior for young lads."

They all start drunkenly chanting, "Kiss the dick! Kiss the dick!"

The young man continues to make the grinding motion towards Harry's face with his toga open and exposed semi-erect dick wiggling in the air. Noam's is now hiding behind the curtains finding the whole scenario quite arousing.

Just as Harry is about to kiss the young man's dick, he bitch slaps him and calls him a faggot and then says, "This old faggot tried to molest me. I'm going to tell Meschel on him!"

Harry nervously says, "That won't be necessary. I can bring you any lady in the palace."

"Fuck yeah, bitch," the young man brags. "We're gonna get laid!"

Harry leaves, and Noam continues to hide behind the red curtains spying on the young men who are now lying on the sofa, some with their erect dicks out waiting service, while continuing to guzzle down their beer.

Harry returns, announcing, "Gentleman, your lady has arrived. Enjoy yourself lads."

She is a famous actress whom Noam recognizes as a teen pop star from when he was in high school. She is a bit older now but still hot. She is brought in tied up by the security robots. She looks terrified.

Harry unties her and leaves her alone with the young men while Noam is still hiding out behind the curtains.

She is on her knees, sobbing and terrified. Noam thought she was cute in high school and remembers her giving off a sweet innocent vibe and is saddened to see another once-innocent teen girl turned into another whore.

One of the young men says, "Let's get our dicks sucked."

The other replies, "We can get our dicks sucked anytime by some teenage bitch. We need to take it to the next level, bro."

One of the young men shouts out, “How about a blowbang?”

The other agrees, “Yeah, let’s fuck this bitch’s throat, make her gag and then cum on her face!”

She continues to sob while they laugh sadistically.

While the woman is on her knees, and the young men are all lined up with their dicks out, they hear a rustling noise behind the curtains.

One of them asks, “Who’s that?”

“It’s probably just a rat,” another replies.

“No I think that sick freak is spying on us,” another says.

They open the curtain and catch Noam curled up in a ball. They order him to get up and notice his massive erection.

The woman screams, “Help me!”

The young men turn to Noam, “Looks like this sick freak has a thing for boys. Let’s teach the faggot a lesson.”

The leader of the young men, who is the lacrosse captain, says, “I am sick of all this shit! Every night after a big game we get some teenage bitch to suck us all off. Yeah getting your dick sucked is fine and all but we are not boys anymore. We are men dammit! Kings on our very own Island and we found this little trespasser, this bitch who dares to enter our kingdom!”

Noam is enraged. He had dedicated his entire life to establishing his aristocratic credentials and now some high school brats are stealing that from him in his very own utopia.

The young man continues, “But I didn’t say we can’t have fun, too. There is no point in being a king if one can’t have his way with the ladies.”

The actress, in tears, turns to Noam and screams, “Get out!”

One of the young men smacks her in the face, and the other turns to Noam and says, “I think he’s that creepy writer that’s working with Meschel. Let’s teach the bitch a lesson.”

Noam turns to them and says, “I am a great aristocrat. You should be worshiping me as my slaves.”

They all start laughing.

One of them grabs Noam from behind, retraining him while the rest rush up. He can feel their hard dicks rub against his back.

Noam was able to capture, castrate, and kill so many muscular and powerful grown men, but the sense of humiliation by these teens brings back memories of the humiliation he had endured in high school.

They then proceed to hold him to the ground, pin him down, with one each holding down his arms and legs, and another sitting on his chest.

They tie one of his hands to a statue and the other to a chair with rope.

Noam gets a massive erection.

One of the young men smirks, “Looks like the faggot is enjoying it.”

Then he takes off his toga and stands straddling over Noam, wiggling his dick in front of Noam's face teasing him.

Noam looks up at the young man and remembers the feeling of being on the floor of the Chadsworth shower. He feels the cold hard marble floor on his back, and can smell the distinct odor of Chads while looking up at the young man, who has now worked up quite a sweat.

Noam tries not to make eye contact with him but looks down and sees his big dick wiggling right in front on him.

Despite having golden-blond hair, he has dark pubes; that and the pale skin from his tan line make his dick pop out even more.

He pulls back his foreskin taunting Noam with his dick then says, "I'll have fellatio!"

He thinks, "School shower all over again? Come on, I can't suck another dick."

He points to the woman and orders, "Fellatio." Noam is confused.

Then he turns around and sits down on Noam's face, his smooth ass smothering him. Smooth like a teen girl's ass but with toned muscles.

He moves to get in a comfortable position, Noam's nose now in his ass while his hairy testicles rest over his mouth.

Noam's thinks, "Teenage balls on a grown man's face. What a disgraceful act!"

The woman sucks him off while he continues to sit on Noam's face, then cums on Noam's chest while the woman licks his shaft.

After he cums, he lets his dick hang over Noam's chin, droplets of cum drooping down onto Noam's hairy chest.

When Noam gets up, he realizes his face is drenched in butt sweat.

Then the young men pull down Noam's pants to reveal pre-cum oozing out of his cock.

The young man laughs, "Filthy faggot!"

Another one of them just rubs his dick and balls all over Noam's face and orders him to sniff his sweaty balls.

He proclaims that his dad bought him tickets to the island for a lacrosse victory at Chadsworth and hadn't washed his balls since the big game.

"Pervert here isn't worthy of your magic balls," the other young man says.

He gets up and says, "Yeah, fuck that faggot. I'm gonna find a hot bitch to lick these balls clean."

He sits down on Noam's face and orders the actress to suck his dick and balls, while he bounces up and down on Noam's face.

Noam can feel the muscles of his buttocks clench around his face, rhythmic motion with every suck. His sweaty ass crushing his face while his hairy musky-smelling sweaty balls sit right on his mouth.

He can now feel his dick contract, about to explode.

Noam opens his mouth to breathe but accidentally licks the young man's testicles.

The young man assumes it's the woman licking his balls and screams "Yeah bitch, lick them clean!"

The woman backs away from the smell of his balls.

The young man in anger sits down hard on Noam's face, suffocating him.

Noam sticks out his tongue to breath, but his tongue is trapped underneath his balls. The taste and smell brings back memories of the stench of the locker room at Chadsworth.

Noam can't pull in his tongue or he will suffocate under the sweaty ass. He licks back and forth from his perineum to the underside of his balls.

He imagines he is instead eating out a girl's vagina. He thinks, "Yes! Smooth youthful skin like a girl."

Noam closes his eyes and imagines his crush is sitting on his face. He continues licking, starting with fast flicks then long slow circular motions.

The young man, who is now in ecstasy and not paying attention to Noam, assumes it is the woman's tongue. He gets up soaking in sweat like he's just got done working out. Then he looks at Noam with disgust.

Noam realizes he has a pubic hair stuck in his teeth.

The young man gets pissed off, realizing it wasn't the woman, "Ewww you fuckin' creep! My dad can have you killed."

Noam thinks, "Fuck that little punk! I am the victim here. I was raped and forced to imagine I was pleasuring my crush. I had no other choice. I will have that little bitch killed as soon as I get things sorted out with Carlos."

The next young man is the tallest and strongest of the group but still has a boyish look.

Noam looks up and admires his golden-blond hair, toned muscles, Adonis chest, dark pubes, and big dick. Like a better looking more sinister version of Nick who tormented him in high school

He smacks Noam across the face, "Yeah, take that you filthy faggot!"

Noam is humiliated that the young man is nearly half his age yet is so much stronger and more powerful.

"I want my throne cleaned before I shall sit. It stinks of sweaty balls," he commands.

He orders the woman to clean Noam up with her tongue.

Her tongue is sticky from the goo, but she has a gift. She licks clean every single spot on his face and then licks the cum off Noam's hairy chest.

She gives Noam a look of lust, like she is pleasuring him and not just cleaning him up for further use.

Then a tear comes from her eye, and she gets up.

Noam viewed her as a cheap whore, but at this moment he feels a tad bit of pity for her.

He thinks, "I have endured great humiliation but maybe there was a miscommunication. Many great Roman emperors engaged in the fine art of pederasty. Perhaps Carlos ordered them for my pleasure assuming I was of his ilk. But no! I am still in control here, dammit! Still the emperor! But her? What a pitiful little creature. She has no free will or control over her destiny. Teen dick is nice for an old perv like Carlos, but it will destroy a lady and make her worthless."

She looks at Noam with admiration, causing the young men to notice and get angry.

One young man shouts, "He doesn't deserve the pleasure of a women's tongue. He has to suffer."

Another young man says, "If the old sicko enjoys it so much, let's make the faggot drink all our cum."

"Smart thinking," the captain agrees, then orders the woman to place a golden bowl on Noam's chest. It is heavy and uncomfortable.

He sits down on Noam's face and violently and grabs the woman's face to his crotch, while he simultaneously fucks the woman's face, clenching his buttocks over Noam's head.

With every suck, he grunts in ecstasy while simultaneously fucking the woman's mouth and humping Noam's face. Noam is no longer able to breathe and opens his mouth, but the young man continues to clench his buttock muscles tighter.

He is drenched in sweat, dripping down his chest and back, onto Noam's face, while the sweat from his buttocks and balls have completely drenched Noam's face.

Noam sticks his tongue out gasping for air but accidentally tickles the young man's anus. While the guy thinks he will get beaten up for being a fag, he feels his giant balls swell up and he continues to sit harder on his face.

Noam continues gasping for air, sticking out his tongue, unintentionally tickling his anus. Noam doesn't want to have to lick an anus and can't think of a more degrading act, but he now has his tongue out licking the insides of his sweaty butt cheeks. Sweat dripping down into his mouth.

Noam closes his mouth and swallows the sweat, but then he clenches tighter, forcing Noam's tongue out again.

He starts to lick around the circle of his anus causing the young man to grunt and contract harder.

Noam backs away, but the young man clenches harder forcing Noam to do the most humiliating thing he could possibly think of and lick his anus in fast circular motions.

It doesn't taste as bad as he thought it would, more of a musky, sweaty taste, kind of how he imagines a teen girl's sweaty buttocks tasting. But the shame he feels is far worse than any of the physical torment.

When the young man cums he just sits down hard, both his dick and buttocks muscles contracting while he grunts in ecstasy, Noam's tongue still stuck underneath his sweaty butt cheeks.

He then moves back and presses his giant dick down over Noam's mouth to cum a second time into the bowl.

Noam can feel the cum moving through his hard dick and envies him for being able to cum twice in a row.

Noam remembers being a teenager and being able to cum multiple times in a row and deeply regrets wasting his sexual peak.

The young man gets up, accidentally rubbing his big cock over Noam's face, droplets of cum oozing out. Noam wonders whether if he were to taste a droplet he would be able to capture his virility but decides not to expose his weakness to his captors.

He looks at Noam in disgust, calls him a faggot, and then spits on his face.

The next young man sits down, gets his dick sucked then pisses in the bowl.

The captain laughs, "I heard this sicko wrote about dudes pissing on him in his journal."

Noam replies, "Excuse me. *My manifesto!*"

The captain mocks him, "You little bitch. You're nothing but a little emo bitch who writes whiny rants in her journal, bitch!"

The young man takes his dick and rubs the piss and cum on Noam's lips.

Then the rest of the young men surround him, forming a circle around the bowl, their dicks right in his face.

He looks at their dicks. Their dark pubes and tan lines make them pop out even more. It was as if all the dicks are there mocking him, reminding him of the humiliation he endured in the showers of Chadsworth.

He is terrified of a repeat of that humiliating incident, but they all just piss in the bowl, lightly spraying him in the face and causing the bowl to become heavier.

After they are done pissing, they wiggle the piss off their dicks, more droplets landing on Noam's face.

They then proceed to rub the piss on their dicks off on Noam's face.

Noam feels even more humiliated than the shower incident in high school. Back then he was a meek young man, but now he doesn't have an excuse.

One young man says to the woman, "I'm a gentleman. I know how to keep my dick clean. Now suck it, bitch!"

After all the young men have gotten blown, the captain declares, "How about round two? Here's the deal. If one of you is unable to cum then you must drink from the bowl, but I know you are all virile warriors, and you will all cum, and then we will make the faggot here drink up!"

Noam is horrified. These young men seem to have an insatiable appetite for humiliating him and they seem to have an unlimited supply of ejaculate.

The next round is even more intense. The first time, the young men would cum in just a few minutes, and get up but this time he is stuck with their sweaty asses and balls on his face for long sessions. Then after they are done they all take a piss in the bowl while sitting down.

Noam thinks, “I’m not a faggot! I’ve dedicated my life to one girl and one girl only. I didn’t choose this situation. I’m the victim here. They are the real sissies, sitting down to take a piss like a little bitch.”

The bowl is so full of piss and cum that the weight is now crushing his chest and he can hardly breathe.

The other young man shouts, “Now it’s time to drink up!”

They bring over the massive bowl of piss and jizz that was placed underneath the girl’s mouth while she sucked off the young men, slowly, as if it is part of a ceremony.

Noam is lying on his back, screaming. One of the young men forcibly opens Noam’s mouth with his fingers, while the other slowly proceeds to pour the liquid down his throat.

Just as the first droplet of cum is about to hit Noam’s tongue, Harry opens the doors.

He shouts, “What is going on lads? And Noam what on earth are you doing here?”

The young men drop the bowl, spilling piss and cum onto the floor and all over Noam’s chest, arms, and hands.

Harry and Noam leave the young men alone with the actress.

Harry turns to Noam and tells him, “You better be careful wandering around these parts. There is a lot of trouble to be had. Those young men’s fathers are financing the film and pull some major strings around here. I would suggest staying out of their way."

Noam is appalled. This is high school all over again where the Chads rule. He thinks, "I'm king here, dammit!"

When Harry leaves, Noam secretly licks the young man's piss and cum off his fingers while he can hear the actress's screams of pain echo down corridors of the palace.

Noam feels so humiliated. He thinks, "I, the emperor, have the sperm of these virile young men festering in my mouth. They should be tied to my bed post, licking my feet and drinking my piss! I'm king here, dammit, not Meschel, not the Chads, nor their stupid rich banker fathers. It's all about Noam Metzenbaum! The one true aristocrat! I wrote that fuckin' manifesto which this entire island is based upon, and I shall change the destiny of the entire human race. I exterminated the Chad elite dammit! And no one shall stand in my way from this moment forward!"

Walking down the corridors hyperventilating in rage and humiliation he runs into Carlos walking a young muscular man on a dog leash who is barking like a dog. Carlos notices Noam's massive erection and remarks, "You like what you see? I'm enjoying the actors but can't wait for all the fresh meat that will be on the film shoot. I'll take you to the Erotic Emporium tomorrow. Everything in your wildest fantasies!"

Noam doesn't respond. Carlos has Harry escorts Noam to his lavish suite, which has crystal chandeliers, and everything is pink.

He is unable to sleep, the sense of humiliation, the dried semen on his chest, the rage that he is not in control of his own palace, and the longing over his one true love keep him up all night in a cold sweat.

He wakes up with a massive hangover and intense anxiety and humiliation. One of Meschel's slaves comes into Noam's room, greeting him. She asks him if he's ok. He replies, "Just a little hungover from last night."

"Wild party," she replies. "Here's something to make you feel better."

She offers him a shot of a tropical fruit juice. Noam has never tasted anything like it in his entire life but feels totally rejuvenated. She notices his massive morning wood and offers him some relief, but he politely declines.

Noam gets showered and dressed and is escorted from his room by Harry to the lobby to meet with Carlos.

The three of them enter the DeLorean and drive off to the Erotic Emporium at the Galleria.

As they approach the Galleria, they drive under a giant pink neon archway which leads to a corridor lined with Roman columns and statues. Noam wonders what the location looks like at night and wants to further explore the architecture of the Galleria, but Harry explains that the entrance to the Erotic Emporium is VIP only.

Carlos jokes, "Noam, you're still such a nerd. The only architecture I'll be exploring is that of the male anatomy."

As the car drives into a tunnel, an electronic sensor detects that they are guests. Once they are validated, animated neon arrows direct the car to another entrance where they go down a secret elevator which leads out to a Roman-themed plaza and loading zone.

Noam notices several limos dropping off groups of pretty teen girls. He wonders whether they are clients or are being trafficked in as prostitutes.

They are dropped off in front and Harry carries all of Carlos's luxury bags for shopping.

Noam sees a giant Roman arch with an animated neon laurel wreath and pink neon lettering which reads, "Erotic Emporium."

At the door there is a security robot that takes everyone's ID and passport and does not return it until they leave.

Obviously, this is no regular mall open to the commoners. Noam's thinks, "Perhaps a place for true aristocrats, not the consumerist masses."

As they enter, Carlos announces, "This is a place where all your darkest secret fantasies come true."

Harry laughs, "We've read your manifesto, Noam. We know you're a naughty lad."

They enter the golden sliding doors into the Emporium. It reminds him of a trip he took to Las Vegas as a kid visiting Caesar's Palace with all the marble, gold statues, and neon.

The atmosphere is like a mall with the scent of perfume, but Noam can already sense something is peculiar about the place.

Noam looks up and sees the ceiling which is painted with a fresco of naked teens in an orgy, but Noam recognizes them as being all the teens he went to school with: the Chads, Wendy, Lisa, Molly, the cheerleaders, and even her, his crush.

Carlos proclaims that, "They cater to the most elite clientele. Any fantasy can be made a reality. We know yours, Noam. This place was built for you," Carlos smirks wickedly.

Noam is very uncomfortable. He realizes that all his darkest fantasies have been turned into some kind of Disneyland for debauched elites.

The first place they visit is called, "The Goo Goo Club." They step inside, and it is like a night club. There is a group of young blond Chads jerking off into cups and even a disco ball that squirts cum.

There are older men tied up forced to drink the cum of the Chads and a gay man (whom Noam recognizes as a pop star from when he was younger) with a group of Chads lined up to cum into his mouth. Another couple hundred show up with enough cum to fill up a swimming pool.

Noam realizes these are not slaves but rich men who pay for the experience. Part of Noam is turned on and wants to indulge, but he is able to suppress that side of himself which had created this whole mess in the first place.

Noam asks Harry how they are able to attract thousands of good-looking teens to the island. Harry explains that it was all part of Blackstone's breading program to create the new Übermensch.

Carlos replies, "I thought Blackstone was a big Nazi when I was younger but now I have an unlimited supply of young blond-man spunk. He was onto something big. I should have listened to you in the debate, Noam."

They leave and approach the next business. It is a two-story storefront with a glass wall revealing the two floors which have two Roman columns, one on either side.

He looks up and sees a large, animated, golden bulb sign in Roman-style lettering reading "Golden Spa."

On the top floor, there is a group of blond teens, even better looking than the ones he went to school with. Girls on the left, guys on the right but separated by a dividing wall. He realizes what is going on. These are their living quarters. Young teens being kept as livestock, like dairy cows that provide a golden liquid.

On the left, the girls have fancy marble toilets that resemble Roman fountains and the boys have similar urinals. There are over a hundred teens pissing and the piss can be seen through glass pipes which lead to the spa.

On the first floor clients enter the spa which resembles a Roman bath with fountain head like showers.

Carlos says, "Harry, hold my stuff. I'm going in!"

Harry helps Carlos get undressed and puts his clothing in the bags.

Carlos is wearing nothing but a speedo. Noam is repulsed by his overweight hairy body.

Carlos steps into the spa. He asks Noam to join in, but Noam remains silent.

Carlos turns on the spigot and yellow liquid sprays down over his brown hairy body. Noam is reminded of his experience in the high school shower but now that he is dominant and in charge he has to keep his honor but is struggling to hide his erection.

Carlos prances around in the shower singing and teases Noam as if he is going to flick urine on him.

Noam stands there trying to keep a straight face and a flaccid dick.

"Do you remember?" Carlos asks.

"Remember what, Carlos?" Noam replies.

"Do you remember your first blowjob?" Carlos says.

Noam assumes Carlos is talking about his oral rape by the Chads.

Carlos starts licking his lips savoring the urine. "Remember that time I got you high, and you passed out in the bathroom and woke up with moisture on your dick?" Carlos starts giving a blowjob motion on the shower spigot drinking the piss from all the teenage guys.

Noam is furious and is about to lunge out at Carlos but holds in his anger.

Noam checks out the left side which offers the luxury of teen girl urine. He sees an older naked Japanese businessman with a tiny penis in the shower drinking the girls' piss.

Noam thinks, "Maybe I'll have to check it out later but come in disguise." Then he punches himself in the balls, "Stop thinking dirty thoughts! You are above this filth!"

After Carlos is done with his golden shower, he is hosed off by the robot staff in a strange cleansing liquid, which smells like licorice.

Harry helps Carlos get dressed and they move on to the next place.

The next place looks like a very discreet club or lounge. Carlos says to Noam wickedly, "I know you will love this place. It's 'women only,' but I got you a VIP pass with a badge that says 'Staff.'"

Noam enters by himself. He looks out and sees Carlos and Harry walking off, laughing hysterically. The manager of the lounge greets him and asks for his ID, checks it and says, "Oh, new boy. For now just hang around the lounge to make sure the clients are happy, but you may be requested for cleaning duties."

Noam scoffs under his lips, "Boy? Cleaning duties? I am a great aristocrat. I shall do as I please."

He walks around the lounge. It is a large luxurious room with red carpeting, pink walls, dimmed lighting, and comfy pink lounge chairs where women and girls sip cocktails.

There is an aura of mystery to the place. Unlike the other clubs, there isn't an explicit theme, but Noam can sense this is no ordinary lounge.

Noam notices a group of wealthy attractive women around his age sitting on a lounge chair sipping cocktails and acting tipsy.

Noam realizes the ring leader of the group is Wendy Silverstein, the girl from high school who organized the cunnilingus party. She is now about 30 but still very attractive. She is with her friend Lisa Goldberg, who is just as hot, both in cocktail dresses which reveal their plump buttocks and legs.

Then Molly Katzenberg joins them, complaining about something.

Molly has put on some weight, but is still hot. They all have cruel arrogant expressions as they laugh, sipping their cocktails.

Noam wonders what happened to them after the fire. They had all survived with perfect skin and no burns. “They must be witches,” he thinks.

They don’t recognize Noam and assume he is a staff member. Lisa orders him to fetch her a bottle of their finest champagne.

Noam quickly grabs a bottle randomly from one of the other tables and hands it to them. Lisa grabs it, refusing to acknowledge his existence.

Noam, being the only male in the room, can tell this is a girls-only club. He feels like he is back in high school, like he doesn’t even register as a human being.

He thinks, “This is supposed to be my island, where I rule as king. Perhaps these are all tests to prove if I am worthy to rule. Yes! That’s it. I shall show them!”

Once they are drunk enough, he starts to eavesdrop on their conversation.

Wendy sees him and gives him a nasty look.

Noam thinks, “Oh great. They caught me. The Emporium has my passport and ID. I’m fucked!”

“We need a foot rest!” Wendy orders.

“Oh, yes ladies,” Noam replies awkwardly. “I’ll go see if I can find something in the …”

They all laugh.

“I see you're new here,” Wendy says. “Get on the floor beneath the sofa.”

Noam gets down and lies on his back, in front of the sofa and underneath the table.

He is humiliated but sees this as a perfect opportunity to eavesdrop.

They all take off their high heels.

Wendy starts by putting her sweaty feet right on Noam’s face. He can get a glimpse up her short cocktail dress and can see her lingerie and some of her dark pubes from underneath.

Then Lisa sits down and puts one foot on his stomach and the other on his mouth. She starts to rub his mouth with her sweaty foot.

Molly sits down, spreads her legs wide open and puts one foot on his dick and the other on his chest. Noam can see she is wearing see-through panties that reveal her massive, reddish-brown bush. As she opens her legs wider he can smell her strong aroma, which is a mixture of arousal and bad hygiene.

Wendy says to her friends, “You are in for the experience of a lifetime.” They are not quite sure what is going on but Noam can tell from their facial expressions and scents that they are getting tingles.

Molly asks, “So what’s the deal with this place?”

“Shut the fuck up Molly!” Wendy replies. “This is a top secret club, and I had to pull some major strings to get us in.”

Molly laughs, “Oh, a secret society! Sounds like fun.”

Wendy looks at Molly sternly and explains that, “The penalty for revealing the secrets of the club is death!”

Lisa giggles, “Yeah, death by multiple orgasms!”

“I’m not fucking around!” Wendy replies. “Now let’s get down to business here. We are all here for pleasure, but this is also a business trip. As you know, I am opening the first commercial line of my spa, and I want to learn from the experts.”

“If they are guarding their secrets with death, aren’t you worried about being sued?” Lisa asks.

Wendy laughs. “This was my fuckin' idea back in high school but that little creep …”

“Noam,” Molly replies.

They all laugh.

Wendy continues, “Yeah that piece of shit, that pervert had to sneak into our private party and put it in his stupid manifesto.”

Molly says, “I haven’t washed since I got on the plane. I want to make ‘it’ suffer.”

Noam is confused as to who this “it” is but remembers Justin and how they left him there to die, his last memory before death being smothered and face-fucked by horny teen girls with stinky, unwashed hairy twats.

Even though Noam didn't care much for Justin, unlike Zack and the Chads, he didn't think Justin deserved his cruel fate.

Lisa carries on the conversation, "Well, my stupid husband makes big money on Wall Street, but he doesn't know how to please me, and I suspect he's cheating, but I don't need the prick. I just pay my pool boy to give me head. I made it extra clear to him that he's just some worthless college dropout. I don't want his dick; he is nothing to me but a toy to use at my disposal! I give him an extra tip, and I just sit on his face for several hours sipping Chardonnay, watching re-runs of the old Twin Peaks from 2017, fantasizing that Kyle MacLachlan is eating my ass."

Noam smirks. He remembers when he visited his grandfather in Palm Springs for the summer when he first hit puberty and started masturbating he would stay up late watching the original Twin Peaks on VHS, fantasizing that he was Agent Dale Cooper tied to the bed at the Great Northern and Audrey Horne would sit on his face, bouncing up and down.

Noam was terrified to watch it to the end when he learned about the Black Lodge and had nightmares just from hearing about it. Perhaps he is now in the Black Lodge and like Laura Palmer, his crush is somewhere out there frozen in time from that horrific night.

Wendy replies to Lisa, "I can't believe you married that dweeb from high school. We all thought he was lame back then, but it was like the high school reunion, and you find out he's worth billions, and you fall for him."

Lisa laughs, "Yeah, I should divorce the prick, take half his stuff and just retire here."

Molly says, "I've just been through a ton of shitty relationships. Dated a ton of Chads in college who all cheated on me, then I was briefly engaged to some dweeby rich doctor who left me for a 20-year-old chink."

Lisa says, "We have to prepare for the future. When we were young, the world was our oyster. We could have any guy on a leash and we were told we could have a career and marry rich, but then that asshole Blackstone comes along with his Nazi breeding program and breeds a new generation of hot girls who are now in their teens who will turn 18 in only a couple of years."

Wendy says, "Fuck Blackstone! That sick fascist freak keeps those young teens in his private harem, but most guys are too pathetic. I know plenty of millionaires who spend thousands at the Vapor Love Hotel on sexbots. It's not about having a rich husband or a young stud on the side with a huge cock. I just want to come home after a hard day of work, sit down, drink a bottle of champagne, and get some good fuckin' head!"

They put their glasses together, "Cheers, to good head!"

Noam can smell their sexual arousal. He is generally not attracted to women his own age due to saving his adolescent purity for his crush, but being underneath these women brings back old memories from high school and the long lonely nights he masturbated thinking about eating out these girls.

He suspects they want him to pleasure them all and can feel Molly rubbing her legs on his erection.

Then Molly grabs Noam's head, pushing it up towards her pussy but the stench is too much, and he falls backwards banging his head on the leg of the table.

Molly laughs and they all get up to leave, Molly accidentally kicking him in the face.

Noam realizes that he had been underneath the table for about half an hour, and the club is now packed with women and girls. He has to follow them to find out what is going on.

He notices groups of women waiting in line to go into the back, all of them attractive but who give off a cruel, sinister vibe.

Noam curiously observes the women and girls walking through the secret door.

A group of stuck up models walk in, then a group of Japanese school girls in uniforms giggling, then wealthy Chinese school girls trying to keep a straight face, then a group of stuck up French girls followed by another group of German teen girls.

Then a group of loud obnoxious high school girls from Long Island walk in. He remembers girls like this from when he visited his cousins in Long Island. They are not as high class as the Greenwich girls at Chadsworth, but they are smoking hot and the fact that they are so rude and arrogant turns Noam on.

The girls push Noam to the side. One girl rubs her breast up against him to tease him.

There is one girl who stands out. She has dark blonde hair, hazel eyes, and an hourglass figure.

One of her friends calls out her name, "Hurry up, Michelle!"

She hands over her ticket and follows the other girls up the stairs.

He watches her walk up the stairs in her high heels and cocktail dress which reveals her plump buttocks. She trips on her heels from being tipsy.

Noam fantasizes about her tripping on the stairs and landing right with her buttocks on his face.

She is the kind of girl he had always fantasized about in high school but knows he has to focus on finding his crush.

He thinks, "My crush would never visit such a place of pure debauchery. I just need to go upstairs to find out what all the fuss is about and then leave ASAP."

Then two teen girls walk by with their personal assistant, who is a hot Korean woman in her mid-twenties.

One of the teen girls has dark brown hair, brown eyes, and pale skin, resembling a cross between a teenage Natalie Portman and Winona Ryder.

Noam finds out from her chit chat with her Korean assistant that her name is Zoe and that she is from Beverly Hills with her friend, a Persian girl named Jasmine. Jasmine says her parents would kill her if they found out. She had told them she was in the Bahamas.

Zoe mentions to Jasmine that she is visiting her close friend, who is the director's daughter.

Noam hasn't met Meschel's daughter yet, but he remembers him bragging that his daughter is the one who pulls the strings around the palace and refers to her as his "daughter-wife."

At first Noam thought that was a bit odd but it caused him to think, "If I am a grown man and my crush is still frozen in her prime teen years, then I am obligated to take on both the role of her lover and guardian. Show her the ways of the world, teach her right from wrong, and then make love to her, licking her sweet nectar all night long."

Zoe starts bragging, "I can't wait to tell my friends back home. They will be so jealous."

The Korean assistant sternly warns Zoe not to brag publicly about the details of the club. Zoe giggles and clumsily drops her cocktail glass, breaking it on the floor.

The Korean assistant tells Zoe and her friend to hurry up because their booths are almost ready.

Zoe is drunk and continuing to giggle. She orders Noam to clean it up, looking at him as if he is dirt. She lightly kicks him in the back with her high heel and then puts her heel on his neck.

He takes extra-long to pick up the glass with a cloth napkin so he can look up her short cocktail dress, admiring her smooth pale legs and thick inner thighs, getting a glimpse of her see-through lingerie panties which reveal her thick dark bush.

She puts her heels harder into Noam's neck, giggling. He can smell her scent of arousal and wants to bury his face between her legs.

After he is done cleaning up, she stops giggling and shouts, “Pervert!”

Zoe’s friend Jasmine (observing the spectacle) sneers at Noam as if to say she is above it all yet turned on at the same time.

Noam stares at Jasmine’s nice plump buttocks as she walks past him while he is still down on his knees.

The assistant shouts at them to stop fooling around, and they rush up the stairs.

Noam imagines the girls in Beverly Hills being best friends with Cher Horowitz from Clueless, but he knows that Cher was a nice girl who helped him find his crush and would never be friends with someone who behaved so indecently.

Noam quickly follows the girls up the stairs. He looks behind him and sees a massive line of teen girls pushing their way forward, one of whom looks almost exactly like Cher from Clueless.

Noam is deeply disappointed, thinking: “Is that really her?”

Noam rushes up the stairs and reaches a long hallway. Everything is red and pink with subdued lighting like an old brothel.

Noam rushes down the hallway which is lined with red padded doors. He passes by the long line of attractive women and girls. The loud obnoxious drunk girls from Long Island, the giggling Japanese school girls in their uniforms, shy cute teen girls nervous and confused, snooty models, bossy career women in their late 20s, and the smug, aristocratic European teens, all lined up and restless to get in.

As he is walking around observing the girls in line, he realizes that the long hallway goes around in a large circle.

He notices that the doors have neon signage that says occupied. All the girls are hanging around the hallway as if they are waiting to use the restroom. Then the signs change to unoccupied and all the girls walk into private booths.

Noam has to think of a way to sneak in to spy on the girls to figure out what is going on. He thinks about sneaking into an unoccupied booth but decides it is too risky.

A maintenance staff member (who is a bossy Chinese woman) yells at him to clean up the chamber. Noam stands there bewildered.

She points to the private maintenance elevator which she opens for him. Noam feels uncomfortable stepping into a strange elevator not knowing what lies beneath.

The Chinese woman yells "Go!" and he steps inside the elevator which slowly goes down making an eerie creaking sound.

The elevator door opens and Noam walks down a long dark concrete hallway with a big sign saying, "Staff only."

The hallway reeks of stale urine. Noam isn't quite sure if it is part of golden spa or a sewage system. Either way, it is a dark filthy place that the wealthy patrons up above are completely unaware of.

The hallway ends in a large dark underground room with concrete floors. There is a drain in the middle, and puddles of stale urine on the side. There is a hose on the side to clean the floors.

Noam assumes his assigned job is to clean the urine, but the smell is too strong and he can barely see in the dark. He remembers the Chinese woman ordering him to bring a flashlight, but he was too distracted and overwhelmed.

Suddenly he hears the sound of doors opening and the eerie red light from above permeating down into the darkness.

Noam looks up and sees openings that reveal small rooms with the same pink and red walls of the lounge. They are pure luxury in contrast to the hellish dungeon he is in.

There are slots on the side of the room, which have coffin-like boxes. He can hear screaming and banging from the boxes. Noam realizes what is going on. There are male slaves trapped inside the boxes.

Noam hears noises coming from up above and looks up to see women in their private stalls pull up their skirts, pull down their panties, and sit down as if they are using a toilet.

Noam wonders if they are toilets but thinks, "There has to be something more to all this, the long lines, the gossip, and the slaves in the boxes."

He isn't able to tell who the women are but can see their pussies and buttocks. He hears a businesswoman in a stall on her phone yelling at a client in her brash New York accent while Noam stares at her dark bush and pale plump buttocks, imagining all her yelling and rage coming down from her cunt and being directed at him.

Noam wonders why all the girls and women are at least reasonably attractive, ranging in age up to about 35. He speculates that attractive women are used to getting all the male attention and dick they desire and are so jaded that they only get off from the most sick and twisted acts.

He thinks, "But my crush is the most beautiful creature alive, and she would never indulge in such debauchery. She has saved her virginity and frozen her youth just for me."

After listening to the vitriol directed at him from the businesswoman's cunt, he looks over to the opening next to her and sees a woman with plump pale buttocks and an extremely hairy reddish-brown crotch which he can smell from down below.

He realizes that it is Molly and remembers her saying that that she hasn't cleaned herself since she got on the plane to the island.

Noam feels that her ass and bush are mocking him, making him feel like a piece of toilet paper soaking in a toilet that she is sitting on above him.

Then she pisses and he observes the piss through the lighted opening go down a drain behind the slaves box and then down into the main room into a big puddle.

He looks next to her and sees Wendy and Lisa. He looks up at their plump buttocks and hairy pussies. He is surprised at how dark and coarse their bushes are for blondes.

When he looks at them, he can't even tell they are grown women. He still imagines the girls who taunted and humiliated him in high school.

He remembers getting a glimpse of their bushes and buttocks the night of their cunnilingus party and had fantasized about eating them out since the moment he met them at the fountain, his first day in Greenwich.

Lisa and Wendy also relieve themselves, both at once. He can hear them laughing sadistically. He wonders if it's some ritual or are they just emptying their bladders after a night of drinking.

Then Noam hears a cranking noise and an elevator device lifts up the coffins to pleasure the clients.

He notices that there are trap doors on the coffins where the heads are located that open up the moment they touch the stalls so the clients don't have to look at their slaves.

He now realizes after great speculation that the slaves are there to orally pleasure the clients.

Noam feels a strong sense of guilt watching such sadistic acts being implemented on an industrial scale for profit.

He has a flashback to the night he saw Justin die in that coffin and did nothing to save him and can smell the fire of burning flesh coming up out of the piss drain.

After all, he had written about all of this in his manifesto (which was dedicated to ending all debauchery). He thinks, "What have I done? Am I truly a great aristocrat worthy of determining the destiny of mankind or just another charlatan? Am I being punished for my sins by being denied reunification with my crush? I must set things right and get to the bottom of all this and go after whomever is behind this."

Noam walks over to the next stalls and sees three more openings. He can hear a group of girls chattering up above. He notices three plump sets of buttocks, one with perfect smooth pale skin and a nice dark bush; must be the young girl Zoe from Beverly Hills. Then he sees the Persian girl Jasmine with her nice plump buttocks (which are pale in contrast with her lightly tan skin). Her dark, hairy pussy gives off a musky scent which he can smell from down below. Then he sees the Korean assistant who has a surprisingly nice curvy ass for an Asian woman and (like the other girls) a thick hairy bush.

Noam says to himself, "How generous of the girls to let their lowly assistant join in on the festivities."

Then the two teen girls start peeing. Noam had noticed them drinking cocktails earlier, and they were obviously tipsy. Noam gets sprayed in the face. He thinks, "At least I know what girl piss tastes like."

The Korean woman reprimands the girls. Zoe tells her to shut the fuck up, or they will have her sent back to Korea.

Suddenly three coffins go up at once.

The girls start pissing again right on the coffin, giggling. As soon as the door opens to the coffin, Noam hears a man scream.

Then he sees the Japanese girls (with their perfectly smooth buttocks and soft pussy hair) giggling.

The coffins rise up, muffling the sound of the giggling Japanese school girls being licked.

Then he sees the Chinese girls, who have much hairier bushes.

He remembers the working-class Chinese girls in Chinatown from when he was a boy, and how they were flat-chested and flat-assed, but these are high-class girls and he is impressed by their perfectly plump porcelain buttocks.

Earlier he noticed they were silent and awkward, but now he can hear them making strange noises: "Ra ra ra."

At first they sound bossy, but then he hears them laughing.

He can smell their fishy pussies from all the way down below. He jokes, "I hope those slaves enjoy stinky fish."

Then he sees the group of school girls from France and Germany and the girls from Long Island.

He looks at the French teen girls. Most have pale skin, a few with tan lines. Most have dark bushes but some have dark blonde.

Then he looks over at the German girls and notices some have blonde bushes, and some have thick dark bushes. Noam starts to keep tabs of pubic hair data but loses count.

Noam thinks, "Would they ever let a lowly Juden like me lie under them and eat them? No! I am still a great aristocrat. Those bitches should be begging me to lick them!"

He notices that the French girls mostly have perfect pale skin. Some have tan lines, but one girl has tan buttocks from nude sunbathing.

He looks out at the bossy girls from Long Island, all packed up right next to each other. He admires their nice teen asses and thick dark bushes and can hear them talking abrasively.

He realizes that unlike Lisa, Wendy, Molly and the businesswoman (who have booths that are larger and more spread out), the teen girls were in small booths the size of a bathroom stall as if they bought them en masse for their school trip.

He wonders if certain slaves are assigned the more expensive booths for the clients who pay more, and whether they are more skilled at their duties.

Noam thinks, “If I were a slave, I mean if I had no other choice, I would certainly much rather be under the teens. I wonder how many of them are still virgins, having their very first orgasm, or would I be licking out a cunt and ass defiled by Chads?”

He sees a girl with nice plump pale buttocks and a nice thick dark bush, much darker than his crush.

He realizes it is the blonde Jewish girl from Long Island, Michelle.

When he was growing up and lusted after these blondes, he always assumed their bushes would match their hair color but he has latter come to the realization that many of these girls have thick dark bushes, and the shock turns him on.

The golden blonde pubes of his crush represent perfect innocence, but there is something about a thick dark bush hovering over him that makes him feel totally dominated.

He automatically gets hard and briefly thinks about sneaking into the box beneath the blonde girl but bitch-slaps himself hard, “No, Noam! You created this mess, and now you have to clean it up!”

Noam tries to open the box beneath her, but it is locked closed. He goes to the one next to him which he is able to open.

It is strangely completely empty with no slave inside. Noam contemplates sneaking inside even though it is very dangerous.

Just as he is about to put one foot into the coffin, all the girls start pissing at once, spraying Noam in the face, all the fancy cocktails turned into a waterfall of yellow teen nectar, relieving themselves before the slaves in the boxes lick them clean and give them the best orgasms of their lives.

Noam can taste the alcohol in the droplets of piss. He looks up at the girls, the Jewish girls with their thick dark bushes, and the German girls with their golden bushes, all soaking wet in piss, with no regard for the men stuck inside.

Noam thinks, "Their future husbands, who are currently studying to get into Ivy League universities, will never know about the pleasures they have had, the torment they inflicted when they were in their prime teen years. They will never be able to give them that kind of pleasure, only used as an ATM. But like the men in the boxes they are also tools to be used at their disposal."

Then the coffins all go up at once to the teen girls, an international feast of juices; Japanese, Korean Chinese, French, German, Persian, and Kosher.

Noam says, "IHOPP; International House of Pussy and Piss."

Noam is trying very hard to suppress his erection, but he knows he is trapped in the labyrinth of his own manifesto, only a sick twisted mind has taken it over and is using it for profit. But he wrote it and knows how things will end, and the controllers cannot change that.

He had come to the conclusion that the only way to get through the labyrinth which he created the blue print for and find his crush is to not fall into temptation of all the erotic tests.

Noam sees a sign that says, "Each session lasts one hour." He wonders how the slaves can last that long. This was his fantasy, he owns it. It was implemented even though he never got to experience it for himself.

Noam imagines what it is like for the slaves stuck in the coffins all day and night. Were they ever released to stretch out their legs, get some fresh air, or was their entire purpose in life to pleasure the clients, one after the other, pussy after pussy, plump buttocks smothering their faces, some clean, some stinky, giving a young teen virgin her very first orgasm right after taking a piss, getting pissed on right in the face, then being sat on by some bossy career woman, eating out her pussy and ass while she talks to her client.

Noam decides that he has learned everything he needs to know about this twisted place and decides it is time to get out before he gets trapped or distracted staring at all the teen pussy and ass.

He heads back towards the maintenance hallway but hears an eerie muffled voice yelling "Noam."

He ignores it and heads back to the elevator.

He hears it again louder, "Noam!"

He looks back and hears it coming from a man trapped in a coffin.

He walks over to the coffin. The man says, "Hurry up Noam, before it's too late."

Noam can tell by the man's voice that he must be middle-aged. It sounds strangely familiar but he can't make out who it is. He thinks, "Perhaps a famous actor? Do those teen girls even know they are being eaten out by a famous movie star?"

Noam inspects the coffin. The man slips him a crumpled up note through the crevice in the coffin and he puts it in his pocket.

Suddenly the elevator pushes the coffin up to the last teen girl and now everything is pitch-black.

Noam rushes back towards the elevator but trips and falls into a puddle of stale urine getting it all over himself.

He looks around and realizes he is trapped in the dark dungeon.

He takes out the paper and can see the paper perfectly in the dark. He feels an intrinsic sense of where to walk.

He walks around the circular room to the other side.

Suddenly a side door opens and there is Carlos out in the garden bar looking shocked to see Noam. Carlos bursts out in a deranged laugh, "Noam you reek of piss! You smell worse than the golden spa."

They look at each other in an awkward silence.

If it weren't for the bizarre situation, the location he is in would be one of the most romantic locations he could dream of, the kind of place he would love to take his crush on their first date.

There is a Roman fountain in the middle surrounded by cherry blossom trees with Japanese lanterns and a rotunda ceiling with a fresco of a magical sunset.

The air has a fresh scent of perfume, a relief after being stuck in the dungeon that reeked of stale urine and unwashed vagina.

Noam wants to just run away and escape from all this insanity, but his entire life he dreamt of his very own utopia and now that he is here, he has to fight to maintain it and deal with the interlopers who are undermining his utopian visions.

He looks back at Carlos, who is laughing insanely and gulping down a mojito he ordered at the bar while talking to himself, shouting, “Everything is just fucking fantastic!”

Then he throws his glass at the gate of the dining area, breaking it. The woman dining screams in horror.

A security staff member asks him if he’s all right, and he just slips him a couple hundred dollars and says, “Mind your own fuckin' business!”

Then Carlos urinates in the fountain as a group of models walk by who just exited the spa.

Carlos shows them his dick, “Yeah, take a look at this big fat brown Puerto Rican gay prick, bitches!”

The models scream. Noam knows their secret, that they have just got back from far more debauched acts than watching some fat gay drunk Puerto Rican relieve himself in a mall fountain.

Carlos grabs Noam by the balls and whispers in his ears, “Tonight, I am going to make sweet love to you. You’re mine, bitch.”

Noam has no idea why Carlos is acting so strange.

Then to interrupt the awkward situation, Harry says, “So Noam, did you enjoy yourself in the spa?”

“Yeah Noam?” Carlos interjects. “I had to pull some major strings to get you in. So I hope you made the fuckin' best of it!”

Harry tries to lighten things up, “Feel a bit sorry for the lads working there. Poor chaps, wouldn’t want to be in their shoes but luckily for them this island has a no-uglies policy, only attractive girls and women are allowed.”

Then Carlos screams, “Dammit!”

Harry asks Carlos, “Where shall we go next?”

Carlos says in a calm cruel voice, “The Club de Sade!”

Noam asks Harry, “What's the deal with the ‘Club de Sade?’”

Harry explains that it is where muscular young men, some college athletes, frat bros, and club douche bags are tricked into a private island spring-break orgy, only to be punished by rich nerds who get off torturing their former tormentors.”

Noam thinks, “Another one of my great ideas! Probably just rich businessmen who were once themselves Chads but want to eliminate the competition from the next generation of Chads.”

Carlos says, “Fuck you, Harry. I wasn’t a lame nerd like Noam. I was always and will always be a power top!”

Harry laughs, “I thought you were into the whole power bottom thing?”

Carlos bitch-slaps Harry, grabs him by the neck, and they enter the club.

Once they get inside there is an area like a petting zoo where young men are walking around on their hands and knees barking like dogs and squealing like pigs.

Carlos walks over to the petting zoo area and takes a muscular young man on a dog leash with a ball gag in his mouth.

Carlos looks pissed and is taking out all his anger on the man, tightening the leash on the man's neck and saying under his lips, "Noam. Fuck you, Noam!"

Then Carlos kicks the young man in his face and says, "Take that Noam!"

Noam has no idea why he is saying his name, but he speculates that Carlos has pent up sexual frustration because he rejected his advances.

Noam thinks, "While I can appreciate the body of an aesthetically pleasing blond teenage man, I utterly detest faggots! They are sick in the head and won't be satiated until the entire world is one massive homoerotic orgy."

Noam walks around the club observing how the men being abused are muscular and tattooed grown men, while earlier he witnessed handsome young blond guys pissing and cumming on older men.

Noam thinks, "Fuck! I am stuck even deeper into my own manifesto than I imagined, like entering another circle of Dante's Inferno."

He remembers writing about how there were two types of males that must be examined; the good-looking blond teens whom he fantasized about, even when they pissed on him in the showers of Chadsworth. He despised them yet admired their beauty and wanted complete control of their bodies.

Then there were the thuggish douchebag types whom Noam found physically repulsive and felt had unjustly acquired the sexual affection of attractive females, sexual affection that he himself was denied.

He never understood the appeal of those thugs, but all he knew is that he wanted them wiped off the face of the earth and to have them suffer in the worst possible ways imaginable.

He wanted them castrated and humiliated and acted out those desires on the men he met at the nightclubs in New York City.

He remembers his history lesson about laws in regard to cunnilingus, fellatio, and irrumatio in ancient Rome and asks Harry if there are any laws on sexual decorum on the island.

Harry, who is now a nervous wreck due to having to deal with Carlos, says, "Oh, why of course, Noam. Despite the Island's reputation for debauchery, we still have our legal codes of decorum, and there are draconian repercussions for anyone who violates them. For example, a grown man may perform fellatio on a teenage man, something I have indulged in from time to time, and a man may also perform cunnilingus and anilingus on a teenage girl. However, if he were to desecrate a teen by having them perform the same acts on him, then that would be punished by the loss of his member."

Noam remembers writing about this in his manifesto. He had fantasized about becoming rich someday and as a grown man he wanted to orally pleasure teens, but the thought of a teen having to suck off some disgusting old perv made him ill.

Noam thinks, "This is my legal code. I am emperor after all! I just need to find a way to rewrite the legal code to say that no part of my manifesto shall be misused for economic gain, and first thing tomorrow I will tell that prick Meschel that he answers to me!"

Noam leaves Carlos alone to take out his anger on the young man and observes the rest of the club.

First Noam notices a young good-looking muscular jock type with long blond hair and tattoos, tied up. There is a short nerdy businessman dressed in leather, whipping him.

Than he sees a muscular black football player, naked and tied up in chains. There is a businessman from North Carolina who is electrocuting his testicles.

A screen shows a depiction of the football player and his black friends defiling a young blonde, white, college cheerleader.

The businessman says, "That's what you get you worthless nigger. For violating my daughter!"

The young black man replies, "Yo daughter's a dumb ho. She came to mah party, and all them white bitches be sucking my big black cock."

The businessman explodes in range, takes out his pocket knife and carves out his testicles. The black man screams out in agony.

The security apprehends the man and says, "You can inflict as much pain as possible but you cannot vandalize the merchandise."

The black man explodes in rage, still in chains. "I'm no slave you white bitches," he says and spits in the eye of the security guard.

The security guard changes his mind and says, "You can do whatever you please to this young buck if you have the funds to reimburse the cost."

The man replies, "Oh don't you worry. I can buy an entire NFL franchise. What's the cost of some state-school nigger?"

He continues to electrocute the young black man in the bloody socket where his testicles used to be.

Next, Noam sees some young douchebag type (who is about twenty-five) covered in tattoos. This is exactly the kind of filth that Noam felt as being totally unworthy of affection from attractive females, but would see them walking around with models in New York all the time.

The video screen comes up and it depicts the man picking up a model at a night club in Miami, doing cocaine out of her ass, fucking her in the ass, and then making her suck his dick, finishing with a facial and a dirty sanchez.

Noam is so disgusted being forced to watch such debauchery, he feels he has to bring the man to justice.

Noam orders the staff to tie the man up naked to a medical operating table. He starts by whipping him until he bleeds.

Carlos approaches Noam and says, "You're such a pussy, Noam. Is that the best you got? You're a fuckin' famous serial killer!"

The man squirms when hears that, "Wait! What? Noam. You're Noam Metzenbaum? Help!"

Carlos hands Noam a cigar and Noam burns the man lightly on his stomach.

The man laughs at Noam, "Is that all you got punk! You're not Noam, poseur!"

Noam says, "I think I should get going."

Carlos says, "Don't you think you let the bitch off lightly? He just insulted your great work. I'll give you exhibit number two!"

One of the staff members turns on the screen again and it shows the man in college with his bros at a party cumming into the mouth of some cute college girl, her mouth overflowing with cum until she vomits and passes out.

Noam says, "I don't think he's gotten enough punishment for his crimes." A staff member hands him a droplet of acid, which Noam's inserts into his wounds from the whipping.

The man screams out in agony.

Carlos jokes, "Noam I was wrong to doubt you. You would put de Sade himself to shame."

Then Carlos takes his hands and grabs Noam's balls hard from behind causing him pain whispering in his ear while licking it, "Yeah, Noam, is that how you like it, bitch?"

A doctor comes by to examine the man to estimate the costs and damages for the bill.

Carlos says, "Put it on Meschel's tab."

The manager of the club comes by, "Meschel? You're a friend of Ari Meschel? The greatest director who ever lived! Don't worry about it, it's on the house!"

They leave the "Club de Sade" and Carlos says that he is going over to the "Goo Goo Club" to have his stomach filled up with boy goo.

Noam says he is going off to get a bite to eat at the food court.

While Noam is tempted to go back to the spa, "Maybe eat out a blonde Jewess or take a golden shower from the young, blonde Aryan teens. No! Because I am on mission to find my crush and restore justice to the world and right my own wrongs."

After Carlos and Harry leave, Noam takes out the wrinkled map the man in the coffin gave him. At first it is hard to read, but then things are clear. It is signed "The Engineer."

He realizes that the map is to navigate his very own manifesto, the world he created but that became a labyrinth so complex that even he, the great aristocrat, could not navigate on his own.

He decides he must go find this "Engineer" who is running the mechanisms of the labyrinth.

The map even shows the current location and where he has to go next, just like GPS coordinates.

He walks back past the secret lounge and sees a new group of women coming in; models, wealthy school girls in their private school uniforms, 30-something career women, and even a mother-daughter couple, like something out of the Gilmore Girls but sick and twisted. The daughter even looks just like the girl from the show.

Then he walks past the Golden Spa and admires the beautiful young blond teens pissing.

Then he looks at the map which tells him to make a left. He walks underneath a small Roman arch and down a long hallway. At the end of the hallway there is a door with a code to enter. Noam looks at the map and enters in the code.

He crosses through a glass tube walkway which overlooks the Galleria. He admires all the bright lights and atmosphere down below, then enters another long corridor which leads to another door where he enters a code.

Noam reaches a courtyard, which resembles an abandoned 80s mall food court.

He feels like he is Indiana Jones discovering a lost temple in Egypt for the very first time in thousands of years.

He looks up at the night sky and stares and realizes that he was at the Erotic Emporium all day.

There is a fountain with an Egyptian frog statue squirting out water. There is something soothing and romantic yet eerie about the sound of the fountain, especially when it is in a strange deserted courtyard.

At the end of the corridor is an Egyptian style, turquoise neon pyramid held up by two columns, with a broken neon sign which makes a buzzing sound and reads, "Pavilion Entrance." Underneath it is lettering in hieroglyphics.

He takes out the map, which has a translator from hieroglyphics and translates the lettering, which reads, "Only those who are worthy may enter."

Noam sees a golden frog icon that is connected to the column. He thinks, "My dream in prison about Shadilay, the frog statue that I took from Moosh that gave me immense power, and now there are frog symbols everywhere! Perhaps some ancient race that worshiped a frog god? Who would have thought?"

Noam puts his hand on the frog icon and there is an eerie stillness in the courtyard. The fountain turns off. The broken neon sign stops buzzing. Complete and utter silence.

Then the ground starts shaking, and the floor of the courtyard starts descending.

An old cage-style elevator emerges from underneath the pyramid. It has golden Egyptian Art Deco frog motifs.

Noam looks at the elevator indicator and sees 93 floors and notices that he is on floor zero, yet looks up at the sky and sees neither elevator shaft nor tower above him.

He enters the elevator and the door closes behind him. He tries to push the buttons of the elevator to reach his destination but nothing happens. He waits a few more minutes and then tries again but still nothing.

Then he starts frantically pushing all the buttons at once. The buttons light up, and the elevator indicator starts spinning back and forth.

Noam feels a jolt of electricity and the elevator starts falling downwards. He notices the elevator indicator showing that the floors are going higher even though he is going downwards.

He pulls out his map but everything is inverted and the lettering distorted, upside down, and backwards. It is no longer of any use to him.

Noam wonders, "Maybe I was right to be skeptical. This is pure entrapment. These dark forces entrapped me on the island to prevent me from implementing my grand visions. The island is not my utopia but a mirage created by accessing my dreams and nightmares, utilizing them to annihilate me, my body and my soul."

The elevator continues to go further down, faster. Noam looks out and sees nothing but black. He cannot tell if he is underground or in outer space

Then he sees balls of electrical currents, balls of warm light floating in the distance towards him. He touches the elevator and gets an electric shock again.

He loses his sense of gravity and grabs firmly onto the elevator railing while getting electrocuted.

Once the elevator reaches the bottom at the 93rd level he gets out and walks out into an underground cavern, where he slowly regains his sense of gravity.

He is disoriented in the dark and takes out his map to see if it is of any use.

He can now see the map perfectly again and looks around. He sees a gold plaque where the elevator was that had engravings in hieroglyphics.

He takes out his map again, and it translates, "Only the great one can overcome the forces of gravity, time, and space with their soul intact."

At first Noam is a bit confused, but realizes that he must have traveled through some kind of vortex where there was no gravity.

He thinks, "This proves that I can overcome the obstacles of time and space by being with my crush as a grown man while she is still a young undefiled maiden. Most mere mortals are taught to improve themselves, yet by the time they do so it is too late to be with their cherished youthful crush, and then they die a little inside, spending the rest of their pathetic lives wondering what could have been. But No! Not me. I have overcome all the odds, and I will be with her. This isn't a trap. This island was created for me, and I must utilize the esoteric powers to annihilate the interlopers who have desecrated my utopia. I just have to find this engineer who will give me the keys to island's mechanisms."

Noam walks through the cavern. There are ancient lanterns that provide dim lighting. At the end, he reaches an underground river with an old rope bridge. Crossing it, Noam looks down at the fast moving water. It is dark, but he can hear creatures in the water.

He hears the sound of the ropes of the bridge tear apart. He has to get across it before it breaks and can sense that the creatures jumping up at his feet must be piranhas.

Noam finally reaches the other side of the water. He continues walking down the cavern but gets to a fork in the cave.

He feels an intrinsic urge to take the right path but consults his map. The map reads, "One path leads to a safe return out, however if you follow your instincts you may reach your destination, or you may reach a fate worse than death. Choose wisely."

Noam is annoyed that the map is not giving him clear directions but at this point he has come so far, and he isn't going to just leave and return to safety, sacrificing everything he had fought for. So he decides to go with his instinct and turns right.

He walks down the passageway and sees engravings of frogs carved into the stone from some lost civilization. Some of the frogs are laughing, some crying, some with mischievous grins, and others engaging in a violent massacre of decapitations.

He thinks, "I thought this was all a joke, but these people really did worship frogs. Just basic grade school biology I suppose. A frog is an amphibian and unlike the lowly homo sapiens, he can morph from land to water. Yes, shape shifting. So unlike our religions it's not about good or evil but achieving a heightened state of being that one can be anything and everything, to shape-shift the world around him to suit his own visions and needs. Things are starting to become more clear, about the Island, and all these visions I have been having."

He can hear strange chanting in the distance, echoing through the cavern but can't make out what is being said.

He continues walking towards the chanting until he reaches what looks like an ancient Egyptian tomb with two giant frog statues but no entrance.

He looks closely and can see the hieroglyphics.

He laughs thinking, “It’s the same fuckin' code as the entrance to the mall courtyard. This great ancient temple has the same code as a fucking mall. Maybe this is just a silly theme park after all.”

He types in the hieroglyphic code and the door slowly opens.

He walks past the massive frog statues into the temple which is dark but lit with candles.

He hears the chanting again and slowly walks past the members, trying hard not to make eye contact.

He hears the chants “Praise Kek,” Praise Kek,” getting louder the closer he gets to the altar, which has a golden pyramid held up by two gold frog statues.

At the altar, there is a priest in gold Egyptian headwear, a crimson silk robe, and holding a golden scepter.

Noam looks out at the followers and realizes that they are all wearing frog masks. Unlike a regular church or temple where conformity is expected, each frog mask represents a different personality type or emotion, much like in the engravings.

As soon as the priest notices Noam, everyone in the temple is silent. They all start bowing down to him as if he is their messiah.

Noam stands there basking in his glory.

Noam turns around and asks the priest, “Are you the engineer?”

The priest laughs, then puts his hand on Noam’s shoulder and says, “Put your palm on the statue of KEK to prove you are the one.”

Noam puts his hand on the golden frog statue.

Everyone waits in anticipation. Some start screeching “Reeeee!”

The priest orders, “Silence!”

Then the statue starts shaking and shoots out a magic beam onto the priest’s sceptre, which he hands to Noam.

Noam holds the scepter in triumphant victory, feeling the esoteric power of KEK running through his veins.

Then the Priest shouts out, “Stop masturbating to lolicon!”

A fat man puts away his loli and says, “Uh, sorry.”

The priest confiscates the loli of an anime frog sticking his dick into a pound of tadpoles.

The priest shouts, “Tadpoles? What the fuck? Blasphemy!”

The only time Noam had ever masturbated to animation was the show Braceface, but that was only because it had Alicia Silverstone in it.

Then the worshipers rise up and start singing the song of praise that the frog goddess Shadilay sang to Noam in his dreams.

Noam asks the priest why they all have such beautiful voices.

The priest replies “I encourage most of my followers to be eunuchs. You can’t truly connect to the powers of KEK when you are distracted by thoughts of fornication. However, I sense that you have the power to have resisted the temptations of the opposite sex. You see those who have engaged in the unspeakable act would have been annihilated by the powers you unleashed. Besides, most of my non-eunuchs spend all their time masturbating to anime or trying to sneak into the palace to spy on the orgies."

Noam never really thought being a eunuch was for him. He needs his testicular fortitude to battle the Chads and win over his crush but the entire philosophy of the temple intrigues him.

The priest says, "Noam, come to me, my son." He puts his hands on him, "We have long been awaiting your arrival, waiting for the one who will usher in the order of KEK. Long before Columbus arrived on these shores, there was once a great civilization on the very ground we stand upon. The tribe of KEK was sent into exile out of Egypt, a long-lost ancient tribe started when Vikings and Germanic tribes took Hebrew women as their concubines to start a new tribe. They ended up in Egypt where they were resented by the pharaoh for their spiritual power and beauty of their women, whom the pharaoh would use for his harems. They found power through KEK, whom they worshiped as their god. They were a caste of artisans who designed all the great pyramids and temples for the pharaoh They were able to take power by using their women to seduce the pharaoh When their blond genes started to die out, they became sick and weak and fled into exile They got on their ships and sailed across the Atlantic to look for new territory to create a new civilization, what you may have heard of as the lost city of Atlantis. However, the civilization was destroyed when the Chads emerged and took the women of more righteous men for their harems. The island was destroyed for its sins but prophecies foretell that a young king of mixed Aryan and Hebrew seed will one day return and find his blonde Hebrew maiden to restore our great civilization. You are the one chosen to restore the order of KEK and the lost civilization will re-emerge and usher in a new order of greatness."

Noam replies, "I am humbled. I admire what you are doing, but will you help me find my crush?

The priest replies, "Of course, that is why I sent for you. She still has her purity and youth. Don't let the wicked Chads confuse you and lead you astray."

Noam asks, "How long have you been down here?"

The priest replies, "A decade before you were in high school I taught ancient history at your school, Chadsworth, so I know all about the wickedness of the Chads. I was and still am the world's greatest archaeologist. I discovered the lost tomb of the tribe of KEK in Egypt, then came to work on the island for Blackstone, but ever since my discovery of the power of KEK, the Chad elite have been trying to destroy me. They destroyed my career as an archaeologist. Then when I taught at your school, one of the Chads' cheerleader girlfriends falsely accused me of sexual misconduct. I went to prison and suffered greatly, but I knew one day I would find you. When I got out of prison, a man approached me and offered me a job to work on a top secret mission. I had no clue who was behind it all, but it was my chance to become an archaeologist again and excavate the Island. I knew there was something special about the place, and there were powerful forces wanting to tap into its powers. I discovered the temple through an underwater sea cave. In case you don't know, your manifesto inspired a great uprising on the mainland that challenged the existing order. I have used the temple as a sanctuary for the revolutionaries, but you must not tell a soul, especially those who are trying to corrupt your work. They are pure evil, but I know you have the power to annihilate them. The uprising will occur. It is inevitable. Now go on Noam and find your maiden, bring justice to the world, and restore the order of KEK!"

The priest hands him a golden key and tells him, "You will know when to use it when the time comes."

He tells him it is dangerous for him to go back to the mall because they have his identification and surveillance of his activities.

He orders one of the temple members to escort Noam to safety.

As they leave the temple, all the men in frog masks bow down to Noam chanting, "Praise Kek," "Praise KEK!"

They walk through the cavern to an old mining railway, which connects to a network of underground passageways that are filled with ancient relics.

The man in the frog mask explains to Noam that the passageways were built when the island was excavated and connect to anywhere on the Island.

Noam asks to be taken back to the palace.

The man says, "I will take you to your destination but the wicked denizens of the palace must not know about our whereabouts. I will take you through a secret entrance."

The mining car enters the floor of the gorge. Noam looks up and sees the glass pyramid and glass sky bridges with cars and monorails running through them.

The floor of the gorge is mostly jungle filled with ancient ruins with cascading waterfalls flowing down into the many rivers and lakes.

The mining car goes behind a waterfall and into another cave.

The man says, “This is your stop and remember when the time comes we will have your back.”

Noam gets off and walks down the cave to the end, where there is another Egyptian-style entrance. He enters in the same code from before and walks up a long staircase, which leads to another long dark corridor.

He looks up above him and sees some peep holes, realizing he is back at Meschel’s palace. He sees some young guy’s buttocks covering up a peep hole, and realizes it is one of the ones who tormented him earlier.

He wonders what they are up to and questions his worthiness, remembering the debauched acts he engaged in, “I’m not a faggot, but engaged in homoerotic acts with these young men. Even though it was forced upon me, I had the option of escaping beforehand, but I stayed because something about them intrigued me, but the only thing that really matters is I am still a virgin and am saving myself for my crush. These young men don’t matter one bit!”

He overhears the boy bragging to some girl, “Yo, the other night we totally made that creepy writer our bitch. He was practically eating out our asses and licking our balls.”

The girl replies, "What a creep. I'm sorry you had to go through all that."

The young man says, "Yo, it's not a big deal. It's not like we did anything gay. We just got our dicks sucked by a hot chick and used him as a chair."

Noam can hear the girl get down to suck his dick and hears him grunt while he watches his buttocks gyrate against the peep hole.

Noam cannot stand to listen to them and keeps running until he finds his way back to the main part of the palace.

He sees Harry with Carlos, who is naked and drunk and flipping out. Carlos says, "Noam! What the fuck! I thought you were dead!"

Then Carlos breaks down sobbing on the floor.

Harry comes over to Noam and says, "You have caused us enough trouble. From now on you are not allowed to leave the premises. I will escort you to your room and tomorrow is our first big meeting with Meschel so you must be on your very best behavior. Do you understand?"

Noam refuses to respond and is escorted to his room by Harry and two of Meschel's security robots.

Noam enters his room and Harry tells him, "Remember, we are watching you."

The next day Noam meets with Meschel at his office. Noam doesn't know what to expect owing to his last encounter with Meschel being rather unpleasant.

Meschel looks Noam in the eye, gives him an angry look, noticing Noam is nervous.

Then he bursts out laughing and orders his assistant to bring Noam a mimosa.

Meschel says, "Look Noam. I'm a big fan of your work. I really mean it, but this celibacy shit and esoteric bullshit you're peddling just ain't gonna fly. People want hot teen tits and ass, multiple cum shots, cute little Asian girls giving messy blowjobs, not some loser virgin who becomes god-emperor after gaining strength through masturbation and angry philosophical rants."

Noam is furious, but he knows he has to play the game.

Noam says, "Well don't you like my cunnilingus scene?"

Meschel replies, "Love it! That's what I want more of. I find it so misogynistic that cinema has yet to catch up with the times. When I was young it was all about blowjobs and blowbangs but from the stories I have heard from my daughter, the girls are now turning the tables on the guys. How about this? A group of teen girls force the Noam character to orally pleasure them? Didn't you write about that in your manifesto?"

Noam says, "I suppose I did."

Meschel says with a big grin, "Wish that happened to you huh? But you were such a dweeb that the girls didn't even want your tongue, let alone your tiny little prick, but your manifesto created a new sexual revolution that you never got the chance to partake in. Ironic isn't it?"

The director's daughter Sarah is hiding in the closet listening in with her recording device while fingering herself.

Noam replies to Meschel, "I guess so."

Meschel continues ranting, "The grand finale, the ultimate cunnilingus party, a historic event in cinematic history!"

He takes out a bottle of champagne and pours himself and Noam a glass and cheers "To cunnilingus!"

Noam thinks maybe if he plays his cards right he can convince Meschel to organize a cunnilingus party with his crush as the actress and him as the main star. Then he can finally take her virginity with his tongue, giving her her very first orgasm.

Noam walks outside to the Roman baths to get a breath of fresh air and contemplate his thoughts.

Suddenly, an actress with platinum blonde hair and big tits approaches him flirtatiously, "Well, hello there handsome."

Noam tries to ignore her, suspicious of all the inhabitants of the palace.

She says, "I'm your biggest fan, Noam. I've been fantasizing about you ever since I read your dirty stories. Naughty boy."

Noam tries not to make eye contact.

The actress then grabs Noam's crotch.

Noam pushes her away and says, "What the fuck do you think you're doing!"

"Well, you certainly know how to treat a lady," she replies.

"You betcha, big stuff," she says. "Now let's see that cock of yours."

She drags Noam into a private room, pulls down his pants, and violently pushes him onto the bed.

She starts sucking on Noam's penis, but he is unable to cum.

He would much rather have a sweet young innocent teen girl with a nice moist bush sitting on his face than being treated like a human lollipop by some late-20s bimbo with fake tits and botox.

After about 15 minutes of fellatio Noam still is unable to cum. The actress is furious, "I give the best blowjobs in the industry, how dare you not cum for me you piece of shit."

"Well, I'm just not in the mood," Noam says.

"I don't give a fuck!" she replies. "Now it's time to prove your manhood, that you have what it takes to clean up your mess. No pun intended."

She squeezes his member hard, "I want your cock in my pussy dammit! And that's not a request!"

She jumps up on him and starts fucking him really hard in the cowgirl position but Noam is repulsed by her shaven tattooed cunt, not like the sweet innocent thick dark golden bush of his crush.

He thinks, "This whore isn't even worthy to lick the gum off my boots. How dare she try to steal my aristocratic seed, which I have been saving for my crush!"

The actress stops and says, “I get it. You’re a faggot, or a virgin, or possibly both. I’ve read your manifesto, Noam, we’ve all read it, and we all know how pathetic you are. We know that you’ve never had a girlfriend, we know about your gay fantasies, admiring the Chads in the locker room, even after they made you gargle their piss, and we all know about your obsessive stalker obsession with that stupid blonde Jew bitch!”

Noam explodes in rage and punches her in the face, causing blood to gush out of her nose, and a tooth to fall out her mouth. She falls backwards onto the floor.

“You have sullied my aristocratic honor with your acts of fornication!” Noam declares.

He looks at her bloody bruised body and thinks, “Is she dead?

He thinks about disposing the body and about where to hide it.

He knows he is already on thin ice but pauses to think, “This is my world. There are no police or courts to judge me. I am the only one here capable of judging the sins of mankind!”

Noam covers up her body with a sheet and heads out.

He ends up back in the big orgy room, which is now packed with the teenage young men who tormented him earlier. They are blindfolded in Venetian masks and have naked women tied up in chains.

Noam rushes through quickly, trying hard not to be noticed but sees Harry and hides behind the curtains.

Harry catches a young man getting a blowjob from one of the chained up women and reprimands him for wasting his seed on the females.

Noam is confused. He remembers the young men treating Harry as their bitch earlier, but he questions whether the Chads are really in charge or are just being given women to keep them aroused and full of cum for homosexuals like Carlos.

Then a naked, drunk Carlos crawls in on his hands and knees going around blowing and rimming all the boys.

Carlos was usually dominant, even as a power bottom giving head to the Chads back in school, but something had happened to him and he is now acting like a submissive little bitch begging the young guys to drink their cum and eat out their assholes.

Noam finally makes it back outside and thinks, "Close call! Carlos has really lost it since going overboard at the spa, and to think that faggot and his bitch Harry have the nerve to blame me for this mess. Without me, there would be no damn movie!"

He makes small talk with one of the butlers about the magical sunset, then takes a cloth napkin and dips it in the pool to wipe off the scent of sex, but realizes that the water has the same sexual aroma from all the orgies, even with all the chlorine (which ironically reminds Noam of the smell of semen.)

He turns around, noticing the actress talking to Meschel, and his heart freezes in fear.

He thinks, "Did she come back from the dead? Is she that resilient?"

He assumes she is snitching on him, but just before Noam is about to explain, Meschel says, "Love your enthusiasm! There is no pleasure without pain. This is the kind of stuff I want in the film!"

Noam thinks about how when Harry punished him it was for rejecting the debauchery of the Emporium by running off to be with the virgin frog men, but the more debauched he became the more he was rewarded.

This angered him but also gave him a tactic in dealing with Meschel.

Despite this new found knowledge, he is devastated by the fact that he lost his virginity in vain. Waiting all these years dreaming about the magical night with his crush and then throwing it all away for a one-night stand with some bimbo.

He gulps down an entire bottle of champagne and wanders around the palace aimlessly.

He says to himself, "I have undone all my great work with voluntary acts of fornication with a woman of ill merit. I am not worthy to carry on the revolution and have lost my one last chance to give my true love my cherished virginity. She would reject me and rightfully so!"

Noam is too drunk to find his way back to his room and falls asleep on a random sofa. He wakes up in middle of night in a cold sweat in a strange dark room. Disgusted with himself, he thinks, "Getting teabagged and face-sat by teen boys is one thing, but intercourse? Fucking sexual intercourse? Inserting my penis into some random vagina! I betrayed my crush and everything I stand for. I am not fit to lead the revolution!"

He wakes up with a hangover and finds himself in the middle of a late-morning orgy.

A flamboyant gay man with a young muscular man on a leash comes by and offers Noam a mimosa.

Noam throws the glass on the marble floor and gets up on the sofa and proclaims, "All of you make me ill! You live you lives purely for the hedonistic pleasures of the flesh. No higher values or visions. Listen up, I am in charge here from now on! I wrote the manifesto this entire fucking island was built upon, and you worthless parasites are reaping the benefits on my great work. Damn you all to hell!"

The people burst out laughing and continue with their acts of fornication.

Noam rushes over to Meschel's office so he can get a copy of the script. Meschel isn't there but his assistant says she can take a message for him.

Noam grabs her by the neck and says, "I'm the fucking star here! I need to read my script!"

The women replies, "Oh, Meschel didn't tell me you were playing the lead role, must have been a last minute decision. Here's a copy."

Noam grabs the script and takes it back to his room to read.

He reads the script and all his worst fears about Meschel sabotaging his manifesto and life's work are true.

It depicts him as just a loser nerd in high school who jerks off to anime all day. At school people try to befriend him at first but he goes out of his way to make the point that he is superior to them because his dad is rich.

He thinks, “Fuck yeah, I am superior to those spoiled high school brats, but they never even gave me the chance to be accepted as their equal, and fuck I was the poorest kid in the school.”

It depicts being a Chad as some kind of spiritual warrior in the high school who values masculine traits and uses them to make the world a better place by encouraging masculine virtue, protecting the weak, and making girls' vaginas tingle.

“Stupid obnoxious oafs!” he says. “I have dedicated my life to exterminating the vile creatures, and then my work is being used to glorify those uncivilized traits.”

Then it depicts his political manifesto as some right-wing Republican Party rant about how poor people are lazy and rich people are fantastic, but that he hates the rich kids in his high school for being too generous by donating to charity and helping the poor and trying to be more inclusive by listening to hip-hop and having black friends.

It portrays Noam as a homosexual predator and the Chads as the victims and that he blackmails them into urinating on him by stealing money from his fictional rich dad to bribe a smart Asian nerd to hack into the school computer to change their grades.

Carlos is depicted as a shy gay kid who is bullied by Noam but who helps Noam come to grips with his own suppressed homosexual urges.

He continues reading and it portrays his crush as a major slut who blows all the Chads in the bathroom, and that he tries to rape her at the party before the massacre but the Chads try to save her before sacrificing their own lives.

It also portrays her as blowing them all and letting them cum on her face to thank them for saving her life and later she starts a charity to protect Chads against hate crimes after the massacre.

This was the final straw for Noam and a realization that it's time for all-out war against Meschel and his cronies.

It also depicts him as a homosexual in prison with a black tranny cellmate as his girlfriend, even though in his manifesto it states that the celibacy and lack of exposure to all debauchery is what made him stronger in prison.

After prison it depicts him as an extreme womanizer who is muscular, covered in tattoos, who uses his fame to sleep with thousands of women and become the Chad he wasn't in high school but feels guilty for his crimes against the Chads so he commits suicide and donates all his money to help up and coming Chads.

He looks at the cheesy title, "Almost a Chad" and then notices that 10% of the proceeds from the film will be donated to the charity, "Chad Relief," founded by Chad S.'s father whose mansion Noam destroyed.

He then rips up the script and stomps on it in rage.

He takes out the treasure map to see if it offers him any clues that will help him defeat Meschel.

He had no idea how intricate the palace was and can see corridors and rooms constantly moving, but with the map he can find his way anywhere.

At this point he doesn't have a concrete gameplan to defeat Meschel, but the map seems to understand his deepest desires.

He follows the map through the many corridors of the palace, finding out the best short cuts and where to avoid danger.

He ends up back in the room where the bizarre sculpture garden of his massacre was, but it is replaced by sculptures of the Chads celebrating victoriously, while the statue of him is crying on the ground like a little bitch and his crush is on her knees, sucking off Chad S.

His screams of rage echo, "Meschel! I'm going to fuckin' kill you!"

He rushes out past the sculpture garden to find the ocean area where he made contact with his crush at sunset, but there is just a wall where the portal was.

He takes the map out again and finds out there is a secret lair where Meschel keeps all his top secret material located underneath the east wing of the palace, where Meschel has his private residence.

The map leads him to another passageway that connects to the location.

He enters a secret library. There are endless rows of books. He notices Alistair Blackstone's Manifesto, all of Roger Blackstone's personal writings as well as his very own manifesto.

He picks up his manifesto, which he has never seen in its entirety. It reads, "Copyright owned by Ari Meschel."

Noam screams, “NO! I wrote this dammit. It isn’t for sale and no one has the right to change anything in it, especially not some disgusting creep like Meschel.”

He wants to spend more time exploring the library for clues but needs to get to the secret lair to find out where his crush is and all of Meschel’s secrets so he can take him down.

He walks down to the end of the library where he sees a sign that reads “Top secret: Trespasser subject to execution.”

Noam’s uses the secret code to open the door to the lair. He was expecting something grandiose but the lair just resembles an office storage unite with piles of boxes filled with documents and tapes.

He finds a small safe and tries to get it open. He remembers that he has a key on him that the priest gave to him and told him that he will know to use it when the time comes.

He opens the safe with the key and takes out the documents. He takes out a small disk puts it in an electronic device and a hologram presentation appears in front on him.

He discovers that his entire life from his internet search history as a boy, high school records, prison records, and surveillance of his activities on the island have been archived on the disk for Meschel.

This is very disturbing, but he needs to find out where his crush is.

He looks through the safe and finds another disk and puts it in. He finally finds out his crush is being held captive in the palace, still frozen in her youth.

He wonders if it was really her he saw out by the sea at sunset.

Then he finds out some urgent news that there are plans to desecrate her at the finale of the film. First they will place bids to auction off her virginity, then commit unspeakable acts in a ritualistic manner. Then they will finish things off by sacrificing her, murdering her in some bizarre satanic ritual.

Noam is terrified and thinks, "I have sacrificed my entire existence to this girl, dedicating my life to selfless acts of heroism. Then when I indulge in acts of hedonistic pleasure I keep getting punished, seduced by temptation that leads to despair and complete and utter failure. Some people just happen to be rewarded for their selfish behavior but not I. I was put on this earth to sacrifice myself to protect the chastity of my one and only love and to show the rest of the wretched human race the way. But now is not the time to think, now is time for action. I know she is out there somewhere in this palace. I failed her the first time and had to suffer for it, but she was reborn as a young virgin, given as a gift just for me, and if I let her down this time then I'm not worthy."

Unfortunately the map does not give him the exact location of his crush but he figures out that the key is to rescue her from the film shoot.

Noam puts the disk back in the safe but feels sharp fingernails clawing into his back.

He turns around, and it is Meschel's teenage daughter Sarah, who is an attractive girl with thick dark hair, dark sinister eyes, curvy, with nice big tits and plump buttocks.

She isn't like the certain type of blonde girls he fell in love with but has a dark sensuality to her and at this moment he is under her spell.

Sarah asks flirtatiously, "What are you looking for?"

"Well. I was just looking for a, ah," Noam stutters nervously.

She laughs, "You look confused. Need an assistant?"

Noam replies, staring at her cleavage, "Uh no. I'm fine, thank you."

In response, she changes her tune, "You like what you see, pervert? I know all about you, your manifesto, your perversions, maybe if I just dyed my hair blonde I could get you to do anything I want, make you my slave."

Noam tries to leave the room but she blocks the door, rubbing her big tits against his chest.

She says, "Look, fucker! Let's cut to the chase. I know you were snooping through my daddy's business files. So I can either turn you in, and you don't want to know what this Island does to punish snoopers, or you can be my personal man slave. It's your choice!"

Noam remembers the girl Zoe at the spa talking about being best friends with Sarah and knows she must be twisted and pulls some major strings around the palace.

Noam doesn't respond, but she notices his erection, which she grabs hard.

She says, "I see you decided. Your little head is wiser than your big one. Now come with me, bitch!"

She grabs him and takes him off to her bedroom. Noam stands there admiring her room. It is a room built for a princess and is several times larger than the entire apartment he grew up in.

She shouts, “Look at this mess. There is clothing everywhere; bras, undies, wine stains. What a disgrace! Now clean it up slave boy! On your hands and knees! Now!”

Noam walks around awkwardly on his hands and knees.

She starts laughing. Then she takes her shoe heel and digs it into Noam’s back.

She points to her undies which have been sullied with a yellowish stain. She shouts, “I’ve read your manifesto. I know about your creepy pantie sniffing fetish, now pick them up dammit!”

Noam’s picks them up with his hands. He can already smell the scent on her panties, which smell like stale urine and vaginal discharge.

“Not with your hands, pervert!” she orders. “With your mouth. I wore those over a long plane ride here. So they are going to need extra cleaning.”

Noam picks them up with his mouth. They taste rank.

She laughs and kicks him again in the back and orders him to lick them clean.

As he licks them, at first he starts gagging.

She shouts, “How rude. How do you think that makes me feel? You don’t want to make me feel self-conscious do you? You’re a very mean little boy! Now tell me how they taste?”

He turns around and says, “Wonderful.”

She pats him on the head like a dog, “Good boy.”

After he’s done licking them clean she says, “You're a good little puppy,” while patting him on the head.

Noam asks, “Can I go now?”

She responds, “Ha! You think I’m going to let you off this easy after all the trouble you caused? Now I just got back from a long plane right and my feet are sore.”

Noam still on his hands and knees is speechless and trying hard to cover up his erection.

“Don’t be a lazy little bitch,” she shouts. “Now take of my shoes and socks.”

She gets up on her bed and puts one foot over Noam’s shoulder and the other one on his lap.

Still on his knees he starts to take of her shoe with his hands.

She kicks him in the face, “Did I fuckin' say you could you use your hands, bitch! Now take them off with your mouth and be a good little doggie.”

He tries to take them off but it is too difficult.

She kicks him again in the face, takes off her shoes and throws them at his head and shouts, “I can’t believe you are so lazy! You can’t even perform a simple task, making me do all the work. How cruel. Now take my socks off!”

Noam takes off her sweaty socks with his mouth.

She playfully rubs her sweaty feet all over his face, "Ah don't they smell nice?"

Noam replies sarcastically, "Just lovely."

"I see you have a little spunk in you left. Now if you kiss them!" she says.

Noam kisses them all over her.

She is ticklish and kicks him in the forehead. "Ooops sorry," she says with some sarcasm of her own.

She pushes Noam's head down and opens her legs wide.

He admires her inner thighs and pink lacy panties, thinking she wants him to go down on her.

Just as he moves in closer she grabs his hair and smacks him on the face shouting, "Pervert! I didn't say you could look up my dress!"

She lies down on her bed and orders him to rub her sweaty feet while she watches TV.

Out of all the shows to come on, it is the cartoon Braceface with Alicia Silverstone, which gives Noam a massive erection but after about a minute or so she changes the channel to some cheesy reality show.

After he rubs her feet for about half an hour she lets out a moan and says, "You know, you're actually really good at this. My friends are spending the weekend and if you're lucky maybe I will offer them your services."

Noam is turned on by the thoughts of pleasuring her and her hot teen friends but at this point he realizes that he has to re-establish his manhood if he wants to be able to get back his crush and defeat Meschel.

Noam is used to establishing his aristocratic credentials but decides to go for a different approach and tries something unthinkable, which is to act like a Chad. He says, "Yo, your bitches need a good banging? I got the big dick for it, ho!"

She slaps him across the face and shouts, "Did I say anything about that, pervert? Now get the fuck out, or I will tell my daddy what you did to me!"

Noam leaves her princess suite and tries to find his way back to his room.

He walks around a part of the palace that he does not recognize, and realizes it must be Meschel's suite.

He finds it odd that unlike the rest of the palace there are no Roman busts, red velvet drapes, neon, or marble checkered floors. Just a generic mansion one would expect to find in Beverly Hills in the early 21st century.

Noam had always strongly believed that one could look into a man's soul by his taste in interior design and architectural aesthetics. This put him at great unease but also further enforced his view that Meschel is no more than a money man and has no real visions, a complete and utter fraud.

He needs to get out and looks for his map for assistance but realizes he had left it in the safe when he ran into Sarah Meschel.

He is disappointed that he lost such a useful asset but was able to figure out the main plans in regards to his crush.

He thinks, “My main objective is to find the right moment when she is alone, and it is just us together as it always should be and always will be. Then I shall snatch her away from that bastard Meschel, and we shall be together for all of eternity.”

He turns around and sees Harry, who is shocked to see him in Meschel’s quarters and shouts “What on earth are you doing here?”

“Well I don’t fuckin' know,” Noam says. “Maybe it’s because I’m the star of the film!”

“Oh, you really are that naive,” Harry replies. “Meschel only wants you there for publicity purposes. I’d advise you stay out of the way if you know what’s best for you.”

Harry escorts him back to his room. He pushes a button and the corridor turns around and then moves downwards as if it were an elevator. Noam finds himself back in front of his room.

Noam suspected that this was the plan all along, just to use the real Noam to get media publicity and he could tell that Meschel and Carlos were insincere when they said he had a major role in the film.

Noam lies in bed thinking, “Tomorrow is the most important day of my final mission, just as the party was for my first and unsuccessful one. I know about the plans for my crush, and this is my last and final chance to win her over and to change the entire course of history. Most people only get one chance at young love but I was granted a second chance to regain my lost youth and retrieve my long-lost love in her pure unadulterated state. This is the time to get things right or spend all of eternity alone, growing old watching future generations of girls reach puberty just to be defiled by Chads while I rot alone as a miserable old impoverished philosopher, ridiculed throughout the entire course of history as the one who could have set things right but failed his mission."

Noam wakes up the next day and finds Harry there in his room.

"Get the fuck out, Harry!" Noam yells.

Harry explains, "Here is the deal, Noam. I am to escort you downstairs for the press conference. Unless it is absolutely necessary I advise you to keep your mouth shut. However, if questioned by the press you are to say how brilliant Ari Meschel is, how much of an honor it is to work with him, and most importantly everything in the film is 100% true. And one more thing, do not talk to the actors!"

Noam doesn't respond but walks with Harry down to the press release gathering.

There is an air of professionalism with the publicist and journalist there that Noam didn't notice in the palace before. It reminds him more of a lot of the press conferences his mom would take him to for her work at Bloom Publishing.

He remembers the second time he saw Natalie after her Bat Mitzvah and before going to Chadsworth at a press event for Mr. Bloom's autobiography that his mom wrote.

He had so wanted to talk to her but was such a coward back then, and Mr. Bloom didn't even have the decency to introduce him because he thought he was such a dweeb and wasn't even worthy of meeting his daughter, but now Noam is a new man who has overcome great obstacles, from massacring Chads in high school, to surviving prison, and now is the beginning of the final chapter of the story that will remake history.

While Noam stands there by himself sipping his chai latte and munching on a blueberry scone at the press banquet, he is greeted by Meschel.

He didn't know what to expect, this being his arch nemesis that is hell bent on destroying his legacy and desecrating his crush.

Meschel grabs Noam's hand causing him to spill his chai latte and proclaims, "Noam! This is it! We are going to make movie magic! We are going to make a fortune, and it's all because of you and your manifesto!"

Meschel opens up a bottle of his finest champagne and cheers, "To Noam!"

All the production staff and cast run up to Noam to greet him. Some ask for his autograph.

The entire cast is there; the actors who are playing everyone including his mom, his teachers, the Chads, the popular girls, the judge, and the prison staff and inmates. His entire life in one room, all there to pay homage to him, even though he knows it is all a sham.

One pretty young female journalist approaches him: "I'm so proud of you for having the courage to speak out. I mean taking a horrific tragedy and using it to bring about world peace. Everyone could learn a lesson from your experience. You inspired me to personally volunteer for Chad Relief."

She notices Noam's look of disappointment and disgust, "Oh I'm so sorry you had to witness all that."

"Witnessed? I was the one of who made it all happen!" Noam replies.

The journalist has a look of complete and utter shock.

Noam walks by the booth for "Chad Relief." There are two pretty young blonde interns at the booth and a picture of two blond high school jocks with the look of sorrow and the caption, "Help us."

One of the interns says, "Noam! I can't believe it's actually …"

Noam is about to scream but is interrupted by Meschel, who gets up to give a speech.

Meschel proclaims, "I've been making movies for over 30 years but never have I been granted the opportunity to do something on this level. Something on such a grandiose scale that will wake up the masses, take them out of their cozy little safe spaces, and wake them up to the rawness that is pure unadulterated sex. Yet with a deep level of social consciousness. Oh the beauty of cum, sweat, and blood. Little teen titties, furry pubescent cunts, multiple cum shots, massive orgies, but also a sad tragic tale about a pathetic young man who becomes stronger by confronting his own demons, bigotries, and insecurities; to become a better man and to show the rest of us that there is a better way."

He gets a round of applause.

Meschel continues, "We are on the precipice of history! De Sade had great visions, used his erotic writings to bring about a greater social awareness and end the tyranny of the Church and monarchy, culminating in the Age of Enlightenment. Then one day film came along and a bunch of prudes stood in the way, preventing artistic expression. Then we threw out all those old puritans, and there were signs of hope for a brighter future, a future of love, freedom, and passion!"

Another big round of applause.

Meschel continues, "But we have entered another dark age where young men no longer know the meaning of free love, and think that it's ok to act out in violence, violence on an epic proportion, but we have to get to the root of this, and cinema is the way to reprogram young impressionable minds who have been lost in a world of anime, sex robots, and holograms. Sure it is great for a quick orgasm, but sex has lost its social consciousness, and we have forgotten what it means to make love, to experience human flesh and desire. This is precisely why we have suffering in this world, because people don't know how to love one another. This is a story of a troubled young man who learns to love despite having closed off his heart to the world and resorts to unspeakable acts of violence, but those acts teach the world that all we need is to love one another and not scapegoat the less fortunate, oh the poor downtrodden American Chad who taught us what it means to be a true American. At first I felt that the American people were not ready for a work of such epic proportions but now is the time for a new paradigm. They will laugh, and cry, and then cum, and then cum some more but develop a deeper social consciousness. We are going to make billions, and most importantly, ten percent of proceeds will go to Chad Relief."

Noam is appalled. No mention of his great work, his philosophy, or grand visions for a utopian society. It is the same trash that he grew up with but on steroids, and worst of all he is the pawn being used to implement it all.

Noam is bombarded with countless people trying to schmooze with him. He shouts, "Fuck off! None of you plebeians have even read my fuckin' manifesto!"

They all smile and say, "Love the passion!" "Can't believe it's actually happening!" "The real Noam Metzenbaum!" "What an honor!"

Carlos walks over to Noam with his arm around a young man from the film and smacks Noam on the buttocks and says, "Noam, we finally did it. Ever since I gave you your first blowjob in school, I knew you were a star. I got you into that party so you could carry out your great performance art act and become a star. We were destined to make this movie together. I love you, Holmes!"

"Excuse me. Performance art?" Noam says.

"I finally get it now," Carlos says. "In school, I thought you were just some bitter nerd who carried out a homicidal rampage, but Meschel helped me realize that all along you were just a great performance artist who sacrificed his own freedom to teach the world that all they need is sex, and this movie will bring your message to the entire world and make us all filthy rich."

Noam is about to tell off Carlos but Carlos says, "I want to introduce you to Aaron Meschel. He's going to be playing you as your high-school self."

Noam thinks, "Meschel's nephew? That bratty little piece of shit!"

Aaron looks at Noam smugly. He is going for the nerd chic look with a thousand dollar haircut and vintage hipster glasses.

The boy says in his whinny voice, "I'm Aaron Meschel. You may have seen me in …"

Noam interrupts him, "Have you read the manifesto?"

Aaron says, "I don't have time for that. I'm an actor."

"Have you ever been in a sword fight? Massacred anyone?" Noam asks.

"Duh," Arron replies smugly. "I was in a hologram medieval action feature about a young prince who gives up slaying dragons for slaying pussy."

"But most importantly are you a virgin?" Noam asks.

Aaron laughs, "What? Not since I was like 13."

Noam grabs Aaron by the collar and says, "Look, you little punk! You are not worthy! Carlos! Fire him and find a replacement ASAP!"

Carlos pulls Noam away and says, "Noam, let me introduce you to some more actors."

Noam sees a large group of young teen actors. Almost identical to the teens he went to high school with but even better looking. The young blonde Chads with their Adonis chests and the young blonde Jewish girls he had always lusted after.

The girls all say smiling, "We love your film, Noam."

Noam knows they have not read his manifesto but blushes over the fact that these young blonde girls half his age admire him and see him as a magnificent being, not just the stupid nerd they saw him as in high school.

The boys all take off their clothes and are in their speedos while the girls take off their skirts to reveal their bikinis. The girls blow air kisses to Noam, and they all run off outside to the pool.

Noam starts pacing anxiously. He still can't find his crush. He knows she's out there somewhere.

He then bumps into the douchy actor (who turns out to be the guy he tortured earlier at the Erotic Emporium) who plays him as an adult. Noam can see the burn marks on his shirtless chest from the acid he used to torture him, but despite that he is still surrounded by tons of young hot actresses.

Noam gives him a dirty look.

"Look, dude," the actor says. "I'm not some loser virgin like you. I've banged so many chicks I've lost count. It's just a gig, bro."

Noam tries to punch the actor in the stomach, but he manages to put Noam in a chokehold. He whispers in Noam's ear while chocking him, "You didn't torture me, bitch. It was all part of the game, for the movie. I had to get in the role, bro."

Noam feels powerless. This was the same man he had tortured and utterly humiliated and now he is going to destroy his legacy and tarnish his image for all of eternity.

Meschel walks over and turns to Noam and says, "You better not pull any shit. If you fuck up my film I'll have your balls chopped off and fed to the sharks!"

"What about the manifesto?" Noam says.

"What about it?" Meschel replies.

"This film is based on me, my story, my visions, and my utopia!" Noam contends.

"I purchased the rights to your manifesto," Meschel replies. "After your trial, the rights were auctioned off. It was a hot issue back then and no one else wanted to touch it, but I saw its future economic potential. Now it's mine and I can do with it as I please, and there's nothing you can do."

Noam notices a sword that is on the set as a prop and he really wants to kill Meschel with it, but at this point his main objective is finding his crush, and he has learned from his past mistakes to not let anything stand in the way of hunting down his one true love.

Walking around searching for his crush, he overhears from one of the teens that Meschel's daughter Sarah is hosting a private cast party after the first film shoot for all the teen actors. He wonders if his crush will be invited.

Noam heads outside to watch the first film shoot which is the pool scene of the party filmed in the Roman baths.

Noam still can't find his crush. He thinks, "Wasn't she there that night, right before she was tricked upstairs? Everything is supposed to happen as planned. Now where was I at this very moment that night? Wait, it is still daytime, the party was at night, not a summer pool party. This completely complicates the entire narrative. I can't find my crush unless I have an exact timeline of events! Maybe I should have kept that damn map. Sarah Meschel probably has it or worse gave it to her father."

Noam gets distracted watching all the young blond teens packed in the pool naked. He sees the boys who humiliated him earlier surrounded by all the hot naked teen girls in the hot tub, who are rubbing their Adonis chests.

Noam is enraged and thinks, "Here I am, the big star, an entire Island devoted to my greatness, and none of these little teen cunts are paying attention to me!"

Noam shouts, "Look at me, basking in my glory, little pubescent creatures paying homage to my greatness," as he paces along the poolside staring at the young teen girls and their cute furry little bushes.

The Camera man shouts, "Cut! Get off the set asshole!"

Noam shouts back, "I'm the star. This is my fucking film!"

Carlos pulls him aside, "This is a film shoot, Noam. Chill out, Holmes."

He offers Noam a margarita which he gulps down.

Carlos says to Noam, "Now I know my bitch Harry told you not to talk to any of the actors, but I can hook you up with any of these fine ass bitches. You know me. I'm the pimp!"

Noam is intrigued but he mustn't let his libido stand in the way of finding his crush.

Noam replies, “Look Carlos, I appreciate the offer, but I have to go find my crush.”

Carlos bursts out laughing, “Your crush? You mean that blonde Jewish chick from high school? You can have any one of these teen bitches, and you still haven’t gotten over your high school crush. I’m sorry, I can’t stop laughing.”

Noam says, “I saw her on the Island and everything that has happened so far, from you inviting me to the island, to my visions, and this very moment. It is all fate!”

Carlos replies, “You got some serious issues, Holmes. But if you wanna know the truth, after the party she quit school, became a ho, got pimped out by some black dudes, and then died of a heroin overdose. Hate to break it to you, Holmes, but you gotta move on with your life. You have a bright future. Stop living in the past.”

Noam shouts, “I cannot solve the puzzle unless I go back to the very beginning and fix my past errors. I will fix the puzzle box so I can find her. She’s out there! I know it! She is still young and pure, waiting for me and I will find her dammit!”

Carlos laughs, “Good luck, Holmes,” and walks off with another young male actor.

Noam wonders if what Carlos said was true and if the girl he saw on the island was just a mirage, but he felt a spiritual bond with her that no mirage could ever create.

He is distraught at even the slimmest probability of that story, but realizes he has to keep his cool if he wants to succeed.

He heads back inside to the main party and realizes it is Sarah Meschel's party.

He looks around for his crush and sees tons of blonde Jewish girls that look like her but who are not her. "Decoys perhaps?"

He keeps looking around for his crush, bumping into blonde Jewesses, one after the other.

Then he feels a tap on his shoulder. It's Sarah Meschel.

Sarah says, "Hi Noam. Glad you could make it to my party."

"Thanks Sarah," Noam replies. "But I have to head out."

Sarah grabs him by the arm, "Not so fast. You remember our deal. Now I want to introduce you to my friend Zoe."

Zoe is the girl he saw earlier at the spa who looks like a teenage cross between Natalie Portman and Winona Rider.

Zoe says giggling, "Hi, don't think we've met. I heard you were like, some kind of movie star."

Noam says, "Yes, of course. I am playing myself, the great Noam Metzenbaum."

Sarah says sarcastically, "Yeah, he's the real deal."

"Wait, you look familiar. Have we met?" Zoe says.

Noam replies, "I don't think so. You probably just saw me on the big screen."

Then her friend Jasmine, who is the Persian girl he recognizes from earlier, approaches Noam. "Oh, aren't you like, some serial killer?"

"Well, I am not some lowly murderer. I am a revolutionary!" Noam replies.

"That sounds like lots of fun," Zoe says.

All the girls laugh.

Then Zoe says, "Michelle, I want to introduce you to my new friend Noam."

Michelle is the blonde Jewess whom he also recognizes from the spa.

She shakes his hand giggling.

This was the first time in Noam's life that he had hot teen girls wanting to talk to him. He feels what a Chad must feel every single day and night, and this made him despise the Chad even more for living the life that he was deprived of.

Sarah says, "Now that we've all been introduced, let's take the party upstairs."

Noam tries to bide his time until he finds his crush and says, "Hold on a minute. I'm going to get a drink."

"Here's a bottle of champagne we can take upstairs," Zoe says.

Noam doesn't know what these girls want from him and is turned on by Zoe and Michelle after seeing them at the spa, but he cannot let them distract him from finding his crush.

He looks out into the crowd of blonde Jewish girls, and there she is, out in the crowd of girls, his crush.

For the first time since high school Noam has the feeling of being a young boy in love, butterflies in his stomach, his heart racing, but now he has the strength and wisdom of a grown man of 31.

Noam rushes towards the crowd but feels a hand tugging at his arm. It is Zoe. Then Michelle grabs his other arm, while Jasmine stands on the sidelines watching.

He looks out at the crowd again but has lost his crush in the sea of blond decoys.

It is just like that fateful night where he lost sight of her, and it was too late because he wasted valuable time peeping in on the cunnilingus party.

Zoe, tugging at him, says, “Don’t you think I’m hot?”

Noam nervously smiles.

“Well don’t you?” she shouts.

Noam blushes in embarrassment. He is sandwiched between two hot teen girls rubbing their tits up against him. He automatically gets hard.

He then breaks free. He thinks, “I have to find my crush! The fate of the entire human race depends upon it!”

Sarah blocks Noam, rubbing her big tits up against him. She reaches over and licks his neck, her luscious dark hair covering his face and blocking the view.

Then Zoe grabs him from behind and whispers in his ears, “Baby, I want your cock.”

Michelle and Jasmine grab his arms while Sarah is still blocking his view from the front.

Noam shouts, "Get away from me, you dumb bitches!"

Sarah says with an evil grin, "Remember our little deal? Now it's time to pay up." She motions to her friends to follow her up the stairs.

Noam thinks, "I have to find my crush. I can't waste my time on these stupid sluts."

Noam tries to break free but the girls drag him up the long staircase.

Following Sarah into her private lounge party, he sees four other teen girls sitting on the sofa sipping cocktails as if they are waiting for someone.

Noam expected some massive teen orgy, but this is a very discreet girls-only party where he is being brought in as the only male.

The room is massive but not like the grand palatial Roman suites that are common in the palace. It reminds him of some kind of set found on old teen-girl shows like "Clarissa Explains it All," like some exotic teen slumber party.

He wonders if this is a set for the movie.

Sarah says, "Noam, I want to introduce you to all my friends. They are waiting here just for you."

The girls in their short skirts, chit-chatting, sipping their cocktails, don't seem interested in Noam.

One hot Asian girl says, "Eeew this guy is old, like 40. I thought you were going to bring us a hot guy."

Sarah says, “He is going to be a famous movie star after my dad’s film is finished, and we are going to initiate him.”

Then all the girls light up in excitement, the same type of girls who ignored him in high school looking at him like a piece of meat even though he is practically twice their age.

The Asian girl says, “I’m Skyler by the way. So happy you could come to the party.”

Skyler is hot, curvy, and resembles some teen K-pop idol.

Next to her is a shy, cute Chinese girl with glasses who reminds Noam of many of the girls in the Mathletes club when he was in high school.

She shakes his hand formally, “Hello, I’m Stacey.”

Next to her are two more girls, one smug French girl (whom Sarah introduces as “Claire”) who has dark blonde hair, pale skin, and thick bushy eyebrows resembling a young Brooke Shields.

Then there is a shy, pretty German girl, tall with golden-blonde hair and blue eyes. She bashfully says, “Hello, my name is Sabine.”

Sarah, Michelle, Zoe, and Jasmine join the other girls on the sofa observing Noam who is standing there in awe, not sure how to react.

Noam is quite excited to be the center of attention, in an erotic pentagram with all eight girls staring down at him.

Sarah says, “Well don’t just stand there, Noam. Pour my friends a glass of champagne.”

Noam opens up the bottle, *"Pop!"*

Something else goes *"Pop"* for Noam.

The girls all laugh.

Sarah smiles. "Don't pop too soon. We have a lot planned for you tonight."

He pours all the girls their champagne.

Zoe says smugly, "That's nice."

He then accidentally spills champagne on Jasmine's skirt. She shouts "What's your problem? This skirt cost several thousand, and it's ruined!"

Noam is insulted. He is a great aristocrat, not some butler. "Can't they find another butler, or does Sarah get off humiliating men of such great stature?"

After the girls start drinking their champagne, they all start chattering in incomprehensible teen girl talk.

Noam remembers how stupid teen girls could be, the gossip, talk of frivolous matters, not great aristocratic ideals, but no, not his crush, she isn't like them.

Noam gets up to leave to go find her. He says to the girls, "Excuse me for a bit."

Sarah looks pissed, "Where the fuck do you think you're going?"

Noam replies, "I'm busy at the moment, need to go somewhere."

"You remember our little deal. Now it's time to pay up," she threatens.

Her friends all start giggling, but Noam doesn't know if they are in on the deal.

Noam rushes out to go find his crush but Sarah grabs him by the arm, "Not so fast you motherfucker!"

Noam had no idea how strong this girl was. Whether it is super-strength or some kind of erotic power over him, she is able to push Noam down to the ground.

All the girls surround him like lions surrounding prey.

Sarah takes something out of her purse: handcuffs. Zoe and Michelle restrain him while Sarah cuffs his hands behind his back.

Noam shouts, "What the hell are you doing?"

"I thought we were going to have some fucking fun! Aren't we?" Sarah says.

Pinned on his knees with his hands behind his back, Noam fell for the trap.

He has betrayed his crush and the feasibility of a successful mission looks bleak.

"Watch me pull out his big cock," says Zoe.

Her friend Jasmine makes a face, "Gross. Like, I'm going to have sex with him?"

Zoe replies, "Someone is sure being an uptight virgin. You will learn once you get fucked for the first time."

Zoe and Michelle take off all his clothes, leaving him on the floor naked, handcuffed with his dick hanging out.

The girls look disappointed and pissed off. They don't like the dick.

Sarah, acting like the narrator of the story, explains, "Now girls, here's what we are going to do to Mister Noam."

She pulls out a briefcase like she is a young businesswoman and takes out some papers.

Noam immediately recognizes what the papers are.

Sarah proclaims, "We've got here his very private notes from high school!"

"Ooooooo," all the girls go.

Noam thought that they wanted his manhood, but realizes now that they are just getting off on his humiliation.

He is not the great aristocrat he had fought to be. At the very best he is like poor Justin from high school, tricked against his will, yet not entirely invisible like Noam's old high school self.

Sarah continues, "And in these private notes read a detailing secret for his inner weakness, and possibly big money for the next Noam movie franchise! How do you like that, you stupid motherfucker?"

She slaps Noam's face.

Noam realizes she must have gotten his private notes when she caught him opening the safe which he forgot to close. He doesn't think that Meschel would have given them to his mischievous daughter, knowing she might reveal the secret that his entire film is a fraud.

Michelle says, “I want to hear the most dangerous thing he’s ever done. I’m starting to really like the guy.”

Sarah continues on, “Well, it says right here in this fine print of Noam’s childhood handwriting that he was raped by the Chads.”

Michelle looks disgusted, “What, raped?”

All of them looked bewildered.

Noam starts to sweat in panic.

Sarah continues, “And most importantly how much he loves cunnilingus! What a dirty boy!”

The girls gasp in excitement, except for Stacey the nerdy Asian girl who says, “Eew, gross!”

“Shut up, Stacey!” Sarah orders.

She continues reading, “And how they did it in Ancient Rome in his history class! What a dweeb! And that he is still a virgin!”

“I can’t believe he’s actually a virgin,” Michelle says. “I thought he was kind of cool.”

While technically Noam had lost his virginity to the actress with the big fake tits, these girls didn’t know that. His last entry to his manifesto was written right after he got out of prison but Meschel had only bought the rights to the manifesto he wrote in high school.

Noam figures out a way he can defeat Meschel, by finding a copy of the new manifesto which documents his evolution from a meek little boy to a great warrior aristocrat.

But now Noam can sense that something really wrong and uncomfortable is about to happen to him.

Sarah looks down at Noam's silent and distraught face. He can't say anything, as if tape is covering his mouth.

Sarah turns to the girls, who had poured themselves another round of champagne and were watching the entertainment. She says, "Clearly you need some experience. Girls, how about we show this man how to be one!"

Noam looks up on Sarah's bookshelf and sees the book, "The Art of the Cunnilingus Party" by Wendy Silverstein, which is dedicated to the memory of her old boyfriend Zack, yet no mention of poor Justin.

Noam knows that Sarah is twisted, and that her friends Zoe, Jasmine, and Michelle already had the "experience" at the spa.

Zoe says, "All right, girlfriend, I know what you're talking about."

Noam is now curled up on the ground in a fetal position, his hands cuffed behind him, and the girls all laughing at him, utterly humiliated.

Zoe pushes Noam off the ground with the help of her friend Michelle.

Sarah says, "Get on your knees, now!"

Noam tries to overcome his sense of humiliation and gets up on his knees while the two girls prop up his arms like a puppet.

Sarah says with an evil grin, "Now you little bitch! It's time to act out on your fantasy!"

Zoe and Michelle drag him over towards the sofa while he crawls on his knees.

Sarah says, "Turn around, girls."

She takes out another page from his manifesto and starts reading, *"I walk around school and see all these stuck up little rich bitches, walking around in their little short skirts, their nice smooth legs, and perfect plump little buttocks. They won't even acknowledge my existence. All I want is to just get down on my knees like a little slave, and kiss their bare buttocks."*

Noam's blood is rushing. He is all for chastity but he had succumbed to his base instincts, tarnishing his manifesto. He realizes that Meschel wasn't exclusively responsible for turning a work about great aristocratic ideals into smut but that he had enabled him by exposing himself at his worse moments.

He has come to the realization that the manifesto itself is flawed and needs to be rewritten if he wants to defeat Meschel and reunite with his crush. He just has to find a way to escape his tormentors, find his manifesto, and rewrite the narrative.

Noam looks up, all the girls lined up on the couch, moving in sync like a marching band, pulling up their skirts all at once, and then pulling down their panties to reveal their bare buttocks up in the air.

Noam notices that all the girls have perfectly pale buttocks and are all nice and plump. He thinks, "There is nothing smoother and tastier then a teenage girl's buttocks."

He automatically gets hard but doesn't want to expose his inner weakness to his tormentors. He had fantasized about being face-sat and kissing the bare buttocks of hot teen girls ever since he was a boy, but this wasn't about sex. This was about submission, and these girls wanted to demonstrate their dominance over him.

"Come here little Noam," Sarah says. "Kiss all our asses!"

Stacey, the nerdy Asian girl, is sitting on the edge of the sofa looking away uncomfortably.

Sarah shouts, "Stacey, don't be such a little bitch. Now show us what you got."

Stacey starts crying.

Skyler, the other Asian girl, takes her plump bare buttocks and starts twerking towards Stacey's face and says, "C'mon little sis. It's just for tonight. No one needs to know."

Stacey looks disgusted and says, "Ok, ok."

Stacey reluctantly pulls up her skirt to reveal her Hello Kitty panties.

The other girls laugh.

Then Stacey says, "I'm sorry. I just can't."

Skyler then pulls down Stacey's panties like a little baby in need of a spanking.

Noam expected her to have a flat ass but she has nicely shaped, smooth, pale buttocks, like a porcelain china doll.

Noam just kneels there observing the girls' buttocks. A scrumptious buffet of buttocks waiting to be feasted upon.

Skyler says, “Let’s get this party started,” and pushes Noam’s head into Stacey’s buttocks, his nose going into her butt cheeks. He dare not give it a kiss.

Sarah notices Noam’s lack of oral attention and says, “Noam, how cruel of you. You want to make this poor little girl feel self-conscious about herself? Do you?”

Noam doesn’t want Sarah to read what he wrote about Asian girls in his manifesto, so he just gives Stacey a little kiss on her buttocks.

Stacey says awkwardly, “Thank you.”

Sarah shouts, “Thank you? He should be thanking you for having the honor to place his lowly lips on your sweet ass. Now thank Stacey, Noam!”

Noam says, “Thank you Stacey.”

“I’m next!” Skyler says.

Noam looks at her buttocks, which are surprisingly plump for an Asian girl.

Noam just stares at them in observation.

Skyler says, “Yeah, I’m Korean. I got a real ass, not like Stacey’s flat chink ass.”

Noam leans in to kiss her but she takes her hands and pushes his head into her buttocks, gyrating against his face, moaning like a porn star, “Oh yeah baby. Kiss that ass!”

Noam gives her a kiss right inside her cheeks.

Michelle says, “It’s my turn.”

Skyler says, "You go girl! Let's show this motherfucker what women want!"

Noam has just kissed the buttocks of the two Asian girls but now it is Michelle's turn.

She has a perfect hourglass figure and not only is she a blonde Jewess, the type of girl he had lusted after ever since he was a boy, she has the perfect smoothness of a young girl's buttocks that make him just want to bury his face into it.

He thinks, "Noam, you're already under the spell of your captors. This is pure degradation. They don't respect your manhood, your aristocratic credentials. They only want to prove their dominance over you. Just get this ordeal over with, and then you can go find your crush."

Michelle says, "What are you waiting for?"

Noam leans in and kisses her smooth plump buttocks.

She moans, "Ooooh!"

Noam wants to savor Michelle's smooth buttocks but Sarah announces, "We have a lot more planned for tonight, so let's get this up to speed."

Sabine is next, the shy, pretty German girl.

He looks up at her from the floor, admires her golden-blonde cascading hair and kisses her smooth plump buttocks.

Sarah is next. She has the biggest buttocks of the girls, but not in a gross way. She is a hot curvy teenage girl who still has her baby fat.

Sarah shouts, "Kiss it, bitch!"

Noam kisses her right in the crack and can feel her coarse pubic hair rub up against his chin.

She taunts him, "You like that, bitch?"

Next is the French girl, Claire. She bumps her buttocks right into Noam's face hurting his nose. Then he gives a light kiss right inside her butt cheek.

Next is Jasmine, the Persian girl who is a close friend of Zoe's. She has light olive skin but pale buttocks from a tan line. He can see her thick bush underneath, which gives off a strong musky scent.

Noam feels intimidated by her buttocks and looks up at her luscious dark wavy hair. He looks down her back and can see she has a hairy lower back.

He lightly kisses her lower back and then kisses each of her butt cheeks. After Sarah, she has the curviest buttocks of all the girls.

He starts kissing lightly inside her butt cheeks and like with Sarah can feel her coarse pubic hair against his chin.

Zoe is next and says, "Decided to save the best for last? Now kiss it, bitch!"

Noam remembers the incident with Zoe at the spa when he looked up her skirt. Even though she is not blonde, he is starting to fall in love with her and feels like they have a special connection but is cautious not to fall for a girl who isn't his crush.

Noam kisses her cheeks. He savors her smooth pale skin with his lips, starting by kissing her cheeks, and then gives her a long moist kiss inside her cheeks.

She makes subtle awkward noises of arousal.

Noam starts tonguing her inner cheeks, until he accidentally makes contact with her anus.

Then Zoe breaks her silence and shouts, "This freak likes to eat ass!"

Sarah says, "That can be arranged. We can indulge the pervert's fantasy." Noam regrets his little gesture.

Sarah and Zoe grab him and push him down towards the ground, but his hands cuffed behind his back make it difficult to lie down. He feels a jolt of pain in his back and shoulders.

Sarah decides to undo the handcuffs.

Noam quickly gets up to escape.

Sarah laughs, "Don't even think about it bitch. You think we're done with you?"

Zoe sits on his chest, her naked buttocks and hairy bush rubbing against his bare chest.

Then Sarah takes out a leather strap from her closet.

Noam isn't quite sure what it is, but it looks like some bizarre sadomasochistic torture device.

Sarah puts Noam's arms into the straps, which have leather handles.

Claire puts a pillow under his head.

Noam says, “Thank you.”

Claire spits on his face and says, “This is for our pleasure!”

Noam notices Claire’s massive, full dark bush and can smell her scent from down below on the floor.

She sits on his face for a while trying to find a comfortable position. Then she pulls the straps straining his back and commands, “Eat!”

He starts kissing and tonguing around inside her sweaty butt cheeks, savoring her smooth skin with his lips and tongue.

She sits down hard, hurting his nose, then pulls the straps again.

He starts to licks out her ass while she starts to gently bounce up and down, clenching her buttocks tighter around his face.

As she bounces up and down, riding his face like a pony, he can feel her wet hairy smelly pussy rub against his face.

He tries to lick her pussy, but she gets angry and slaps him on the face shouting, “Did I say you could do that?”

As punishment, she pulls the straps tighter as he continues licks out her anus, her pussy juices draining into his mouth and causing him to choke.

She gets up and looks at him with the utmost disgust, and then it's Sarah’s turn.

Sarah straddles him, teasing him with her big ass over his face.

Sarah sits down, her cheeks completely engulfing him.

Sarah presses her buttocks down hard and shouts, "What are you waiting for?"

She pulls the straps restraining Noam's arms and back as punishment.

Then he starts licking around inside her sweaty cheeks.

She lets out a moan and starts gyrating.

She pulls the straps again harder and shouts, "I want your tongue out on me!"

He tries to lick around her anus, but she clenches her buttocks muscles tighter and shouts "Lick that shit you fucker!"

"Gross," Stacey says, watching from the corner of the room.

He was too close, he couldn't breathe. The tongue has to come out in order to save his life. He licks around her anus in circular motions but the more he licks the more aroused she gets.

She clenches even tighter, her sweat and pussy juices drench his face as the aroma is too much to bare, a mixture of butt sweat, stale urine, and female arousal.

The other girls grow impatient. Jasmine says, "It's my turn!" Then Zoe says, "No, I have him next!"

Sarah says, moaning from pleasure, "He's mine. I own him. I'm just being a good friend and lending him out."

Noam with his head down continues to lick out Sarah's asshole. The taste and suffocation make him dizzy.

He starts to get an erection. How could he?

He thinks, “No, no, no!”

The girls notice his erection.

Sarah says, “Yeah baby! Lick it!”

Sarah gets up, his face drenched with her butt sweat and pussy juice.

“Ha! The bitch actually enjoyed it,” Sarah boasts. “I don’t care if he has a tiny dick. He’s good with his tongue.”

Jasmine insists, “I’m next!”

She inspects his face but notices one of Sarah’s pubes on his lips, and her fluids drenching his face and complains like a bratty little princess, “I want him cleaned up first.”

“You have a problem with my juices?” Sarah scoffs.

Jasmine replies, “No, it's just basic hygiene.”

Sarah says, “Well Stacey, since you're such a little prude, why don’t you clean up Noam’s face for Princess Jasmine here who thinks she’s too good for the rest of us.”

Stacey rushes over to the bathroom and cleans up Noam’s face with a baby wipe.

She is very gentle and carefully cleans every inch of his face.

While most of the girls looked at Noam with disgust, she treats him with care.

He always wondered why some guys had Asian girlfriends and thought it was just that they were the biggest dweebs who could not attract hot blondes, but now he can start to see why.

Jasmine sneers at Noam, then places her entire skirt over him to keep some level of modesty.

Noam briefly gets a glimpse of her plump buttocks and hairy bush hovering over his face but is now completely engulfed in the dark.

She puts her feet up on his chest causing further pressure of her buttocks on his face.

She demands, “I want my foot rub too.”

“Don’t be such a greedy little bitch,” Sarah remarks.

Noam starts licking her inner cheeks.

Then she orders him to lick her in really fast circular motions.

He follows her request, and then she starts gyrating on his face in rhythmic motions.

“Faster!” she demands.

He continues to lick faster in circular motions but keeps getting her ass hairs in his mouth.

When Jasmine finally orgasms, she sits down hard, moaning.

She gets up, and he gasps for air.

She sees the pubic hairs stuck in his teeth and laughs.

“And you have the nerve to complain about my hygiene?” Sarah says.

Stacey cleans up his face again and plucks out the pubes from his teeth with tweezers.

Sarah laughs, "You'll be a great dental hygienist someday."

"At least I'm not a lazy spoiled Jew!" Stacey responds.

"Silly Chink. You will never be like us," Sarah says.

Stacey proclaims, "I would rather die an honorable death then sink to your level."

"Sorry bitch," Sarah replies. "You already got your ass kissed. You're on the dark side now, and there's no turning back."

Despite being shy, Sabine is now turned on by the situation.

She politely asks, "May I go next?"

The other girls are too busy chit-chatting and arguing to respond so she just hovers over Noam awkwardly.

Noam fantasizes about her calling him a filthy Juden and then suffocating him like in some Nazi dominatrix porn, but she just politely sits down on his face.

While the previous girls gave him a hard face-fucking, she just sits down awkwardly like sitting on a sofa.

Her smooth skin and plump buttocks feels amazing on his face.

Noam starts licking inside her cheeks, then does quick dart motions on her anus.

She starts slowly gyrating in pleasure.

She orgasms, making cute little noises, then clenches her buttocks over his face while he continues to tongue out her ass.

"I'm next," Zoe says.

“You already got your ass eaten,” Sarah says. “We have to move on.”

Zoe is pissed, “Yeah, like one little kiss. I’m next!”

“Okay, since you're my best friend I’ll let you ride him,” Sarah replies.

Zoe rushes over to Noam.

She really wants to tease him and make him work for it.

Noam is really turned on by Zoe and wants to give her the best experience.

She pulls up her skirt. He can see her dark bush, then places her buttocks right on Noam’s face.

She starts giggling, rubbing her ass and pussy all over Noam face.

Then she pulls the straps straining Noam’s arms and back like he is a toy.

Noam starts slowly tongue kissing her inner cheeks like he did earlier.

She moans in pleasure, clenching her buttocks on his face.

Then he starts licking her anus in circular motions, then does quick tongue darts.

He knows he is not supposed to break the rules, but he is so turned on by Zoe that he stretches his tongue lightly tickling her clit.

She gets so aroused that she starts masturbating, stroking her clit, while Noam eats out her ass, her pussy juices and butt sweat drenching his face.

Sarah is cross. She says, “Did I say you could masturbate on him? We have to do things in order, based on the manifesto if we want to release the powers of sex magic.”

While Zoe is gyrating her buttocks against Noam’s face, he remembers learning about sex magic from Alistair Blackstone’s writings.

The key is that if you perform certain sex acts in ritualistic order you can release the powers of the occult. Noam was just a boy and writing about his own sexual fantasies, but after discovering the powers of the island maybe there is some secret occult power, and if it did exist, Noam has to tap into it to find his crush before Sarah can.

Sarah says, “All right, girls. Next on the menu is cunnilingus!”

Michelle looks annoyed. She was left out of the festivities.

Even though he felt a stronger connection to Zoe, the fact that Michelle is a blonde Jewess really turns him on.

Noam gets up and says, “You know, Sarah, I think you're being quite unkind not letting your friend Michelle have a turn.”

Noam thought this kind gesture would earn Michelle’s affection, but she just sneers at him.

Sarah rolls her eyes, “Ah you're pathetic, Noam. Michelle, go ahead but we don’t have all day.”

Noam had remembered looking up at Michelle at the spa, her dark bush in contrast to her golden-blonde hair.

She sits down on his face hard, suffocating him while grabbing the straps sadistically as he gives her a nice thorough tonguing, starting with her inner butt and then her anus.

She has the perfect plump buttocks, and they are clenched around his face.

She clenches harder, making funny noises as she is about to orgasm, but Sarah orders her to get up.

Noam looks up and sees Michelle's thick dark bush dripping with pussy juices right above his face.

Michelle looks pissed but takes out her anger on Noam by spitting on his face and pointing out that even when erect he still has a micropenis.

While lying sideways on the floor, he notices that Sarah has carelessly left his manifesto and her pink feather pen underneath the couch.

Perhaps Sarah isn't the powerful villain he thought she was but just a bored mischievous spoiled rich girl.

Noam thinks about writing in the ending of the manifesto while pleasuring the girls with his tongue, and since Sarah forgot to put his handcuffs back on he decides it is a better strategy to use his hands for writing then to try to escape again.

Zoe and Skyler drag him back over to the couch.

Zoe suggests, "All right girls, let's drink another round of champagne while he pleasures us!"

Sarah says, "Hell yeah girl!"

She orders Stacey to get another bottle and pour the girls glasses.

He is now back on his knees, the girls sitting on the sofa fighting impatiently over what order they will get serviced in.

He looks over at Zoe, who is sitting smugly on the sofa in her short skirt, admiring her smooth pale legs.

He is starting to fall for her and so badly wants to savor her most intimate parts.

He looks over and realizes that the manifesto is under Sarah and that he is going to have to spend a long time pleasuring her if he wants to rewrite the manifesto.

The girls are now drunk and distracted.

A drunk and giggly Zoe grabs him by the hair and pulls him over towards her.

He lands on her, his face falling on her breast, then slips down to her lap.

Zoe starts petting his head like a puppy, giggling.

Sarah says sinisterly, "Don't get too attached. I have some real fucked up shit planed for him tonight."

Jasmine says, "What? Like a smut film? That would be awesome!"

The girls all laugh.

Zoe pushes his head down beneath her and opens up her legs.

Instead Sarah has Stacey crawl under the sofa to clean up Noam's ejaculate with the baby wipes.

Zoe grows impatient and grabs Noam's head back between her thighs while Stacey is still underneath them cleaning up the mess on the floor.

Noam starts lightly licking at Zoe's hairy labia majora, moves in on the labia minora, and then he lightly flicks her clit with his tongue.

The more he licks the wetter she gets, and the new wetness mixes in with the build-up of prior vaginal secretions and stale urine, creating a more pungent taste and scent.

He continues licking around her labia and flicking her clit until she orgasms.

Moaning, thrusting her pelvis in his face, and squeezing her thighs, trapping his head, she then pulls his hair hard as she moans.

He keeps tonguing her faster as she fucks his face having multiple orgasms, her pussy juices gush into his mouth.

He gags a little but is intoxicated by her juices.

The other girls are looking in awe, begging for their chance, but Noam has a special connection with Zoe and doesn't want it to end.

Zoe lets out a sigh and then orders him to lick her clean.

She continues to drink champagne and giggle, while he cleans up her pussy juices with his tongue.

He tickles her urethra causing her to giggle. He wonders if she's ticklish or just likes having her urethra licked. He continues until she pisses right in his mouth. But he doesn't mind it, savoring her yellow nectar.

Sarah says, "Zoe, stop being a selfish bitch hogging him all to yourself. Our cunts need service too!"

He looks up at Zoe and she notices him gargling her piss. She looks at him with the utmost disgust.

He thought they had a special connection, but realizes she was just using him like she did with the slaves at the spa.

Sarah then looks over at Stacey, who is sitting on the edge of the sofa looking away and laughs, "Looks like you need some experience."

Stacey is about to cry, "No, please no! Don't. This is sick!"

Sarah then turns to Noam, "Now Noam you've made poor little Stacey feel left out. That's not very nice."

Skyler grabs Stacey by the arms.

Stacey screams, "No! Please! Stop it!"

Skyler and Jasmine, grabbing both her legs, spreading her open like a Barbie doll.

"What are you doing? Please! Stop it!" Stacey cries.

Sarah looks down at Noam, "You're going to munch on this nice Chinese pussy and you are going to like it!"

Noam looks at Stacey, a china doll with a black hair bowl cut, and looking so innocent.

Unreal, Noam with an erection, approaching a hairy, fishy-smelling vagina.

She continues crying, "No! No! No!"

She doesn't want to go through with this and Noam is feeling the same way, too. In this hour of horror, he and she could relate.

While Skyler and Jasmine pin Stacey down, Sarah pushes Noam's head down between her legs, closer, closer, getting closer to that hairy bush.

Noam's face is smothered in the hairy, wet, stinky vagina. How wet it is.

Stacey is humiliated.

The girls are all laughing.

Noam's dick is dripping. He feels ok.

He didn't think about Asian girls before. Something is happening. "Who is my crush again?" He is starting to lose his mind. "This girl… is different. If my crush were here she would have saved me from this rape. She would have told me how much she really loved me. Nope. But this girl. Stacey is her name? She is different. She's probably never had sex before until now. I am her hero. Yeah, that's me!"

But her pussy… it is … fishy.

Maybe he should have chased after Asian girls during his school years. Skyler is hot, too. He could have. Why bother going after the unique phenotype of his crush, when he could have gone after all the hot and nerdy Asian girls in his biology class.

Who cares about all the Roman stuff when the history of East Asian people is much more fascinating. The philosophy too, like Confucius, Lao Tzu …

Noam is losing his mind.

Stacey is crying, upset, angry, and violated.

His face finally pulls away from her tight pussy, sticky wetness all over his face.

After munching on Stacey's fishy pussy, Jasmine is next.

Jasmine just pushes him down hard on his knees.

He starts licking her inner thighs, savoring her musky scent, but Jasmine wants it now.

She pushes his face into her hairy bush.

Like Stacey had a fishy pussy, Jasmine has a strong spicy musky scent and flavor.

He realizes that different nationalities of girls have different scents and flavors and wonders if this is what all the fuss about diversity his teachers ranted on in school was really all about.

He wonders what a big-bootied black chick or a feisty young Latina might taste like but remembers that those were the slave classes of American society.

There is a special kind of diversity that exists in elite circles, but he was never taught that in school and now he is learning a real political lesson.

Noam stops thinking about esoteric philosophical concepts and gets back to work.

He continues licking out Jasmine's hairy wet cunt while she fucks his face, grunting.

He keeps spitting out her pubes but she gets insulted and smacks his face.

When she orgasms, she crushes his face with her thick thighs still thrusting her crotch against his face.

Then she pisses right onto his face like how he remembers with Zoe at the Spa, but at least Zoe pissed in his mouth, and he was able to swallow.

Now he is completely drenched, the others girls are shocked.

Sarah orders Stacey, who is now completely nude, to wash his face with a wet towel.

Skyler gets a wicked idea.

Skyler says to Sarah, "We should handcuff that little bitch Stacey. She's a fuckin' spy!"

"Really?" Sarah asks, taken aback.

Skyler says, "I overheard her speaking in Chinese about how she is infiltrating the island for the Chinese to steal your dad's film, which they will use to incite angry Chinkcels to kill Americans."

Sarah replies, "We can't let that happen. So then what should we do with the little cunt?"

"Let's give her the Noam treatment!" Skyler suggests.

Stacey runs to escape, but Skyler and Sarah grab her and put handcuffs on her.

Stacey starts crying.

Then Skyler says, "Let's not let this little bitch ruin our fun!"

Skyler gets up on the couch and demands, "Bring them both over."

Sarah laughs, "Are you fuckin' serious?"

Skyler orders a naked Stacey to lie on the coach.

Stacey screams.

The other girls pin her down.

Skyler sits down on Stacey's face, suffocating her, "How do you like that, you flat-assed chink?"

Then she orders Noam to come over to service her cunt.

Noam gets up and starts to lap at her pussy but Skyler is more interested in fucking Stacey's face.

After she is done she pushes Stacey down on the floor, hurting her back because her hands are in cuffs.

Stacey just curls up there in a ball, sobbing.

Noam looks over and sees that his manifesto is still under Sarah. He had written about every single one of these girls in an erotic fiction story, and knowing what he would have to do to Sarah it wasn't going to be pretty, but it was the only way for him to finish the manifesto.

Sabine, who is now drunk and out of her shell, orders Noam over.

She roughly pushes his face into her thick dark blonde bush and squeezes her thighs tight against his face and orders, "Now eat!"

Her pubes are much softer than the other girls' but just as thick and smelly.

As he laps away at her labia he fantasizes that he is with his crush, having the honor of placing his lips on her golden labia, but this girl is hot and he can't help himself and licks every corner of her cunt.

Then she grabs his head and violently fucks his face as she orgasms, moaning and spraying his face with pussy juice.

Claire is next. Earlier she had denied him the right to eat from her hairy, moist, smelly cunt, and this only increased the anticipation.

Noam's tongue and neck are pretty sore from all the pussy eating, but he knows that he still has a lot of work to do.

Claire, who must have some kind of gymnastic skills, puts her feet right onto Noam's back and moves her body up into the air so that both her pussy and buttocks hover over Noam's face.

She orders a sobbing Stacey to use her hands to prop up her buttocks so she can properly fuck Noam's face.

Stacey cries, "I want to go home!"

"Yeah, let Stacey go home!" Noam says.

Sarah replies, "Ah, how sweet."

Meanwhile, Claire is growing impatient and opens up another bottle of champagne, then hovers over Noam's face.

While she had sat on his face before she is in a position now right above him where he can see everything in full view; her buttocks, vulva, pubic hair, taking in her beauty and aroma.

A sobbing Stacey walks over and holds Claire from the side but is very uncomfortable.

Then Claire orders Noam's tongue out, and she quickly fucks his face while he tongues her hairy moist cunt.

Stacey's hands slip and Claire lands right on Noam's face hurting his nose again.

Noam screams out in pain.

Claire is pissed off, so she decides to piss in Noam's mouth. Then orders him to gargle.

Sarah laughs, "Yeah, we've all read your manifesto. At least you get to drink girl piss for a change, faggot!"

Then Claire sits back on Noam's face and orders him to lick up all the piss from her pussy and her pubic hair.

His mouth is now full of piss and pubes, but he did this to himself. He had written about all of this in his manifesto and feels that he is just another cheap smut peddler like Meschel and deserves his fate.

Noam briefly passes out from all this tonguing, face sitting, and golden showers. Everything is a blur.

But then Michelle slaps him on his face, "It's my turn now bitch!"

He had pleasured most of the girls, but Michelle was the last girl before his long ordeal with Sarah Meschel.

Michelle was the specific type of blonde girl he had always lusted after.

Dark bush, musky scent; he had always wondered what a certain type of blonde tasted like, especially while fantasizing about his crush. This was his chance, but his tongue and neck were so exhausted.

Noam, down on his knees, buries his face in Michelle's bush.

He starts licking at her labia. The taste and smell are so intense.

He remembers from the horrific night when he saw his crush desecrated he got a faint whiff of her scent. This was a similar scent but slightly different.

As much as he wanted to bury his face in this girl's labia for hours, she wasn't his crush.

Noam finishes up and licks away at her labia while she fucks his face, having multiple orgasms.

Noam is about to pass out but remembers that Sarah is next, and that brings attention to the fact that in his manifesto he wrote an erotic story when he was in prison that was inspired by Justin's story where he was rented out as a slave to rich teen girls, and his ordeal ended in his death, just like Justin's short life ended by being face fucked to death by horny teen girls.

This had nothing to do with his aristocratic ideals. He was just bored, horny, and alone in his prison cell, but he knows that he has to finish the manifesto before he is facefucked to death.

Sarah says, "So here's the deal. I want you to write your entire manifesto on me with your tongue. If you complete your task you can remain here as my servant, but if you fail you will die a horrific death."

"Why? Why are you doing this to me?" says Noam.

Sarah says, "Don't you see? I am here to ruin your career. I know about the revolution. Don't play dumb, Noam. I know your whole game about being a virgin is a charade. A phony lie to get your point across! We don't need an army of virgins."

At this point Noam realizes he was mistaken to underestimate Sarah Meschel and her motives, but he has no choice but to cooperate.

Noam gets down on his knees wanting to quickly get this ordeal over with.

He had become so skilled with his tongue that everything he wrote on Sarah's pussy he was able to write with the pen in sync, every detail of the great manifesto, from his deepest desires, and grand visions to all the obstacles he has overcome.

Noam's tongue is exhausted and gasps for a breath of air but he has to finish his manifesto.

Now Sarah is screaming from pleasure completely oblivious to Noam's writings.

Noam finally gets to the crossroads, the final part where he left off that Meschel had seized. Now is the time for a new beginning, but he needs inspiration.

Having his face buried in Sarah's filthy cunt doesn't exactly inspire the romantic desires that would bring about the perfect ending to this story.

He frantically tries to thinks of something, but just before he is about to give up hope he looks down at the manifesto and sees a sketching he did of his crush when he was in prison.

Even though it was created when he was in prison and separated from his crush he was able to take the longing for her and create the most beautiful masterpiece.

Then he realizes that his true love for her was imprinted in his own subconscious, and it didn't matter that his tongue was up in Sarah's hairy smelly cunt.

Just like that the perfect ending to an epic journey came to him.

Sarah is still fucking his face, his tongue and neck sore, causing him to suffocate.

She screams, "I'm going to fuck your ugly little face until you suffocate. Just like in your little story!"

Then Noam blacks out. Where is he now? Is this the end?

Noam is trapped in the dark, but Sarah and her friends are gone. He cannot hear, taste, or smell them.

But wait, Noam can smell the sweetest pussy, not like Sarah's or like Zoe's whom he enjoyed, or even like the blonde Jewish girl, Michelle.

This was a smell totally unfamiliar, not just stimulating erotically but a scent of love, pure love that he hadn't experienced with any of the other girls.

Was this all part of his ultimate cunnilingus fantasy?

Noam realizes his face is still buried between a girl's legs but it isn't Sarah or any of the other girls.

He wonders who this mystery girl is. He is still blind in the dark, but he can sense he is no longer in Sarah Meschel's room.

Opening his eyes, he looks at the most beautiful pussy he had never seen, something familiar yet mysterious.

This was the girl of his dreams, angel-like legs, and then he sees her vagina for the first time.

Amazing, crazy, he didn't know what was going on anymore.

Perfect sweet vagina, dark blonde golden soft pubes he just wants to bury his face in for all eternity.

He goes in for his taste. This time, though, it isn't an ugly fish smell. It is sweet. Sweet like a magical rainbow unicorn prairie. Pink! Pink like the smell. Like she's still a virgin. He can tell.

But he is trapped underneath and could not see who this dream girl is.

He goes in for a taste. He doesn't feel dizzy or exhausted anymore. He has the energy to eat pussy for hours.

How long has it been? Noam is used to it. He is in heaven. Sex. Sex is good. Pussy eating is good. Pussy eating your crush is good. "Wait? Is this my crush?"

His theories about life are coming back to him. Socrates, Plato, Aristotle, those great men. Did they ever eat pussy like this?

Hours pass by. Munching on pussy.

The perfect dark blonde golden bush, then he looks up and it is her, his one true love.

Dark blonde hair, hazel eyes, dimpled smile.

But she doesn't even notice him. She is just sitting in her chair like a princess enjoying the nice little sensations of a tongue on her vagina.

She is a princess in her throne, and he is her slave, still naked and chained underneath her. Does she truly love him or is she just using him like the other girls?

He goes in to prove his love for her.

She starts moaning in pleasure as he continues to lap away.

This isn't an illusion, a mirage. He knows it's true. This is what he wrote when he wrote the ending to the manifesto.

He caresses his crush and looks into her eyes and can tell the feelings are mutual, both young lovers naked, with their perfect bodies as one.

He thinks, "Am I a Chad?" Laughs a little and then the two lovers float up above into the clouds, their souls connecting as they ascend into the heavens.

Noam just stares into her eyes. This was the girl he had dreamt about for most of his life, and she is right there in front of him.

Most of Noam's life, he had spent dreaming about romantic utopian ideals or fantasizing about vengeance against his adversaries but for the first time in his life he could just enjoy the moment, live in the present as the cliché goes.

But at the very moment their souls are fully in sync, the clouds float away and he is back at Meschel's palace.

Perhaps it was all but a dream after all, too good to be true?

But no, his crush is by his side, and he is still a young warrior, but things are about to get ugly.

Noam looks around and sees people running out of the palace for their lives, bombs going off, and military helicopters swarming the premises.

Many of the people are missing limbs and some are even decapitated, still holding onto their heads then looking at their corpses and dying of shock.

It was much like the night of the great massacre but the only difference is he is not alone; he has his one true love beside him.

An alternate ending to the story of Noam? When he saves his crush from that fateful night and takes her away to paradise. Or did his rewriting of history usher in the apocalypse?

It is now a complete war zone at Meschel's palace. The military helicopters land and robot police enter and order everyone in to a zone.

Then the robots start rounding up specific individuals, those who have been selected for arrest.

Noam wonders if the military invasion was because they feared his manifesto would usher in a revolution, but luckily for him he resembles a young boy, and they can't identify him.

As the robot police continue a mass arrest of the palace's inhabitants, out of nowhere a group of men in frog masks show up with swords.

First they start massacring groups of the douchy young men who desecrated the palace, starting with the douchy actor who stole Noam's identity.

The man screams Noam's name out in pain, right before his decapitation.

Then the robot police come in for the frogmen, armed with swords they have no chance against the high tech police force.

But then they start screeching, "Reeeeeeeeeeeeeeeee," which causes everything to vibrate.

The Robots starts malfunctioning.

The frogmen catch Carlos blowing a young Chad, they behead him; the Chad cums the very same moment of decapitation, shooting blood and cum all over the frog masks.

Then the human police come with guns as backup.

Meschel, who has just awoken, comes over and screams, "What the fuck is going on?"

The chief of police proclaims, "Ari Meschel, you are under arrest for the production of child pornography, using underaged actors in your film."

Meschel replies, "No! This was all Noam's idea. This is was from his manifesto. I wanted to change it, to make it more family friendly and remove any reference to underaged sex, but he insisted on the accuracy of the manifesto and threatened to have me killed by the virgin frogmen if I didn't cooperate."

The police chief asks, "Where is this Noam?"

Meschel points to him, "That him!"

The police chief says, "But that is just a boy."

Meschel replies, "No, he's a-"

Meschel's security attempt to help him escape, but the frogmen get to him first.

One of the frogmen beheads Meschel.

Sarah Meschel is there crying hysterically.

One of the frogmen gets down and starts performing cunnilingus on her.

Sarah starts moaning in pleasure.

Then her moans draw in all the palace inhabitants to start fornicating again in one massive orgy.

The frogmen take a torch and light the orgy blob on fire.

Then their leader turns to Noam, “Follow me.”

Noam and his crush follow them.

Noam looks back and sees the palace on fire and the massive orgy turning into a blood bath of beheadings.

Noam was given his second chance to relive that night, and get things right and he had succeeded, but he needs to get the fuck out.

As they run, a Roman column falls down behind them. The palace is collapsing.

He follows the frogman through a corridor back into the palace.

He thinks, “Is this a trick?”

But Noam has no other choice and follows the frogman indoors. Inside are more naked people, their orgies disrupted by bloodshed, and they are now rushing to get out.

The frogman takes out his sword and starts beheading the people escaping, then directs them down a staircase, where they end up in a long dark tunnel.

The frogman says, “Run!”

The frogman stays behind, and Noam grabs his crush and they run as fast as they can down the long dark tunnel.

When they get to the end they find themselves back at the sculpture garden, marble statues in mysterious purple and blue florescent lights.

Noam looks back, and the door has closed behind him. He is trapped but at least he is with his crush.

Are they to die together in this dungeon? Better to die with the one you most love than to spend the rest of your life alone.

But then Noam looks at the sculptures and things are different now, no Chads, just a statue of him and his crush holding hands together, as things always should have been.

Warm light pours in, and they walk out towards the light, ending up back at the magical water front location at sunset.

Noam proclaims, "Natalie, I love you so much. I created all of this just for you."

Natalie giggles.

Noam says, "This is it! The happy ending and it's all because of you!"

Natalie says, "Noam, to be honest, I thought you were a total dweeb. In fact, I barely even remember you from high school."

Noam is crushed and puts his head down, all of this for nothing?

But then Natalie says, "Wait Noam. We are not at Chadsworth anymore. I wasn't this magical maiden you wrote about. I was just a girl who liked shopping, traveling, and hanging out with her friends. Yeah, I wasn't that different from those other girls but you, you created this new universe where dreams become real and the past doesn't matter."

Noam asks, “Do you love me?”

“Of course,” she replies. “This is your fantasy. You created this new world, and we shall repopulate and create a new utopia.”

Noam’s dreams had come true but he was confused. The girl he had put up on a pedestal was just another pretty rich girl, but this girl, she gave him his youth again and a new start at life.

His crush hugs him to comfort him, and he stares into her eyes. He loves this girl, but this wasn’t his crush from high school. In fact, this girl was much prettier.

“Perhaps this girl was created by me, a figment of my imagination,” Noam contemplates.

But there was more to all this, his fantasies and desires used to create the perfect girl from scratch. She is real, standing right there in front of him, still pure, innocent, the perfect teen girlfriend, and through all the torments, trials and tribulations Noam went through he finally has his romantic movie happy ending, and no one could steal that away from him.

Noam reaches in to give her a kiss, but she says, “Your breath stinks like pussy!”

They both hold hands and continue to stare into each other's eyes. Sex doesn’t matter, it’s just about being with the person that you love, together in paradise, and no one else there to stand in the way of true love.

Noam hears frog noises, “Ribbit, Ribbit.”

He looks out and the frog goddess, Shadilay, appears.

She proclaims, “Noam, you finally did it.”

Noam bows down to worship the frog goddess.

Shadilay says, "Noam, I am not a god or goddess. I am merely a meme. You see, when you rewrote your manifesto, you disrupted the order of history, the spacetime continuum creating an alternative reality, another dimension in a sense. You see, your manifesto had such an impact that it shaped so many events that the course of history could not handle such chaos, and it split into two courses."

This is what Noam wanted his entire life, but part of him feels that there is something artificial. He wanted the entire human race to worship him as a god-emperor, build monuments to him and implement his visions of grand new utopian civilizations, but even when he became famous and had an entire island devoted to his greatness, his adversaries and the rottenness of human nature still stood in his way. Part of him just feels like he is living in virtual reality.

But then he looks over to his crush. She isn't some sex robot or hologram. He could look into her eyes, and see it was pure love, and that they were destined to be together from the very beginning.

Shadilay says, "Noam, you have a choice, you can go back to the world as you know it or see the world you helped create."

"I just want to stay here with my crush in paradise," Noam replies.

"Noam, you can't stay here," Shadilay responds. "This is not paradise. This is just Vapor."

"Vapor?" Noam replies, confused.

"Yes, Vapor," Shadilay says. "A void where all your fantasies are stored, unrealized concepts that have not been implemented and discarded into the abyss."

"So basically everything I have ever dreamed of but have not successfully implemented?" Noam says.

"Exactly," Shadilay replies.

Noam asks, "So why can't we just stay here?"

Shadilay says, "Anything that you have dreamed of that has not come into fruition is in essence non-existent. You must have entered a portal at some point, but if you stay here too long you will get so attached to your unrealized fantasies that those fantasies will seize control of you, and you will become vapor in an essence."

Noam asks, "Are you implying my crush is Vapor?"

"That is for you to figure out," Shadilay replies. "But all I can say is that once you become Vapor there is no return. You will be trapped in your subconscious for all of eternity. And from what I've read, I wouldn't want to be trapped in *your* subconscious."

Noam wonders if all his bizarre experiences on the Island; Meschel's film about his manifesto, The Blackstone Tower, The Palace, the Erotic Emporium, the strange experience with the teen boys, and the cunnilingus party with Sarah Meschel and her friends were all just figments of his imagination. Things he had fantasized or wrote about but that did not exist. But then he thinks about how those events all led up to the moment of reunification with his crush, and *she is real.*

Then he asks Shadilay, "So what is on the other side? Have all my grand visions been implemented?"

"I cannot give you the answers," Shadilay replies. "You created this new world. I am merely a messenger."

Noam looks out at the sunset and sees many of his unimplemented dreams floating towards them. Some of them things he deeply regrets dreaming about and doesn't want his crush to see.

Shadilay insists, "We must leave now before it is too late."

Noam doesn't know what is in store for him in the new world, but all he wants is to love one girl and one girl only. He grabs his crush tightly, and they get onto the back of Shadilay and ride off into the neon sunset. As Shadilay serenades them, Noam holds Natalie close to him and knows that they will be together for all of eternity.

www.ingramcontent.com/pod-product-compliance
Lightning Source LLC
La Vergne TN
LVHW050917080826
845145LV00001B/110

* 9 7 8 0 6 9 2 9 8 0 0 8 8 *